Bonded by Ash
Cadence Connor

eBook ISBN: 9781068839313

Paperback ISBN: 9781068839337

Cover Design by Moonpress, www.moonpress.co

The Princess

Screw the goddesses and their constant meddling. And screw this place, too. It could wash away into nothing, along with the rest of her dreams.

The water beneath her hands pooled and circled, clawing its way down the drain in a plunging vortex that mirrored her own inevitable descent.

When the last drop vanished, Isla stepped into the soft towel Alynna held, her damp hair billowing behind her for Susanna to tame with a brush. All Isla could do was stand there, feeling like a stranger in her own skin—as she had since her escape—incapable of dressing herself, running her own bath, or... anything at all.

She slipped into a silk dress and was guided to a seat in the center of her darkened room. Isla had always preferred deep colors and stained walnut to furnish this space, and nothing had changed in her long absence. It was as if she could never truly escape.

As Alynna and Susanna fussed over the best way to fashion her hair, finally settling on a half-up style meant to bring out her eyes, Isla curled her hands together and wished she were anywhere but here.

One deep breath drawn to steady herself and hold the darkness at bay. She had become skilled at that since leaving the mines, after nearly destroying everything with her outburst. Even now, she had to remind herself she was safe within their draped castle in the capital city of Aurial. It had once been the only home she knew, yet now she felt like a stranger parading in a princess's skin. She didn't belong anymore, though no one seemed to notice.

No one cared.

"Which one would you like to wear today, Princess Isla?" Alynna held out two silver-flamed tiaras for inspection. One was strung with iridescent pearls, the other adorned with black diamonds across the front.

Isla shook her head.

If she had a choice, it would be neither. She never wanted to wear one again for the rest of her life, if she could help it. Today, she felt the furthest thing from a princess.

The framed portrait of her mother wearing her lost circlet seemed to mock her. Thank the goddess she and Edmund had taken after her instead of their father—in looks and, she liked to believe, in temperament, though she had never met her.

But her father demanded she continue wearing a tiara, especially after the first day she went without, when she felt most like a fraud. He insisted it was necessary to display their status and remind everyone that she was a princess of Velotia.

Alynna conferred with Susanna, and together they decided the diamond tiara would best complement her silk dress. They placed it atop her head. The weight felt unnatural, but Isla smiled in thanks.

She winced at the headache pressing in. The latest of many symptoms that had plagued her during the two months of freedom, despite how many healers examined her. She slipped on a pair of lace gloves her father had commissioned to keep her from parading around the palace with those 'nasty' scars.

Once polished into absolute royal perfection, Isla set out to join her father in the throne room, where he was to receive guests from Bastilo. A silver-clad Siica shadowed her every step, his onyx badge catching the daylight. The irony wasn't lost on her.

People paused to bow or curtsy as she passed, and she nodded back like a gracious princess. A good princess.

A perfect princess.

The fine white marble beneath her feet echoed, its sound too close to metal striking rock. The halls, wide enough to fit ten men abreast, felt as constricting as the narrowest tunnel in the pit.

At least no one here gave her withering glares or leery stares—not openly. She still felt their lingering eyes long after they passed, and knew they whispered once she turned the corner.

Whatever.

She reminded herself that she was used to this. She hadn't cared about them before, so there was no reason to start now. Not after everything.

Towering pillars led to the throne room. Her eyes skimmed over the familiar white-and-silver arches, the black flames etched into the three-stepped dais, and the onyx throne it framed.

The King of Velotia, her father, sat upon it, his double-layered crown of flames resting on stark blond hair. His bright green eyes barely flicked toward Isla as she entered. Thank the goddess she and Edmund had inherited everything from their mother. Isla often wondered if she was a painful reminder of his late wife—that would explain some of his cruelty.

At least two dozen silver-clad Siicas lurked in the alcoves lining the walls, watching every entrant. Her escort peeled away, slipping into the shadows with the same bored expression fixed to his face.

Her father was already deep in discussion with Commander Baran and his top advisor, Tyrone. His eyes flicked to her for the briefest moment before returning to Tyrone as they introduced Skallen's replacement. Isla slid into place at his left, ever the obedient daughter. The seat at his right, Edmund's seat, remained painfully empty.

Neither Tyrone nor her father acknowledged her for hours. No one asked her opinion—not that she had ever expected them to.

So, she stood there, hour after hour, dreaming of anywhere but this cursed room.

At last, they were dismissed. Her father didn't spare her a second glance as she slipped away before anyone could call her back.

The stony-faced Siica outside her room nodded at her. This one was her brother's favorite, Beau. What was he doing here?

The wooden door clicked shut behind her, and she leaned against its cool frame, praying to Halia, goddess of mountains and forests, for strength. She had grown used to praying to Halia during her time in the mines and still found comfort in the goddess's name despite there being no forests nearby, except for the few dozen walnut trees that had given their life to furnish her room.

A shadow coughed, and her heart nearly leapt out of her throat.

Edmund sat on the long couch, clutching a lacy pillow in his lap. Who knew how long he had been waiting in the dark of her room?

She hissed, snatching a book from a nearby wardrobe and hurling it at him. "Don't do that."

It was caught with ease. The room was dim, but she could picture him rolling his eyes. "Always with the dramatics."

Isla lit a gas lantern to clearly see his face. "Your absence was noticed today. Father asked where you were, and he didn't seem satisfied with my answer."

Edmund scoffed, as though their father's fury meant nothing. It must have been easy, being the favorite—always escaping the brunt of his wrath, as he'd done for years.

No. She shook her head. It wouldn't do to dwell on their tangled past, not when they had promised to focus on a new future together.

She slumped into the seat beside him, massaging her temples. The question forced its way out against her will. "Any improvement today?" she asked, already dreading the answer.

Edmund's head slowly edged from side to side. Then he paused, his gaze fixing on the portrait of their mother, as if he too felt her lingering eyes from beyond the twelfth gate.

Isla sighed, the day's weight easing as she peeled off her sweaty gloves and tossed them to the floor.

Not surprising. She hadn't expected much progress after the way things had ended. Everything had unraveled into a mess, and the burning sting of betrayal still gnawed at her insides. She didn't know how to stop it from spreading.

Edmund leaned his head against the plush backing, and Isla followed suit.

"Ready for the Celestial Solstice ball?" he asked with a smirk.

"Don't remind me." She let her eyes flutter closed and clasped her hands together. Though she was glad to be done with Slin's chaotic year, when nothing seemed to play out in its proper order, she worried what the star goddess Hierel's year of blessings and truth would bring. "I have no desire to be paraded around, or to see him again."

"You have no choice," came the simple reply.

Nothing had changed. She'd never had much choice before, and she still didn't now.

"I know." She flung the diamond tiara onto a carved walnut table. Gods, her life had shifted since the black comet appeared, heralding the sister-goddess years. Once so certain of her place, now she was filled with uncertainty, doubt, and a longing for something more than this. "I'm dying here. Literally dying. I hate it."

Edmund straightened and turned to face her. It was almost hard to recognize her brother. His soft cheeks had vanished during his time away—his time hunting her down. Now his face was taut, his eyes carrying a strange fiery glow, as if he had glimpsed Rallion's first gate and stared Sister Death in the eyes.

If anyone were to ask, she was certain she looked the same: a completely different person from the girl who had left Aurial screaming and fussing about her upcoming wedding.

A shiver ran through her body at the thought.

Edmund only raised an eyebrow.

"What is it?"

"Come with me tonight. I mean it this time."

It was Isla's turn to scoff. "As if Father would ever let me step beyond those draped walls, unless it's to march straight to Koliat."

"We'll slip out once everyone's asleep. Your ladies will cover for you."

Guilt curdled in her belly. Alynna and Susanna would keep her secrets, yes, but she could never forgive herself for putting them in such a compromising position again. She had asked too much of them already.

"I don't think that's a good idea. And what exactly do you mean by sneak out?" Her voice shook despite her best efforts to keep steady.

Edmund smirked, the vein in his temple throbbing. "I've been ducking out of this place for years, sister. I know the secret passages—I mastered them long before you were—"

He stopped. For a heartbeat, panic flickered across his face.

Isla didn't have the heart to be angry at his slip. Before you were born. Those were the words he couldn't bring himself to say. The truth of what he lost that day, and the reason he had spent years resenting her.

Edmund swallowed. "I used to frequent the drinking halls, is what I was going to say."

No, what made her chest tighten was the thought of all those years she had been stuck here, helpless and trapped, while her brother slipped out, probably to drink and laugh with his friends. He had never once thought to show her the passages.

She shook her head. New beginnings. Don't dwell on the past. Remember.

Remember.

Still, it was hard not to wonder what else her brother kept from her. There was no way he had been sneaking out for years merely to find a jug of ale. He still hid things from her.

Edmund went on as though nothing had happened. "You should come. Before I take my men and leave. Before Father decides to visit the camp outside these walls."

"I'd rather not involve my ladies—"

"Then don't." He arched a brow. "I'll get you out. I'll show you the passages—all of them—so you can use them later."

Her heart fluttered.

"I think it's time," he said softly. "Don't you want to question our prisoners for yourself?"

One

The General

The goddesses seemed determined to curse his very life. They shadowed his every move, careful to absolutely fuck up everything he did. There was no way he was escaping expulsion after this.

No fucking way.

Hells, he'd gladly trade his uniform for the chance to drive a fist into this man's jaw. He'd even settle for a sharp kick to the shins. Anything to bleed off the fiery rage burning through him at the sight of the man standing in this half-dead forest as if it hadn't already tried to kill them several times.

Rian stared at the Velotian crown prince, fists clenched so tight his knuckles ached. Gods, it took everything not to choke the life out of him right then and there. How bad could the consequences really be for murdering the crown prince?

As if in answer, a breeze stirred the twisted branches, flinging a spray of dark leaves into Edmund's face. His stupid brown eyes and stupid brown hair looked painfully like Isla's, and Rian didn't need the reminder—not when he was this close to knocking him on his royal ass.

"You were supposed to stay behind," he hissed through clenched teeth, his voice carrying louder than he meant. An Agicae wielder drifted closer, curious why the Pedite general was shouting at one of them. "You said you were staying behind. You're going to get us all killed."

Edmund rolled his thin eyes, and the gesture sent Rian's blood boiling.

They'd been searching for Isla for months. Months. And now, in the choking dark of these forests, where every step reeked of danger, the one thing most likely to ruin their mission had decided to tag along, wrapped in a stolen wielder's cloak and glaring at Rian as though he were the problem.

He jerked his chin toward Malin and Freya before he did something unforgivable. They had already moved closer, hands on their hilts, no doubt wondering if the Agicae had stepped out of line and needed to be dealt with.

This Agicae wasn't part of the hunting party Rian had hand-picked to cross into Muratian lands in search of Isla and he sure as hells shouldn't be here. If the king learned that both his children were lost behind enemy borders, not even the star-goddess Hierel herself could save him.

"You fucking idiot." Rian knew full well that speaking to a royal like this edged on treason. But this particular royal moron? He could be tossed off that cliff they'd passed earlier, and Rian wouldn't lose a hint of sleep.

"Did you know about this?" He turned to Freya and Malin, jabbing a finger toward Edmund's stupid face. The royal pain even had the gall to look offended.

"Absolutely not," Malin said, laughter tugging at his voice as he adjusted the band binding his shaggy blond hair and leaned against a rotting tree. "But this is an incredible turn of events."

"Me neither," Freya added, though her gaze flicked to the disguised prince for a heartbeat. Her thumb traced Bone Breaker's edge.

For a moment, fear cracked through the prince's carefully stoic mask. An emotion Edmund had never let slip in all the time they'd been forced together. He clenched his jaw.

"I came on my own. She's *my* sister."

"You cannot be here," Rian said again, each word clipped. "Do you know what will happen when we get back?"

The prince only shrugged, indifferent to any consequences. Easy for him. Edmund didn't have to care. He wasn't the one who would pay dearly for this.

Rian's arm throbbed again.

It had been happening for hours now. At first, a sharp stab had dropped him to his knees, forcing him to feign a stumble over a vine while he tried to make sense of it. But the pain was only growing worse. Searing and relentless.

Something was wrong. Something beyond Edmund. And discovering a stowaway prince in their ranks was suddenly the least of his concerns. A darker, quieter part of him even considered leaving Edmund behind in the woods. No one in their party would object. They might even cover for him if the prince happened to get lost.

Tempting.

But he couldn't.

The cavity of his chest tightened, rib by rib, slowly crushing inward. Stabbing. Suffocating. It started nearly a week ago. An icy burst of pain that jolted him awake mid-dream, tearing through his side like a blade. For one heart-stopping moment he'd thought he was dying. When he calmed enough to realize it had only been a dream, he understood the truth: something terrible had happened.

Then it stopped.

Four endless days of silence, when he was certain Isla was dead. They'd wandered the forest aimless, directionless, with nothing to guide them.

Relief had struck when the pain returned. First a dull throbbing, then a steady, merciless stab that never left him. Twisted as it was, he welcomed it. Pain was better than nothingness. Pain meant she was still alive.

And now he knew exactly who waited on the other end of that pull.

"We need to push forward," Edmund said at last. His lips pressed into a hard line, his chin lifted in royal haughtiness. "We're wasting time here."

This man had never been told no in his life, except by his father. It shouldn't have surprised Rian that he'd slipped past the borders without a thought for his own safety or that of Rian's men. Edmund was as naive as his sister had once been when it came to the dangers lurking in these woods. More so, if that was even possible.

Rian exhaled, the weight of the entire forest pressing against his chest. There was a reason he had left Edmund behind... or thought he had. And this was exactly it.

"I know that. What do you think we've been doing these past days? Camping out here for fun, idiot?"

For emphasis, he punched Edmund's bad arm. The prince clutched at his old injury, lips working soundlessly like a stranded fish.

Rian opened his mouth, ready to layer more scorn on the prince. He deserved it, and more, but—

Pain tore through him. Burning. All-encompassing. Familiar. He couldn't explain it, only knew it urged him forward, the same way it had for months since she was taken. Since the day Rallion's comet appeared. Since Commander Skallen's betrayal.

But this time, something was different.

The source was close. He would have wagered every frayed piece of his soul on it.

Another pulse shot through his arm.

Rian bolted, leaving the bewildered prince behind. Freya shouted something, but her words drowned beneath the thunder of his heart and the crunch of the forest under his boots.

The throbbing stopped, and so did he. He strained to listen. Leaves rustled. Branches crashed together. A shard of light cut through a gap in the canopy, spotlighting the twisted limbs ahead.

Everything was too loud. Too bright. Too distracting.

He crouched in the leaves, straining for the forest's sounds, when footsteps crashed up behind him. Heavy breathing. Pretentious gasps. He didn't need to turn to know who it was. He shut his eyes and prayed to the goddess for one more scrap of patience, even as his fingers tapped the hilt of his blade.

Something was wrong.

"Don't run off like that," Freya scolded as she caught up, jerking her chin at him. Her double-looped braids still bounced from the run.

When he turned, most of the others had followed from camp. Perfect.

"The prince," someone whispered. Edmund's hood had slipped back, his face exposed for all to see.

Rian groaned. If not for the tingling crawling from his arm to his fingertips, he'd have sent Edmund back with Freya. But he needed her here. She was his best fighter. They couldn't afford to waste her skills with escort duty for an infantile prince who'd strayed too far from his cushioned palace life.

Gods, he hated this man.

Why did Edmund have to insert himself into everything, making it worse every single time, without a single useful thought to stop him? Rian should have known the prince was with them from the start. Back when he'd gotten stuck in that first mud pit.

Edmund rubbed his side as he struggled to catch his breath. Freya stepped around him, her eyes lingering a little too long on the prince's movements.

Rian made a mental note to bring that up later. When she didn't have Bone Breaker within reach, or any of her other weapons.

He seized Edmund by the collar and hissed, "Look what you've done now. Everybody knows you're here."

Edmund rolled his eyes. "And I'm certain they won't tell another living being once their general commands their silence."

The venom never seemed to leave his tongue whenever he addressed Rian by his new title. A title Edmund himself had forced on him and now deeply regretted. He reminded Rian of that at least once a day.

Rian sighed and rubbed his temple. The throb in his arm crawled into his skull and pounded away at the last dregs of his sanity, shredding what little patience he had left.

"I'll talk to them," Freya said. She seized Edmund's arm in what must have been a brutal grip, judging by the grimace that twisted his face.

"No, it's fine," Rian muttered, his gaze sweeping the dark forest as the hairs on his neck prickled upright. "I'll handle it."

Edmund pursed his lips, about to demand exactly how Rian meant to handle anything, when—

Something brown darted from a dense cluster of trees, too far to make out clearly. Instinct drove Rian forward. He lunged after the shape, ignoring Freya's sharp scolding as he plunged headlong into danger.

The creature vaulted over a fallen trunk and slowed to a light trot, dipping its head.

It whinnied.

Rian froze. Every beat of his heart stretched into eternity, and breath abandoned his lungs.

A horse. A matted, filthy horse.

But not just any horse—this one was missing an ear.

River.

"Come here, boy."

River thrashed his head and pawed at the ground. What had happened to him these past months? What was he doing—

A gasp cut the air. A figure was slumped across his back.

Rian's chest cinched tight, blood roaring in his ears. Impossible. He had to be daywalking. And yet, the pain in his arm still pulsed. Still burned.

And she was here. On River.

She was here.

She was here.

She was here.

The words echoed in his mind like a chant, a prayer to the goddesses. He never thought they would listen. But today, at least one had.

"A sign from the one-eyed goddess," a soldier whispered, pointing at River's missing ear.

Rian closed the gap, fingers finding the horse's mane before he could bolt. The animal swiveled his head and stomped. Something metal clattered to the ground. She shifted weakly on River's back.

Edmund moved first. He caught her before she slipped, nearly collapsing under the weight.

Rian pulled her from Edmund's arms with ease. His heart sang the moment she pressed against his chest. Warm, real, and alive. He couldn't believe it. She was here. She was here, and—though she looked as if already halfway through the second gate—still breathing.

"Grab the horse," he snapped at the soldier who had muttered about goddesses. Turning, he started for their makeshift camp.

Her head lolled lifelessly against him, a sight he hated. Was she awake at all? Aware? Her long brown hair hung in filthy mats, and the rags on her body barely counted as clothes. What horrors had Laian put her through? Surely the goddess of wrath and retribution was watching tonight.

Then he saw it. A dark red stain spreading across her side, fresh and wet.

They needed a healer. Now.

"Stop. Stop!" Edmund hissed, circling like a frantic crow. "Put her down. Put her down, now!"

Before Rian could spit a cutting word, he saw what Edmund pointed at and his heart stuttered.

The tips of her fingers were black.

"Don't touch her," Edmund snapped, his breath unsteady.

"You don't touch her," Rian shot back.

"Well, I'm not touching her," Malin muttered, edging closer.

"Give her to me." Edmund held out his hands as if he hadn't nearly dropped her moments ago. Then, barking to the soldiers: "Someone grab the wielder. Get the healer."

Idiot.

"No," Rian said, voice flat with resolve. He sank to the ground with her still in his arms. "Everyone, back to camp. Take the horse and pack only what we need for a quick departure. They'll be close behind."

"Not if she escaped on horseback," Freya countered. "Even our best mounts wouldn't cross the forest edge. If theirs are the same, we have some time."

"I said back to camp," Rian snapped, sharper now. Months after his promotion, it still felt strange to bark orders. Yet the weight of command pressed through every word. "Now!"

"Tell the healer to be ready," Edmund said, glancing at Isla's side and angling himself to block her from view. "We'll be right behind you."

A united front, at least on this matter. Even the trickster goddess Slin had to pause her chaos some days.

The soldiers exchanged uneasy glances but obeyed. One looped a rope around River's neck to lead him away. By some miracle of Rallion, none of them spotted Isla's hands.

Freya hesitated. As did Malin. They shared a wary glance before Rian gave a single nod. Permission enough. He ignored the way Edmund cursed and threw up his hands. They could stay.

There was no one he trusted more.

Edmund dropped to his knees, a vein pulsing in his forehead as his eyes locked on Isla's hands. Sweat slid from his tangled hair down the curve of his neck.

He needed to pull himself together. Had he never witnessed an outburst before?

Rian's chest constricted. Likely not. Edmund had spent his life avoiding his sister and her deathpuller powers.

Idiot prince.

His arm throbbed. The black retreated an inch before creeping higher than before. The power needed to be let out. It needed to be released.

"That's it. You can let it go. Let it all out if you need to. I know you won't hurt me—us," he added quickly. He glanced at Edmund, still kneeling and pale, then to Freya and Malin pacing the perimeter. "Don't move," he murmured.

His friends froze like predators catching the scent of wounded prey. No hesitation, thank the goddess. Edmund, on the other hand, resembled a terrified toddler and likely couldn't have moved even if he tried.

"I got you. Let it go."

His arm pulsed again, and darkness burst outward.

Two

The Princess

She must have slept for days. Days trapped in the swirling darkness of her mind that had become a new prison.

There had been a horse. She was sure of it. It had carried her somehow, though she could barely cling to its back as she followed that golden thread calling her onward. Hours or minutes, she couldn't tell. Then there were soldiers, and she was pulled from the horse. For a brief, terrifying moment, she thought Devlin had found her, dragging her back to the mines. Back to that prison.

And then darkness ruptured everywhere. After that, nothing.

Now she was warm, lying on something that wasn't rock. Her body felt as if an entire mountain had been dropped on it, her head pounding beneath the weight. That cold dagger still sliced through her skull, memories clawed at by Beretta's powers, hollowing her out from within.

Vicious tremors rippled through her body when she tried to move. A huge mistake. Each shudder set off fresh waves of pounding in her head.

A warm hand touched her arm, and she recoiled. Pain shot up her side, and she vowed never to move again. Even her eyelids were too heavy, too drained to open.

Was any of this real? Had she been recaptured and this comfort nothing but another cruel trick to win her trust? She half-expected to open her eyes and see dark stone walls closing in again.

"Are you in pain?" a female voice asked—soft and gentle, not cold and cutting. A hand brushed her forehead this time. "Shall I fetch the healer?"

No!

The word refused to form in the wasteland of her throat, though her heart darted frantically in its cage.

Not him. Never him.

"Here," the gentle voice said again. "Drink this."

A cup—not a ladle—pressed to her lips. She took a hesitant sip. Water. Plain and simple, cold and delicious, not tainted with dirt or gods-knew-what else.

Even the act of swallowing a few mouthfuls drained her bones and her mind. If this was another trick, she had no desire to open her eyes and confirm. Better to let ignorant sleep overtake her than fight the darkness.

New voices tugged her from the depths, but she didn't move. Couldn't.

They spoke low and hushed, as though afraid to rouse her. Not angry. Not calculating. Another trick?

"—We have to move."

"What if it sets her off again? I don't want the others to see."

"I'm more worried about what happens if they catch up. They know these woods—"

"I thought you said _you_ did?"

"I did—I do. But they know them better. We can't let them get to her again."

Silence stretched, heavy as a held breath.

"Fine. But at the first sign of anything, we send the others away. Far away."

"Agreed."

"And don't let the others near her. I don't want her out of our sight."

A murmur of assent. Then, nothing.

The dreams returned. Nightmares, mostly. Walls pressing in, tunnels narrowing until she couldn't breathe. Black skies, shadowed by something vast sweeping overhead. And always, that same sunrise, breaking through the forest's edge to engulf her in its warm embrace.

At last, she dared to open an eye—a dry, heavy eye. Beige sand loomed above. No... not sand. A canopy, stretched wide, enclosing everything in sight.

She lay low to the ground, in a makeshift bed softer than anything in the mines. At her side sat a blond-haired soldier, hair bound back with a strip of silver leather. His black-and-silver uniform hung loose at the shoulders, a sword-and-hammer badge gleaming on his chest. That badge mattered—she knew it, even if she couldn't yet place why.

The instant their eyes met, the soldier leapt up and hurried out of the tent.

Moments later, a figure burst inside. She shot upright, heart pounding. They'd found her.

But no. It wasn't a wielder. Only someone draped in a wielder's cloak. She knew that light brown hair and slightly drooping nose. Her brother.

He breathed a name—her name—and dropped to his knees beside her. His hand pressed gently to her shoulder. "Lie back down."

She let him ease her back onto the bed, or rather, onto a pile of layered blankets that still felt wondrously soft against her tired bones. How long had she slept? Years, perhaps, judging by the dryness in her throat and the hollow pit gnawing at her stomach.

Brown eyes searched hers. "How are you feeling?"

She winced. Terrible. As if death herself had come to claim her.

The bile in her stomach churned as Devlin's words slammed back into her. Rallion's comet. Her powers. Her mother. Sister Death. All of it tangled in a muddled rush her mind couldn't unravel.

He didn't seem to expect an answer. "Rest while you can," he said softly. "We can't stay long."

She frowned.

"We don't know where the others are, and we have to move before they find us."

That frantic rhythm restarted in her heart, as though it longed to flee. Flee from here. From *him*. He would be furious once he learned she had slipped from his grasp.

"Do you remember where they took you? How many there were?"

She blinked. Her head was too heavy to form words.

"That's all right. You can tell us later."

He kept speaking, but her mind refused to focus, letting his words drift over her like a warm breeze.

Then he said a name.

Again.

And again.

"Isla." His grip on her shoulder tightened.

Right. She shook her head.

Isla. He was talking to her.

"I'm going to take care of you, sister. Do you understand?" His gaze burned with such intensity she almost wanted to believe him. Almost. But a small, persistent voice clawing at her skull whispered that she shouldn't.

The next time she woke, her body no longer felt a step away from the first gate. Instead, it was as if she'd been lightly stabbed in the side... over and over again. That had to be an improvement.

With great effort, she managed to sit up, aided by, of all people, Edmund, who appeared in her sandy enclosure the moment she stirred. His timing was impeccable. Almost too impeccable, as though someone were reporting her every movement.

Her brother called for food and water, and the angry howls in her stomach finally quieted. The first bite nearly made her retch—some kind of broth, thin and flavorless—but she forced it down. It had been days since her last meal. Months, perhaps, since anything resembling a proper one. The thought hollowed her further. Months, except for the small treats Devlin had stolen away for her. But she refused to count those.

Edmund stared at her, waiting. Or maybe building the courage to find his voice.

There were things she wanted to say, but the words slipped, always out of reach.

They would have to wait. She threw back the layers of blankets.

"What are you doing?" Edmund stepped forward to press her down but froze when she flinched at his touch.

"I can't stay in bed any longer. I need to move. I have to," she insisted when his expression wavered with doubt.

"You need to—"

"I thought we had to leave soon," she cut in, refusing to meet his eyes. "Let me stretch my legs, only for a minute. It's been so long since I... since I... just let me breathe fresh air for a moment, then I'll come back."

Edmund's eyes darkened, and part of her wanted to recoil at the sight. "I don't want to push you—"

"You won't," she said firmly. Not after everything she had survived.

He looked ready to protest, but after a silent battle within himself, he only nodded.

Though she'd been unconscious for who knew how long, her legs carried her surprisingly well... until she promptly tripped over nothing but air right outside the tent.

They wandered for a while, her hand resting on his arm for balance, though she had refused at first. He'd been immovable in his insistence, and she eventually relented, slipping her hand into the crook of his arm while her eyes tried to make sense of the forest. All she saw was a tangle of twisted branches and a thin carpet of dark moss spread over the ground.

The soft rustle of leaves sent a stab of pain through her skull, but she kept it to herself. Her brother's presence should have been a comfort. It should have but unease threaded through her despite his encouraging words. Something was wrong, even if she couldn't name it.

Their short walk around the clearing brought no relief. Most of the soldiers gave them space, but a few watched her too closely. The blond soldier she had glimpsed in her tent lingered at the far edge of camp, his gaze tracking her every step. Another, her hair looped into braids, shadowed them from a steady twenty paces, never closer.

It was unsettling.

Isla bit into the stale pastry clutched in her free hand. Edmund had pressed the oversized biscuit on her before they left, insisting she carry something to eat. She was grateful, if only because it gave her hands something to do.

They never wandered far. Her tent—the only one in the small forest camp—remained in sight at all times, as though Edmund expected her to crumble without warning and need to be carried back. With the way her body protested each step, she couldn't entirely fault him.

A shimmer of violet caught at the corner of her vision, half-hidden in the thicket of red-vined trees. It vanished before she could check if it had even been there at all.

Edmund's hand tightened around hers, and they walked on, tracing the same loop for the third time. The stretch of her legs felt almost liberating, as though she hadn't moved them freely in weeks—or was it months?

She frowned.

How long had she really been down there?

Everything had blurred into one tangled knot, impossible to separate memory from dream, truth from invention.

At least Edmund didn't press. He seemed to understand how hard it was to recall. And truthfully, she didn't want to remember, except to know which pieces were real and which belonged only in her fractured mind. Not only the memories Beretta had stolen and torn apart.

At least she was away now. Safe.

Or as safe as one could be, given the circumstances.

What did safety mean here? Who—or what—counted as a threat? Even now, the faint rustle of leaves ahead sent her pulse racing, a sheen of sweat breaking at the back of her neck.

It felt like she was being watched. And technically, she was, by more than one pair of eyes.

This was just a forest, she told herself. Nothing more. Devlin wasn't lurking behind a thick trunk or crouched in the shadows of some scraggly bush.

There were only trees here. Rows upon rows of pine and brittle leaves.

Only trees.

Until the rustling came again. This time chased by a low snarl.

Her breath caught before Edmund even noticed. A dark, serpentine shape, no larger than her head, slithered from the bushes.

It opened its narrow jaws, but only a strangled growl escaped, a half-cry as if it didn't yet know how to roar. The thing tumbled forward on feline-like limbs, its long neck craning toward her and blood-red eyes locking onto hers.

Edmund drew his sword, confidence gleaming in the motion as he stepped between her and the beast. It bared its teeth—smaller than she expected—and released a thin, wheezing war cry.

The creature prowled closer, onyx claws sliding in and out with every step, as though it hadn't yet mastered the use of its own weapons.

Before Edmund could test his blade, the blond soldier appeared—axe raised high. She moved with ruthless precision, already swinging as the creature sprang.

"Stop!"

The word tore its way out before she realized it came from her. Everyone froze. Dozens of eyes prickled her skin, but she ignored them.

Against every instinct, she slipped free of Edmund's arm and crouched, hand outstretched.

This wasn't some feral monster come to devour them. It was a cubling—no more than a few months old. And from the desperate hunger glinting in its red eyes, it had been alone far too long.

The blond soldier hesitated, axe hovering. Her jaw tightened as she cast a fleeting look behind her, as though expecting orders from the trees themselves. Then she stepped back, barely a step, keeping her weapon ready.

"It's a youngling," Isla rasped, her throat still raw from thirst and the mines. She broke off a corner of the hardened biscuit.

"I really don't think that's—" the soldier started, then cut herself off with another quick sideways glance.

The first piece landed beneath its nose. The creature sniffed, lifted its long head, hissed at them, then gulped the crumb in a single swallow.

It skittered back, dead leaves crunching beneath its stubby legs, but froze when another scrap hit the ground. This one closer. Its back arched and teeth flashed, before it crept forward to snatch the second piece.

The third went the same way. Then the fourth.

Each bite drew it nearer, while Edmund muttered beside her, sword hand twitching, watching as though the tiny thing were a nightmare given flesh. To him, it was a monster. To Isla, it was merely hungry.

By the fifth bite, it was close enough to touch. She could have seized it then, but she knew that would end in blood. Instead, she offered her palm, the last of the biscuit crumbled in her hand, and nudged it toward the creature.

After sniffing the air and hissing once more, a rough tongue flicked across Isla's palm, stealing the last of the food. Then—before she could breathe—it lunged, curling its wiry body tight around her arm.

"Get it off her!" Edmund barked, sword flashing up.

But the creature only cooed.

The blond soldier, axe half-raised, froze mid-step. She shot Edmund a sharp look, then glanced past him toward the clearing. "I don't think it's dangerous," she said to the same patch of trees behind them.

Edmund's mouth tightened. He spoke her name like a blade slicing through the air.

"Isla."

She snapped her head toward him.

"I said hand it over. I'll dispose of that—thing."

The cubling gave a plaintive cry, pressing into her chest. Isla cradled it instinctively, crouched low to shield it from them. Her voice scraped out, rough but fierce.

"No. He's only a baby."

Edmund scoffed and seized her arm.

The blond soldier was there in an instant. For a heartbeat, Isla thought she meant to wrench the creature away. Instead, she pried Edmund's hand off with iron precision.

The cubling squawked and clung tighter.

"Don't be ridiculous, Freya," Edmund snapped.

"Back off, prince," she shot back. "Before you make things worse."

Worse. Isla almost laughed. Wasn't that all they lived in now? After what she had endured, she was certain she'd walked through every gate Rallion had to offer. And yet, she still couldn't bring herself to surrender the creature.

"It's fine," another voice cut in.

Edmund stiffened. The soldiers shifted, pulling back without a word.

Isla cleared her throat.

Bootsteps scuffed the dirt, stopping before her. Careful, deliberate, not daring to kick up dust or jostle the creature curled around her arm.

"It's dangerous—" Edmund tried.

"It's a baby," the voice said darkly. "Orphaned, most likely. It won't harm anyone. Let it be."

A sharp sigh from Edmund, then a low groan. "I'm not feeding it."

She pressed her cheek to its scaly head. "I will," she said fiercely. A spark of confidence she hadn't felt in days surged through her. "I'll take care of him. Or... her?" She ducked her head, searching for some sign of its gender.

The creature thrummed against her.

At least someone else felt as lost as she did. At least someone else didn't belong.

"We'll get it some food," the voice said again. "Keep it from turning feral with hunger."

Edmund's head snapped up, his eyes flashing.

Freya's fingers twitched toward her axe. "It'll be fine," she said, her voice carrying undertones Isla's muddled mind couldn't quite unravel.

They were letting her keep it, for now. She'd have to keep it happy and fed or they'd take it away. She knew they would.

She tore her gaze from the creature's crimson eyes and let it climb the length of the soldier's black-and-silver uniform and over the chipped hilt of his broadsword, until it met his storm-gray eyes.

Her breath caught, heart fluttering violently. She knew him. The dark curls. The sharp jaw. Those thin, unsmiling lips. She remembered them.

Isla opened her mouth to thank him, but the general turned on his heel before she could utter a word, leaving only a cold hollow in her chest.

Three

The General

If it weren't for the half dozen Pedite soldiers—soldiers who barely recognized him as their leader—watching him and the prince, Rian would've already decked Edmund square in that smug face and stepped over his writhing body to get to the tent behind him.

He'd been patient. He'd stayed away, all in the name of 'avoiding a scene' while she recovered, according to Edmund. Now she was up, walking around, and apparently well enough to cuddle with a seropa, the larger version of which had tried to kill them months ago. And she refused to let anyone take it from her care.

And yes, maybe he froze when he saw her with the creature. When her wide brown eyes met his, his brain stopped working, no matter how much he shouted at it. So, he ran away... well, more of a brisk walk. Not that he was proud of it.

Which was exactly why he needed to talk to her now. Now Edmund had suddenly decided he knew what was best for Isla. That was rich, considering he'd never once done a single thing right by his sister since the day she was born.

By some miracle, they managed to keep their voices down, so no one picked up on the discourse. Edmund, of course, was making that nearly impossible. Thank the goddess they hadn't brought any Listeners or there'd be no corner of this godsdamned forest left with even a scrap of privacy. Rian didn't need anything else the other generals could twist against him when they got back.

"She barely remembers her own name," Edmund muttered. "Don't make things worse."

"I refuse to lie to her anymore," Rian said, gruff as ever. "And what do you mean, 'not make things worse'? Is your grand plan to get back and hand her straight over to *Brenner?*" His derision couldn't be hidden—there was no point. Every soldier here thought that man was a cursed asshole who belonged in a cell, not wandering these lands with a title he thought meant he could do whatever he wanted.

"No." Edmund shook his head. Rian didn't bother hiding the shock that crossed his face. "I'll deal with my father, but there's no way in all of Rallion's twelve gates that I'm handing her over to him in this state."

"Oh, so get her healed up a bit, then hand her over? Sounds like a brilliant plan."

"Don't be an idiot. We're returning to Aurial first, then my father can decide what to do next."

Rian laughed.

Nothing Isla had said gave him any confidence that the king would do the right thing. He was the one who had traded his daughter to an imbecile simply because he could no longer stand the sight of her.

Gods, as reckless as Rian's father had been—gambling and squandering all their money chasing a better life—at least he would never have done something like this to his children. His choices were irresponsible, yes, but they had only landed his eldest sons in the Pedite Corps as a result.

"No fucking way are you taking her back there after everything," Rian said.

Edmund closed the distance and poked his chest. "I'm trying to do what I can. I'm doing the best I can. Right now, the only option is to take her home. If we don't, my father will march straight into this forest with his contingent of Siicas to drag me back to Aurial, and send her straight to Koliat, no matter what condition she's in. This is all I can do."

Rian jerked his head toward the tent. "Then *try harder*."

Edmund scoffed. "We'll go on foot. We can buy time on the journey back by avoiding transporters. I'm sure they aren't suitable for someone who's been through what she has. That's our best shot."

"And if he shows up?"

Edmund made a disparaging noise and gave him a dark look. At least there was *one thing* they agreed on.

"Enough of this," Rian huffed. He'd delayed long enough. "I'm going in."

He brushed past Edmund, ignoring the curses of indignation, and strode into the small tent. They'd gathered what blankets they could spare to create a makeshift bed, and Freya helped change Isla's tattered clothes that first night into spare slacks and a tunic. Rian burned the old rags immediately after.

Isla sat in the bed with the serpentine-feline curled in her lap. Both were bathed in a golden hue from the sun filtering through the beige canvas. The moment he burst in, the small creature jumped up and hissed at Edmund, who had crashed in behind him. That blasted royal couldn't even give him a moment alone. Was he really that worried Rian would pull something? *Now?*

Isla tucked her hair behind her ears and held the seropa with both hands to keep it from leaping at Edmund. The scars on the back of her hand made all the blood rush to Rian's ears. They hadn't looked so bad before, but now, with a clear view, the sight rekindled his insatiable rage.

"Don't get up for us," Edmund said, beating Rian to it. "It's fine."

She shifted back on the mess of blankets. A bowl of raw meat sat before her. Food they'd found for the creature, which had quickly grown tired of stale bread.

Rian half-thought it might do the beast a disservice being fed this way. It'd never learn to hunt on its own once they left. And the only other thing he and Edmund could agree on was that the seropa would have to stay behind.

Isla's eyes flickered up for a moment before returning to the seropa. Rian scratched his elbow.

How long had it been since he'd last spoken with her? Months.

It felt like an eternity.

An eternity spent losing pieces of his mind every day, then scavenging the scraps just to keep moving. He had led their group as a hollowed-out version of himself, half of him missing since she'd been taken. And now, he didn't know what to do with the rest.

"Are you feeling better?" Edmund asked, still annoyingly attached to his side.

"Much better," she said quietly, keeping her gaze fixed on anything but the two men in her tent.

Rian opened his mouth, then closed it. What was wrong with him?

It was unclear exactly what had happened to her, and even less clear what she remembered. The last thing he wanted was to make things worse. And the one thing he excelled at was precisely that: making things worse.

When their eyes met after finding the seropa, she looked right through him, as if he were a complete stranger undeserving of her attention. Perhaps that was all he was now.

It was hard to accept, especially when she had become his reason for breathing. His reason for existing.

"I don't think you've met the general yet," Edmund said smoothly. "He's been *assisting* with your rescue operation."

A faint smile tugged at Isla's lips at the irritated tone Edmund used.

"Thank you," she said softly.

Memories of a laboriously pulled apology, drenched in barely concealed derision one night by the fire, returned to him. He'd never be able to make it up to her now.

A knock against the trunk they'd used as a post jerked him out of his brooding thoughts. He relaxed his grip on Dark End when he spotted the Agicae healer.

Ben bowed his head and pushed back the hood of his cloak. "I wanted to take a quick look before we leave, Your Highness."

Isla's lips pressed into a thin line, but she nodded and tried to pass the seropa to Edmund. It hissed again. Rian plucked the squirming creature from her hands, cradling it against his chest as he backed toward the edge of the canvas.

The creature vibrated warmly against him.

Edmund was too busy scowling at the seropa to notice Isla's subtle grimace when the healer touched her. It was barely perceptible, but Rian caught it. He knew her moods well enough to recognize when something was wrong, even if she didn't fully realize it. Something about this wielder—this healer—had set her off in a way he'd never seen before.

Sensing his scrutiny, she held her chin high with a grim smile, as though reassuring him all was fine.

The healer's hand glowed faintly as it passed over her body, checking for any pressing injuries that needed attention before the journey home. Isla clasped her hands together, her wide eyes following every movement. The small seropa squirmed and squawked, trying to reach her.

Edmund continued his long rant about the weather and the mushy ground they'd crossed, oblivious to the tension in the small enclosure.

When Ben finished his check-up, he nodded to Edmund and Rian, pulled his cloak tighter around himself, and edged around the two before scuttling out of the tent, as though afraid of them.

Ridiculous.

They were here to watch over her. Nothing more. Not like either of them had experienced their share of absolute freak-outs and meltdowns over the past months.

Not at all.

The creature squirmed from his arms and flopped to Isla's feet. It twisted its head toward Rian and Edmund, curling its upper lip.

Isla looked between them expectantly.

A moment passed.

Then another.

She picked at the ends of her hair. "If we're expected to leave, I should prepare."

Rian hesitated, every instinct tugging him in opposite directions all at once. "We'll leave as soon as you're ready."

Isla sucked in a breath. The creature circled in place.

"These forests are cursed," Edmund said. Panic flickered across her face. "And we don't know how long we have. We need to move right away."

Exactly the opposite of keeping her calm. Idiot prince.

"Then we can get you someplace safe," Rian said, suppressing a convulsion from rippling along his spine.

Safe.

As if he could do anything about that. He'd promised to keep her safe and had yet to follow through. He'd failed in every sense of the word.

Edmund stepped forward, oblivious to his sister's recoil, and asked, "We need to know where you were and who took you?"

Something flashed in her eyes, and Edmund's gaze jumped to her hands before he seemed to catch himself. He scratched the back of his neck and shifted uneasily.

Isla shook her head, and the creature made distressed noises.

Moron. They'd already agreed not to press her for information until she was ready. Did Edmund forget all sense?

Freya burst into the tent without a care to Slin. "Both of you idiots, get out," she said confidently. Not a hint of contrition as she addressed two of her superiors. Though that had never stopped her before. "You are not helping."

Edmund had the grace to sputter only a little.

Rian didn't move. He wasn't afraid of Isla or her powers, unlike Edmund, who couldn't stop glancing at her hands. She hadn't harmed them in the forest when she found them, despite losing total control. Only trees and shrubs served as casualties that time.

Edmund had turned into a pale, blubbering fool afterward. It was likely the first time he'd seen his sister's powers with his own eyes. Perhaps now he realized his father's error in refusing to teach her to control them. To fully embrace her gifts instead of the debilitating fear he'd instilled in Isla her entire life.

"Your ladies aren't here, Princess, but I can help you dress." Freya tossed one of her uniforms onto the makeshift bed and knelt. "We'll have them back after we leave the forest, and they'll be able to—"

"It's fine," Isla said, toying with the fabric. "I am capable of dressing myself."

"As you wish." Freya's eyes darkened, but she didn't push. She grabbed Rian and Edmund by the collars and pulled them out with her, ignoring both of their heated protests.

Four

Prince Edmund of Velotia

He swiped at his foe, pouring every inch of frustration into making the hit land. A thick slice cut through branch and bark, right on top of the first. He made another. Then another before backing away to assess his work.

He winced and rubbed his shoulder. It was acting up *again*. Just perfect.

Once they were back in Aurial he'd have his father's top medics check if there was a better way to push the pain away for good this time. Nothing the healer had done helped for long, and since Edmund had been hiding his identity since entering this forest, he couldn't ask for help.

And now, the wielder needed to conserve his strength to help Isla. She needed it more.

"Your form is improving, Prince. Less like a toddler who got hold of his father's sword, and closer to a young novice."

Leaves crunched as Freya approached. He hadn't heard her sneak up on him. He'd have to learn to pay better attention to things like that. Maybe once she deemed his sword skills passable enough, he could ask her to go over some of the tracking basics that every man in the military seemed to have received except him.

Their lessons had been going on for some time now, away from the others so as not to embarrass him, or *her*, with his deplorable lack of progress despite having an excellent teacher.

"You seem troubled," she said, leaning against the tree he was practicing on, its branches dead at the bottom but fresh green sprouted at the topmost branches. "Distraction will get you killed out here. It will get *me* killed trying to protect your sorry excuse of a royal ass. Why are you holding back?"

Edmund grimaced, allowing the insults to slide over him as if she'd sent him a glowing compliment instead. He sheathed his sword and dabbed at the trail of sweat making its way down the side of his neck, joining his already drenched back.

He kicked a small bush with dark berries, exactly the kind Freya had warned him against eating.

"Your restraint is impeccable," she said. "Who taught you that?"

Edmund ignored her and clenched his hand into a ball. This was stupid, and he was getting nowhere today, despite it being the first time in days he'd managed to sneak away from the group.

"At least he didn't throw you out like we'd feared," Freya said with a grim smile. "Though your timing was impeccable, I'd have to say. Perhaps Imoten's fortune is finally sliding our way."

"Perhaps." He pursed his lips and turned on his heel, determined to return to camp before anyone noticed his absence, motioning for her to follow.

He did not doubt that the general had told Freya to tail him since being discovered in their party. The thought that he needed a guardian sent his blood burning. Deep down, he knew it was warranted.

So much for helping with Isla's rescue. He'd hardly contributed anything to the search since stepping foot in this forest, and once they'd found her, he'd remained equally useless.

Not to mention cowardly. When he finally found himself alone with his sister, the apologies he'd rehearsed refused to leave his lips, and he stared at her stupidly. Did she remember the words he'd said? The blame he'd laid on her all his life?

He often thought of their mother and what she would say about all of this. There was no way she'd approve of what he'd done these past years. She'd be so ashamed... ashamed of *him*.

He certainly was.

Maybe that was why he'd pushed this off for so long. If he didn't say the words out loud to Isla, he'd never have to face the depths of his shame.

"Want to practice?" Freya asked, her brows knotted together in some unspoken question.

Edmund shook his head. Someone would notice.

He flexed his fist and forced his face into passive disdain as they entered the camp.

The two Agicae jumped and backed away. Now that they knew his true identity, everyone decided to skirt around the prince with hushed whispers, more than they ever had at the prior camp. Perhaps it was because this mission was so small, so intimate, that no one had expected him to join. No one had thought he'd do something this risky and idiotic, as Freya constantly reminded him.

The moment he was in the relative safety of the small group, Freya peeled away from her prince-watch duties and went off in search of Rian.

Edmund's eye twitched at the confirmation. He prayed she wasn't reporting all his secrets back to the Pedite general. She'd promised as much, but Edmund knew where her loyalties truly lay.

He found himself standing outside Isla's makeshift tent. Nobody had offered him such covering, and he'd been forced to sleep on his bedroll on the ground again, despite the soldiers knowing who he was. He had no doubt who had instructed them to do that.

The blame couldn't lie solely with them, considering he was the one who had sneaked in after countless warnings about how dangerous this journey would be. He was the one to put himself at risk. All to try to make things right before it all got too complicated.

And yet, here he was, unable to move.

Argh. Why was he hesitating now? Wasn't this the chance he'd wanted?

Fear leaked from him when her power clawed its way out that day. He'd stood there, doing absolutely nothing. Paralyzed. It was a good thing she hadn't been able to see the look on his face, though the others had: Freya and Malin... and *him*.

Edmund was certain they'd be using that against him until they returned to Aurial, and the thought infuriated him.

Before he could decide whether to enter or slink away like a coward, a black spot darted out from the small tent, followed by his sister.

"Get back here, you—ooh!"

Isla froze mid-scoop and straightened. There was a shift in the way she carried herself now that she wore the black-and-silver uniform. Edmund was certain she'd balk at wearing a Pedite badge on her chest once she was back to her normal self.

Her hand jumped to the thick braid running down her shoulder, and he hated the way she looked at him. Would things ever return to normal between them? Whatever that even meant anymore.

The creature hissed and twisted in the dirt, so she bent to retrieve it. It gnawed on the tip of her finger.

"You shouldn't do that," he found himself saying. Hadn't Rian mentioned that certain genders of this creature carried a potent toxin?

Isla's eyes jumped to his, a brief flash of anger crossing them. "It's not dangerous." As if to prove her point, she held the creature out, but it merely swiped a tiny paw at Edmund.

Isla grinned when he scrambled back. At least some things hadn't changed. Maybe that was a good sign.

The grin disappeared as quickly as it came, and she cast her eyes down. Edmund whipped around.

"Are you ready to leave, princess?" the shaggy-haired soldier asked, approaching with the general right behind him.

Annoyance flickered through Edmund. At least Rian looked equally unhappy to see him.

"Yes." She turned toward the small tent. "But I'll need to—"

"Someone will pack for you," Rian said quickly. "And we have Ri—the horse ready."

She nodded, something hidden in her eyes that she refused to reveal to anyone. The creature squawked again.

Edmund opened his mouth.

"I'd like to keep him," Isla cut across. "He's so small and won't get in the way."

"Absolutely not," Edmund said confidently. Then he realized Isla wasn't trying to bargain with him.

Her gaze was fixed solely on *him*. She held the creature out again, as if the sight of its red eyes and sharp teeth snapping at the air might sway him.

"I don't think he'll make it on his own," she added gently.

Rian sighed and his face softened annoyingly. "Fine." He reached out and scratched the creature's head. "But don't let it spook the horse—or terrorize the men," he added with a grin, eyes flickering toward Edmund, as if he were the only one that last category applied to.

"I won't. I promise." The seropa cooed its own strange confirmation.

Edmund didn't bother mentioning that their father would spear the creature and hang it from the rafters the moment they returned to Aurial—he'd probably make her watch as its heart was ripped from its chest. She'd have to figure that out for herself before they arrived.

Instead, he focused on the winning smile his sister sent the soldier and the tentative one that matched hers.

Fucking nope.

No way in all the cursed hells. Edmund would have to keep a closer eye on that. He wasn't about to let anything like that happen again. Not even if his sister had been to Rallion's first gate and back. He needed an excuse to keep those two separated.

Edmund stepped between them, ignoring Malin's chuckle, and held out his arm. "Let's get you and the horse ready."

The general allowed them to leave without a fight, though Edmund could feel his eyes following as they approached the mangy horse whose hair had been haphazardly brushed out. It was missing an ear and bore several scuffs, as if it had gotten into a few scraps out here.

"What's his name?" Isla asked, reaching out to scratch along the horse's nose. She'd smartly tucked the seropa into her oversized jacket, which—Edmund realized with a start—bore a general's crest. How had he missed that important detail before? They needed a different one, *immediately*.

"It doesn't matter. The horse is half-dead, but it brought you here, so it should be able to do his job."

His job. That's it. That was the key.

Freya had mentioned that Rian wanted to work on military reform within the Pedite Corps once all this was over. Something about better conditions and regulations for the conscripts. A noble cause. One that would hopefully keep the general busy with his duties and his gaze far from Edmund's sister.

A line formed between Isla's brows. She allowed him to help her onto the horse's back while the others packed up her tent. The horse was less jumpy than he'd expected, given how long it must have been living in these woods. It must have had owners before, judging by its familiarity with human touch and how it didn't seem anything more than slightly annoyed by the seropa's presence.

The soldiers made quick work of clearing the camp and erasing any lasting traces of their stay. Another skill he wished he'd been taught during his training, though he never imagined he'd be roughing it like this. His father had said he had no need for such training, well, look at him now.

Though his father would be furious once he found out what Edmund had done.

He winced. Both he and Isla had a reckoning waiting for them once they got home.

Five

The General

After traveling for hours, they stopped for a brief dinner. Edmund complained about wanting a break and had grown more vocal now that he wasn't hiding under the cloak of an Agicae wielder. Though Rian would rather remove an index than grant Edmund even a hint of reprieve or comfort, Isla had turned a hint pale so he called the group to stop.

Edmund sank to his knees the moment the words left his lips.

Rian sent Freya to help Isla and River, while he and Malin went off with Aldan to see if there was any edible game in this part of the forest. They caught sight of a family of hares, which Aldan was setting a trap for, while Malin and Rian edged away, scanning for other life. Malin's gaze lingered on him, too closely, as if he expected Rian to sprout a pair of antlers or grow scales along his side.

"What?" Rian bit out, sharper than he intended. "Stop staring like that."

Malin laughed and looped his thumbs through his belt. "Wasn't staring… but since I have you alone—what's going on?"

"Nothing." Rian turned on his heel and gathered branches to start a fire. Stewed hare would be perfect, if they could manage it, and if this forest didn't interfere first. Aldan was astute at hunting and tracking, and Rian had every ounce of confidence in him.

He planned to work with Aldan more, to hone his skills and help him become more than just another soldier trapped in the Pedite Corps like so many before.

"You've been extra jumpy since…" Malin lowered his voice dramatically, despite Aldan being wholly focused on his task. "Since we found her. What was all that about with the…" He scrunched his face and flexed his fists like claws. "With the hands and the dead forest and… stuff?"

Rian shook his head. Not here. Not with anyone within earshot. Aldan finished setting the last strings of the snare, dusted off his pants, and surveyed his work.

They both jumped at the hint of rustling, hands flying to their pommels, but it was only Freya. And someone was behind her.

Isla.

Freya's self-satisfied smirk was too much.

"The princess wanted to find some food for… it," Freya said, her voice clipped. "And I didn't think it wise to let her wander alone." The seropa poked its dark head out from the jacket he'd given to Freya to give to Isla and sniffed the air.

A light blush crept up Isla's neck, but she held her head high, that old self-righteousness resurfacing.

"Well." Malin brushed his hands together. "You're in luck, princess. We found a family of hares we were about to coax out."

Isla wrinkled her nose.

"Perfect," Freya said happily. "Why don't you help the general here, and you can find something for that… that thing to eat. Malin, I need your help back at camp."

Rian had never hated his friends more. Especially when Malin called for Aldan to join them now that the snare was ready.

Isla watched them go with a strange expression, then shoved the creature back into her jacket, the bulge almost comical.

"Can I stay here for a bit?" She gestured at the stump Aldan had vacated. "I don't want to go back to the camp yet."

Rian's chest nearly cleaved in two. "Can you keep it quiet?" He pointed at the jiggling lump.

She nodded eagerly and sat on the dark log, clasping her hands over her knees as she stared at the snare's opening, as if their meal might leap through at any moment. At least that bite of impatience hadn't left her.

Rian lowered himself to the ground, keeping several paces between them and letting the silence stretch comfortably.

They'd have to return soon and push on as far as they could for as long as they could. The Muratians had found them once before in these very woods, and he feared they would again.

Even if they crossed the borders, she still wouldn't be safe. His insides squirmed. It was unclear when—or where—she would ever be. Did that place lie with the Koliats, or within their own kingdom?

Only the goddesses knew the answer to that mystery, and they weren't known for making things easy for the mortals who walked these lands.

"Do you think..." Isla began, her voice wavering. He looked up, and she had finally torn her gaze away from the snare. "Do you think they're coming after me?"

"Yes," he breathed. He doubted they'd ever stop. "Was it the same ones from before? Their prince?"

She shook her head. "Things are still foggy, but yes. It was him." She hesitated, and he spotted a shine in the corner of her eyes. "I thought she was my friend. I didn't—I didn't know who she was."

"Nobody blames you. Not for any of it. She was a powerful wielder."

It must have been the one hunting them down. The mindweaver.

He flexed his hands. He'd seen firsthand how powerful that one was—and how much she enjoyed causing pain.

The seropa peeked out at its keeper's distress and crawled up to her shoulder, nuzzling its long nose into her neck. Rian tilted his head, watching it curiously.

"Thank you," she said, so soft it was nearly lost in the forest wind.

"What for?"

"Coming after me." He opened his mouth, but she added, "Edmund said you led the rescue efforts."

Right. Right. His stomach churned. She didn't remember anything else yet. Didn't remember him.

"I also know that you helped me the first time," she added, more tentatively.

Rian raised an eyebrow.

"Freya told me."

Naturally. His friend loved interfering wherever she could, despite his strict orders *against* it

"Sorry if I was a lot of work. It sounds like I was."

"I'd do it again," he said plainly.

Her smile faltered, then returned stronger. The creature cooed from beneath the jacket.

"What's its name?" he asked.

"What?" She peered at the bulge.

"You should give him a name. Or is it a she?"

"I think it's a boy." She chewed her bottom lip. "I don't know a good name. Any suggestions?"

He sighed, staring at the dark canopy overhead and imagining the dancing lights that would soon appear in the concealed sky. "How about Ophis, for the serpent constellation?"

"I like it." She cradled the bulge. "Opi for short."

"It's perfect."

A flash of violet appeared in the distance as a wisp darted from branch to branch before disappearing into the shadows. He fully planned on capturing the next one that tried spying on him. What were the old tales about wisps and their link to the goddesses again?

A crash came through the bushes, coming from the direction of their camp. His hand didn't even twitch toward Dark End as he recognized the erratic stomping pattern—coming to ensure Rian didn't lay a hand on his sister—followed by the quiet gait of Freya close behind.

Isla rolled her eyes, and he couldn't suppress the laugh that clawed its way up from his previously chilled chest.

Edmund stopped in front of them to glare but couldn't seem to catch his breath enough to brandish any admonishments.

Freya happily strolled past the wheezing prince. "The prince wanted to check if you needed anything to drink, Princess Isla."

Rian had to hold back his retort; Isla scoffed. "I had some water right before leaving," she replied smoothly.

"Ben wanted to check in on you," Edmund said. "It's been a long journey so far."

There was no mistaking it. Isla definitely grimaced at the mention of the healer. Once again, Edmund either missed it or didn't care.

Freya grabbed the prince's shoulder. "I'm certain the princess is more than capable of determining her own health at this point. Let's go back."

Edmund opened his mouth, and Rian, knowing the insult ready to spill out, cut him off before the prince could make even more of a mess of things. "I can take care of things out here, if you want to return with them, Princess."

Isla's face dropped, and she stood.

For some reason, that was the wrong thing to say. If only his brain could come up with something better. *Anything* better to fix this than staring at her awkwardly.

They would be safer at the camp. Edmund was right to come get her. What had Rian even been thinking in the first place?

A gurgled howl broke the discomfort.

"What in Rallion's twelve hells is that?" Edmund muttered, his eyes jumping to Isla as if expecting Opi to be the source of the racket.

Rian scrambled to his feet as a pale body tore out from the bush facing them. Splinters and thorns showered down, bouncing off Rian's uniform. Long ivory claws dug into the dirt as it propelled itself toward him and Isla. The creature was almost human in form, twisted and deformed beyond recognition. But when it opened its mouth, it was like staring past Rallion's seventh gate adorned with rows of thin teeth.

Black goo—blood of some sort—leaked from the corners of its gaping mouth and a thick cut that ran down its torso.

Freya was there, hand on Isla's shoulder, pushing her back, much to the annoyance of Opi, who had popped out again to growl at the intruder before being jostled to the ground along with his master.

The beast missed its target and crashed into a tree, nearly toppling the giant birch that towered above them. It climbed to a thick branch before leaping back into the middle of the group.

Dark End was settled in Rian's hand, a full extension of himself, while Freya's Bone Breaker was already drawn from its spot at her side.

Rian angled himself in front of Edmund and swung at the creature, ignoring the chill that gnawed at his bones at the sight of the gaping mouth that dripped blackness everywhere.

Isla didn't move or scream from her spot behind Freya; she stared at the creature with her mouth agape, clutching the writhing seropa. It cried and yelped, instincts pulling at it to flee.

When the death's-gate creature turned back to them, Rian felt the same instinct rising—to drop everything and run. That was the only logical response when facing a beast far beyond Rallion's first gate.

The air in his lungs chilled, and his heartbeat slowed to a dangerous pace. He'd never seen anything like this before; he didn't even know where it had come from. Its hollow eyes conveyed no emotion, not even the hunger one would expect. What could anyone do when confronted by a creature such as this?

His swing missed, barely scraping the creature's arm. It didn't flinch or howl. Nothing indicated he had hurt it. It didn't even slow down, except to snarl at him and swipe a lengthy claw, catching the edge of his jacket, missing skin and bone.

The seropa yelped, drawing the creature's attention.

No. Not her. Anybody but her.

Throwing all sense to the dark forest, he dove for the creature, tackling it to the ground with a deep roar. They became a tangle of limbs and claws and shouts and growls, but somehow a clawed foot—or hand—hit, pushing him out of reach of that haunting jaw.

That foolish plan worked. The creature redirected its focus onto the annoyance—onto him. Dark End was out of reach, and he was certain none of his daggers could pierce this horrible creature's skin. He was powerless. Defenseless.

Pure, foolish adrenaline kept him moving, and he flung out an arm to punch it again. The blow did nothing against its tough hide except to annoy it further.

His vision blurred, locked on that sharp void of a mouth determined to swallow everything in its path. Each pulse of his heart thundered through his body, begging for release. For something, anything. Yet the sight of the creature rendered him useless. He couldn't move. Couldn't think.

It snarled and hunched, readying for its final leap.

This was it. The true end.

A shining star barreled toward the creature. Bone Breaker.

Freya's aim was true; her axe landed squarely on top of the creature's head, sending it plummeting to the ground.

Rian remained still.

The creature scrambled, scratching the dirt with its bone-like claws as it attempted to right itself. Gods, what in all of Rallion's gates was this thing?

Edmund picked up Dark End and swung the sword down. It cleaved the creature's head from its body, dark ichor splattering their boots and half of Rian's face. All he could do was stare at the unmoving body of that—thing—while his limbs struggled to respond.

What the fuck?

What the fuck?

What the actual fuck was that?

Edmund dropped Dark End and scrambled over to Isla, ignoring the disparaging scowl Freya sent his way. "Are you alright, sister?"

She was equally transfixed by the body and the pool of blood forming beside it. It seemed to drain the life from the few blades of grass below. Her mouth moved wordlessly as her eyes bulged dangerously.

Opi leapt from her arms with his back arched, hissing at the dead creature as if he had been the one to fell it.

"What in Dia's unknown insanity was that?" Freya wiped Bone Breaker on her pants and held out a hand. At least she didn't comment on how he had just frozen there.

Rian shook his head, finally feeling his limbs return to life. That was a good question. He took Freya's hand and leapt to his unsteady feet.

Edmund shook Isla's shoulders. "Did it get you? Are you hurt?"

"We should get back to the others," Freya said in clipped tones. All the color had drained from her face, yet she wasn't the one who became completely paralyzed by it.

Isla still didn't move. Opi now pranced around the dead creature, alternating between crooning at his owner and hissing at the body.

"Do you need me to fetch the healer?" Edmund asked, worry coloring his hoarse voice.

Silence again.

Rian picked up Opi before he decided to taste the dead beast and dropped him back into Isla's arms. He crouched in front of her, wishing he could elbow Edmund out of the way, but knew better than to try anything right now.

His insides were still a sputtering mess, and he was certain he'd left his stomach back on the ground. Somehow, he managed to keep a steady hand as he touched Isla's shoulder. The contact made her jump, but recognition flitted across her face, and she snapped out of the trance that had held her.

"What is it, Isla?" he asked. Her brown eyes met his and flashed dangerously. He understood.

She had seen this creature of Rallion's deathful curse before.

Six

The Princess

The chill in her bones wouldn't leave, despite the thick jacket wrapped around her and the glowing warmth of the moonlight filtering through the gaps in the leaves above. It had been hours since they'd killed that thing. Hours.

They'd put considerable distance and countless trees between themselves and the disintegrating mess of its body.

Her brother and Rian exchanged hushed, heated words once the creature was dead. That dweller—or a Nothing, as the others whispered—had found them, which meant the others were close. Her blood curdled at the thought.

The general's face, despite being streaked with dark blood, was as pale as the moonlight that managed to slip through the thick canopy. He hadn't shown much emotion since she'd escaped, but the sight of that creature seemed to rattle him more than the others. It rattled her the same.

Even now, the others whispered about what it was and how it had crossed the gates as it did. They only stopped when the general snapped at them. It was almost comical how he and Edmund tripped over each other to take charge, though the soldiers—mostly Pedite, according to Freya—looked to the general more than her brother.

Opi croaked from his safe nest, refusing to leave after being unnecessarily yelled at by Edmund. At least he had been quieted by some dried meat Freya handed her with a wry smile. She thought they were out of their supply, but Freya said someone had a few morsels hidden away.

At least not everyone hated the creature. A few seemed to find it as endearing as she did. Opi wiggled in her arms, a relieving warmth against her cold body. How could anyone hate such a cute, harmless creature?

The horse whinnied softly. He was sturdy and kept a decent pace all night. Some of the men had tripped on the forest's traps or fell into hidden pits, but not this horse. She reached over and patted his neck. At least he had brought her to safety. Somehow, he knew where she needed to be, even if she hadn't realized it at the time. Now he was taking care of her again.

So much for a nice respite. So much for having a moment to get to know her saviors a little more, and so much for time to sort herself out before being hoisted back onto the horse and whisked into the dread of the Black Forests.

She had been through most of Rallion's gates and back again, and this forest, despite its odd quirks, was nothing compared to that. In fact, the steps she took almost felt familiar, like she had seen the twist of the branches in a distant memory.

This forest wasn't a stranger to her. It was vague and foggy, but each twisted branch sang to her in a familiar, yet strange, way. The fact that she couldn't remember more than that frustrated her to no end. It made her toes curl and the tips of her fingers prickle.

Freya passed her a waterskin, and she took a tentative sip before helping herself to a healthy chug. They gave her fresh water or food whenever she asked, and there was no reprimand despite bracing for one each time. She was still unable to shed those parts of her forged in the mines, even after knowing it had all been an elaborate farce created for her.

But now they had sent that—that demon—after her. It was dead, or so she thought. She had seen Devlin kill it with her own eyes. Even with her memory in shambles, she knew he had killed it before.

They found a way to bring it back and sent it after them. After *her*.

It was a message: he was coming. And once he found them, what he'd done to those villagers would happen to every single person here. Because of her.

It was nearly too much. Yet, everyone seemed to understand why it was here, without a hint of blame cast her way. She had enough guilt on her own.

Times like this, she wished she had a friend to talk to. She wished she had—

No. She shook those thoughts away.

Beretta was *not* her friend. She had none, not even before this.

The soldiers kept a close eye on her. There was always one or two within arm's reach at all times. It was hard to tell whether they were watching for dangers or simply keeping track of her.

Eventually, *he* crept up, flanked by the shaggy-haired soldier with the band around his brow, pretending to casually wander as if he didn't know who traveled with this part of their group. Something shimmered in her chest. An ember that was snuffed out so quickly she was unsure if she'd imagined it in the first place.

He patted the horse on the same spot on his neck she'd just tended. "How's River doing?"

River.

That name brushed against her skin like a soft petal. So, that was the horse's name. Fitting. Like a piece of an everlasting puzzle in her mind that she couldn't fully loop together.

The horse's ear flickered, echoed by a brief scratch at her chest from Opi. "He's doing great." She allowed her body to shift and flow with his every movement. "Was he—was he yours?"

The way the horse's ear perked up when he neared, and the familiar head bump he gave the soldier, made her certain they knew each other.

"In a sense," Rian said. "We found him. Together."

Opi popped out of her jacket, and she grabbed him before he could spook River. "I think he likes you better."

"I think so too."

She opened her mouth to scowl, but when she turned her head, he was laughing. It was a joke. Only a joke.

Rian dug into his pocket, grabbing a piece of dried meat, which Opi happily gobbled up. A warmth simmered in her veins at the sight.

"You may not remember this," he said with a half-smile, "but we crossed paths with another seropa ages ago. That one wasn't as kind as Opi."

There was no judgment or blame for her lack of memory, just understanding and a simple explanation. It was refreshing compared to Edmund's constant hovering and demands for answers.

"Maybe it was searching for its next meal," she said wryly.

"Oh, it found it for sure," he said. He winced, and something dark crossed his features. What happened to that one again? Trying to think that far back made her dizzy.

Right. Too soon for that.

This was so annoying. How did she remember more about her last three months beneath that dark rock than she did the rest of her life? It was like every time she tried to pull at a distant memory, everything around it unraveled like a thread, threatening to take her sanity with it... all thanks to Beretta.

She sighed. Slin really had it out for her.

"We're losing a lot of the moonlight," Edmund said from her other side, causing Opi to jump.

When did he manage to sneak up on them? She thought he was at the back with Freya, yet he always seemed to show up at the worst times.

Edmund clutched his side, likely in pain from the brisk pace they'd kept. She'd offer him the horse again, but knew he'd decline thanks to his pride.

There was something inside her that filled with unease at her brother's presence, and it didn't help that he seemed unsure what to say around her most of the time. When he did speak, his pompous demands reminded her painfully of Devlin's degrading demeanor. It made her sick to her stomach.

She hated herself for the thought, but the others didn't send her into a similar spiral.

"We'll keep going," Rian said confidently. "The clouds will clear soon, and we can't afford to linger any longer than necessary." His eyes flickered toward her and the horse—only for a second. "You should know that better than anyone here."

Edmund huffed. "I know exactly what's at stake here."

Rian muttered under his breath. Clearly, the two had some issues they'd yet to fully resolve.

Freya told her how Edmund had sneaked into their party without anyone knowing, and he and Rian had done nothing but fight ever since.

For some reason, she still couldn't open her heart to the man who was her family, despite his clear desire to protect her. What did that say about her?

"That creature," Isla began, desperately needing a distraction from her own thoughts, "what did the others call it—a Nothing?"

"Yes," Rian said darkly. "Something that has come back after passing through Rallion's gates. It's not the same as what first went through, so in a sense, all that is left... is nothing."

"How is that possible?" Isla asked, her voice hitching. A princess shouldn't show her emotions so easily, and, as much as she had recently forgotten it, she *was* one.

Rian's face darkened. "I don't know."

"That's not for you to worry about," Edmund added. "Whatever caused that creature to return from the gates is far away."

But what called it here? Isla feared the answer to that question. What had Devlin said about the gates again? She knew it all linked together somehow but didn't have enough of the picture to piece it together yet.

And she had a sinking feeling that Edmund knew more than he let on. There was something he kept from her. Maybe that was the reason she couldn't allow herself to fully trust him.

Both Rian and Edmund trailed behind, exchanging more heated words that only sent Freya and Malin into gleeful spirits. One of them was always by her side whenever her brother and the general disappeared. It didn't feel as smothering as she'd expected. In fact, it was rather comforting to have someone watch over her, unlike in the mines, where she had been constantly monitored.

The forest was alive in a way she hadn't realized during the first few days but had become glaringly obvious now. Soldiers constantly got tangled in moving vines, and a swarm of birds attacked three who had ventured too far during a respite.

Good thing River had found those wayward trees before it was too late. He even warned them of a hidden crevice lurking beyond a curtain of branches.

The moonlight ebbed in and out of the cloud cover, forcing them to pause when it grew too dark and resume their pace when it reappeared. It was currently hiding behind its shield of clouds, and an odd stillness settled over the forest.

The ground rustled, different this time, and her pulse quickened.

The others heard it too. Rian and Malin were at her side, the former quietly reassuring River. Soldiers fanned out to investigate the source, and she prayed to the forest goddess Halia that it was nothing more than a restless creature. A fuzzy, friendly one, and not a blood-seeking demon straight from the worst gates of the twelve hells.

She couldn't see Freya, but knew the soldier was at the back with Edmund.

"What is it?" she whispered, too afraid to move. She wished she were on the ground with the others rather than perched atop River, where she could do so little... though she reminded herself that she'd likely be equally helpless on the forest floor.

But she hadn't been useless before. She'd managed to break out of that horrid prison, all on her own. She'd found her way back to them despite the horrors inflicted upon her and the demons hunting her—both mental and literal, she thought with a shudder.

Dark memories of the mines returned, sharper this time, as if she had never escaped and this was all a giant ruse once again.

"Malin," Rian's voice was sharp. "Go help Aldan and the others."

Isla opened her mouth, about to ask why he abruptly sent him away, when she looked down and realized her fingers had begun to blacken.

Seven

The General

It pained him to keep his distance, but after exchanging a flurry of heated words with Edmund, he wasn't sure how to proceed. He wanted to find out what she knew about those creatures, but distance was what she needed.

Edmund had made one or two valid points. Isla would be married—whether to Brenner immediately upon their return or sometime later, once she was fully healed. Her father would make certain of it. That was her fate in life, and Rian had his own mistakes to make up for.

Plus, he had plans to make a real difference in the Pedite Corps. He didn't want what happened to his family to happen to others: trading off children to the conscripts to pay down debts, leaving soldiers trapped in the corps for life. That cycle was one he intended to break.

Despite his promotion coming through the most scrupulous of means, he had every intention of using it to reform the Pedites and help prevent unnecessary killings in the days to come.

Convoluting any of his own twisted feelings would only hurt Isla more, especially now, even if it still pulled against his instincts to lie or withhold things by omission. He wasn't certain this was the right path. Until he knew, he wouldn't confirm anything. All he knew was that he was here to make sure she, and now her brother, too, returned home safely.

But then the horse spooked, as did the men.

Something was out there, hiding in the shadows of the dark forest.

He was so distracted by whatever was circling them that he didn't notice what was happening with Isla. Not at first. He didn't even think she knew herself, not with the way her eyes glazed over while she stared at the shadow-filled trees. When his gaze passed over River, checking that the chestnut would remain calm—though he should never have doubted it—that was when the darkness began pooling at the tips of her fingers.

It reminded him of the icewielder's power, how it stretched up his arm when they fought, growing and spreading until it exploded outward.

Now was not a good time, not that it ever was, with everyone so close. So, he sent Malin away with a brisk order.

By now, Isla realized what was happening. They didn't need a full explosion like Ackerslie, or when they found her in the forest. Though, depending on what was out there, it might be useful if she could learn to control it.

"I can't control it," she said, raising a hand toward him. It hadn't spread much, not yet.

He ignored the scrape of metal as swords were drawn from their sheaths. Branches lurched and swayed, as if anticipating whatever was coming.

Rian pulled Isla off River and took Opi, who had peeked out from the safety of her jacket. He set the seropa on the ground, where it curled around Isla's feet, letting out a low growl.

"Yes. You can." He gripped her shoulder as she leaned against the sturdy beast, using his body to shield her from view. They were the only two that mattered right now. Just them. "I've seen you do it before, Isla."

Her eyes shot up to his.

It tore his heart in two to see the uncertainty and the layers of pain treading beneath the surface. He hated the dark smudges under her eyes, her gaunt appearance, and the marks on the backs of her hands. Every image of her suffering ripped through his thoughts, urging him to drop everything and hunt down those responsible.

He grabbed her hand, and she tried to yank it free. Fear flashed across her face, and Opi let out a high-pitched yelp.

"You know what to do," he said, nodding slowly.

Her gaze stayed fixed on their joined hands. She was worried she'd hurt him. But he had never feared her before, and he certainly wasn't now.

"Deep breaths, and it'll pass." He pressed their entwined hands to his chest so she could feel his steady rhythm and match it.

There was shouting and soldiers darting in every direction, but he angled his body so she was perfectly wedged between him and River. It was hard to see the fear on Freya and Malin's faces at the first glimpse of her powers, despite their attempts to hide it. He couldn't let the others see it too. So, it was only him and Isla.

That was all he needed to focus on.

The feel of her hand against his sent ripples of warmth through him, and he cleared his throat as though something lodged there, preventing him from speaking. Did she feel it too?

Blue-clad soldiers had broken into the camp, slipping past the sentries scrambling in panic.

Fuck.

He didn't move. His focus remained on keeping his breaths steady, on calming her.

Time was short, but he'd make all the time in the world for her. She drew two deep breaths, her fingers twitching beneath his. He finally looked down.

The darkness had retreated.

"You did great," he whispered, though Isla still stared at her hands.

Boots scrambled around the other side of a massive tree. Rian grabbed her hand, tugging her around River's flank. Opi yipped at their ankles but padded after them without hesitation.

Freya stayed with the prince, and if Hierel still smiled upon them, hopefully the Muratians wouldn't notice the crown prince was among their party. Though the sky goddess was known as the bringer of gifts of life and truth, that hardly boded well for them. Edmund had hidden himself easily enough when they entered the forest. Rian prayed he stayed that way. Useless royal ass.

He dug into his pocket for a small blade, his fingers brushing past his father's dagger, the one he had once given Isla, but he couldn't part with that. Instead, he seized a jagged little blade and sent it flying into the back of a blue soldier's neck.

Isla allowed herself to be pulled through the chaos as the forest erupted around them.

Now would be the perfect time for some deathpuller action to take care of them all, but there were too many Velotians around. Too many witnesses. And he'd never ask that of her. Not after Ackerslie and what it had done to her.

Aldan and another soldier struggled against a pair of Muratians, but Rian kept his grip on Isla and ducked behind a thick trunk. Those two would have to fend for themselves.

Isla's shoulders shook as she drew in a ragged breath. Rian squeezed her hand, channeling every ounce of strength he could muster into hers.

"You got this," he reminded her.

A burly Muratian with pock-marked cheeks stepped around the base of the tree. Isla gasped.

"You're coming back with us, you little bitch," he spat.

A pulse thudded across Rian's chest. His broad sword was already in hand. Not while he had a breath in his lungs.

The man wielded a thin rapier in his left hand and charged at them. Rian met him head-on, blocking the strike.

Isla clutched the dark trunk behind him, frozen but alert.

When the man raised again to strike, Opi darted out, sinking his tiny teeth into the soldier's ankles. The sudden attack startled him, his guard faltering for a heartbeat. That was all Rian needed. He drove Dark End into the man's gut with a brutal thrust.

Isla covered her mouth, eyes wide, but didn't utter a sound. She scooped Opi back into her arms and edged closer to Rian, trembling but safe. He didn't comment on the dark streaks left on the trunk behind her.

"Stay with me," he grunted, pulling the sword free and wiping it on his pants. "Did you recognize him?" He gestured to the body sprawled at their feet.

"Yes," she breathed, clutching Opi closer. "He was a guard there. Down below."

Down below. The words crashed over him like fire. They had taken her. For *three months*. Three months he'd imagined what he would do to those responsible. Now, none of that mattered. Protecting her came first. Revenge would have to wait.

They needed to find someplace before the Muratians realized where she was. His hand went to her back, keeping her close. Her fingers brushed his for the briefest moment, a touch that stretched into an eternity.

Then a blue-clad Muratian stepped into view.

Rian didn't hesitate. It didn't matter who the soldier was aiming for; all that mattered was her safety. Dark End sliced through the air, forming a lethal, invisible barrier between them. The man ducked under the first swing, but Rian was already in motion, flipping the blade backward and driving it into the soldier's side.

He stepped around the first body, hand out toward Isla, feeling the air she breathed, ensuring she stayed with him. Behind them, Opi squawked, the sharp, frantic noise somehow grounding him.

Rian kept an ear tuned to the creature's distress while slipping through the shadows of the towering trees, dodging Muratians as they appeared. In the chaos, it was easy to move unnoticed. They hadn't yet realized where Isla was—or that the crown prince was hidden among their ranks. That knowledge had to stay buried.

Keeping track of the sounds and movements around their small circle of safety was exhausting, but he trusted his men. The soldiers he'd brought into this forest were the best he could find.

Isla stayed close, pressing against him as he wove through the chaos of flashing silver, scanning for Malin or Freya, anyone who could help keep her safe.

A new noise cut through the din. Different.

It was Opi. The seropa was whining.

Rian whipped around, but Isla remained pressed against him. Instead of squirming, Opi tried to bury himself in her chest, his whole body trembling as he curled tighter into her embrace.

Instinctively, Rian moved closer, keeping a protective arm around her as his gaze swept the grove for the source of Opi's fear.

There.

Movement at the far edge of their clearing, sliding closer with terrifying stealth. Each shift of shadow sent his heart racing and icy tendrils crawling up his spine.

A cloaked figure slithered along the edge of the foray. At first, Rian thought it was another wisp, but it moved too deliberately. Those tattered dark robes... he had seen them only once before.

When it reached out a hand toward the nearest dueling pair, the two crumpled to the ground, drained of life. Rian finally understood what they were facing. His heart stuttered, threatening to stop entirely.

The clang of combat and the metallic tang of blood in the air had beckoned it. The elemental had arrived.

Eight
The Princess

A dark shadow passed over the forest and settled into Isla's bones. Opi cried out, claws digging into her chest, terrified of the newcomer. She knew this creature. She knew it.

The scent hit her first—stale and metallic, like the air in the mountainside—and her stomach twisted. A bony blue hand lifted from beneath its wispy robe, and the Muratian and Velotian soldiers nearest it collapsed as if the air had been stolen from them.

Strong hands gripped her shoulders, and a bulky form pressed her down, crouching over her. "Don't move," he whispered into her ear. The faint scent of morning sun, pine, and grass cut through the stench, a fragile thread of comfort in the dark night.

Every limb froze. Even Opi stopped whining, pressing flat against her, shivering uncontrollably, but staying perfectly still.

She swore that creature turned its head and stared straight into her. A shiver rippled up her spine, but he continued holding her against his chest, trying to shield her from something terrible.

The elemental's shadow spread, and all the soldiers slowly turned toward this new threat as they realized they'd caught the attention of something horrible. Muratian and Velotian steel pointed toward the creature, several men cautiously backing away while others seemed transfixed by the intruder.

"Drop your weapons," Rian shouted. "Drop them *now*."

Freya lifted her chipped axe even higher, aiming directly at the elemental.

"Freya, don't!" He gripped Isla even tighter. "Please."

The blond warrior shifted her gaze between Rian and the elemental, hesitation blazing in her eyes.

Where was Edmund?

One of the closest black-and-silver soldiers charged at the creature with a throttled roar. He collapsed before making it two steps.

"Drop it. Now."

"Kill it!"

"*Get down!*"

Freya slowly lowered her axe, letting it fall limply to the ground. Most of the soldiers mirrored her, but a few turned and ran. A trio in blue and gold seemed to have succumbed to madness, charging straight at it.

Opi let out a small whine.

Rian twisted his body to shield her, and she didn't see what happened next. She was calmed away from the twisted screams and the thudding of bodies by focusing on the warmth wrapped around her and the steady heartbeat pressed against hers. She absorbed the soft thuds like a melody played against her eardrums late at night.

She felt it when his heart sped up and he curled around her even tighter, nearly cutting off all access to her lungs. Each thudding beat stretched sluggishly as time bent and slowed. After about thirty seconds, he finally loosened his grip.

The noise around them disappeared altogether, and she hadn't realized she'd closed her eyes until she cracked one open to check.

Bodies lay scattered, as if the soldiers were merely resting. Yet many black-and-silver soldiers crouched low, heads bowed, waiting for the creature to pass.

Its back faced them, but Isla still felt its attention on her. She prayed to Hierel that it wouldn't turn around. That it would leave. Anything but facing that chilling gaze again.

Thank the goddess, it slithered out of the clearing.

She released a deep breath, the most glorious she'd had in a long while. Opi uncurled himself and sighed, still hesitant to move.

Rian's hands slipped off her as he stepped back slightly, eyes scanning the scene. He froze when he spotted what she had already glimpsed.

Something was in front of them. A shining blood lily, fully bloomed, lying inches from her foot.

A trail of wilted flowers marked the path the creature had left.

She twisted her head to meet Rian's horrified gaze.

It took everything in her to remain still as the healer's hand glowed against her side, spreading relief—relief, not pain—through her body. She'd barely been scratched, yet Edmund insisted on tending her first, though he seemed more shaken by the elemental than anyone. He wasn't the only one worrying needlessly. Everyone insisted she be treated first.

Everyone.

The difference between here and the mines was still hard to grasp. It was as if she were precious cargo to be protected, not a useless dredger doomed to work endlessly underground, even if she now knew that was all a lie. A savage, elaborate lie.

It didn't change how she felt inside, despite regaining new memories each day. She was confident enough to understand her place in all of this. Her place with all of them.

Most of them.

Several memories continued to evade her, no matter how hard she focused.

After the elemental, everyone was beyond exhausted. They'd settled in an open spot for the night, with a few willowy trees as cover.

Opi happily pounced around, crushing leaves or chasing wayward roots away, crooning proudly from his *help* earlier that day. When they tried to create a makeshift tent for her, she refused. It was a fight, but one her stubbornness managed to win when Freya declared that all the shouting was making things worse and insisted they trust her if she wanted to sleep on the dirt and leaves. She said that last part with far too much delight in her smile, but Isla was determined to get back to normal as best as she could, and that included no more special treatment.

Though... shouldn't she be getting preferential treatment as their princess? The thought brought on another splitting headache, so she let it go. For now, she wanted to be the same as everyone else. She wanted to blend in.

That meant lying on the mossy ground, wedged between Edmund and Freya. They must have spoken about this before, decided somehow with the general, as they both took up their spots without a fuss.

The healer settled beneath the weeping cedar next to them.

She sighed and scooped Opi against her. So much for blending in. At least they gave her a small semblance of independence and allowed her to sleep out here with the rest of them, even if it pissed off Edmund. That part made her heart thrum even more in her chest, so she knew it was the right decision.

Edmund's snores slowly filled the forest, yet sleep evaded her despite how drained she was. The plan was to rest for a few hours before setting off at an even harder pace. One soldier had suffered an injury the wielder couldn't fully heal, and Isla had every intention of giving him the horse tomorrow. Though she was exhausted, she could push through. At least her time underground had taught her how to do that.

Eventually, she grew tired of watching the swaying branches and counting the leaves overhead. She pushed the thick blanket back, leaving behind a sleeping Opi and Edmund, and decided that a walk around the camp might help lull her mind into a peaceful sleep.

Freya stirred the moment she stepped away, bolting upright with thin eyes that glinted in the moonlight. Those eyes flicked from where Isla stood frozen to her spot and around the camp where four sentries were stationed. Her gaze lingered on one at the far end before she shrugged, pulled the blanket up to her shoulders, and threw herself back down.

Well, that was easier than she'd thought. Too easy.

Something tugged her in the direction Freya's eyes had shifted, and she quietly made her way through the small camp, wincing each time a branch cracked beneath her boots.

The forest was still. Calm, even. Something about it soothed her nerves—or maybe it was simply the peace and quiet that came with no one around to fuss over her.

The general was settled at the base of a twisted redwood, its dark leaves almost fully hiding him in shadow. He gently worked a blade through a piece of bark, and she knew he had heard her approach when he dropped the wood to the ground and scratched his chin with the back of the blade.

"Can't sleep?" Rian asked. He wore a thin jacket despite the crisp forest night, the silver stitching barely visible against the shadows.

Isla shook her head, then realized he couldn't see her face from this angle, so she sat on the ground across from him.

"We'll be out of the forest tomorrow or the next day," he said confidently—more confidently than any of the others had when she asked. "Then we'll find you better accommodations... your brother, too."

Something in his voice tightened. It reminded her of the way Edmund's brow scrunched when they spoke of what was next. What waited outside these woods that had them both on edge? It couldn't be worse than what she'd left behind.

Nothing could be more terrible than the overwhelming feeling of an entire mountain closing in on you, with no end in sight, no light, no fresh air—or—

Stop it, Isla.

She dug her nails into her knees and took several deep breaths. "What are you carving?" She nodded at the block of wood in front of him.

"Nothing special," he mumbled, handing it over to her. It had the beginnings of a feline body with a long neck, but the rest was incomplete. "It didn't work out like I wanted."

She examined the smooth bark and poked at the start of a claw. "You should finish it. I like it."

He chuckled. From what little she could see of his face, she imagined his mouth turned up in a smile.

"Are you having nightmares?" he asked.

She swallowed the lump in her throat. Heat bloomed in her chest, telling her she could be honest with him. "Yes. I keep imagining I'm down there again. I keep seeing *their* faces when I close my eyes. I don't want to sleep, because I know it'll get worse."

"Don't let them," he said.

"What?"

"Don't let them win," he said. "They wanted to break you. They wanted to turn you into a shell of yourself. You can't let that happen."

She choked down her reply and blinked back the burn starting in her eyes. He wouldn't take the wood seropa when she tried handing it back. Gods, he was so difficult.

"Why don't you like me?" she asked.

He ran a hand over his face. "What makes you think that?"

"Why are you avoiding me?"

"I've been scouting. Keeping us safe. I haven't been avoiding you."

"Freya thinks you are," she said slyly, still clutching the half-formed seropa in her hands.

He scoffed. "Freya needs heavier assignments if she has so much free time to gossip."

"That wasn't an answer."

"No, it wasn't."

"Neither is that," she pressed, feeling bolstered by the ruse of privacy under the dark skies above. Here, nobody listened to their words except the goddesses, and they had better things to do than gossip about the pathetic mortals that walked these lands.

He nodded, refusing to give her more... but there was something there. Something he held back, and she didn't think she could convince him to tell her what it was. Not with that wall, whatever it was, carefully erected to keep everyone out. To keep *her* out.

What was it?

Each moment since escaping was slowly coming together as part of a larger, fuzzy puzzle. That creature from the mines. The elemental. The wilted blood lily. It all led back to Rallion. It all led back to her.

The leaves rustled as she fixed the strands that had loosened from her braid. She scratched at her leg, itchy from all the forest bugs and leaves that hounded her day and night.

A vine crept up, snaking around her ankle, twisting and grabbing her. It was alive.

She gasped and—

A blade sliced through the vine before she could blink. It returned to his hand, where he flipped it casually, as if the forest hadn't just tried to claim her.

"You have to watch out for the forest here," he said plainly. "Sometimes it acts out."

Right. Right.

Vague memories of lashing vines and creeping roots stirred in her mind. When she tried to pull on those precious fragments, her head protested ferociously, and she gave up.

"Thanks." She tugged her jacket tighter and shook off the renewed bout of nerves coursing through her body. She hated feeling so off-center and not knowing why.

Maybe it was the forest. Or the remnants of Beretta's powers, lingering at the edge of her sanity. All she knew was that she was safe with him.

Safe enough to ask, "Why do I hate Edmund?"

A bite of laughter escaped him. The question had caught him off guard.

"He is a pompous ass," Rian said. "And so were you, once." He shifted, rustling the leaves beneath him. "He hasn't been kind to you, not for a while... I don't think you hate him. He's been trying really hard. It may not seem like it, but he is trying."

She tossed the wooden seropa from hand to hand. "That explains this baffling annoyance I feel every time I look at him."

"It's his face. I get the same overwhelming urge to punch it every time I see it. It'll pass."

She smiled, the first real one in a while. "It *is* very punchable."

"It's a sibling thing, I think."

He spoke as if he had siblings of his own. She wished she could remember more about them. About him. Surely, he'd told her about his siblings before? There was an older one, she thought. Maybe younger ones, too? It was hard to pull on that memory.

Another moment of silence passed as the leaves bristled above.

"And Freya," she started hesitantly. "You two are friends?"

He dropped his head, and there was no mistaking the laughter he struggled to contain. "This isn't the first time you've asked me that, you know?"

"That's still another non-answer."

He chuckled and rubbed his chin. "Yes, we are friends. *Just* friends. Malin too, in case you were wondering."

She picked at a loose patch of moss. "And they don't hate me, despite what they've seen."

"No. They were just... surprised at first. But you didn't hurt anyone. They promised not to tell another soul."

"Then why do you?"

Even in the dark, it was easy to notice the way his body stilled, freezing completely as the pulse of the forest swelled in and out around them.

And then, so quietly that she thought she'd imagined it, he whispered, "I could never hate you, Isla."

A hammer tapped at the edge of her heart. Then came that usual stomping and rustling of leaves she had come to loathe with a fiery zeal.

Nine

The General

That was way too close.

For once, relief filled him when that thunderous stomping approached, Edmund rushing at them like a hammerboar. Rian didn't know how he was going to get out of that conversation without lying—or revealing something he shouldn't.

Every passing minute she was here made it harder. Almost impossible. It felt like a sharp knife running along the inside of his skin, trying to burst free along with all the wrong words. And that couldn't happen.

He laughed at the way she rolled her eyes when Edmund stormed upon them, a chirping seropa skipping around his ankles, carrying a dead treemouse in its mouth like a prized possession.

There was no fight as she allowed Edmund to lead her back while he muttered nonsense about regaining her strength and resting her mind. She glanced back and gave him a grimace, as if apologizing for something.

There was nothing to apologize for. If anything, it was he who had overstepped again. He really needed to pull it together. Fuck. What was wrong with him?

They returned to camp, and Isla settled in the spot between her brother and Freya—who hadn't budged when either of the royals left. He'd have to speak to her about her guarding abilities slipping.

Rian sat against a nearby tree to keep an eye on things, as clearly no one was as concerned with their movements as he was. Isla continually shifted and fidgeted, Opi squeaking a protest every now and then. He'd been useful for alerting Rian to Isla's whereabouts around the Muratians... though that didn't mean he liked the beast.

They'd have to get rid of it before its venom kicked in. Cute as he was now, once the males matured, they could paralyze with those little teeth.

No thanks. He had to go. Rian first needed to figure out how to break the news delicately.

Isla huffed and sat up, locking eyes with him. His heart contracted under her gaze, pattering against the walls of its cage.

They held that contact in the dark, Rian keeping his expression as blank as possible despite every instinct yelling at him to *do something* and stop sitting there like an idiot. She sighed, dramatic as always.

He raised an eyebrow, a silent question he prayed she understood. Edmund's throttled snore punctuated the heavy silence.

She pulled the blanket up to her neck and mouthed *I'm cold* before squirming back into place.

He turned his head to hide his smile, feeling her eyes burn into his soul, threatening to break down every remaining ounce of resolve he had. Why'd he even sit so close to her? This was far too dangerous for his flimsy self-control.

Another few minutes passed, and when he deemed it safe, he returned to watching her movements. He couldn't help it. He should be watching the perimeter, but Aldan and Malin were on it, and Les was further past the camp, ensuring no creatures or men snuck past.

Rian should feel calm. He should feel safe. Yet, for some reason, unease settled into his bones and chest, clawing its way deeper and deeper.

Isla sat up again and turned toward him. He sensed a silent question looming between them, stretching and reaching its way out. There he was, sitting in the middle of their camp, unable to sleep, and she was so close—tucked between Freya and her brother, her brother who had uttered countless warnings and threats his way since the moment they found her.

A beat passed as the question lingered in the air.

She moved a fraction of an inch, her intention obvious. But he shook his head.

Those brown eyes darkened, something flashed across her face—hurt—and she tossed herself back to the ground, not moving.

A claw reached out and touched his shoulder, and he almost wet himself.

"What was that about?" Malin asked smoothly. "Lovers' quarrel?"

Rian clutched his racing heart. "That was not funny, Malin."

His friend shrugged and flopped onto the ground. "Maybe you should be a better sentry. Anyone could have snuck up on you."

"Aren't you supposed to be watching for threats?" Rian said, expending a considerable effort to keep his voice low.

Malin clasped both hands behind his head and stared at the dark canopy above. "Shift's over. So is yours. *I* was trying to get a bit of sleep while I can. What's your excuse for still being up, besides being so distracted you didn't notice the watch changing shifts?"

Rian didn't grace him with an answer. If he had half a mind, he'd think of the appropriate reprimand to ensure Malin didn't speak out of turn again. But for some reason, his thoughts traveled elsewhere.

"Fine." Malin turned onto his side, resting his head on a mound of dark moss. "If you want to keep brooding and do nothing but scowl and sigh all day, fine by me."

The insides of Rian's stomach churned. Still, he said nothing.

"You need to figure out what you plan on doing when we get back," Malin said.

Rian swallowed.

"You're the first of us to be promoted in ages. Usually, they hand over rank to one of the promoted Divites when they're green and learning. You're definitely green and not sure how much you're learning, but you have the title. What are you going to do with it?"

Rian tilted his head, focusing on the steady movement of the group across from him as she settled into a deep sleep.

"I hope it's worth it," Malin mumbled, his gaze following Rian's before he turned onto his side. It took less than thirty seconds for his light snores to punctuate the forest's breathing.

They planned to rise before the sun, which he could sense waiting beyond the horizon. They were almost home. He could feel it.

At some point, he drifted off. For an hour or two at most, he swore.

A breeze rustled his hair, jerking him alert as the forest quieted. The darkness that had blanketed the night wavered as the sun started to make its journey past the horizon. Then a light clash sounded in the distance, echoed by similar noises, one after the other. Rian stilled.

Something stirred in the forest. Something that drew closer.

Not an elemental this time. Not a wisp or a boar or a seropa—who slept silently beside Isla. Something *else* was out there.

His hand slid to Dark End's chipped hilt. He hadn't taken it off since they entered the Black Forest, not even to sleep, and he *especially* wouldn't let it out of reach now that they'd found her. Without his blade, he was nothing and couldn't do the only thing he was barely any good at: protecting her

The stillness that settled over the forest was unnatural, broken only by the heavy breathing of their sleeping party. There was every possibility it was merely another forest dweller, intent on passing by without harm. Perhaps another seropa, searching for an early morning snack.

He wasn't willing to risk everything on that gamble.

Rian shook Malin awake and moved into a crouch, one hand skimming the ground to sense any movement. Aldan froze. He was their best tracker by far, unnaturally so, and it wasn't surprising that whatever lurked in the forest had already alerted him.

The creature barely rustled the earth as it moved, but he could pick up half a dozen faint footsteps. And those footsteps were headed straight for the sleeping group.

Malin moved faster than Rian, shaking Freya's shoulder before moving on to the others.

By now, Rian was on his feet, blade drawn, edging toward the camp's perimeter. He positioned himself directly in the path of its intended target.

A loud rustling announced Edmund stumbling to his feet. Isla was already up, clutching a struggling Opi as the creature emitted a low throttle. She pressed a hand over his mouth, but the sound persisted. He sensed what the rest of them did.

Danger.

A figure stumbled into the camp, his features illuminated by the soft light filtering through the trees.

Except it wasn't a man. Not anymore. His skin was pallid, almost ivory, stretched taut over his bones. Dark blood trickled from the corners of his eyes and a gaping wound at his neck. It was the same as before.

The man—the Nothing—stumbled and turned, catching sight of the frozen party.

This time, Rian was ready. He refused to be rendered completely useless by these beasts again, despite his body urging him to flee or curl into a ball. If Freya hadn't been there the first time, a shudder ran down his spine at the thought of what might have happened.

Not this time. He swallowed the fear and locked it away.

He advanced on the Nothing, driving Dark End into its gut. It gurgled and groaned, staring at Rian with onyx eyes that recalled Rallion's first gate. Whatever remained of this man had been reduced to nothing, a soulless creature wandering the forest.

And he wasn't alone. Other Nothings began trickling into the camp. Slowly at first... then faster. Godsdamnit.

The one impaled on the tip of his sword twisted its head, almost curiously, before swiping at Rian with a clawed hand. Rian leapt back, pulling Dark End free with a sickening sound.

What in Slin's name was happening? That strike hadn't slowed it.

This demon was cursed far beyond the holds of Rallion's first gate.

He stabbed at its heart again, but it pressed on. Even severing its arm failed to stop the creature—once human—from moving with singular purpose. Now that it had found its foe, it was determined to keep moving, until it was all over. Until it killed them all.

No. He'd never let that happen. Not after swearing under Rallion's comet to bring her back safely. To bring them *both* back.

It growled, crawling toward him, thin teeth bared to rip him limb from limb if it got close enough.

Where was Isla? Rian stole a precious second to spot her, pressed against the base of a tree with Edmund. Freya and another soldier stood before them, weapons ready.

His Nothing lunged, clawing down the side of his arm, searing past the mark he treasured so dearly.

Rian hissed and swung, taking out a chunk of its shoulder, but the creature remained undeterred. There had to be a way to stop it for good. Freya swung her axe, nicking the nearest creature's neck. It hissed furiously before Bone Breaker returned, fully decapitating it.

Right. The head. That's how she'd stopped the other one.

He took Dark End and swung with all his strength, cleaving the once-man's head from his body. The Nothing finally stilled.

Malin must have seen it, for he began shouting orders to the others to aim for the head. Rian shifted toward the siblings at the tree, keeping himself in front of Freya and Gord, making sure none got close to either of them. Even so, he was half tempted to let one take a bite out of Edmund to see what would happen.

There were seven wraiths—or Nothings—depending on which goddess you prayed to at night. Either way, they were the same: undead beings, similar to the dweller, pulled back from Rallion's twelfth gate, neither fully here nor there.

Abominations. And he knew exactly who sent them.

What had they been doing under that mountain? And who even possessed a power like this?

Rian's eyes caught something in the distance: movement that didn't align with the Nothings' patterns.

"Stay with them," he shouted at Freya. His instincts protested, urging him to stay and do the same, but there was something else out there. *Someone* else.

Rian took off, dodging around a groaning Nothing that had once been an old man, and chased after the figure in the woods.

He nearly slammed into a low-hanging branch and caught his foot on a root but managed a glimpse of tattered grey robes sliding through the forest.

Before Rian could get close enough to stop him, the man spun on his heel, embroidered robes flaring in the wind, and vanished.

A fucking transporter.

He'd brought those creatures here. But who was he? And more importantly, who sent him and those Nothings?

A pang ran up Rian's arm, a foreign sense of worry crawling into his body. Worry and fear that didn't belong to him.

Right. Realization hit like a boulder. He'd left the others in the midst of that chaos. Whatever possessed him to leave like that? Rian whipped around and ran toward the fray. Toward her.

The sun finally made its full entrance in the distance, the first rays of thick light guiding his path.

By the time he made it back, all the Nothings lay dead on the ground. Only one Velotian soldier lay with them. Gord. His heart sank.

Isla and Edmund were unharmed, though Freya had turned a shade paler. When Isla's eyes caught sight of him skidding back into the camp, relief flooded her face. She hugged a struggling Opi closer to her chest and exhaled a heavy sigh that Rian felt deep in his lungs.

Then all the remaining color drained from her face as her eyes fell on the Nothing beside Gord. At first, he thought it was the way the moss around the body withered and died. Then his gaze traveled to the creature's head and—

Rian's breath captured in his chest. He felt as cold as the lifeless body before him.

He recognized this Nothing. At least, the person it had been before... and, to his utter horror, so did Isla. It had once been a villager from Ackerslie.

Ten

The Princess

"You recognize it—him too," she hissed. It was not a question but a statement. Surely, *surely*, there was no way he could deny the recognition that fluttered across his face at the sight of the man she had once named Gummy.

It was him. She was certain. Mostly certain, as his head still dangled from his body, and if she looked again, her stomach might turn itself inside out.

Except now he wouldn't look at her or confirm it. Edmund hovered precariously close, moving as if to edge the soldier away entirely. She elbowed him aside, ignoring the way he scowled at Rian, and not her, when she did so.

"We need to move out," Freya said, sliding her axe back onto her belt. Her eyes shifted to the burning pile of bodies Malin had suggested they set ablaze to return their souls to Rallion. "That smoke will attract more *things*, and I, for one, don't want to be here when they come calling."

"Are there more?" Edmund asked, his voice hitching slightly.

Freya turned dramatically, pointing at nothing in particular in the distance. The sun finally peaked over the horizon, and Isla finally got a clear view of the grove they had settled in. "How would *I* know? If you want to check it out for yourself, you're more than welcome to."

"Do not," Rian said quickly, as if he expected Edmund to take her suggestion seriously. "There was something else in the forest." He still wouldn't meet her gaze. "Someone brought those things here, I'm certain of it."

Edmund drew himself up. "That settles it. We need to evacuate. Immediately."

Despite the authority in his voice, neither Rian nor Freya paid him any attention. They were currently having a silent conversation—or perhaps an argument. It was hard to tell.

"Those things came from those mines," Freya said aloud. "Perhaps the gateways between the hells have weakened since the appearance of Rallion's comet."

"Maybe somebody has been weakening them," Rian whispered, carefully wrapping a shallow wound on his arm. When did he get that? "The same ones who brought them here."

"Enough," Edmund said. "We don't know anything yet. But we do know it's not safe here."

Freya stared at Rian. "What do you want to do?"

"Cursed hells," Malin sauntered over, looping his thumbs through his belt. "That's one awful wake-up call directly from Rallion herself. Definitely makes the list of the top three worst ways to be woken. Up there with being thrown out on my ass by someone's angry brother."

Rian rolled his eyes. Freya looked disgusted.

But Isla still had questions, and she was fed up with being ignored. She grabbed Rian's sleeve and pulled him aside. He sighed and nodded at the others, who scattered to finish packing the camp. Edmund stomped twenty feet away, then turned on his heel, watching with arms crossed like an overbearing milkmaid.

"They killed them," she said. The words rose from the bottom of her tattered soul, dredged up from a time she was desperately trying to forget. But those miners were fragments of another part of her past, dangling in hazy pieces. "They were with me... and he killed them."

"I know." He hung his head and shook it slowly. "It's hard. I'm sorry. They did nothing wrong, except for letting weary travelers into their village when they should have turned them away. I'm just as much to blame for it."

Isla chewed her bottom lip. It all led back to her. It was her fault. Why wouldn't he say it? She clenched her hands into fists as Opi rubbed against her heels.

A trio of soldiers whispered loudly, glancing in her direction. She knew exactly what they must be saying. And *who* they were blaming.

For some reason, she couldn't meet his eyes. "They were down there... in the mines... with me... because of me."

"Not because of you," he said firmly. "Because of the Muratians. Because of him."

Her heart felt as though it carried the weight of the entire mountain, and she was certain her nails would pierce her skin. Devlin only did this to get to her. It always led back to her.

A hand lifted her chin. Softly. Delicately. This show of kindness felt undeserved after everything she'd caused.

"I know what you're thinking," he said. "There was no way you could have saved them. Their fates were decided by Mannop's justice long ago. Don't let the guilt eat you alive. Don't let it take over."

Warmth spread through her, a heat as blazing as the morning sun that had yet to rise.

She opened her mouth, but Edmund cut across. "We're ready to go, *General*."

The hand on her chin dropped, and her stomach plunged.

Cold fury burned in Edmund's eyes, all of it directed at Rian. Opi yipped at his heels in protest. "Keep that creature in check, or it's staying behind," he snapped, steering Isla away.

She shot a glance over her shoulder and saw Opi cradled in Rian's arms like a precious babe.

Exhaustion weighed heavily on her, compounded by the lack of sleep. She couldn't explain it, but something felt... off. A pull she couldn't ignore had kept her awake most nights. Now she knew exactly where it came from.

Who it came from.

And she was determined to find out more. This was the final piece of her missing memories. He couldn't avoid her forever. She was persistent. She was determined. And she *would* get her answers.

Once again, she let the wounded soldier take River. She needed to move her limbs, despite every fiber of her body begging for rest. She'd rested long enough.

The uniform Freya had given her was comfier than anything she'd worn under the mountain, though loose around the hips and shoulders. The jacket, several sizes too large, was so cozy and warm. It even had space for—

Where *was* that creature?

She whipped around. That furry sap was draped over Rian's shoulders, completely asleep, judging by the way his limbs flopped about. If he wasn't passed out, he was certainly a master at pretending.

It didn't make sense to disturb the sleeping creature, so she let him stay there. As they walked, she devised a plan to silence that constant nagging in the pit of her stomach. She just needed the right moment.

There wasn't an opportunity until after they'd settled for the night. They'd traveled most of the day, and the days began to blur together. The group had to circle around several sinking pits, a soldier got trapped in a ferociously thorny bush, and then a trio of sharp-clawed birds, the size of small horses, attacked, nearly taking the head off their healer before Malin carved their wings off.

The moon had returned to its usual spot above them, small rays of white light filtering through the thinning canopy. Now was the time.

It was her only chance as Edmund had grown worse in his refusal to let her out of his sight. He'd gone off to search for firewood with Freya, both shrugging off Malin's offer to help with vague excuses. Apparently, gathering wood in the middle of the forest, despite already having a pile ready, was more important than watching his sister's every move.

Not that she was complaining. She finally had a moment to breathe air that wasn't exhaled by her incessant sibling.

She scooped up Opi, who had returned to her after being carried for half the day, and sought out her target. With Freya occupied by Edmund and Malin patrolling their setup, it was a rare chance to get him alone, especially when he seemed as determined to avoid her as she was to corner him.

He sat at the base of a curved tree, staring at a small fire and whittling something again. She thought she was being sneaky and quiet, but he glanced up before she even got close.

Unless she was mistaken, his eyes lit up when he spotted her and Opi. Perhaps he was excited for more cuddles from the small beast.

Before he could utter any excuses, she plopped down next to him and let Opi crawl into his lap for scratches.

"I remember something new," she said.

The hand scratching under Opi's chin froze. "Oh?"

She smiled. "We've been here before... well, not exactly in this spot, but in these woods. It's repeating in a jumbled mess in my mind thanks to Slin's jest. Some of it, at least."

A small treemouse scuttled past their boots, but Opi was too distracted to notice the moving snack.

He returned her smile and scratched behind Opi's delicate ears. "And no headaches today?"

She shook her head. The healer had been attending to her whenever he could, as much as he could without draining himself. It was helping... somewhat. Overcoming a mindweaver's work was never easy, but having a fully healed, rested body helped combat it, or so

Ben had said. And they wouldn't get a true night's rest while in these cursed forests.

"What else do you remember?" he asked.

She picked up the carving Opi had kicked out of his hand to demand his attention. It was a horse's head. A one-eared horse's head.

"Much better this time," she said. He raised an eyebrow, but she refused to elaborate. If they were all determined to keep secrets from her, she could do the same.

She lifted her gaze to the skies above, now almost entirely visible thanks to the thin branches, and watched the stars dance. They were near the forest edge, and the anticipation twisted her stomach into strange knots.

There was a larger party they planned to rendezvous with, Edmund said. The thought of having to hold it together around more people was too much. She clutched her hands together, heat rushing to her cheeks for some unknown reason. Well, the reason was known, but she refused to acknowledge it.

It was the same reason she couldn't sleep, and it had nothing to do with nightmares. Quite the opposite, in fact. Now she didn't know what to do with these new—or old—feelings. Everything confused her mind, but her body remembered.

She reached out, fully intending to grab Opi, but instead ran a finger along Rian's lip.

He froze, probably from shock, as did Isla. Both equally terrified of what just happened.

Moments passed.

Seconds dragged on, agonizingly, in which neither of them did anything. Why wasn't he moving? Isla's entire chest caved in on itself. Oh gods, what had possessed her? She'd truly lost her mind back under that mountain.

He didn't push her away. That had to count for something, right? Isla didn't know what to do next. Fuck. Do something.

A flash of violet. Rian's head whipped to the side.

"What is that?" she asked, clasping her hands together in her lap and praying her face wasn't as red as she suspected. She could blame the fire in front of her for the rising blush.

"A wisp," Rian said, relaxing his hand. Was that relief on his face? "There are a few wandering these forests but they're not harmful. I think they're curious."

A wisp. What was the old saying about them and their links to the goddesses again? Isla couldn't remember and she had a feeling that wasn't from Beretta's powers but rather from not paying attention in a lesson ages ago.

Sulfur filled her nostrils, and for a blood-freezing moment it reminded her of the deep tunnels in those mines.

A shadow passed overhead.

Then another one, lower this time, nearly scraping her scalp.

Isla cowered under her arms when a winged creature went for her hair again. The bat was there one second, then Opi leapt up and grabbed its wing. He tossed it in the air, and it was down his throat in seconds.

She sat there, dumbfounded for a moment, before bursting into laughter when Opi scrambled onto Rian's shoulder and launched himself at another one. He grumbled when he missed, landing silently on the ground.

Rian smiled, and her stomach tumbled in a chaotic series of flips. "At least he hasn't lost *all* his hunting instincts."

Opi crawled up his side and tangled his front paws in Rian's hair, trying, unsuccessfully, to get a better angle on the next flock of flying creatures.

Isla smothered the smile aching to break free and poked at the fire with a stick, imagining her insides churning like the hot embers.

A few soldiers edged closer at the commotion, but once they saw there was no danger, they returned to their tasks. Malin, who had returned from patrol, caught her eye and winked.

Something in her chest stirred, begging to be released. But when she turned back to speak to Rian, he was already handing Opi to her, muttering an excuse to leave. The words she'd wanted to say died in her throat and stayed there.

She'd pushed too hard. Crossed an invisible barrier that upset him somehow. Would apologizing help, or only make things worse? There was no one she could ask. In the mines, she'd had Beretta, but Rallion knew how that ended.

And now, despite her brother at her side and several soldiers sworn to protect her, she felt oddly alone.

That night brought another restless sleep, plagued by shame, hurt, and dark visions. Memories. Memories pierced only by the brilliance of the morning sun.

When they awoke, he avoided her. He let Edmund hover instead, throwing not-so-subtle glances her way, with Malin or Freya never far. Always watching. Always near. Never letting her be truly alone.

River was given back to the injured soldier, though Isla sensed the frustration radiating off Edmund. He wanted her to ride, and he didn't think another should claim the only horse willing to venture into these woods. Isla didn't care. She hadn't cared enough about the other miners, even back when they'd still been villagers, not miners... and now they were all dead. She'd lived enough lifetimes being selfish and blind to others' pain.

She vowed to be better. It was the only way forward.

The forest grew greener. Less dead here. No swooping beasts, no Muratian soldiers, no Nothings clawing their way back through the gates to kill her. Still, he refused to speak to her and stayed at the back of the group.

And then the forest opened. The canopy thinned, and with it, it felt as though a heavy cloud in her mind finally broke apart.

River had never looked happier, moving with a new spring to his step, while Opi curled into the safety of her oversized jacket, less certain of this strange land so far from his Black Forest home.

She frowned. Would Edmund keep his word and leave him behind? Opi would never survive, and she couldn't bear the thought. So, she kept him hidden, tucked close and out of sight. Maybe, if she was lucky, her brother would forget about him until it was too late to send him back.

They'd left the forest around midday, entering a grassy plain. Scouts rode ahead to summon the rest of the military, along with her ladies, Susanna and Alynna. The names didn't come easily, and Edmund had to remind her.

When the scouts returned with horses and supplies, Edmund stiffened. The injured were lifted onto a cart, and Rian claimed River's reins. Isla and Edmund were given a pair of white stallions, their thick manes flowing like banners in the sunlight. She almost missed the one-eared chestnut. He'd been far more entertaining than the pristine purebred beneath her now.

Then came the others. More Velotians.

No, not only Velotians. A scattering of soldiers stood out in dark maroon among the black-and-silver ranks.

One of them strode toward her. At once, two bodies closed in tight at her sides. She might have been flattered by their overbearing protection—especially from Rian, who'd spent the past two days pretending she didn't exist—if the man looked dangerous. But he didn't. His only weapon was a gleaming blade at his hip, polished so bright it was hard to believe it had ever known the taste of blood.

Even Freya's hand drifted to her axe, her gaze tracking every step the man took toward them. Toward her.

He wore a fine maroon jacket, dark buttons lining the cuffs and front. His freckled face, framed by light brown hair, was set off by amber eyes fixed squarely on her.

His gaze flicked to Edmund for the briefest moment, a curt nod of recognition, before dismissing Rian entirely. A ripple of annoyance stirred in her chest for reasons she couldn't name.

"Princess Isla," he said, his voice smooth as silk. He caught her hand and pressed his lips to the scarred skin on its back. "I'm so relieved our efforts have succeeded."

Isla glanced left; Rian wore a vicious scowl, while Edmund's disdain simmered beneath the surface.

"I'm Prince Brenner," the man continued. "Your intended."

Eleven
The General

Fuck it.

He'd fully intended to back off once they left Murat. His plan was to throw himself into training his men, fighting the Divites and Agicaes, and finally getting better equipment for the Pedite Corps. Changes had to be made, and it was the perfect distraction now that his main task, his very reason for breathing, had been achieved.

He had every honorable intention in all ten Rocian kingdoms to keep his distance. He swore it. He'd even managed to tear himself away when she cornered him in the forest, despite every part of him raging against it.

Seeing Brenner's preening face the moment they stepped out of that forest was too much.

He'd heard the rumors back when they were camped together. Freya's attempts to hide Brenner's missteps had been amiable, if misguided, but others in the camp had let slip what happened. He would've rather heard it from her, even if she tried to soften the truth to keep him from throwing the obnoxious royal off a cliff and sparking *another* war.

Now that the rest of the war camp had caught up with them and, annoyingly, Brenner along with it, he wasn't about to leave Isla alone with him. It was irrational, and he knew it, but the flare of emotion in his chest refused to be smothered. Ensuring her safety was the only thing keeping it from breaking loose.

Brenner's slimy grin did nothing to cool the fire inside. Neither did the calculating looks he sent her way, nor the way his hands trailed over her hair under the guise of checking for injuries.

He finally left her when Isla loudly declared she had a headache and needed to rest, but not without posting two maroon-striped guards from his personal retinue. The grim smile Isla sent Rian's way was enough to tell him she hadn't appreciated Brenner's veiled attempt at monitoring her either.

Rian didn't buy it for a second, but there wasn't much he could say. Not without risking his title and position. So, he left to eat with his friends, giving Brenner—and Isla—a respite. She was already overwhelmed by the attention, and Rian didn't want to add to her stress.

The promise he'd made to Edmund could be damned to Slin's chaotic grace.

Especially now, with Isla standing outside *his* tent. Alone, wrapped in one of her ladies' white cloaks.

Was she lost? Both royals had been outfitted with plain beige tents despite the Divite general's protests. Edmund kept getting lost try-ing to find his and complained about the lack of size and comforts. Isla, on the other hand, had voiced no such protest. If anything, she looked relieved to have something softer than rock or dirt to sleep on.

So why was she here?

Rian scooped up Opi, whom he'd been watching while the royal siblings toured the camp with Brenner, and held the guy out as an offering. He'd been cold to her these past few days, too focused on holding himself together.

"What are you doing here?" he asked, taking in the borrowed cloak and the absence of Koliat escorts. It amazed him how easily she slipped away, likely with the help of one of her ladies, whom he fully intended to speak with so it wouldn't happen again.

Freya, with whom he'd just been discussing the wielder who deposited those Nothings in the forest, vanished as quickly as the Agicae transporter they'd been talking about. He'd have to track her down later, too.

"I couldn't sleep," Isla said sheepishly. Color had returned to her cheeks, and she no longer resembled the wraith she'd been when they first found her.

He glanced at the dim light from the sun still sinking toward the horizon. "It's a little early for bed, isn't it?"

"I needed to get rid of him—both of them, actually." She jerked her head at his tent. "Are you going to invite me in?"

His heart sped up. "I—I don't think that's a good idea."

She grinned. "And staying out here where hundreds of passing soldiers could wander by is better?"

He opened his mouth, then closed it. Godsdamnit.

The widening smile told him she knew she'd won. He hated the way it stoked that ember in his chest.

He exhaled. "Fine. One minute only. Then I have to take you back before your brother comes and—"

"Demands your title and your head," she finished, flicking back the flap of his tent and ducking inside. Opi scrambled to her shoulder and yipped at him to follow.

His heart hammered, painfully reminding him of the last time they'd shared a tent and the misery that followed, as self-inflicted as it was. Edmund would surely murder him once he heard about this. *Again.*

This time he was determined to be on his best behavior, all the gods be damned.

There hadn't been time to set up anything beyond the basics and he hadn't even secured a bedroll yet. The tent held only a plain, undressed cot and his discarded bags. Now he wished he'd taken the time to scrounge up some chairs. Anything, really.

She sat on the edge of the bed, staring at a spot on the old canvas while he lingered by the door.

"I feel so out of sorts here, even though I know I'm home. I know I'm safe, but I can't help but feel..."

"Like an outsider," he finished. He'd lost count of how many times he'd felt the same in these camps, even among his fellow soldiers. "I get it. It'll pass with time, and before you know it—"

"Can I sleep here?" The words tumbled out of her in a rush. Rian couldn't stop the shock from flashing across his face.

"I don't want to stay with the others. I can sleep on the floor. I'm—I'm used to it."

Yes. That was the answer his insides begged him to give. It almost slipped out. Fucking hells. He should send her back to her brother, but he wasn't doing what he was supposed to right now either, and something deep inside urged him to keep going. To believe this was a great idea.

He silenced that voice.

"First off, I may be a Pedite, but I'd still like to think of myself as a gentleman, and there's no way I'd let you sleep on the floor while I took the cot. But secondly... no." The word felt dredged from his very soul. He ached to give her everything she asked for. It felt unnatural not to.

Her eyes widened. She went still.

"Why not?"

The same question. The same pleading look she'd worn back in the forest.

He sighed, his resolve cracking. "We didn't exactly part on the best terms. I—I did things I'm not proud of, and I hurt you."

She frowned. "I remember some of it. Not all, exactly. Small pieces here and there. More now. I remember you. I remember us."

His breath hitched, as if his lungs had forgotten how to draw air.

Eventually, he managed, "But you don't remember all of it."

"Then *tell* me."

He couldn't look at her. "It would only make things harder for you." The pain in his chest surged, sharp and unfamiliar. "Trust me."

Her face hardened. She clenched her hands at her sides. "I'm really tired of hearing that. And I'm even more tired of everyone knowing what's going on except me."

"I'm—"

"Don't you dare say you're sorry. I want people to stop lying to me."

"Nobody's been lying to you."

"You're not telling me what I need to know." She flexed her fingers, studying them as if checking the darkness stayed at bay. "And I know enough to know that."

"I—" He stopped himself, jaw clamping shut. There was nothing he could say that wouldn't bend the truth, and he owed her more than that.

"Is it Edmund?" she asked sharply. "Did he do something?"

"No. He's a complete idiot, but nothing like that."

"Then tell me. Please. I need to know why. I need to know why I feel like a stranger in my own skin, why I feel like I'm dying on the inside and no one can tell, and why I feel just as trapped as I did in those mines… except when I'm with you. Why is it that the only time I don't feel like my world is burning away is when you're near?"

"Because I feel it too," he said quietly.

The words slipped out before he could stop them. It was out now. The truth his body had been aching to release, consequences be damned.

At least the shock on her face wasn't revulsion. There was that, at least.

She swallowed and nodded, as though confirming something to herself.

"Was it—was it always like this?"

He laughed. Might as well let it flow, since he already leaked the first truth. He was terrible at this and they hadn't even officially entered Hierel's year yet.

"Gods, no. Not at first. It crept up slowly, silently, but it was there, building into something more before I realized it. I think it was the same for you, and something like that doesn't go away easily..." He rubbed his arm—the mark where she'd been burned into his soul. "At least, I don't think it can. What do you want to know?"

A knock on the post outside his tent. A warning.

He shot Isla a look. A promise that they'd finish this conversation later. Helping her up, he kept her hand in his grip until they stepped outside.

Freya was pacing, one hand on the hilt of Bone Breaker.

"The prince—" She winced, her gaze moving to Isla. "*Princes* request an audience with you, Princess Isla, now that you're up from your rest."

Isla rubbed her wrists. Did she imagine the scars already burning into her skin? He hated to think of her bonded to that man for life.

"Give us a second," Rian said, lifting a pleading hand.

"Fine." She scoffed. "But he ordered me to stay here until you came, so I'll just—" She strode over to a dead firepit and dropped onto the edge of a log. "Wait right here."

Isla turned on her heel to face him.

"You can't stay here tonight... or tomorrow night," he added quickly, cutting her off before the thought could even form on her lips.

Was that disappointment? If so, she masked it fast.

She shifted onto the balls of her feet, tucking a strand of hair behind her ear. "Then I want you to help me."

"With what?"

She stepped closer, lowering her voice even though the only one nearby was Freya, who was gracefully distracted with lacing her boots.

"You're going to train me. I want to learn how to control *it*. They called me deathpuller. Ashfeeder. I want to know why—and I want to change it."

"I don't..." He scratched his chin. "I don't think I'm the best person to help you."

Isla shrugged. "You're the only one who's ever helped me. And one of the few who even know about it. I can't go to anyone else." A devilish glint sparked in her eyes. "If you don't help, I'll tell Edmund you slipped into my tent and took liberties. Something tells me it wouldn't be the first time."

"Trouble," he murmured. Nothing changed. He still wouldn't confirm anything for her. It didn't feel right to add another burden to her weight.

"After dinner," he said at last. "When it's dark and the patrols change." Opi squirmed in her arms, and she handed the creature back to him.

"And no noisy pets allowed."

"I can keep him quiet," she pressed, a hint of desperation in her voice. "We can't leave him."

"He'd give us away. It's only for the night, I promise. If not, no deal." His chest pulsed. "Think about it while you enjoy the meeting with your brother and Brenner."

Her eye twitched. "Maybe your presence will also be required, General."

"Doubtful."

Freya reappeared at their side, eyes dancing dangerously. "Is that an order, then, Princess?"

Isla turned back, studying his face for far too long. "No. It's fine for now. I'll spare you from those two. We'll catch up later. But you'll need to find someone to watch Opi."

Wait. What? Why did seropa supervision always fall to him?

Freya smirked as she followed Isla out. At least one problem was already solved.

"Are you sure she's alright watching him?" Isla glanced toward the dark mounds in the distance. A thread of lightning ripped across the sky, heralding the storm. "If he causes a scene, Edmund will send him away."

"Freya can handle Opi," Rian said, taking careful steps to avoid divots. He should've brought a torch, but the wind had been too fierce when Isla appeared. "It's rare I call in a favor from her, and believe me, she owes me plenty."

"Doubtful," Isla said.

Rian snorted. True enough. If anything, he owed Freya far more than the other way around. Not that he'd admit he'd practically thrown Opi at her with a rushed explanation before bolting, promising to make it up to her later.

He hadn't expected to see Isla again that night, not with Edmund and Brenner tailing her every move. Yet here they were, slipping into the dark, about to practice... something. He definitely hadn't thought this through.

"This is far enough," he said as the first drops of rain touched his wrist.

They stopped in a small grove beyond a grassy hill that would perfectly block them from view. No one would see through the downpour as the drizzle swelled and grew.

He lowered himself onto a flat patch of grass, motioning for Isla to sit opposite him. Between them, a thorny plant sagged under the weight of the rain, its petals heavy and its spindly branches bowing in the gale.

"What's the first lesson, guru?" She dropped to her knees in the wet grass. That white cloak would be mud-brown by the time they were finished.

"Not being a snarky pupil," he shot back. Her grin only widened. "I told you, I'm not the best at this. I've got next to no experience beyond the basics."

"And I already told you, that's fine. I want to practice with some-one who won't bolt screaming for Laian's wrath."

"I still might." He flicked rain from his shoulder and tipped his head toward the plant between them. "Can you try to summon it?"

Her eyes widened and hesitation tugged at her features. She rocked back on her heels. "I don't know if that's a good idea."

"You're the one who wanted to practice. We snuck out for this."

"Just like that?" She snapped her fingers. "No warm-up first?"

"I don't know how else to go about it besides leaping off the cliff," he said quietly. "And you're ready. I'm certain... Now try."

The mark on his arm prickled for the first time in days.

She rubbed her palms together and leaned forward, eyes locked on the thorns as thunder cracked, rumbling through the ground beneath them.

"Summon it and control it," he said.

"Summon it. Control it," she echoed, her voice oddly light, her gaze never wavering.

While she focused on the plant, he let himself study her. Her lips pressed into a thin line and her nose was scrunched up from concentration. Even in the dark, he could recall every curve of her face as if it were burned into memory. He had dreamed of it often enough these past months, no matter how he begged the nightmares to leave him alone.

Another crackle overhead. Hierel must be busy preparing for her year to allow so many to slip through.

Isla shook her hands, flinging off the streams of water that clung to her skin. "You got this," she muttered to herself.

Raindrops slid from her nose, but she still stared at the plant. Minutes passed as they both knelt in mud and water. He refused to break her focus.

Maybe she had drained it all. How long did it take between outbursts? Days? Weeks? He opened his mouth to ask, then snapped it shut.

A nudge of darkness curled and stretched. He couldn't see it, but he felt it. The mark on his arm burned white-hot. Not painful, more of a *curious* sensation.

He stared at the topmost thorn. A black spot bloomed across its leaf, whirling outward until it nearly touched the edges. Then it pulsed and stopped.

Isla shifted from knee to knee, her eyes kept locked on the ashen leaf. A vein throbbed at her temple.

"You're doing it," he whispered, then quickly added, "Sorry."

"No, it's fine." Her eyes shifted to his for only a second. "I need a distraction. Keep talking."

"About what?"

"Anything. Ask me a question."

"Tell me about them. The ones who took you. The wielder." He winced as the words left his mouth.

A crease formed on her forehead and she gritted her teeth. A thin line of ash puffed up, but the darkness didn't spread. "I thought she was my friend. But she never was. I didn't even remember being taken, she was that powerful."

"Did it hurt?"

The darkness slid down the stem, then recoiled back to the leaf.

"Yes. She liked making it hurt."

The words knotted in his chest, twisting tight. For a heartbeat, he wanted nothing more than to leave. To find her captors and make them pay for everything.

The ash bubbled and coiled, still clinging to the single leaf. "Devlin and her knew each other. I think they were familiar, maybe even friends. But they definitely knew each other. He protected her when I—when I—"

Again, the darkness curled outward, only for her to snap it back.

"He saved her, but not the others."

"How?"

"The firestone. It suppresses wielder powers. He had a dagger—your dagger, actually." Her eyes jumped back to his before settling on the plant again. Darkness pooled at her fingertips and stayed there.

"I took it off you when we found you in the woods. You can have it back, if you want. It's yours." He'd kept it tucked in his jacket all this time, pressed against his heart.

"Why did you take it?" Her voice cut sharp. This wasn't about the dagger anymore. "It was my mother's. And you took it."

His pulse quickened. "I didn't know what it meant then."

Her eyes dropped. She turned her hand over, keeping the ash trapped to the same trembling leaf. "But you did later."

"I know. I don't have a good excuse, just that I was weak and afraid. But I promise I'll make it up to you."

"How?" Her voice cracked under the strain. "How do you expect to do that? It's gone now. The last piece I had of her."

His heart stuttered.

The ash thickened, pooling until several tendrils branched down the stem. A crack of lightning struck nearby and they both jumped.

The tendrils burst outward, swallowing the entire plant and racing toward the ground, stopping an inch from where he sat. The plant shriveled into a heap of ash.

Isla swore and threw up her hands. The darkness had spread past her knuckles.

"This is your fault!" she screamed.

"Just—just calm—"

"I'll let it kill you if you finish that sentence."

"Then stop it. Do something." He shifted back as the dark path crawled dangerously close to his leg.

"You're supposed to be helping me!"

"I. Am. Trying."

A flash of light burst beside them. Not lightning this time. The spirit vanished before he could even turn his head. Fucking wisps.

The darkness surged. A nearby tree cleaved in two before collapsing into dust.

"You're not doing anything useful." She flung her hands to her sides, and twin streams of black shot out, draining the life from everything behind her.

"And you're not even trying to control it!" he shouted back. "You know how, so do it. Let go of whatever's holding you back, or it'll drag you under."

"You're an idiot!" she screamed, echoed by another bout of thunder. "A thieving imbecile!"

They stood locked in a glare, both soaked to the bone and shivering in the storm. The swell of darkness trembled in and out but didn't fade.

"I hate you," she said.

"No, you don't." His voice rang with reckless overconfidence. "Or I'd already be ash, Your Royal Magnanimous." He pointed to the ground around them, darkened and withered everywhere except the two spots where they stood.

"Pompous asshole," she breathed.

Their eyes locked. One look into those swirling brown depths and then they collided. Crashing against each other with the force of the storm. All thoughts of the decay vanished as her body pressed to his, lips meeting with the next thunderous shake from the heavens. The world beyond this small alcove disappeared, leaving only her. Her scent, her warmth, and her presence filled every crevice in his mind.

Every inch of his chilled skin hummed at her touch, and he swore her heartbeat pounded in unison with his own. He held her close, a hand braced at the back of her head, while her fingers slid through his soaked hair, velvet against the storm.

Desire spread through him like a fever, growing and curling tighter with each breath. He never wanted it to end. He never wanted to get his fill of this.

It was impossible to tell where his body ended and hers began... and he never wanted the answer.

At some point they stumbled back against something solid. The rough base of a tree pressed into his palms as he braced his hands on either side of her, refusing to break their connection. If he did, he might combust into himself completely.

Nails scratched the back of his neck, igniting him over again. He wanted her to claw all the way through and break him apart piece by piece. She pushed against him and he groaned, his mind at war with itself.

Every thought was consumed by her and focused on the places where they were bound together—and still it wasn't enough. His lungs burned for air, but he didn't care to breathe if it wasn't with her. How had he ever survived those months apart?

Water streamed down his back from the branch above, cold and relentless, but he barely felt it. He could have been thrown into an icy river and it wouldn't matter, not when she was here.

The mark on his arm pulsed frantically, and he could almost feel the lifebeat of the tree beneath his palms. Or was that only his own heart?

Despite being drenched, her scent still drove him mad. Lilies and honey and *home* filled his senses, and he wanted to drink it in forever.

A bolt of lightning struck the topmost branch, sending it crashing down beside them. They sprang apart, Isla letting out a startled yelp swallowed by the storm's fury.

He dropped his grip on her.

When she realized it was nothing more than a broken limb, she laughed nervously and cupped his face in her hands. The darkness had almost fully retreated. He'd forgotten all about it in his frenzy. The same as the black grass that crunched beneath his boots.

Well, that was *one way* to get rid of it, he thought smugly.

Another crack split the sky, and a burst of wind sprayed them with fresh sheets of water. They'd both catch a sickness if they lingered too long.

He sighed and forced the words out against his will. "We should get back before we're swept away. Either that, or before Edmund drags himself up here with a full battalion."

His hand lingered on her cheek and brushed slow circles into her damp skin.

"I doubt he'd ever set foot outside his tent in this weather without at least three fur-lined jackets. We're fine." She leaned into his palm and pressed a quick kiss there. "But you're right."

A small frown formed on her lips, gathering the stray water sliding down her face. What was she hiding from him?

Twelve

"Where in Dia's all-seeing lunacy have you been?" Freya demanded, shielding her eyes from the downpour. The derision in her gaze was sharp enough to make Edmund proud.

The camp behind her was nearly swallowed by the heavy rain, but Isla's vision, her entire being, was consumed by him. She wanted more, but reality had dragged them crashing back here. Even soaked to the bone, every inch of her skin buzzed, alive and crawling over itself in a desperate attempt to regain that lost contact. Half of her longed to give in, but she knew he wouldn't allow it. Not with the rest of the soldiers lurking beyond the curtain of water.

They must look like drenched wrecks, especially with her white cloak matted in thick mud. Alynna and Susana would never forgive her for that. But she didn't care. The last piece of her fractured memories had fallen into place, and now she understood.

Rian spoke first. "We were just—"

"Actually." Freya cut him off with a raised hand, shoving Opi into his face with the other. Isla didn't even bother asking for him back; Edmund had already banned the sweet thing from both their tents.

"Don't answer that," Freya went on. "I don't want to get blamed for this. Alynna is waiting for you, princess. She'll get you—ah—sorted out." Her nose wrinkled at Isla's mud-caked robes. "Before anyone notices."

Isla gave Opi a quick goodbye, watching him happily snap at the falling drops. She had no idea what to say to Rian, so she yanked the hood over her face, spun on her heel, and followed Freya through the dark camp, wincing at her own awkwardness.

Gods, why was she like that? She hadn't even asked if he wanted to watch Opi again. She'd just assumed. But he hadn't said no, so... that had to count as a yes. Right?

Their little session in the rain answered *a lot* of questions, even ones she hadn't remembered until she was standing there, soaked. Surprisingly, not a trace of guilt stirred in her body despite being engaged to another man.

She trailed Freya through the rows of tents, easily spotting her unmarked one among the throng. She'd already memorized the turns during her earlier escape. If she could navigate those mines, she could manage a camp.

Six black-and-silver soldiers and two maroon-clad ones stood posted near her tent, stopping the pair as they approached.

"Do you realize the hour?" a barrel-chested maroon soldier said, spitting into the mud beside Freya. "The princess is asleep and won't wish to be disturbed."

"Yes, I understand that," Freya shot back testily. "But the princess gave explicit instructions that her lady Alynna return immediately upon arrival."

The soldier's eyes narrowed. He tilted his head, trying to peer under Isla's drenched hood. "Where has she been so late in the night? And why is she so filthy?"

"That is her and the princess's concern," Freya cut in. "Shall I fetch your prince and tell him you're delaying us, or may Alynna return to her lady?"

"Let her pass," a black-and-silver-clad Divite told the Koliat. "Trust me. You don't want to incur this princess's wrath."

Isla grimaced but kept her head low.

The Koliat guard, convinced by the Divite's sharp warning, dipped his head and stepped aside.

Freya seized Isla's arm, making her nearly jump out of her quivering skin. She said, loud enough for the watching soldiers to hear, "Have your princess come directly to me or the Pedite General if these guards trouble you again, Lady Alynna."

The Divite scowled. The Koliat muttered threats under his breath. But Isla slipped past the safety of her tent flap, where she was met with a hushed berating for the late hour and immediately accosted by the real Alynna, who set about scrubbing half a mountain's worth of mud from her.

And all the while, Isla replayed the last hour in her mind, terrified that memory too might be somehow whisked away with the storm.

⁓

The stubborn yawn refused to be stifled and escaped behind her hand in an embarrassing display of weakness.

"Try this, my lady." Prince Brenner offered a wineskin. "Far better than the sludge from Prominent—or even your own vines here. It's from a few years back, before our crops were hit by the blight and ruined. Exquisite, I promise."

Isla grimaced. The last time she'd accepted wine on horseback didn't end well. "I'm quite fine with water for now, thank you, Prince Brenner."

They'd just settled atop their steeds after the camp was packed with impressive speed. The Koliat prince was determined to keep her close for the entire journey, and he had said as much.

Surprisingly, he hadn't protested when Edmund declared they would return to Aurial instead of pressing on to Koliat as was the plan or—the original plan, before it all descended into Slin's fitful chaos. Rian and Edmund were braced for a fight, but the Koliat prince surprised them by taking it in stride. He said he didn't wish to hinder Isla's recovery, and if that was what the healers recommended, he wouldn't argue. Instead, he added, he was glad for the chance to experience the Velotian middlelands for himself.

Still, Brenner insisted his Koliat healer examine Isla, much to her dismay and Rian's outright displeasure. Every time their hands touched her, the mountain came rushing back. It took everything to keep the shakes and darkness at bay.

Nothing seemed to curb it. Nothing except—

"Would you look at that," Brenner exclaimed, pulling his horse to a stop. Her milky mare trotted up beside him, and Edmund was at her side in an instant. "Something's killed everything in that grove."

Heat rose to Isla's cheeks. It was the same grove they had practiced in last night. The ground was scorched in a vine-like pattern, the plants shriveled into nothing. A spruce had split in two with its ashy branches littering the ground.

"Strange thing," Brenner mused, stroking his chin. "Well." He sat up, more chipper than before. "The lightning must have gotten it."

"Yes," Isla said, praying to Hierel that her face stayed calm and unflushed. But the star goddess relished in new beginnings and glorious truths, so she doubted it. "It must have."

A muscle ticked in Edmund's cheek, but he said nothing.

They moved on without further mention of the deadened grove. By the time they broke for lunch, Alynna and Susana had taken over care of Isla's horse. The Pedite soldiers were nowhere in sight. Edmund had pointedly explained they were sent to scout the road ahead.

"My men tell me your lady was out in the dead of night," Brenner remarked, pulling out a chair for her.

They had set up a small table, weighed down with an unnecessary amount of food. Edmund and the Koliat general joined them, while the rest of the soldiers tended to the horses or gathered in small groups with their own rations. Pedites, Divites, and Agicae each kept to themselves, as did the Koliats.

A red-haired Koliat soldier brought Brenner a jug of wine—and Isla's heart stopped. For a moment, she saw Beretta's face on that soldier. She blinked and it was gone. What in Dia's name was that?

Brenner was still watching her, waiting for an answer.

Pull it together, Isla. "Yes. I believe she was out rather late."

That was it? What was wrong with her? She was a princess, not a cowering dredger, despite how most days she still felt like that miner trapped below.

"You know," Brenner said, easing into his chair while one of his soldiers filled his plate. "That is not wise given the current political climate. Even if she is *only* your lady, the danger remains."

"What do you mean?" she asked sweetly, masking the rage churning beneath.

Brenner leaned closer, his voice low so the nearby soldiers couldn't overhear. "What if she were captured and turned? Or replaced by someone trying to get close to you. One can't be too careful, not after everything that's happened."

Isla took a measured bite of her sliced fowl. "Yes, of course. I'll speak with her about her movements."

Brenner smiled—it wasn't the haughty leer Edmund so often complained of, but a genuine one—and poured her a glass of sparkling fresh water. He tipped his own against hers, and the crystals sang. "Or more discreet, at the very least."

Edmund, who'd stopped eating and was watching them with furrowed brows, cleared his throat loudly. "What do you think about stopping in a village tonight, Brenner? Slomat is nearby and should have several inns for our top men. The rest can camp outside. It would be good to rest in something other than a camp before the more grueling stretch of our journey." He cast a pointed look at Isla. "I believe the healers would agree."

Isla swallowed her scoff with a gulp of cold water. Once again, they spoke of her as though she wasn't even there.

Brenner's eyes shifted from Edmund to her. "I won't deny that a night in a proper bed sounds glorious. What do you think, princess?"

Spending the night in lush quarters while the rest of their men slept on the hard ground or in cots? Absolutely not.

But she knew what was expected of her. What was expected of a Velotian princess. So she offered them a winning smile and murmured her agreement. Rest in a wooden structure and an actual bed would be nice for her weary bones. That's what she told them, at least, and it satisfied both men.

Soon Brenner and Edmund were locked in a heated debate over the best kind of sword for sparring, and Isla lost her appetite. She pushed aside her half-eaten plate and excused herself from the table.

As soon as she rose, the Divite general—hungry for face time with the princes—slid into her seat. He had a sniveling, crooked nose and a pasty demeanor she loathed. It didn't help that their last commander had been the one who handed her over to the Muratians. Since then, she'd developed a distaste for the Divites and trusted none of them.

Still, she'd better get used to them, considering they were her father's favorite... besides his own personal Siica Corps, who never left his side. Once they returned to Aurial, they'd be attached to her every movement again.

So much for relative freedom. It had been nice while it lasted, and she intended to stretch it out for as long as she could.

Her stomach sank at the thought of her father's wrath waiting in Aurial. Edmund had promised to handle him, but Isla knew where the blame would fall, as always. He'd be furious at the further delay to the marriage ceremonies instead of continuing to Koliat as planned.

At least Brenner hadn't fought their change of course. He'd accepted Edmund's word about returning to Aurial without protest, and surely that had to count for something with her father. Surely.

She stopped near a cluster of Pedite soldiers. Her feet had carried her there out of pure instinct. At least, that's what she told herself.

Rian was already rising to excuse himself before she reached them. Freya stayed put, and Malin elbowed the soldier beside him. She ignored their stares; she'd had plenty of practice by now. Still, the Pedites here were less likely to roll their eyes when they thought she wasn't looking—and she had a feeling she knew why. A few who had been with them in the forest definitely skirted around her now, even though Rian swore from Rallion to Luriel, that none had seen her powers except Freya and Malin.

"Something I can help you with, Princess Isla?" Rian asked, bored and loud enough for all to hear.

"I need you for a moment, soldier."

He arched a brow, silently asking 'for what?'

She didn't know yet. She hadn't thought that far ahead.

He motioned toward the edge of the battalion, where a group of horses were tacked and feeding on long grass. She spotted the one-eared steed at once and nearly skipped over to River.

The horse stomped his hoof in greeting and nuzzled her shoulder, demanding attention. His mane was smooth and silky—someone must have finally brushed it out—and if she wasn't mistaken, he was less lean than when they'd sent him off at the forest's edge months ago.

Rian handed her a coarse brush with a smirk. "Planning to run off without a proper goodbye again?"

"Maybe." She drew the brush along the fine hair of River's neck, careful to follow the flow of the strands.

"I've been riding him since we got back," Rian said, scratching at his chin. "They tried to give me another mount that wasn't half-dead, as they'd said. It didn't feel right after everything. He's been getting all the treats and scratches."

Naturally.

She missed the even-tempered horse. Edmund would never let her ride a scraggly beast like this again. Their time in the forest had been a special, desperate circumstance.

At least River would be cared for now, since he had no place to return to. Her stomach flipped. Whoever his owner had been either died in those mines or back in Acker—

"What are you thinking?" Rian was closer now, studying her face intently.

Isla dropped the brush and examined her hands, half-expecting to see black-tainted tips forming, but there was nothing.

She scooped the brush from the dusty ground and said lightly, "I was thinking it's good you'll have a sturdy steed to look after you, since I know how much you enjoy wandering straight into trouble."

Rian chuckled and rubbed his arm. He definitely didn't believe her story.

"We're staying in a village tonight." Her mood plunged from cloudy to complete darkness.

"Hey." His hand settled over hers on the brush, warmth rushing up her arm and straight into the hollow cavern of her chest. "It means nothing. We're merely going to stay the night in a place where those two royal princes won't be forced to sleep on a lumpy cot."

A muscle in her mouth twitched, though she couldn't tell if it wanted to laugh or cry. "I'm sure the cots in Slomat will still be too lumpy for their tastes."

And the quicker they left that place, the better for everyone involved. Isla had a habit of cursing anyone and anything she touched. If that weren't enough, she kept catching visions of Beretta lingering around the camp, only for the Muratian to retreat back into the shadows of her mind whenever she blinked.

Those visions were proof enough that Rallion's deathly luck trailed her every step.

"Exactly." He released her hand, and a wave of cold rushed in. "Prince Edmund," he said loudly. "What can I help you with today?"

Isla didn't bother pulling away. She simply resumed brushing River's thick coat. The more pieces that clicked into place in her fractured mind and the more time she spent around him, the clearer it became why she felt uneasy around Edmund.

He was a pompous dick, as Rian would put it. And he was her brother, no matter how much she wished otherwise. Especially in this particularly infuriating moment.

Edmund strode right up to them, horse wrangler in tow, caring nothing for propriety. "We have plans to stay the night in—"

"Slomat," Rian finished with a winning smile that sent the tick in Edmund's cheek racing. "Your sister just informed me. Kit, he looks much better today. Must be the extra grain we gave him—you were right."

Rian thumped River's neck while the red-bearded Pedite ducked to examine the horse's front hooves. "No bruises or injuries to the soles. Rather lucky, considering he was in the wild for Hierel knows how long."

"He's light on his hooves," Rian added, bending over to check them himself.

"Were you not hungry, Edmund?" Isla asked sweetly, still brushing River's mane. "You had a full plate when I left you."

Rian and Kit murmured about the horse's potential load, with Rian assuring that River was sturdier than he appeared.

Edmund scowled. "As did you." Rian cast Isla a quick glance, but she turned her head to the side. "I was checking to make sure you were feeling well, sister. It's been a long morning, perhaps you need to rest before we leave again."

It was Isla's turn to scowl. They were twenty feet from the rest of the camp, and with a horse wrangler pretending to be engrossed in conversation with Rian, so she kept her more colorful comments to herself.

"I'm perfectly healthy, as you and the healers are well aware, brother. If you're concerned about the strenuous ride, perhaps *you* are the one who needs a respite before heading back out."

Edmund's face scrunched in indignant outrage, and he sputtered. Rian hid a laugh behind his arm, masking it as a cough, and gently turned a shocked Kit away from the siblings.

"Do you think we can get him a new saddle next time we pass a blacksmith?"

"If we have the time," Kit muttered.

"Can you check with the quartermaster to see if we have anything with more padding until then? I'm worried the current one is rubbing his underbelly too much."

"Let me check." Kit gave a jilted half-bow to her and Edmund before running off toward the camp.

Edmund had finally collected himself. He stepped closer, his eyes traveling from Rian back to Isla. In a low voice, he said, "Your intended is wondering where you are, sister, and he has his men watching for your *safety*. You should come back with me before anyone takes notice."

Rian's smile faded. It was as if he, too, wanted to ignore the looming truth of their circumstances. Isla preferred to pretend there was no cruel reality waiting for her with every step they took toward Aurial. All she wanted was a few minutes to herself, but Slin had other ideas.

She nodded, giving Rian a fleeting smile, then grabbed Edmund's arm and allowed him to lead her back to the rest of their party. She dropped the brush next to a pile of muddy boots.

Thirteen

The General

Rian ran his fingers through the swirling water and scooped another handful to throw onto his face, trying to scrub off weeks of dirt and grime he hadn't been able to remove in the bath.

The tavern room he'd been assigned was dark and smelled like a moldy cloth, but it was better than the forest floor. Plus, the water was far more welcoming than a frigid stream fed straight from the mountain glaciers, so he had little to complain about.

Water splashed from the bathing room next door, hidden behind a musky curtain that was definitely growing a new species of mold.

"Are you almost done in there, or have you used up all the water in the village?"

"Hey," came Freya's cutting voice. "You're the one who offered your room for a clean bath, and it's not like I took as long as Malin."

"Excuuuuuse me," Malin said from his spot on the lumpy mattress. He tied a band around his half-dried hair. "These locks take time and dedicated scrubbing to keep as silky smooth as they are."

"Pampered softie," Freya murmured.

Malin spat a string of curses toward the curtain.

Rian chuckled and turned back to the rusty mirror. He examined the new marks at the base of his neck. A faint trail left by the feathered touch of fingers he could still feel quivering along his skin. His high collar would hide them until he could find a way to delicately tell Isla what she'd done. It wasn't as pronounced as the mark on his arm, and he could easily pass it off as a birthmark or scar. No need to worry her unnecessarily.

A burst of hot breath tickled his neck, and he jumped.

"How did that one happen?" Malin asked gleefully, pressing the marks with his thumb. "When did you two sneak off again?"

"*In the middle of the freaking night*," Freya screeched through the curtain. It was loud enough to wake Opi from his nap. He jumped up, hackles raised, as if expecting a foe in the middle of the room. "When it was raining half of Hierel's fury on us."

"Ah." Malin clucked his tongue and flopped back onto the stiff mattress, motioning for Opi to jump up despite Rian's explicit orders that the creature stay *off* the bed. "How does she do it—without killing you?"

"You know what," Rian grumbled, throwing on his jacket to hide the marks. "Why don't you ask her yourself?"

Malin wagged a finger at the ceiling. "No. Thank. You. I don't want to get blasted into nothingness."

"You know." Rian bit the inside of his cheek. "I already regret inviting you two over here. I should have left you to sleep in the dirt with the rest of—"

"Us lowly Pedites," Freya finished, throwing back the curtain in a grand display. Her uniform pants and tunic clung to her, while her soaking blond hair flowed freely down her shoulders, drenching the back of her shirt. She threw herself onto the bed beside Malin, lying on her stomach and leaning on her elbows to scrutinize Rian directly.

"You're the only one of us who was given a room," she said. "Most of the Divites got one, as did the Koliats."

"Yeah, well, Brenner is a pretentious jerk who threw a fit at the thought of some of our soldiers being assigned better quarters than his. And seeing as I was the only one who thought otherwise, there wasn't much debate."

Just as Rian had made small strides to get his men better tents and a few extra weapons for sparring, Brenner had to come in and snatch everything away for his own camp. Turning the Pedite Corps into a group the others took seriously was harder than he'd thought, especially with the self-absorbed Koliats around. He had been incredibly naive in his prior optimism.

"You and the princess, you mean." Freya glanced his way. "I heard the debate."

"Well, she couldn't push against him too much, he is her—"

"Betrothed," Malin said boredly. "We *know*."

The thought of that preening royal marrying Isla—of him getting to kiss her, hold her, and spend his life with her—was nauseating. Rian liked to pretend that future didn't exist.

Freya rested her head in her palms. "And we also know you only invited us because you didn't want to be left alone with your sad, sad thoughts."

Malin sat up and scratched under Opi's chin. "Don't you mean because he was assigned lodging at the complete edge of Slomat? As far away as they could get him from—"

"Yes, I'm aware," Rian bit out. Inviting them over had definitely been a mistake. "I'm fully aware that not only was I given the worst room of them all, but it's the furthest one away from Isla."

Malin and Freya exchanged a look. He hated when they silently discussed him while he stood right there. They probably thought he was being overdramatic. If he had half a mind, he'd order them back to the camp outside the city limits, not that they'd listen if he tried.

They barely listened to him before his promotion, and none of that had changed, especially when, as Malin put it, it was only a half-assed, bribe-induced promotion to begin with.'

He knew where this was headed. They'd start in on him about survival after they got to Aurial. *After* the point where he would never see Isla again. Rian refused to think about any of it. He didn't know who he was anymore if he didn't have that driving mission in life. Plus, he had a whole battalion of Pedites to care for while they were ramping up for one of the worst wars Velotia had seen in years.

"Now he's going to sulk again," Freya said dramatically. "Look what you've started."

"He always was a brooding bastard," Malin barked. "Even worse... now he's a brooding bastard with rank." He wiggled his nose in disgust at the last word.

"The worst kind." Freya threw her wet hair back, spraying Opi and Malin with droplets. She'd always grown her hair out despite it getting in the way in battle, unlike her sister—

A knock at the door, and Opi was back on all fours, growling. Rian's hand flexed at his side, where Dark End was missing from.

"What now?" Malin whined.

Freya sighed and jumped off the bed. "I swear upon Rallion's fiery gaze, if it's that moron Shaw coming back with more questions, I'm going to—"

She swung open the door and froze.

Rian blinked stupidly.

Isla stood there, one of her lady's cloaks draped over her shoulders with the hood pushed back. She stilled upon seeing Freya.

"Oh hiiiiii," Malin said, smacking his lips together loudly.

Opi puffed out his chest and crooned.

Isla tilted her head past Freya. Her expression softened when she spotted Malin on the bed. Then she broke into a timid smile.

"What gracious goddess do we owe this late pleasure of a visit to?" Malin said, struggling into a seated position. "Need to review tomorrow's travel plans again? I hear your last session got rained out. *Drenched* is the word I've heard thrown around."

Isla shrugged, peeling off the white robe to reveal a tight-fitting black corset with a silver flame emblem over the chest. Her hair was in a fancy updo, pinned with ivory and pearl barrettes, and she still somehow resembled a goddess reborn, despite the dark smudges under her eyes.

She took a deep breath and sat next to Malin. "I couldn't stand it over there for another second. Do you know how much one person can listen to the pair of them discuss which type of broadsword is better for sparring, or which goddess is best to pray to for a fruitful harvest and plenty of rain?"

"I am *not* getting in trouble for this," Malin said slickly. He slid to the floor and leaned against the small dresser, looking entirely too smug for Rian's liking.

"She's going," Rian said, pointing at Isla like an idiot.

Isla shifted further back onto the bed. "No, she's not."

"How'd you get here?" Rian asked. How did she even know which of these lodges he was assigned?

She grinned devilishly. "Susanna is quite the curious one and has a wicked memory."

That wasn't an answer.

Every ounce of blood pumping through his body—every muscle, every inch of skin—begged for her to stay. All he wanted was to throw out his friends and finally get that precious alone time. Proper time where they weren't being assaulted by the forces of a vengeful storm. But they would notice her absence, and Edmund would throw a fit unlike anything they'd ever seen.

"Why don't you offer your guest a drink?" Freya suggested. She crossed the room, sat next to Malin, and pulled her hair into a quick bun on top of her head. "I could use one too."

Isla smiled and tapped her lap, which Opi immediately jumped into for chin scratches. Rian swore that beast had grown an inch overnight; he was taller, and his neck reached further than before. Plus, his belly was protruding on both sides—they'd have to cut back on his feeding schedule, or he wouldn't make the rest of the journey home. Actually, they should find someplace safe to leave him before they set foot within Aurial.

Rian rubbed his temples and sighed.

"What?" Isla said innocently. She and Opi both tilted their heads at him. "Edmund said we couldn't be seen together alone. We're not alone."

"Exactly." Freya scanned the room. "Now... about that drink."

Malin kicked open the pack he'd discarded in the middle of the room upon his boisterous entrance. "Lucky for you all, I bought two jugs of ale from a rather talkative innkeeper on the way in." He popped one open and wrinkled his nose. "Smells like Rallion's hairy elbow, but it's all he had."

Freya snatched it from him and took a swig.

Rian ground his teeth. He was outvoted. He really should have sent them back while he had the chance.

Malin passed the other jug to Isla, who took it with a tentative smile. She coughed up the first gulp. "Gods, that tastes like piss."

"It tastes even worse than it smells." Freya grimaced. She shrugged, then took another large helping. "Better than nothing."

"I've drunk worse," Isla said before taking another sip.

"Where would you have—riiiiiiight," Malin dragged out the last word far too long. He awkwardly snatched the jug back from Freya and started chugging.

Rian sat next to Isla. The bed dipped in the middle and pressed them up against each other's sides, both leaning against the wooden headboard.

Freya smiled over the lip of the jug she had just tugged from Malin's grip. "How are the two delicate princes handling their accommodations?" She snorted. "I bet the Hayfield Hare didn't quite provide the luxury they were expecting."

Isla brushed the fabric of her pants and continued scratching Opi. "Definitely not. My brother had someone give his room an extra cleaning before setting a single precious foot in it. I'm not sure about the other one, but I can imagine it was a similar reception."

"Do you think either of them has ever had a hard day in their life?" Malin mused. "Edmund certainly wasn't part of the same Divite training as the others. He had a special class. Have you seen him swing a sword?"

"He's getting better," Rian said. "Perhaps those months spent in a real camp finally ground something into him."

Freya grimaced.

"I'm sure Aurial will stamp that out as soon as we get there," Malin said.

Isla's shoulders shook in a silent chuckle. "You have no idea."

Malin took another giant gulp and lay on his back, arms clasped behind his head as a pillow. "I've only been outside the capital. They don't let us Pedites stay in the main barracks when we're stationed there."

A thin line formed between Isla's brows.

"But they have some fine tents set up outside the city walls," Freya said with a bitter laugh. "At least you've never been stationed at that dreary excuse of a stable in the cold months. I thought I was going to lose a toe at the very least."

"Guys," Rian warned.

"What?" Malin jumped to his knees. "It was only a joke," he said hurriedly. His eyes traveled to Isla's hands.

The movement did not go unnoticed. Isla splayed them out in front of her. Opi immediately started licking her fingertips. "I'm fine. I didn't take any offense."

"Well... still," Rian huffed. "No need to be insensitive jerks."

He knew the treatment of the Pedites was unfair. They all did. Making Isla feel guilty about something she had no control over was not the way to go about building change.

They didn't know how much Rian had to fight with the Divite General Garin to even allow the Pedites to travel with them all the way to Aurial. He had wanted to send them to a neighboring city to await orders, but Rian pushed back. The Pedites had been instrumental in rescuing the princess and knew these lands better than the rest. Edmund surprisingly backed him up and helped tilt the case in Rian's favor.

One small win for the Pedites. He'd take what he could get.

"I can handle it but appreciate the sentiment." Isla sent him a small smile while Freya and Malin exchanged another gleeful look.

"Well," Malin settled back into a more comfortable position. "Now that we know you aren't about to suck the life out of any of us, Freya wants to know what it feels like?"

This time Freya punched him before Rian could even open his mouth. The resounding smack to his shoulder made Opi jump.

"Idiot," Freya hissed.

"What?" Malin rubbed his shoulder. "He said I could ask—you could ask."

Rian dropped his head into his hands. "Not like that."

Isla pressed her lips together. It was hard to tell if it was in anger or to hold back a smile. "Were you talking about me?"

"No," Rian said.

"Yes."

"Absolutely."

Isla let her smile slip through. "I heard you soldiers were terrible gossips, but I didn't think you'd be worse than the courtesans back at Aurial."

"Well," Malin started. "Things get a little boring when you have nothing to do but set up camp and march around all day... back to Freya's question, though."

"I don't know how to describe what it feels like," Isla said darkly. "But I assume it's similar to other wielders. It starts deep inside you and spreads out like a storm, or an unstoppable wave. Sometimes you can control it... sometimes you can't."

"Hm. Doesn't sound all that fun."

"Definitely not," she said. "They say that when a woman is pregnant, she can pray to her favored goddess to bless her child with gifts.

My mother must have really hated me to pray for Rallion's curse like this."

"It's also passed down through bloodlines," Malin said. "Maybe she didn't mean for all this to happen." He motioned at her hands. "Does your brother have the same... the same thing? It usually runs generationally."

She shrugged. "If he does, I've never seen it. Like you said, he can barely swing a sword properly so it'd take a miracle for him to have practiced that unnoticed."

Freya raised an eyebrow and continued drinking the ale. Rian nearly choked when he accidentally took too large of a swig, and Isla's face lit up devilishly. She handled the disgusting sludge well, though he knew the conditions she'd been held in before.

A shudder of rage ran through him, one only Isla seemed to notice. He shook his head. Not now. They would pay, one day. He'd make certain of it, no matter the cost. He'd made a vow to make things right with her and was determined to see it through.

A little nagging voice in his head asked: *as he was once determined to take her safely to the Koliats to complete the alliance?* He shoved that thought into a dark box and locked it tight away. The reminder on his arm protested, but he quietened that too.

They stayed like that for a while, with Isla next to him on the bed, enjoying the little time they were given, while Freya and Malin argued about who was the quickest during their training courses.

It was Freya, for the record, but Rian didn't feel like adding any heat to the current argument. Doubtful that Malin would listen to reason after all the piss-ale he'd consumed.

The pair's arguing voices floated past him like a smooth wind on a mid-season sunny day. Isla's head was a warm weight against his shoulder, comforting his weary soul. Months of searching, of teetering on the brink of insanity and exhaustion, were finally over. Yet it was still hard to tell his mind and body that they could relax.

They couldn't. Not while danger still lurked under that mountain and in that forest... perhaps even tracking them this far into Velotia, as it had before.

Isla sighed and pressed into him further; all thoughts drifted away as warmth bloomed from deep in his chest and spread to his fingertips. He rested his cheek atop her head and allowed their breathing to sync up. Opi lay curled at the foot of the bed, snoring contentedly.

His eyes grew heavy, and at some point, he must have drifted off. Someone was shaking his shoulder, and he lurched forward, hand instinctively reaching for Dark End.

"It's only me," Malin said, his face inches away. "It's super late." He nodded toward Isla, who was already off the bed and petting Opi goodnight.

He stared at her, and she stared at him. He didn't want her to go, especially if she had already made the effort to sneak out...

"She needs to head back before they notice the switch," Freya said pointedly. "They're not completely stupid. Brenner's men have been snooping around, and you don't want to give them anything to go off of."

"Or anything that leads back to certain people," Malin added, shoving his thumb into his own chest. "I feel like we just made it out of the trenches, and I have no desire to go back."

Isla snorted, tossing the white cloak over her shoulders. Rian tugged the hood snug over her head, hiding her face in the shadows. "I'll take you back."

Freya scoffed, tugging on her black-and-silver jacket. "Rallion's gate, you will not. I'll take her back. If we're spotted, it won't be great, but it'll be less suspicious than having the princess wandering the late hours with another man. With *you*. Trust me."

Stupid friends.

"You can have five minutes. I'll wait downstairs." Freya grabbed Malin's arm and tugged him along, giving them a pointed look that

Rian knew meant they had to be quick or she'd be right back up here with Bone Breaker to tear them apart.

Isla fluttered her eyelashes at him, despite barely being able to see past the hood of her lady's cloak. Rian tilted her chin so it fell to her shoulders.

"Thanks for coming to visit," he said. "I'm sorry about that pair."

"I like them."

Rian chewed on the inside of his cheek. Gods, why was this so difficult? He knew the proper thing to do was take her downstairs immediately. It was the respectful thing.

Then he decided to fuck it all. He ducked his head, pressing his lips against her silk ones. It wasn't like the kiss in the grove. For starters, they weren't soaking wet and being tossed around by the winds. In fact, he was toasty warm everywhere. And most importantly, it wasn't the fiery, chaotic kiss from that day in the rain, it was soft and measured. They took their time exploring each other. It was painfully slow, but the way she hummed against him held onto that thin thread of sanity he barely managed to keep.

She was his sanity. His reason for breathing. He knew that for certain after so long apart. When she had been taken, it had felt impossible to breathe. Now, every breath tasted like sweet honey and the lilies that grew back home. Pure bliss.

He deepened the kiss as much as he could, keeping the delightful pace they'd set. He breathed in her glorious scent as if it were sustenance, and the feel of her body pressed against his was all the nourishment he needed.

This time, he hit the wall as she pressed against him with more strength than he thought she possessed. The wooden frame groaned against his back.

She pulled an inch away and whispered against his lips, "Are you certain I can't stay a little longer?"

He groaned. *Stay,* that inner voice begged again. Yes, that was a great idea. There was no better plan than that.

Except...

He leaned his forehead against hers. "If you do stay, then I won't let you leave... and Edmund will show up with three battalions to drag you out, and I'll be sent for lashes."

"At the very least." She sighed and rubbed his arms, lingering for a second over the mark burned into his skin. Did she know what was there, and *how* it got there?

She smiled as if in confirmation. All of her memories must be within her grasp now. *All* of them.

The only ones who knew about that mark were Freya and Malin, even then, he'd only shown them once, making them swear upon the goddess of wrath's name to never tell another soul. Even during training, he kept a shirt on to cover it, despite how sweaty he'd get. He definitely didn't want Edmund to ever find out.

"Will I see you on the road tomorrow?" she asked hopefully.

He nodded, despite knowing Edmund would assign his Pedites to scout ahead or take up the rear as usual. He didn't have the heart to tell Isla.

Isla threw her hood back on, and he guided her downstairs to meet Freya. His friend was right, and there'd be too many questions if he were seen escorting the princess at this hour, especially with Brenner's men lurking nearby.

Malin and Freya were seated around a small table with another jug of that piss-ale resting between them. Freya stood and ushered the cloaked Isla out the door without a word.

Malin stared at him for a few seconds, then pushed the jug toward him.

Excellent idea.

He threw himself into Freya's vacated seat and helped himself to the terrible swill once more, letting Malin distract him with a long-winded rant about the recent increase in both Rian and Freya's moodiness, and how it was affecting his usually cheerful disposition.

It wasn't until they were halfway through the jug that a terrible pain radiated from Rian's arm. Something was wrong.

Fourteen

The goddess Laian, was determined to test his patience, likely due to some long-forgotten slight he'd committed against the keeper of wrath and retribution. Surely, there was no other reason for the torture of keeping this pretentious swine occupied.

Isla had already abandoned them after a few bites of dinner, excusing herself to her room as a headache began to throb. Edmund had the same headache but couldn't escape his hosting duties the way she could, especially when she insisted she was perfectly fine, healed, and whole.

Fully healed except for the moments when Brenner weighed on her patience.

Abandoning her duties wasn't like her. Yet the sister who had returned from Murat was not the same one who had been taken. Not really. He refused to accept it. Their father would surely not approve of her newfound impertinence. Edmund knew the source of it and tried everything in his power to keep them apart, no matter how much Isla despised him for it.

Nothing would change once they reached Aurial. Their father would demand she follow through with the marriage ceremony. He would likely insist it happen the moment they stepped through the gates. Once the scars were burned into flesh, there was no going back.

He instinctively rubbed his wrists, as if it were the first day they had been engraved into his skin and soul. He never understood why all ten Rocian Kingdoms still upheld the old tradition of maiming oneself in a mirror image of the ancient goddess bonds.

"Missing the wife?" came that irritating, grating voice.

Edmund closed his eyes for the briefest of moments and smiled grimly at Prince Brenner. "It has been many months since we were last together."

Thanks to very thoughtful planning.

His father hadn't been pleased with their long separation, but Edmund had managed to step around that issue the last time it arose. He didn't know if he'd get so lucky again.

"I'm sure the reunion shall be a fortuitous one," Brenner simpered, chugging the glass of wine he had complained about being too tart only five minutes prior.

Once Isla had left, the Koliat's demeanor shifted from engaged dinner guest to bored royal hunting for his next distraction. He lounged back in his chair, feet on the table, spinning a jewel-encrusted knife on its edge as if the conversation wasn't interesting enough for him.

With no one else around, Brenner dropped all pretense of civility, letting the heavy silence settle. The only person he seemed to care about impressing anymore was Isla, and sometimes her ladies—only sometimes. Edmund saw through the chameleon act, and it annoyed him more than Isla's feigned illness to get out of things.

"She may not be in the city when we arrive," Edmund said casually.

The knife stopped. Brenner raised an eyebrow, but Edmund didn't elaborate. There was no way he would give this ingrate anything to use against him later, not before uncovering Brenner's true reasons for tagging along so quietly.

There was something else he was after. Something else he was interested in.

"A shame," Brenner said, resuming the spinning of the knife. That dull clink would haunt Edmund's nightmares for weeks.

As soon as they reached Aurial, he could finally be rid of the man for good. He'd return to Koliat, where hopefully Brenner would remain for a long—

The cured ham he'd eaten churned in his stomach. Then Isla would also be gone to Koliat, stuck with Brenner. Forever.

Edmund winced.

"Ham upsetting your stomach?" Brenner asked.

"Yes... something I ate." Edmund grabbed a glass of water and downed it to maintain his composure.

Brenner nodded. "The root vegetables were off. Likely a bad harvest. Koliat has seen its fair share of rot and drought over the past years. Luckily, your lands seemed to have escaped thus far, except that one grove."

No wonder Isla was always slipping away, loath to spend more time than necessary with the prince. She had a lifetime of misery ahead, and she knew it.

He supposed that if Isla was condemned to life with this man, he could stomach him for a few weeks. It was the least he could do after *everything*. The guilt weighed on him heavily. More now that they'd found her safe. He wanted to make things right, but admitting his wrongs was never easy, especially since there was still *so much* she didn't know. Every time he tried to talk to her, cowardice claimed him, and he stayed far from the truth he most longed to speak.

At this rate, he might never make things right with Isla.

What was that word the soldiers had used before? *Cordrai.*

Fitting.

No one else knew the full truth of how terrible he'd been to her. If they did—if that Pedite did—he'd never be able to stomach it. There was so much more she didn't know about, and he had no clue how to even start that conversation.

The hand around his glass tightened hotly.

"Who else knows?" Brenner asked, dragging Edmund back into the stifling heat of the room.

"What?"

"About your sister?" Brenner's feet dropped from the table and he sat up straight. "I asked—who else knows about your sister?"

Edmund's breath caught in his chest for a moment. Thank Imoten they were alone. "No one."

This Koliat prince knew far too much, thanks to Edmund's own gossiping men. He needed to find out more about Brenner—something that could be used against the man, not just the fact that he was an absolute asshole. That much was a given with most royalty in Rocia.

Shiaarl shared an important border with Koliat, and his wife was from there. Perhaps he should reach out to see what information she could dig up on Prince Brenner and the Koliats. He'd send a letter first thing in the morning.

"The Muratians know," Brenner said. "You know they do. I know they do."

"Fine. Some of the Muratians *may* know."

"Your soldiers. Which of them know?"

"None," Edmund lied, hoping his voice was steadier than his frantic heart. "I don't even think her ladies are fully aware."

Brenner picked up the knife and spun it again. "Then why the sneaking around?"

Another frantic beat of his heart. "One of her ladies is involved with a soldier in the Pedite camp. We spent a lot of time with them while searching for her."

The knife clattered to a stop on the table. Brenner nodded to himself. "Everyone needs their distractions, I guess."

Edmund was proud of the quick lie. He'd have to talk to Isla about her indiscretions again. Brenner wasn't an idiot. He was calculated and possessive and *would* notice soon. This had to stop... for real this time.

"The Pedite that was with her knows," Brenner said sharply. "He has to. He was there in that village in Murat. How much does he know?"

"You know," Edmund said hotly. "It doesn't feel proper to speak of my sister in such a manner while she is not present. If you have questions, why don't you ask her?"

Brenner looked taken aback at the suggestion. He quickly adjusted his expression, as if actually asking Isla had never occurred to him.

That guilt in Edmund's stomach bubbled up again. He had never encouraged asking his sister her opinion in the past, so why be surprised that Brenner simply continued with the foundation he'd already set?

"Apologies." Edmund rubbed his face, stretching the skin on his cheeks. "It's been a long ride today..." He hesitated, searching for the proper wording. "The general is *aware* of some of her gifts."

Brenner's throat bobbed. "Will he be a problem?"

Absolutely not. "He won't be a concern."

Once again, Brenner nodded to himself. "My men tell me he was recently promoted to Pedite General. That would explain the reasoning. Smart move over force. It would make the others suspicious."

Edmund wrinkled his nose. He did not need this pretentious hen's praise. And the promotion wasn't *only* to keep his silence on Isla's powers, but he'd rather be dragged through all of Rallion's gates than admit that to Brenner.

"He's loyal and won't say a word."

"That's not what some of the men say," Brenner said.

"I'm aware of what they've said about his past actions. He's more than made up for it now."

Gods, why was he defending that incompetent soldier so fervently? Edmund must be coming down with an ailment—or slowly losing his wits.

"If you say so." Brenner plucked the knife from the table and tucked it into his belt. "Your mother must have strong wielders in her family line."

Edmund winced. He'd long suspected that their mother's bloodlines stretched back to the High King's daughter. Others had come to the same conclusion, and now it seemed Brenner was zeroing in on it too.

Brenner nodded. "They say the High King's line was forged through a bonding with Rallion herself, if you believe such tales."

"I'm not one to live by the word of old folk stories and twisted legends," Edmund said bitterly.

"Neither am I, but there is some truth to it. All of our lines can be traced back to the same lineage. The same High King and his son. I've been doing more research since the events of the past months. Does your sister know?"

"I'd rather not share gossip about my sister like this," Edmund said pointedly.

"Understandable," came Brenner's smooth reply. "Why aren't your special guards with you?"

"Huh?"

"The Siicas. I heard about them from my father. I'm surprised they weren't sent with you—or the princess, for that matter. Especially given all the reports of unrest and strange happenings across your lands."

"They were needed back in Aurial. Plus, I don't always travel with them—"

"When you're disobeying your father, you mean?"

Edmund ignored that. "We don't always have them. They're meant to guard our father and other important members of the noble court."

He didn't bother sharing his concerns with Brenner. The Koliat didn't need to know what Edmund had started to suspect, and he'd been piecing together Skallen's betrayal long before Brenner came into the picture. A man like that would have never acted alone.

"And your father didn't think to send them with her on the original journey?"

"He sent her in the care of his most trusted commander—"

"The one who betrayed you?"

"And two battalions of soldiers as well. *You* were supposed to protect her once they got to Bluemoon Bay." Edmund fixed Brenner with an accusatory glare.

"They never arrived at Bluemoon Bay, did they?"

"What are you trying to insinuate—that my father planned for this? That he was trying to back out of the agreement or something?"

"I would never dream of implicating our partners in something like that." Brenner refilled his wine. Red crystals splashed into the cup. "But you certainly are keen on delaying the inevitable—both of you. If I were another man—a smarter man—I'd say you have no intention of going through with our contract, and I'd be curious why you're so intent on dragging us all back to your capital city when it would have been quicker to continue to Koliat."

Edmund slapped the table and slowly rose from his seat, his glare locked on Brenner. "How dare you. My sister is in poor health after what happened to her, and I have no plans on handing her over while she is in such a condition."

Brenner's grin widened. "So, you do want to stop the marriage contract."

"I never said I did."

"You may as well have."

Edmund felt his carefully curated temper fraying. "How do I know *your* people haven't conspired with the Muratians?"

"How dare you!" Brenner snapped, standing so quickly that his chair toppled. "Listen to me. This marriage contract is happening. Our fathers have both agreed to it, and nothing anyone does can stop it. If you attempt further delays once we reach Aurial and your sister's health is cleared by a healer you deem capable, there will be dire consequences."

Edmund's fists shook at his sides. The air in the room felt like it was boiling. "Is that a threat?"

Brenner's gaze remained ice-cold and unyielding. "It's not a threat. It's reality. One we all need to accept, especially you and your sister."

Edmund's chest heaved harder than after a training session with Freya. He ground his teeth until they ached, carefully weighing every word. One misstep could ignite war against his kingdom and his family. They couldn't afford it. She couldn't afford it. Not with everything Brenner already knew.

A commotion rose in the hallway, likely quarreling soldiers. The Koliats and Velotians barely tolerated each other on the best of days. They didn't need to witness their princes squabbling like green recruits.

Edmund steadied his voice and said, "I am—we both are—all in agreement with the marriage contract and want this alliance to go through. Our father rejected many suitors before this."

"Including Murat," Brenner added slickly. "They were quite adamant about arranging their own union before all this."

That was years ago. How did he know that? "Our king wouldn't have accepted your father's terms if we weren't willing to see this through. If you have any doubts, I apologize for planting them. You have to understand that things changed after she was taken, and we all want what is best for Isla. That includes finalizing this partnership in burns. You have my word."

Brenner leaned forward. "We shall see if your words ring true, prince. And allow the goddess Wallienne to judge all." He picked up the glass of red and drained it. The shouting outside intensified. "What is that incessant yelling? We are trying to have a civilized meal here."

Brenner strode to the door and yanked it open. A maroon-clad soldier stood there, arm raised as if about to knock.

"My prince," the soldier said. "There is a fire next door, and it is spreading quickly. We must get you to safety. You too, Prince Edmund." Several black-and-silver Divites rushed down the hall.

Edmund and Brenner exchanged a look, and he was delighted to see brief fear flit across the Koliat prince's face. It seemed he, too, hadn't spent much time near a real battle or fight, just as Edmund hadn't... a fact he'd begrudgingly come to terms with thanks to Freya's constant battering.

The soldiers ushered them past a window, and Edmund caught sight of vicious flames licking the wood of the next building. There was no way, in all of Slin's cruel jokes, that this was a mere coincidence.

He was already halfway up the stairs, intent on grabbing Isla himself, when a white-clothed figure ran out of the hall.

"Susanna." He froze with his foot hovering off the next step. "Where is..." He trailed off as Isla's trusted lady shook her head.

"She was feeling sickly, prince, and Alynna suggested some fresh air to help with her ill composition."

"They went alone?" Brenner barreled up the stairs behind him. "What could have possessed them to do that?"

Edmund closed his eyes and sent a prayer to Hierel.

Susanna held her chin high, not cowering under their scrutiny. "The town was well guarded, and we did not see an issue. I believe some of the Pedite soldiers may have watched over their progress."

"Very well." Brenner had already turned on his heel, missing the pointed look Susanna gave him.

Edmund did not need her confirmation; he already knew where she had gone. He whipped around. "Where are you going, Brenner?"

The prince did not slow his pace as he leapt down the last set of stairs into the main tavern, where soldiers barked orders at another. "To find your sister, obviously."

Edmund stuttered.

Brenner turned, amber eyes blazing fiercely. "You were right before when you said she should have been handed to me and my men for safekeeping in Bluemoon Bay. Clearly, your troops have a lackluster system and have allowed safety to slip. No more."

"This is hardly necessary, as my men will—"

"If you truly meant what you said about this partnership working, then I see no issue starting to repair things by working together, as true partners, right now. What do you say?"

A warning bell chimed, alerting the rest of the soldiers to the fire.

Edmund wanted to groan. He wanted to scream, to throw things—throw the prince right into the flames raging feet from their rooms. But he did none of those things. Instead, he found himself issuing orders to his Divites to help fight the fire, while directing several others to aid him and the Koliats in finding his sister.

Fifteen

The Princess

The walk back to her room at the Hayfield Hare was painfully slow and awkwardly silent. She wasn't sure if the strong-willed soldier liked her or saw her as an incredibly annoying nuisance to take care of. Couldn't the loud one have taken her instead? Malin's constant quips would fill the eerily silent night air.

It would have been as bad if she was caught with him. Running off in the middle of the night with Freya, while it came off as terribly suspicious and idiotic, would pass off better than wandering alone with a male soldier.

But she was disguised as one of her ladies, and nobody paid her any attention. Likely thinking that the princess had sent her off with another message for the general. She'd have to start talking to the Divite general every now and then so people didn't grow suspicious. What was that prick's name again? She needed to learn it fast.

"You don't have to take me all the way, if you don't want," Isla said, desperately needing to break the silence.

They passed a duo of Pedite sentries who nodded at Freya.

She scoffed—a bitter laugh—and ran her thumb along the edge of her double-sided axe. "I may as well cut off my own arm if I let you go on your own. They'd both gut me, no questions asked."

Isla snorted, then tripped over a gap in the cobblestone. "You're probably right. It's a bit much at times."

"And they say they are the more rational of the genders."

"Doubtful."

"I haven't seen him like this in a while. Not since…" Freya slowed her pace, taking two languid steps before turning to face her. "Do not hurt him. I know he's an idiot sometimes—most times—but he's my idiot friend."

"I'm trying not to." Isla's pulse quickened. "I really am."

"But we all know the last pages of the great story. The end of the path we tread upon."

"Yes." Isla rubbed her wrists as if she could already feel the burn. "I don't know what else to do, though."

Freya tilted her head. "I guess in some ways you have even less choice than those of us who had this life forced upon us at fourteen."

A twinge of guilt, even though she wasn't the one who set up the conscripts. That system had been in place in Velotia for centuries. "We all must stick to our own trials."

"Well…" Freya pivoted and started walking again. "I am most certainly excited to see Aurial this time of year, even if it is from outside the city walls."

"I'm certain we'll be able to make arrangements once we get there." There was no need for only the Pedites to stay outside the castle walls… no reason, besides centuries of prejudice against that corps.

"Doubtful." Freya shrugged. "And it would be peculiar to those who know the old ways. They'd ask too many questions. We're used to it. It's fine."

Isla frowned. Everyone was resolved to the same swaying of Mannop's sour justice.

"What lies ahead for you after this?" she found herself asking.

Freya smiled, a puff of air forming from her breath. "A giant casket of ale… and sleeping for a fortnight straight."

"That sounds lovely."

"I bet you could have a month's worth of rest if you played up being sick."

"Which I'm not," Isla quickly corrected. They already thought she was frail and losing it, and she hadn't told another soul about seeing waking visions of a certain red-headed soldier around camp. It only happened when she was tired, and the visions disappeared long before she could blink twice. Nothing to worry about... or was it?

"You're not sick *unless* your brother or Brenner are around," Freya said smoothly.

"Exactly. At least my time away does have its benefits." She paused. Surely, Freya was a safe confidant? "Although some days I feel like I'm still there."

"Down... below?" Freya said slowly.

"Yes." Isla rubbed her hands down the sides of her dress. "Sometimes I feel like she is around. Watching me still, but then I snap out of it."

"You should tell him," Freya said, and she didn't mean her brother. "Let him know, and maybe Ben can help relieve some of the past traumas."

"I don't want to worry him. I just—argh." Her world spun as she was thrown into the side of a building, and whatever words she had were squashed beneath a clammy palm.

"Hush," Freya whispered, her breath hot against Isla's ear. "Someone is following us."

Rian? She was going to murder that soldier.

Freya shook her head, understanding the newfound fire burning in Isla's eyes. "Not them." Her eyes widened, and she quickly removed her hand from Isla's mouth.

The sting came quickly when she realized Freya was afraid of touching her. She told herself it was because she was her princess, not for any other reason. The lie quelled the tears threatening to break free.

A loud bang echoed in the distance.

Right. Someone was following them. Priorities, Isla. *Priorities.*

Freya turned and reached behind her, grabbing Isla's hand with no wince in sight. "Follow me and do exactly as I say."

Follow the rules and don't wander off. Isla was used to this, despite what Freya might think about her refusing to listen to those beneath her station.

A tug on her hand and Freya led her down the dark alley behind them, away from the lit street they'd just vacated.

"Just keep moving. It could be nothing," Freya said, one hand casually sliding over the hilt of her axe, as if she longed to hold it but didn't want to upset Isla.

A flicker of annoyance spread through her. When would people stop trying to coddle her—when she was one foot past the first gate?

Freya quickened their pace—nearly a run without actually running—and Isla struggled to keep up. Okay, she wasn't quite as healed as she pretended to be. Months spent digging in the mines hadn't prepared her for sprints like this.

Another turn, and they were down an even narrower alley. It reminded Isla of the tunnels near the pit. The ones that seemed to close in with every step. Except these weren't tunnels, and she wasn't a trapped prisoner anymore.

Freya noticed her struggle. It wasn't hard based on the way Isla's breath came in labored gasps. Her side ached, and for a panicked moment, she thought the wound there had split open, despite being fully healed. But the pain was only a stitch from muscles unused to this kind of exertion.

How embarrassing.

Freya slowed once the alley spilled into a new street, pausing briefly as her head whipped in every direction. Then she pulled Isla along at the same careful pace.

"I'll have you there in a minute," Freya said confidently, though her gaze still darted around.

A flicker of movement on the rooftop across the way. Isla heard something whizz past them.

A scream ripped from her throat, and she clamped her own hand over her mouth before Freya could, but it was too late. Another object hurtled through the air, and Freya dove at her, knocking her out of the path of whatever it was.

They landed hard on the ground. Isla's shoulder and hip took the brunt of the fall, but Freya was already tugging her up before her body could even register it had fallen.

Cold fear threatened to claw its way into her heart and veins, and a foreign throb of emotion bubbled up from her chest.

A bell chimed ominously across town, a loud warning or plea for help—Isla had never bothered to learn the soldiers' signals, despite spending weeks among them.

Light flickered in the buildings across the way as the occupants were roused by the strange noise in the dead of night. Perhaps the Pedites stationed outside the village heard it too. Maybe they were readying themselves to help.

Freya's axe was out. When had she managed that? She used her spare hand to usher Isla back towards the nearest building wall.

An orange glow bloomed in the distance. It came from the direction of her room at the Hayfield Hare.

Her throat bobbed. Edmund was there. She prayed his trusted Divites were with him.

A trio of dark-cloaked men approached. The hems of their robes were ripped and stained with what she hoped was mud. Drooping hoods shadowed their faces, yet she could feel their focus on her. A thread of ice spread down her spine and into her fingertips.

Isla's own hood had been thrown back during their frantic pacing. There was no need to hide her face, for they'd known who she was long before now.

"I would stay back if you know what's good for you," Freya said, twisting her axe in a way that would make Isla immediately drop any weapon she carried and beg for mercy.

The men in front of them did no such thing, nor did they slow their approach. They moved with feline-like grace, each at least a head taller than Isla.

They spread out before Isla and Freya. The one in front stepped forward, pulling back the grey hood of his cloak.

Freya inched back, and Isla gasped.

Scars. Everywhere.

Burn marks fully covered his hands, half of his face, down his neck, and the portion of his shoulder she could see. Now that he was closer, etchings of a flower gleamed in the middle of his cloak, which she realized wasn't torn but burned at the bottom and cuffs.

His hair was thin and white, half of it singed away, and the whites of his eyes were far too thick, giving him the look of a half-crazed ghoul. The others pulled back their hoods, revealing similar burns across their bodies and faces. Isla's stomach churned at the sight

What had they said about the old Rallion followers? Zealots. Crazed lunatics who burned their own flesh as an offering to the goddess. Mutilating their bodies in a rite they believed would sway her for a touch of power. She had never seen anything so mad in her life.

"Blasphemer," the man spat at Freya.

"Lunatics," Freya whispered.

The first man raised his hand, and a small flame flickered to life. A godsdamned firewielder.

A pulse of fear pricked Isla's heart and spread faster than she could stop it. The tang of power flooded into her hands. There was no need to check the color her fingertips had turned.

No. She closed her eyes as the trembling started along her spine. Not now.

There were people all around in these buildings. Families and children and animals... and Freya was too close and she didn't know how to control it. It was Ackerslie all over again.

Images of the villagers' faces, twisted in horror as there was nothing they could do to run or hide from it—from her—came crashing into view. Her breath caught somewhere between her chest and her lungs, pooling there.

"I'm not going to tell you again," Freya said.

It was impressive, the way she kept calm—at least on the outside. Isla, by contrast, was a mess inside and out, certain an explosion loomed near.

Please, not now, she prayed—to Hierel, to Rallion, to Imoten. She wasn't sure who would answer while the goddess of chaos still reigned.

The man's mouth twisted into a cruel smile, and the small flame in his palm twisted into a sphere. It pulsed three times before shooting at them, missing by inches and flying right over their heads, clinging to the wood and paint of the building behind them.

Isla threw her hands above her head to shield herself from falling sparks and splinters. All that was left of the wall behind them was a giant crater—a flaming crater that grew by the second.

He had missed on purpose.

A second flash of silver shot by, and Freya's flailing arms batted the arrow away with her axe. Gods, she was quick. Smoke tickled Isla's nose, and heat licked at her backside as the fire spread behind them. More bells chimed from the southern end of the village.

Another bright flash. This time the firewielder formed a new fireball, passing it between his hands as his eyes sparkled at Freya. The other two had yet to move or attack. What were they playing at?

Freya didn't give him another chance. She charged, axe swinging.

The wielder on the left stooped, and an old cart transformed into a sharp pike that Freya nearly ran into. At the last second, she dodged, the end of the pike grazing her sleeve.

A shifter. One of Slin's chosen chaotic wielders.

The third man didn't appear to have any wielder powers but drew a long scythe, its edge flashing in the firelight.

Freya groaned and rolled onto her knees, her axe was tight in her grip, while Isla remained frozen in place. Terror held her there. Afraid to move, afraid she'd get in the way, or worse. Everything she did always made things worse.

The man lifted the scythe, and it met the blade of Freya's thick axe. Another arrow shot from a building top, its tip ablaze as it struck a new spot behind them.

The heat at her back intensified, and she inched away from the wall.

Freya grunted and kicked the man in the abdomen. He doubled over, wheezing in pain, while Freya limped back to Isla, hand outstretched to keep the others at bay.

Isla's attention snapped back to the firewielder. His raging ball had now doubled in size, rolling from hand to hand as he stared at them with bloodshot eyes. It was almost as if he was taunting them. Waiting for something.

Freya planted herself in front of Isla, blocking the rush of burning nothingness aimed their way.

Someone shouted down the alleyway, and a door across the street burst open. Soldiers. It was hard to tell the color of their uniform through the flames.

The ground churned beneath their feet, thanks to the shifter. Isla dropped to her hands and knees on the cobblestone, now softened into dirt, trying to keep her stomach's contents inside. Freya somehow managed to stay upright amidst the chaos of moving ground determined to swallow them whole.

Freya roared and hurled her axe toward the shifter. It struck true, embedding itself squarely in the wielder's chest.

The movement beneath her feet stopped, but Isla's stomach didn't stop rolling.

The firewielder shouted as his companion fell, his fingertips were now licked by flames. His eyes glowed, with that fury entirely focused on Freya. Isla watched in horror as the fireball pulsed, just as it had before he last shot it.

She shouted, reaching out as if she could bat it from his hands.

The darkness shot forward before she could stop it or even think. It slithered and stretched along the cracked cobblestones, searching for anything within reach.

Not that one!

Isla couldn't rein it in. She wasn't strong enough, but she focused every ounce of herself on pulling it back, pulling it away from Freya.

The power surged toward the wielder, drawn by the heat of his flames.

As the dark energy touched him, consuming the fire in his hands, he tilted his head back, euphoria flashing across his features for a brief second. Then he was reduced to ash.

It took everything in her to draw the darkness back as it begged to explode further and devour everything in its path. The rush of power back into her slammed her into the wall behind her. She slid to the ground, her vision fading in and out. Freya crawled over as other voices shouted. Panicked.

Soldiers ran up to her. At first, she thought their uniforms were bloody, but they were maroon, not red. Someone in black seized her shoulders a little too harshly and shook her until her vision snapped back.

Edmund. A man wearing the Koliat crest stood behind him, his face stark-white as he peered at her.

Isla clutched her brother's arm to steady herself as he helped her to her feet. Her fingers tingled, the same way they did after staying in the cold too long, but she refused to look at them.

"Sister, are you all right?" Edmund's eyes scanned her, taking in the dirty cloak he must know did not belong to her.

A pair of black-and-silver soldiers rounded the corner at a sprint. Several Koliats unsheathed their weapons at the intruders. For a fleeting moment, one soldier's face twisted into Beretta's grim smile, then it was gone. With a quick nod from Brenner, they relaxed and allowed the new pair into the semi-circle that had formed around them.

Isla wanted to sob at the relief flooding her body, warmth returning to her fingers and toes, but Edmund's face silenced any such thoughts.

She'd never seen him this furious as he surveyed the two new arrivals, especially when they went to help Freya. Isla sensed Rian's eyes dragging across her face, but with so many people around, and Edmund watching, he wouldn't be allowed any closer.

Freya groaned as they pulled her up. A flowering bruise marred her cheek, but she was alive. "Did you get the last one? He ran off."

Rian shook his head. "There were more of them."

Now that they were closer, Isla detected a streak of blood across his cheek. Something growled deep in her chest at the sight, but she forced herself to calm down. It was likely another's blood, and they were probably already dead.

Edmund whirled toward Rian. "I thought your men were on watch. How did Muratians get past the sentries?"

"They weren't Muratians," Malin whispered. "They were Velotians."

Edmund's mouth hung open.

"And they were here before we arrived," Rian continued. "Some zealous sect or another. I think they were the same ones from the forest with the—ah—creatures." Brenner shot him a sharp look. "We found a healer with our group."

"Where is he?" Edmund asked, shaking his head.

Malin smiled devilishly. "He put up a fight and won't be speaking to anyone for a while."

"That's not helpful."

Rian threw up his hands. There was no way he was ever going to do anything right with her brother, he should have realized that by now.

Brenner, who had been silently observing the exchange, swiveled his head toward Isla. "What were you doing out so late?"

Isla stared at her hands, avoiding his narrow gaze. "I couldn't sleep and went out for a walk."

Edmund rolled his eyes, unseen by Brenner, who ordered his soldiers away. One of them eyed her skeptically before shuffling about twenty feet back.

"Where were you?" Brenner asked, gentler than her brother had been.

Isla had never felt smaller than while under their two unwavering gazes. "I didn't think anything would happen," she said sheepishly.

"You weren't in your room like you said you'd be," Edmund said.

"What were you doing wandering outside?" Brenner asked again, sterner this time. "This isn't the first time, is it?"

Edmund's eyes widened, warning her. But Brenner wouldn't leave without an answer, and he wasn't foolish enough to believe she craved fresh air in the dead of night.

Think.

Isla stepped closer to her brother and Brenner, even though only Rian and Freya lingered nearby. She put on an annoyed expression, as if the answer were painfully obvious. "If you must know, Freya has been helping train me."

"*Train you?*" Concern laced her brother's voice, mixed with a healthy dose of that Velotian anger. "Train you on what?"

"You know what," Isla said calmly. "Just to help me control it. Nothing more."

She could see understanding flicker in Edmund's eyes, as if his mind had finally caught up to her lie. He shook his head and turned on his heel, rubbing his temples.

Brenner already knew about her wielder powers. There was no other reasonable explanation for sneaking around at night. Plus, it wasn't entirely untrue. It was a partial lie, and that made it easier on her conscience.

"You've taken a ridiculous risk," Edmund began, swinging back to face her. "How could you—"

Brenner cut him off, stepping closer to edge out Freya and Rian. "You should have said something if you wanted help with your—ah—gifts." His eyes shifted to her hands, and she was relieved to see they were perfectly normal now. "I have gifted wielders among my men—"

"Thank you, Prince Brenner, for the offer, but I feel more comfortable with our own soldiers, for the time being."

"And I'm certain the princess did not want to impose on you," Edmund added quickly, a trace of forced civility in his voice. She knew it pained him to treat the man courteously, but they were stuck with him—*she* was stuck with him—and they had to try.

Brenner's eyes searched hers for a moment. "Understandable, I suppose. And I, for one, recognize the need for secrecy, but the dangers—"

"She won't be out alone again," Edmund supplied, ignoring the glare she sent his way. "You have my word."

Isla scoffed.

Her brother's eyes blazed with the same fury as when they first found her. He was angry. And he'd make her pay dearly for the near slip with Brenner. She really was cursed. Why else would those zealots have been out at the precise moment she had snuck away from under Edmund's clutches?

A guilty ping in her stomach told her why.

Edmund waved angrily at Rian, barely meeting his eyes. He already knew the truth about why Isla had left her room that night, and no story she could spin would save her. "Gather your men, *General*, and have the Divites provide aid to the citizens of Slomat.

We'll try to get some rest and leave as soon as it is safe. You will remain outside the village limits with the Pedites tonight to ensure there are no more slip-ups."

Rian nodded, barely giving her a second glance. He didn't shy away from the clear punishment Edmund had given him. As a Pedite, he and his men were used to it. This time it was different. More personal.

When he turned to leave, Rian's fingertips brushed the edge of her cloak. It was no more than a whisper of contact, but it might as well have been a comforting embrace against the cold darkness.

Naturally, Edmund would send him outside Slomat. As if he wasn't already nearly out of reach. As if they didn't already have so little time left together, and now Edmund was determined to cut that even further.

Imbecile of a brother.

You're going to do your job, and maybe you'll finally contribute one good thing to this family since killing our mother. The words he had spoken to her that day in the camp came back as vividly as a painful slap. She was stupid to believe he had changed even a bit, and an idiot for ever allowing herself to hope.

Sixteen
The General

Freya stomped back to their fire pit, her face screwed up in an emotion she rarely let slip through. She kicked at nothing in the air. "Yuuuup. Still pissed... and refuses to see me."

Malin groaned, kicking his scuffed boots out and sending a fresh dusting of dirt into Rian's face. This section more closely resembled a dried-out swamp than a royal military encampment, not that he had expected better conditions for their dilapidated tents.

Since the ambush in Slomat, Edmund had become utterly unreasonable. He'd gone back to blatantly ignoring Rian during their daily regroup with the other generals and made a point of sending him and the Pedites far ahead to scout the terrain every day. He refused to let them set up camp anywhere near the Divites and Koliats, where he'd moved his and Isla's tents, abandoning the well-concealed beige ones that Rian had painstakingly arranged to the prince's exacting standards.

Rian tried sending Freya to talk with him, but judging by her huffy entrance, she'd been equally unsuccessful. Edmund had turned Rian away with a ridiculous assignment anytime he came within sight of Isla or any of her ladies, finally catching on to how she'd managed to sneak out each time. That intelligence hadn't been shared with Brenner, who was already acting strangely around Isla—at least according to reports passed to Rian by Freya or Malin, who could only get close to Susanna or Alynna for updates.

"Here." Freya shoved something into his chest. "I didn't see her, but Alynna passed this over. I assume it's not a love note expressing the princess' hidden feelings for *me,* so it must be for you."

"Which one is Alynna again?" Malin asked. Rian and Freya ignored him.

A smile crept across his face as he unfolded the parchment.

Malin kicked his feet out in front of him. "It was nice while it lasted, wasn't it?"

Freya raised an eyebrow and bent down to give Opi scratches along his back. Edmund refused to let the poor creature anywhere near Isla, and he'd started crying at night, keeping Rian awake and at his wit's end.

Malin added, "It was nice being treated like a regular person for a little bit there, instead of being tossed around like the scum of the military. All until Rian had to go and screw it up."

Rian scowled.

Freya replied quietly, "It was only because of him that Edmund ever changed his attitude, even if it was short-lived. We appreciate the efforts you've made on our behalf, Rian."

They might be the only two, from the way the rest of the Pedites were talking. While they still followed his orders, Rian sensed a hint of disdain lurking beneath the surface. As a new general, they still eyed his leadership with a healthy dose of suspicion, and at this point, he didn't blame them.

"It's worse to see the other side than having to come back to this." Malin pointed at his dinner. The leftovers after the other groups had already picked through the rations. "At least we're used to it." He sighed wistfully.

That set Rian's temper boiling. Edmund could be as mad as he wanted at Rian, but he shouldn't take it out on his men, especially after everything they'd done to prove their worth. He was nearly about to march straight to the pompous prick's tent and give him a piece of his mind before he checked himself.

That would only make things worse, years of experience in the Pedite Corps taught him that.

Rian re-read the note briefly, tucking it into his jacket pocket before Edmund could pop up and snatch it from his hands. Judging by the way that dastardly prince was behaving, he fully expected it.

Malin wiggled his eyebrows. "What's it say? Flowery confessions of feelings, or a promise to get us better rations?"

"Neither," Rian said. "And it's private."

"I already read it," Freya said. "And you're about to get into even more trouble, Rian Accultus."

"Oh, last name too," Malin said dramatically. "She's serious. Not that you'll listen."

"He's beyond reason," Freya said, speaking over his head. "It's like he's gone mad."

"We already knew that."

As did he. Still, Rian was on his feet and striding away from his friends before they could attempt to dissuade him with words, or through force.

First, he went in search of Shaw, who always needed help remembering his orders, then helped Aldan go through their weapons inventory, and double-checked the patrol schedule with Les until their camp was set so perfectly that even Edmund wouldn't be able to find a single fault.

They had briefly considered leaving soldiers in Slomat, but it looked like the zealots had moved on. Rian didn't want another excuse for Edmund to strip him of his title, so he decided to take all their soldiers. The target was in their camp, and the pursuers would surely follow. They needed every man they could get to keep her safe...and keep Edmund off his back.

Once he started to feel like a half-decent leader again, the sun passed the horizon and the last of its rays slowly disappeared. He approached River. A maroon-clad figure stood at the horse's head, speaking to the beast in rich, velvety tones that twisted all of his insides into one jumbled mess.

"How'd you escape?" He pointed at her outfit.

Isla tilted her head back and giggled—a glorious sound. "I told my brother that Brenner and I wanted a private supper to get to know each other better." She winced. "Luckily, he's fully fed up with Brenner and agreed after a heated discussion, which involved him explaining many times that I was to only treat with Brenner before immediately returning to my tent."

"And he bought that?" Rian grabbed the hand twisting through River's mane and brought it to his lips.

"Brenner helped. I told him I wanted to meet with his teacher, and he helped cover."

"And where is his wielder now?" Rian peered around, half-expecting to find a Koliat wielder hiding behind River's backside.

"I did a couple of exercises with him, nothing that showed a hint of actual powers. Then I had a fainting spell from overexertion, and he helped me to the tent to rest. He was worried about Brenner and my brother's response if they found out he'd overworked me and begged for my silence. He's hiding out among Brenner's men, and neither he nor my brother will be any wiser for hours."

Pride pooled in his chest and spilled out like liquid gold. Clever girl. "That explains the lovely outfit."

"Brenner sourced it for me. He didn't want anyone else to know about the work I was doing and thought no one would look twice. Apparently, many wielders in Koliat prefer to stay in hiding since they don't have a special corps like we do." She spread her arms and twisted so he could see every inch of the tightly fitted maroon jacket. "What do you think?"

Rian toyed with the maroon lapel and pulled her closer. "I prefer you in black."

"Me too."

"But I prefer you right here, right now, so I'll take you any way I can... Not like that," he added when she rolled her eyes. "You know what I meant."

Her eyes traveled to his lips, then back up to hold him captive in her gaze. "Do I?" She spun away from him—and it was only then that he realized River was tacked and saddled. She pulled on the saddle for emphasis. "I need fresh air. This camp smell is giving me a headache."

His hand followed hers, pulling it away from the horse. "I don't think that's a good idea. Your brother... he's a little crazy right now. Remember?"

And he was determined to take his anger out on every single Pedite here, not only Rian.

"Rallion can be damned before I care what my brother thinks. He's practically held me hostage for a week. I'm done doing what he says."

Rian tilted his head and thought up a hundred reasons why they should care what her brother thought and did.

Isla continued, "Creatures are returning past Rallion's gates, some crazy lunatics tried to kill us, and I'm pretty sure all these bad things keep happening because of me. I want to go for a ride on the horse that saved my life, and with the soldier I've grown rather fond of to protect me."

"From vicious vines and hidden mud pits?" he asked. He hated that she felt such heavy guilt. He'd give anything to take it away. "I don't think there's any out there right now, Your Supreme Stunning-ness."

"Rascal." She pressed into his chest, and he could feel her heart beating beneath the far-too-many layers that separated them. "Just for a little bit. I need to clear my head. We won't go far, and you'll be there in case anything happens. You wouldn't let anything happen to me, right?"

"Never." He'd sooner carve out his own eyes than allow any harm to befall her.

"Good." She stared at him, and he warred within himself, remembering Freya's warning. River shook his head side to side and pawed at the ground. It was settled. He lifted Isla onto the horse's back and swung into place behind her.

She shifted back so she was fully pressed against his chest. *Fully*.

He reached around her to grab River's reins and tilted his head. "Where to, Your Majesty?"

"Not the woods." She rested her head back against his shoulder, a silken weight against his eager body. "I've had enough forests to last two lifetimes now."

"Got it." River edged around a group of Koliat horses. "Some nice, flat lands with not a single tree in sight."

"There can be one tree—maybe two—that's all I'll allow."

"Thank you for your graciousness." River kept a slow steady pace as they passed drying saddles and equipment, ready to grab for the next morning. "How'd you get him ready on your own?"

He imagined a smile filling her face, though he couldn't see it. "I bribed that horse wrangler to help me. Ah—Kip?"

"Kit."

"Right. Kit seemed more than willing to help, and I gave him some coins in case he became talkative later. The gold was courtesy of Edmund's stash, too."

Rian curled the hand around her waist even tighter. "I can help show you next time. But if you want someone who may have a hint of patience, Freya is your girl. And if you want to end up hanging off your steed midway through a trot, then ask Malin."

"I'll keep that in mind." Isla hesitated. He could sense indecision swirling underneath the surface.

"What is it?" he asked.

"Those zealots. Why do they keep coming?"

"I think you already know the answer," he said. The time for coddling her had long since passed. She'd proven herself more than capable of handling the truth. Likely already suspected it by now.

Her body tensed against his. "My powers."

Rian nodded, pressing her close with his spare hand. "It's all connected. I'm just not sure how."

"The link to Rallion," Isla said, as if musing over her morning tea. "The tainted blood that flowed down the High King's line, straight to my mother, and down to me. It all leads back to this curse somehow."

That word sent his insides scattering. He hated how she viewed any part of herself as a curse when all he could see was pure sunshine and godliness. If only there was a way to make her see herself the way he did.

They turned at the end of the camp and—

"No fucking way," Isla muttered.

Rian mock-gasped. "Language, princess." He'd already slid off the side of River and winced at the coming barrage. Edmund might actually try to have him killed this time.

"You're dead," Edmund said, vocalizing what Rian had known all along.

"Just going for a jaunt up and down the rows," Rian said stupidly. "River's a bit older and not used to the pace, so his muscles need some stretching in the evening."

Edmund marched over to them, at least he was alone. He snatched River's lead rope out of Rian's hand. The horse pawed at the ground angrily. "I can't keep having the same conversation with you, Isla."

She held her chin high, despite the withering glare from her brother. "Neither can I."

Edmund turned to Rian. "Do you want all your men dismissed without pay? Is that what I have to do, since you clearly don't seem to care?"

Heat bubbled to the surface, but Isla was quicker. "Don't you even dare threaten your—*our* men like that."

"Then what will get through both of your firestone-filled heads? I don't know what else to tell you, Isla."

"And I don't know what to say either." She slid off the opposite side of River, keeping a soothing hand on the horse's neck. He had been ready for a nice little jaunt outside the camp, and now he'd be cooped up for the night... and River wasn't the only one.

"Isla." Edmund sighed and ruffled his hair. The dark circles under his eyes were more pronounced than last time. "We're not talking about this again. Do you want father to—"

"Throw me in the stocks? Lock me up? Whip me senseless? What do you think he's going to do that hasn't already been done? I don't care anymore."

"Isla—"

"You said you wanted things to change. To be different. But it's all the same. You haven't changed one bit. You're exactly like him!"

Edmund looked like she had struck him. Rian tried to edge behind River, feeling like he was intruding on a private family conversation... but there was nowhere to run or hide. He'd rather be facing that icewielder again.

His arm prickled at the rising heat coming from Isla. It wasn't a physical heat he could feel. He could just tell, as if an invisible thread connected them. The same one that had guided him when she was under that mountain.

Edmund found his voice. "That's going a bit far, don't you think?"

Isla stared at him for a moment before shrugging. "Stop being an asshole, Edmund."

He opened his mouth, likely to comment on the colorful language not becoming of a Princess of Velotia.

"Just..." She stared at his boots. "Just give us two minutes, okay? Then I won't make a scene."

Edmund's nostrils flared. He pointed between the two of them. "Not a second more." He turned on his heel and strode twenty paces away. He sat on the ground and watched them intently, despite the last of the sun's rays having fully disappeared.

"Sorry about him," Isla said, walking around River to come face to face with him.

"I'm used to it." They had spent months nearly skinning each other alive while searching for her. He didn't want to tell her how much of a prick her brother had been during that time. He'd rather not relive it and he'd rather not be the axe that widens the wedge between the two siblings.

"I guess you would be." She sighed and leaned against River. Edmund moved to a new spot to keep sight of her. "I... don't know if he's going to be reasonable. I tried talking to him after Slomat, but he was *so* mad. I know he's giving you guys a hard time. I'll try speaking to him again."

"He's worried about you... with good reason. Things are different now, and Brenner is here. His men are watching, and despite whatever front he is putting on for you, he can't be trusted."

Isla scoffed. "I know how to read people and form opinions for myself."

"Do you? After everything that's happened, maybe you aren't fully..." He didn't finish the sentence, trailing off after a withering stare from her. The pang from his arm was hardly necessary this time. "I didn't mean it like that."

"Then what did you mean?" Her eyes blazed. Even River swayed his head away. "Explain it to me like I'm stupid."

"I—uh—I just meant that maybe things are still a bit confusing and we're not sure of the lasting effects. I meant that you should..." He didn't bother to finish that sentence either. That was even more of the wrong thing to say.

She rolled her eyes. "Whatever. Edmund's about to blow a fit, and I have to get back. Should I handle that myself, or do I need to ask someone's permission first?"

He opened and closed his mouth like an imbecile, but not a single useful sound came out.

"I'll talk to you later... if I'm allowed. Maybe I need approval for that too." She turned on her heel and strode toward Edmund, who was already on his way to declare that their time was up.

Rian knew he heard the end of that little argument, judging by the smirk playing on Edmund's lips. Stupid, pompous royal.

River stomped his feet and nestled his head against Rian's. "Not today, buddy."

Rian wanted to find a cliff and throw himself off it. He led River back and handed him over to Kit, then went off to sift through how spectacularly he had managed to fuck that up.

⌒⌇⌒

What an idiot he was.

That was all Rian could think as he made his way through the rows of black tents. This was after Freya had kicked him out for sulking too much and ruining her evening, all while Malin tried convincing him it was a grand idea to drown his sorrows at the bottom of a tankard.

Rian had tried that, and it was after the second one that his feet somehow found the courage his brain didn't. Now he was here, standing in front of the black tent he knew was hers. If the thrumming on his arm didn't confirm it, the soldiers clustered in a formation that failed to be casual or unassuming was all the confirmation anyone would need.

They really didn't know how to be discreet, these royals.

A black-and-silver soldier popped out from the shadows. His dual-sword Divite badge glared at Rian with as much force as the owner. "Go back to your camp, Pedite. The princess is ill and asked for no visitors."

They'd certainly grown more vocal in their disdain after Edmund had freaked out on Rian in front of the entire camp. He had practically given them free rein to resume their usual harassment of the lowly Pedites.

The Koliats had never held back their disdain. One stared at him with ice-cold eyes, as if wishing she could gut him right there—but held back.

The Divite, Eliot, scowled. "Well, move along, soldier. What's the problem?"

Rian stood there with a pint and a half of ale sludging its way through his brain, trying to think of a valid reason why he was standing outside the princess' tent. His feet hadn't thought of that part while dragging him up here.

Great. He was about to get himself expelled.

He lifted his foot, determined to turn around, when a voice called out: "What's going on here?"

If there was one person he wanted to see less than Edmund, it was him. Rian had taken great pains to avoid the man all week and had succeeded, until now, when his luck ran out.

"Prince Brenner, what can I help you with today?" he asked sweetly.

Brenner strode up to him, amber eyes blazing in the torchlight. For some odd reason, his boots were muddy and covered in grass. "Perhaps I should be asking you that. Was there a meeting I wasn't made aware of? Where is your prince?"

The Koliat soldier who had been glaring at him smirked and turned her head.

Rian rubbed his temples and held back the retort he wanted to release at the idea that Isla needed her brother-guardian at all times. Things were different in their world in ways he could never understand... and he never wanted to.

"Probably off giving more foolish orders or brandishing his sword like an overgrown toddler." Rian winced the moment the words slipped out. He was certainly bound for the stocks now.

To his surprise, the Koliat prince laughed. "Most likely." He turned back to the tent. "Were you looking for the princess?"

Rian didn't answer. What reason could possibly satisfy this assuming, no, *arrogant*, asshole?

"I was—ah—sent to check on her after her—ah—"

"Ah, right." Brenner nodded as if he understood any of that stammering. "I don't think it went so well, from what my man reports. Perhaps tomorrow she can try with him and your soldier. The blond one, was it?"

"Freya. And no. I mean, *yes*, she was working with her, but not anymore. Not after what happened in Slomat."

"Ah, yes. The zealots." His eyes whipped back up to Rian's. "Your troops have certainly been slacking in their patrols—"

"We haven't since then," Rian said gruffly. "And that night was not our fault. Those crazies were already—"

"Yes, whatever. I honestly don't care." Brenner dismissed him with a wave. "Either way, tell your prince to keep his men in check."

That part was laughable, considering how little Edmund actually knew about the workings of the men around him.

"Well." Brenner jerked his head at him. "Go on. Dismissed."

"Right. Thanks, prince." Rian hesitated, but the prince didn't move. He cast one last glance toward the tent before turning on his heel and leaving, feeling more defeated than ever.

Seventeen

The footsteps faded into the dark of night, yet she stood there a moment longer, hoping one set would return. When it became clear he was not coming back, she sighed and threw herself onto her bed. The cot was comfier and the tent more spacious than the Pedite one she had before. Falling asleep *should* have been easier, but the black fabric felt like it was closing in on her.

Her stomach swirled. Was that disappointment or anger? It was hard to tell with her mind so muddled. She was about to step out to save him from that soldier's questioning when Brenner appeared. Good thing she hadn't.

But she wanted to see him. Hear his apologies. Just *see him*. That would have to wait.

Or did it? Could she somehow slip out and find him again? Did she even want to, right now?

No. Make him wait. He could stew in his guilt overnight, she thought with a small measure of satisfaction, but still...

There would be nothing but thick loneliness to soak in all night, and she didn't even have Opi for cuddles, since Edmund had banished him too. Hopefully, Rian was taking care of him despite his initial protests. Who could hate a creature as cute as that?

She snorted. Edmund definitely could. He hated anything that brought her joy.

Their walk back from where she had left River and Rian was silent and tense. She refused to acknowledge Edmund, and when he tried to speak, she shut the tent flap on him and announced loudly that she felt too ill for visitors.

It was a half-truth, seeing as merely standing in her brother's presence gave her the most vicious headaches. Likely due to the way her body tensed at the sound of his voice.

She flipped onto her back and pulled the thickest blanket over her. It didn't cover half of her left leg, but she lacked the energy to fix it.

Idiots.

There were idiots all around her, *including* Rian. She was glad he had to wait to see her now.

Eventually, she drifted off, dreaming of alleys that closed in on her and tunnels that never ended. The dreams shifted slightly each night, but they always ended the same way: morning rays bursting through the darkness to warm her from the inside.

At least she had some form of protection, even in the dreamlands.

Something pricked at the back of her mind, like a sharp jab from inside her skull. It hadn't happened in days, and she had thought the last remnants of Beretta's hold were completely gone. Even today, she thought Beretta lingered in the camp, but then she blinked, and she was gone.

Perhaps he was right and she wasn't fully in control of herself. That was something she refused to ever admit to him. No way.

Isla groaned and turned over. Maybe her personal security had gone for a break and she could try grabbing some fresh air again.

She snorted at her own attempt at a joke. As if they'd let her out of—

A shadow moved, and she scrambled out of bed. What little air was in her lungs was cut off, as was her scream, thanks to the hand clamped over her mouth. It was hot, sweaty, and smelled like musty dirt.

She couldn't see beyond dark shapes, but the chill in her bones and the way her heart tripped over itself weren't good signs. Cold metal pressed against her neck, and she stopped struggling.

The rancid breath from the man behind her tickled her ears. "Shut up, or I'll slit your throat." The dagger broke past skin, while his other hand pressed hard across her ribcage.

Blood pounded against her skull and throttled her veins. She could hear nothing except her own shallow breaths and the man's threats.

"You're coming with me."

No. Not again. She refused to be taken prisoner by—whoever it was. Not back to the rock and tunnels that never ended.

Panic filled her. It threatened to consume everything she was, but she would not go anywhere. Not like this.

She remembered those nights in the forest where Rian had taught her to use a dagger, despite her dismal failings. There was no dagger here besides the one the man held, and she needed it.

It was now or never.

One deep breath, and she grabbed his arm, dropping to her knees and flipping him over.

Even *she* was surprised that it worked.

Triumph was fleeting. The man was back on his feet. At least she managed to get a better view of his face—his scarred face... the one that had escaped in Slomat.

Her heart stuttered and skipped several beats.

The flip only made him angrier. She didn't remember what she was supposed to do once she got him off her, so when he scrambled to his feet, she ran for the tent opening. He was faster and yanked her back by her hair.

She let out a strangled cry as she landed in the hard dirt.

A furious shape darted through the canvas opening and latched onto the zealot. The creature snarled as it clawed and swiped at him, trying to tear anything it could.

The man roared and threw the dark creature off, where it landed against a pole with a sickening crunch.

"Opi!" She reached for him, but was kicked. Pain erupted at her side from her injury that had barely stopped throbbing. She cursed and rolled over; he tugged her back to her feet.

"Let's go." The steel pressed into her side this time. "Or you'll regret it."

That rancid breath choked her lungs. "No. Thank. You." She shoved her elbow into his gut, and he dropped his grip.

She scrambled until the backs of her knees met the bed. That was all she remembered. That was all he had taught her to get out of a situation like this. Isla was at a loss for what to do next.

Opi wasn't. The seropa growled and sprang up. The tightness in her chest loosened. He leapt between them with his head low and hackles raised. A low growl rumbled deep in his throat.

The man's attention lowered to the beast between them, as did his blade.

Rage. Blinding fury filled her, and she felt the darkness start to seep out. The shadow curved past Opi and straight for the zealot. It neared his feet, and she pulled at it to stop. The seropa continued growling, unafraid of the dark ash clawing at the ground around him.

"Get out," she said through clenched teeth. A bead of sweat dripped down her forehead from the effort of holding everything back. Dozens of tents surrounded them, and she couldn't lose control. She had to contain it.

Summon it and control it.

The man's mouth twisted into a cruel smile. "No, cursed one." He drove the dagger into his own arm, slicing through the flower-stitched cloak and skin. A stream of red dripped past his fingertips onto the darkened ground as he muttered a string of strange words.

What in Rallion's cursed—

The edges of her powers tugged, physically yanking her forward. A fog clouded her mind, and she swayed on her feet, gasping for air. Opi warbled low and flattened against the ground.

The darkness had fully reached the man's feet, and he tilted his head back as it touched him.

Another yank pulled from deep within her core. This time she tried to rein it in, to draw it back into herself and simmer that fire, but it only burned hotter.

The man continued chanting, and the scar on his face spread until it consumed everything.

Isla's vision wobbled in and out, and a high-pitched buzzing in her ear drowned out everything else.

The ground around them curled and crumbled to dust. The darkness clawed and pulled, but this time it was pushed away from her. Towards him.

Her heart strained to pump life through her body. It pounded slowly, then frantically, as if something were draining it. Draining *her*.

She couldn't see, but she felt it pooling in the ground before her. Swirling and digging and clawing for something below. No scream escaped her lips, and no breath worked its way in. Opi whimpered as the darkness closed in on him from all sides.

Then it stopped. And everything came rushing back at her. She gasped from the force, nearly toppling backwards.

The man's eyes widened in shock. A wet mark bloomed across his chest and spread. A drop of blood trickled from the corner of his mouth before he crumpled to the ground, the chipped hilt of the broadsword still embedded in his back.

Freya ran over and steadied Isla by the shoulder, while Rian kicked the body and plucked the sword from it. The tent flaps hung open, framing a Koliat soldier sprawled in the dirt.

Isla couldn't form words to thank them. She could barely remember how to stand, let alone speak.

Blood. Blood was everywhere. It mixed with ash and dirt to create an ungodly pile of mud.

Freya glanced back at the body, her face unusually pale. Had she seen what happened? "Let's get you out of here, princess."

Rian grabbed her other arm, and together they guided her around the pile of muddy ash and out of the tent.

"What in all of Rallion's cursed gates happened here?"

Edmund was already there, out of breath, as was Brenner, whose own men held him back while assessing the area. Isla still struggled to calm her own breathing, instinctively hiding her hands from a soldier who came too close. A flash of red hair in her peripheral vision made her catch her breath, but no one noticed her stumble.

Opi pranced loudly around the pile of ashes, brimming with pride for another killing blow he hadn't actually delivered.

"Are you alright, Isla?" Brenner asked, breaking away from his men and silencing their protests with a steely glare.

Isla hid her grimace by pretending to adjust the tie at her night-gown. She *was* inappropriately dressed in front of her betrothed and all his soldiers but that was the least of her concerns.

What in all of Rallion's gates was that? It felt like she was being drained. Drained and reshaped into something terrible. The spot on the ground remained intact, yet she swore she could still feel that pool of darkness lurking beyond a thin veil.

Brenner's eyes followed her hands to the darkened ground, and he seemed to catch on to the supposed source of her discomfort. He untied the cape pinned to his maroon uniform. "Here, let me—"

For once, Edmund's overbearing attitude was welcome. Her brother was quicker, removing the long robe he wore and draping it around Isla's shoulders, all while throwing a withering glare at Brenner.

"Thank you," she murmured. The words felt strange directed at her brother. Louder, she added, "I am fine, Prince Brenner. Thanks to *our* men."

Edmund rubbed his temples. Considering all the condescension aimed at the Pedites lately, she couldn't help the dig at the Koliats' lack of any real protection.

Brenner's head whipped from the pile of ashes to Freya and Rian. "How did you get here so fast?"

Freya made a face and gestured at Rian to answer.

Opi knocked at her knees and let out a long, preening keel.

Rian smiled. "Opi alerted us that something was wrong."

Liar.

He looked at her, eyes sparkling in confirmation.

"Opi?" Brenner's gaze traveled to the seropa dancing circles around Isla's legs. "You named it?"

Isla held her chin high. "Yes. For the serpent constellation. Fitting, don't you think?"

The creature hobbled over to Rian, who immediately scratched under its chin.

Brenner grimaced. "Lovely." He stepped over the pile of ashes. "We should find the princess another place to stay—a *safer* location."

"We had safe tents set up for the prince and princess prior," Rian cut in. A hint of guilt flashed across Edmund's face.

Freya stepped toward Edmund, who scrambled backward. "If it weren't for—ah—Opi, your sister would be dead. This stupid tent was far too obvious."

"We had guards set up—"

"Some help they were." Freya grumbled and turned on her heel. Isla had the distinct impression she would have said a lot more if Brenner and half a dozen Koliats weren't standing feet away.

A commotion arose as Malin shoved his way through a pair of maroon soldiers, throwing on a wrinkled Pedite jacket. "Everything all taken care of here, then?"

Rian cursed under his breath and beckoned him over, murmuring about setting up new tents for the royals while Edmund tried to insert himself with requests that both soldiers ignored.

After several assurances from both Isla and Edmund, and after viewing the new beige tents with outright disgust, they finally convinced Brenner that all was well and to take his leave. The man seemed more than happy to withdraw from this section of the camp, which he'd taken great care to avoid thus far.

The four soldiers he left behind lingered several tent spaces away to give them some semblance of privacy. Not that they'd do much good if anything happened.

Once everyone had dispersed, Isla allowed the exhaustion from the night to wash over her. She swayed on her feet, and Rian caught her elbow, much to Edmund's chagrin.

"It's been a long night," he said. "You should get some rest."

"Wait," Edmund interjected.

Now that the others had dispersed, Rian seemed comfortable enough to openly sigh in front of the Velotian prince. "What is it *now*?"

"How *did* you know before the others?"

Rian narrowed his eyes at Edmund. "We already told you that. Good night, prince."

Isla stifled a laugh at her brother's shocked expression. The same face that was unaccustomed to hearing the word no or being blatantly ignored.

"Fine. Fine. But there's something you aren't telling me," Edmund said, nostrils flaring. "What happened back there, Isla?"

Isla felt four sets of eyes on her. She squeezed Opi tighter as the memory of that strange feeling returned. The sensation of being sapped of *something* and unable to stop it. She'd only begun to understand her powers, and now this. What had happened to her?

"I don't know," Isla said. "It all happened so quickly, and then I let my powers go. He tried to hurt us, so I stopped him."

Lies.

She pushed that inner voice deep down. Whatever it was, she didn't want to admit that her powers had grown unstable and beyond her control. They'd lock her up.

Rian wasn't convinced. She had a feeling he'd try to bring it up later. It depended on what he and Freya had seen back there. Maybe she could swing it—convince them they'd imagined things.

Or she could just talk to one of them, but that would be the logical option, and she wasn't quite that mature yet.

Edmund bit the inside of his cheek. "Good thing for your powers, then." Isla was shocked as he'd never said anything positive about her gifts before. Her brother took a couple of deep breaths and leaned in close. "Oh, and if anyone asks, Alynna is involved with a Pedite soldier." He looked around, then pointed at Malin. "This one."

Malin shoved his thumb into his chest. "Me?"

Opi tilted his head and chirped.

"Yes," Edmund said. "Brenner isn't an idiot. I had to come up with something."

Malin's mouth opened and closed several times. "But I don't—"

"You couldn't have found anyone more believable?" Freya cut in, gifting Malin a disgusted glower.

"Apparently not." Edmund's expression softened as he surveyed Isla. "I am glad you are alright, sister." His eyes traveled to Rian for the briefest of seconds. "Thank you."

Before anyone could respond, he turned on his heel and stomped off toward his own tent in the dark, several Divites peeling away to follow him.

Opi barked happily once he was out of sight.

Rian turned to Freya, who threw both hands up. "Don't look at me, I don't know what that was about."

Exhaustion crept into every limb, but Isla grabbed Rian's arm before he could leave. "Can we have a minute? Out here is fine," she added quickly, stopping the rejection before it could slip from his tongue.

Freya and Malin exchanged a single glance and were gone before Rian could object.

"How *did* you know?" she asked. Quick and to the point, before he could conjure another fake story. "How did you know something was wrong?"

Rian looked everywhere but directly at her.

He balanced on the balls of his feet and ruffled his hair. Then he rubbed a spot on his arm. A spot that had once been marked.

That was how.

Those zealots were right. She was cursed.

"I'm sorry," she said quietly, dropping her gaze to stare at his boots.

"You didn't mean it at the time. You didn't hurt me."

"But—I—I did something to you. I marked you."

Rian shrugged. "I have worse scars from more terrible memories."

Right. *Right.*

Liopen.

He bent down to pet Opi's head. "He knew something was wrong and was much faster than I was. Good thing, too."

"I know. What a good boy," she cooed, bending to pet the opposite side. "You can stay with me tonight. I don't care what Edmund says, you are a great protector. The best one in all ten kingdoms."

Relief washed over Rian's face. Was the creature really that cumbersome to take care of?

He smiled, and she thought it was a delightful sight. "Good night, Isla."

Isla. The name sounded velvety and warm coming out of his lips, a stark contrast to the grating ice she felt along her skin when Brenner said it.

He lifted his foot, then set it back down, and started digging in his jacket.

"Here." He placed something cool in her hand. "I think you need this back. It's yours now anyway."

The dagger.

The same black-hilted one Devlin had taken and used against her. It was laced with firestone, even if she hadn't realized it the first time she held it. Why did Rian even have a firestone dagger in the first place?

"Keep it under your pillow." He gave a cheeky wink toward where Edmund had disappeared. "To keep away any unwanted attentions at night."

Eighteen
The General

Rian walked along the rows of horses and supplies as Malin updated him on the morning checks. After last night, they'd doubled the patrols and secured the camps, including the Koliat sect.

It took a twenty-minute verbal sparring with Garin and Kolan to convince them to rotate all their men so the Pedites didn't burn out. This time, he didn't even need Edmund or Isla to back him up to get them to relent.

Progress.

Slow and steady. *Painfully* slow.

Though he wouldn't call any of this a win. Not after last night.

Thank the goddesses they'd made it to Isla in time—and that Opi had been quick enough to buy those precious seconds he so desperately needed. The soldiers Brenner and Edmund assigned had proven useless, though they weren't the only ones to let the enemy past their lines.

The horse wrangler, Kit, was found dead, along with several others on the east barrier. That weighed heavily on him. He'd been the one to promote Kit to that position in the first place. Another thing he'd gotten wrong. And now, Rian didn't have the heart to tell Isla, especially since she had been gushing about how well he cared for River and the other horses.

After giving up on any hope of sleep, he made several patrol rounds around the Pedite camp, passing one particular tent more times than was appropriate.

Opi's snoring echoed from inside, a small comfort that everything was fine. The creature had impeccable instincts, and Rian knew he'd protect Isla with his life. Still, he couldn't quiet that small, nagging voice that said something was wrong.

When he had reached her tent last night, a terrible coldness overcame him. Something he'd never felt before, and it seemed to pull at him, tugging from that mark burned onto his skin. Whatever it was stopped when he killed the lunatic, and there was nothing amiss in Isla's tent beyond a few scorch marks. He'd convinced himself he must have imagined it, but Isla seemed... off afterward. Had she sensed it too?

He had every intention of asking her, if he could ever form the words to explain what he'd felt back there without sounding insane. Instead, he paced the rest of the night away.

When the sun rose, Alynna and Susanna appeared with a swath of clothing and entered the tent to get Isla ready. Both offered curt greetings to Rian before disappearing inside.

He imagined how nice it would be to have someone clean and prepare his clothes every day. Then he remembered the strict rules royals had to follow, including how they weren't allowed to step foot where their father didn't deem appropriate, and decided he didn't mind cleaning his old uniforms from time to time.

About ten minutes later, Isla emerged, fully dressed in her black travel leathers with silver flames stitched up her arms. She looked every bit the royal princess, even while trying her best to blend in.

Rian approached her, fully set on delivering a smooth compliment that would land him in trouble, when footsteps approached, carrying the weight of a small limp that Rian recognized.

It was Shaw. An almost useless private, but he was a Pedite nonetheless, and Rian felt some loyalty toward him. Determined to improve those under his command, he'd assigned Aldan to work with the lackluster officer. He had a duty to him, but it was difficult to remember that right now, with Shaw's eyes lingering far too long over Isla. It made him want to kick the soldier to the far end of the camp—or the borders of Velotia, if he could manage it.

"Can I help you, soldier?" he said, voice tight with irritation.

Isla hid a laugh behind her hand. He didn't care if he was terrible at concealing even a hint of jealousy, at least he kept it in check around Brenner. Shaw, on the other hand, knew better, and should show some respect to his princess.

"Yes." Shaw licked his lips. "Prince Edmund and Brenner are requesting your presence. There's been an update on the Muratians."

Rian and Isla exchanged equal looks of revulsion before taking off toward the shiny black tents that stood out far too much.

It was easy to find Brenner and Edmund, who were talking with General Garin and Brenner's top commander, Levi, outside a three-peaked tent with a flag sticking out of the top. They were huddled over a makeshift table, and Freya was already there, standing behind Edmund.

When they approached, Edmund's eyes flickered toward Isla questioningly, then back to the tent, where the maroon-striped soldiers Brenner had assigned to watch her finally caught up. He mouthed something incoherent before returning his gaze to the map.

Brenner's head popped up, and his eyes followed every step. The royal wore his dark maroon cape again, paired with tall boots. A smile curved along his face as he said, "Princess Isla. Glad to see you're feeling better. I'll have to have a word with my guards for slacking on their duties."

He moved aside for her to view the map, but Isla squeezed in beside her brother and General Kolan. Brenner's smile faltered for a fraction of a second before he pointed at the map.

Rian peered over Edmund's other shoulder, eyeing the outline of the forest's edge and a few nearby villages roughly sketched in. What now?

"The Muratians have been following us," Edmund said.

Rian's eye twitched. That was the obvious statement of the year. It wasn't only the Muratians. Someone had sent those Nothings after them too. Just because Brenner hadn't seen it with his own eyes and didn't believe what they'd witnessed didn't make it any less true.

"We believe they are headed to Vaner," Brenner said. "We have our best trackers on it, mapping every step they take."

Isla's eyes darkened. What was going on in her head?

"How do you know it's them?" Rian asked. "We talked about the *others* who might be following us. I don't think they're related. How are you certain?"

Edmund scratched his neck and looked around every way except at Rian or Isla.

"What is it?" Rian pressed. Freya wouldn't meet his gaze either. Something cold sprouted in his chest. His fingers flexed, itching to wrap around a smooth hand.

"There've been casualties," Edmund said quietly, his focus locked on the map in front of him.

"On the way to Vaner?" Isla asked.

"No. Larger." Edmund's throat bobbed, unable to form the words.

"They razed several sects of Slomat to the ground," Brenner said bluntly. "Two dozen buildings completely decimated after we left."

The contents of Rian's stomach churned violently. His blood pounded against his skull. It was *his* call to take all their soldiers with them. It had been *his* decision.

Not again.

"What about the people there?" Isla asked in a hollow voice.

Edmund shook his head, words failing him.

Brenner, the callous asshole, had no problem finding his voice. "About fifty villagers, from what we've heard."

"Hierel save us," Freya whispered. General Garin shifted uneasily.

It was Liopen all over again. Two years ago, they'd set that village aflame as a message to Velotia, and now the same hell had been unleashed once more. A shot aimed directly for Isla, even if the arrow's head clipped Rian as it passed. A direct blow straight to his chest. To his past.

Isla's eyes drifted to his. Did she remember? Did she know what he'd done and what he'd caused?

"May Rallion guide them through all twelve gates." She hung her head and inhaled deeply. When it lifted, fiery resolve blazed in her eyes. "You can still catch them if you hurry," she said. "They have wielders and will know you're coming. They're stronger than they look, and you can't underestimate them. You'll need your own wielders if—if that's the plan."

Rian opened his mouth, ready to insist they should definitely—

"Absolutely not," Edmund cut him off. "We're not placing everyone in the camp at risk for the sake of petty revenge."

Isla's face scrunched. A quick pulse of anger ran down his arm.

Edmund's expression softened. "I want justice for what was done, but not like this. Not now, Isla."

"They'll come again," Isla said quietly.

Rian understood. More than she could possibly know. It wasn't her own safety she feared, but the devastation wrought in her name... and, once again, no one was listening to her.

He'd already failed Liopen. He'd failed Velotia. And he had no desire to fail Isla next.

"If we could capture them," Rian said, surprising everyone, himself included. "Then we can bring them to answer for their crimes. We'd have leverage to potentially end this war before it spreads further."

"No," Edmund said. "It's too risky."

"We should leave. Immediately," Brenner added, glancing at Isla. "Before they find us."

"For once, we agree on something," Edmund muttered.

The Divite lead, General Garin, nodded fervently at Edmund's suggestion.

Rian looked at Isla. That carefully constructed mask slipped enough for him to see past. She clutched her hands together and shifted her weight uneasily. He knew what those people had done to her. What the thought of them sneaking into the camp was likely doing to her right now.

She would never be able to rest knowing they were still out there. Knowing *he* was still out there, hunting her, even when she was safely beyond the Koliat borders.

They wanted her. She told him what Devlin said about her wielder abilities and the link to the old High King's powers. They wanted that power back in Murat—and they would never stop.

And Rian could never rest while they remained, leaving a trail of bodies behind.

What he wanted didn't matter. Neither did the desires of either of those two witless princes.

He faced her, ignoring Edmund and Brenner entirely. "What do you want, Isla?"

She pursed her lips and dragged her eyes to meet his. He ignored the flutter in his stomach at that precious contact. There were far too many people around for her to acknowledge him more than that lingering second.

"I want him dead," Isla said, loud enough for all to hear.

And he would do everything in his power to give her that.

◈

"Did you not hear a word I said?" Edmund seethed, following Rian's every step as he unfurled the cloth with his throwing daggers. He counted them, making sure they were all there, except his father's. The one he'd given to Isla.

"No, sorry," Rian said, a thinly concealed grin tugging at his lips. He stopped, and Edmund nearly ran into his back. "What did you want, prince?"

He scuttled back. "I said we are to pack up and return immediately to Aurial. We've been ordered back by my father."

"Right," Rian drawled. "Are these the same orders you've ignored for months?"

Edmund said nothing.

"I thought so." He whipped around to grab a small pack. They'd need rations for the journey to ensure the soldiers stayed ready. "Don't pretend you're suddenly going to listen to him after all this time. No new communications have come from Aurial, thanks to your brilliant plan to cut off all missives before we left for Murat."

Edmund lowered his voice. "It doesn't matter what my father wants. I'm the crown prince and—"

Rian brushed past him and approached the two soldiers hovering nearby. He tried convincing himself this was all Edmund's fault. But Edmund wasn't the one who had chosen the safety of their traveling party over the village.

"Freya, check on Haldren's group. Malin, do a count of how many able horses we have, and make sure Shaw doesn't get one." That soldier was abysmal at best on a horse, he'd go with the rest of the infantry.

"I was talking to you." Edmund scuttled in front of him again, breath hitching. "We are not putting anyone in danger—I am not placing my sister at risk, *again*."

Freya rolled her eyes and turned on her heel, calling for Haldren.

"Neither am I," Rian said, lowering his voice so passing maroon soldiers wouldn't hear. "If we don't act now, they'll hunt us all the way back to Aurial. And trust me, the body count will only grow."

Edmund looked aghast. "How do you know?"

"Because I know what they want. And they've already shown they'll do whatever it takes to get her. That includes burning down any piece of Velotia between here and Aurial along the way."

They'd already lost one city because he'd underestimated them. He wasn't about to give up half the countryside because of Edmund's cowardice. They had to do something. Anything to stop it.

Edmund stared at a pair of muddy boots. Rian knew what he wanted to say: that he didn't care about that. He only wanted to get them home. Blood consequences be damned.

If he had half a sane thought left in his head, Rian would want the same. That was their mission after all this. To bring the two royals home safely. But the Muratians weren't rational. They were singularly focused on their goal, indifferent to the destruction left in their wake.

"If we strike first—if we act before them—she'll be safe." They'd all be safe. "Isn't that what you want?"

"Of course," Edmund snarled. "You of all people know I'll do anything to keep her safe."

"Then we get to him before he gets to her."

"I don't like this," Edmund muttered, kicking at the mud. "Not one bit."

"You don't have to," Rian said. "Just don't be stupid... and keep her in your sight at all times."

With that, he turned on his heel to finalize the plan with General Garin and divide their soldiers appropriately.

He'd take Malin with him as there was no one else he trusted to have his back after everything. Brenner was glued to Edmund and Isla, annoyingly so... but it made it easy to keep watch over all three of them together.

Aldan went to prepare River. Rian already refused the other war-mount they'd tried to assign him, despite the confused looks from the quartermaster. River was solid. Steady. Reliable. His instincts were sharper than even the fanciest royal horses the Divites and Agicae rode.

He left Freya with Edmund, fully intent on finding River and mounting him. That was his true, swear upon Wallienne's watchful eyes, intent.

But then she was there.

She was there.

His heart caught in his chest, and he nearly killed himself tripping over nothing in the dirt.

The smart thing would be to turn around. The smart thing would be to check on the remainder of his men—that still felt strange after all these months. And the absolute smartest thing for his life and sanity would be to run as far away from here as possible.

His feet hadn't caught up to the realization his mind had already made.

She opened her mouth, and he answered, "No."

"I want to come with you," she said. "I want to help."

Not the same argument. He needed her to understand *why* she couldn't.

"How exactly would you help?" he asked, keeping his tone calm. "Your brother will tag along, so will Brenner, and they'll get in the way."

"He's after me." She flexed her hand, eyeing it suspiciously. "I have better control now... I think. I can help. He burned Slomat to the ground as bait, and you're riding straight into it."

"I know," he said. It didn't matter. They could handle it.

He refused to allow her anywhere near Devlin. If things went sour, they had a plan for her and Edmund to escape. The transporter would go with them and, if necessary, take her as far as he could. Rian refused to place her in any more danger than necessary.

She stepped closer. His breath hitched in his chest, and his arm pulsed.

"He can do things I've never seen a wielder do before," she said. "And she's powerful. So powerful. It's like I can still feel her in here." She tapped her temple. "Digging around."

"Exactly why you're staying behind with your brother." He began to move away.

"Nobody ever listens to me. Not before. Not now. I'm telling you it's a stupid move. You're underestimating them."

Rian sighed and prayed to the goddess for strength. "I have a plan, I promise. Can you trust me on this?"

Her eyes whirled as she warred with herself. She couldn't fight like he could. The best she could do was keep herself safe. That's all he wanted in this world.

He pressed the side of her riding jacket, where his father's dagger was tucked away. Edmund had somehow edged closer, watching their every move from a few paces off.

"Remember to use this if you have to," he said. "And not just for keeping away unwanted suitors." He jerked his chin at Edmund, and he loved the way her eyes lit up.

"Thanks." She clenched her fist around the spot where the dagger's hilt would be and leaned over expectantly, her intent clear to all observers.

Instead, Rian grabbed her hand and pressed a kiss to the scars on the back of it. There were too many around to risk more contact, despite the way his skin hummed and craved more.

"You sure about this?" she asked again.

"Are you?" His eyes trailed from her face to the dagger in her hand.

"Absolutely." She straightened and motioned at Edmund, who hovered nearby.

The two vaulted onto their horses, and with a terse nod at Rian, rode out of the camp. As their backs shrank into the distance, the mark on his arm protested. Then, as if Hierel herself had heard their plans, a crack of thunder split the sky.

Nineteen
The General

Malin bounced on the balls of his feet, his hands constantly flexed as he was itching for a fight—or so he reminded him every thirty seconds.

It shouldn't have surprised anyone that his friend was so impatient. They'd been pushed past Rallion's first gate these past days, and Malin was in a foul mood from the measly rations and a night of patrolling in the mud, all thanks to the relentless rain.

Now, the ridge they waited on, with a perfect view of the rolling plain below, dotted with hundreds of small hills and bumps, was covered in a foot of squishy ground, making everyone grumpy after the tumultuous crossing.

"When this is over." Malin whipped his head toward Rian. "You're getting us better provisions or Hierel help me..."

He let the threat hang in the air, unfinished. It was foolish to goad the goddesses on a day like this.

Rian's reasons for wanting to get this over with mostly involved ensuring they could never get to Isla again. Needless to say, they were both itching for this long-overdue fight.

And yet, they were nowhere near where the main clash would take place. Rian watched as General Garin and most of the men set up their formations in the vast field below, ready for the coming ranks of Muratians who had caught up over the course of the day.

They'd moved slowly, to tempt the Muratians close enough and give the impression they were unprepared and sloppy. Rian prayed their gamble paid off. They had close to a hundred troops with them. A hundred Muratian soldiers who couldn't be allowed to roam these lands filled with innocents.

They *needed* the Muratians to come to them. And their enemy obliged.

When the Muratians hit their main cavalry below, Rian braced as if feeling the impact himself.

River huffed and shook his head. All he could do to reassure the horse was a gentle pat along his side. The sounds of metal unsheathing and groaning leather must have been harsh for him to hear. It was hard enough on Rian to sit and watch the blue-clad soldiers approach their men and do nothing.

This was the plan Garin and Edmund had settled on, and Rian had no choice but to follow.

It was a team effort, after all. Despite the Pedites pulling most of the weight, and despite being the ones who'd pay most in blood. That's how it always was for the Pedite Corps.

Some days, Rian cursed his father's weakness that led to his mounting debts and the conscription of his two oldest to pay them off. It set him and his brother on a path with little hope of escape. That's why he pushed so hard for change, even when it felt impossible. Every movement he made was judged harshly, and every misstep made an example of him for the troops. He couldn't afford another failure.

So, he sat on a ridge with a perfect vantage of the main group. He'd selected six men to stay with him, praying the Muratian prince would rise to the bait.

If it didn't work, Garin and Kolan would never let him near the planning tent again. Edmund would never let him near his sister again... well, that part was a given.

Not a breath was loosened while the seven watched the Muratians charge across the plains, reckless and blind. They didn't know these lands as well as the Velotians. They didn't know the type of grass that grew or the dirt lying beneath it.

If they had, they would have realized that a field like the one below was riddled with pits and sticky mud—chaos waiting to happen. And chaos was exactly what unfolded.

Hooves sank into the ground. Mud sprayed into the faces of the soldiers behind, nearly blinding them. In the confusion, the Velotians struck, taking advantage of the sturdiest ridges among the hundreds of small hills below.

Rian allowed himself one small smile as the first part of the plan worked. That was all he allowed.

"There." Aldan pointed toward a shadow of movement at the far end of the field. It flickered once and was gone before his gaze could double back.

There was no way Aldan didn't possess a trace of wielder abilities. It was rare, but some people developed abilities later in life, or hid them for years, for reasons known only to themselves. One day, Rian would ask him about it.

That was it.

It *had* to be.

He dug his heels into River's side and gave the order.

"Finally." Malin vaulted onto a cream horse, and they surged forward, Aldan and Haldren close behind.

That group wasn't as concealed as they'd hoped. The prince really ought to recruit better wielders. The one hiding them now was barely competent. The only truly skilled wielder was that godsdamned mindweaver.

The clamor of the forces behind them faded into the steady pounding of hooves along the edge of the field. The same spot that Rian and River had tested earlier and knew to be stable.

Another shimmer in the enemy's camouflage marked the wielder struggling to maintain his shield for that long. Rian counted the figures ahead as fewer than twenty. It was as he had hoped.

It was easy to spot *him*. The sparkling gold badges and too-polished uniform that had never seen real hardship. Rusty brown hair. Dark blue eyes that swept the battlefield with fiery hunger. Definitely him.

Several commanding officers flanked him, though Rian couldn't tell their rank as the meaning of Muratian badges was foreign to him.

They didn't seem to expect an ambush, confident in their supposed hiding spot. But Aldan's expert tracking left no room for luck.

Malin went for one of the general-type soldiers while Rian kept his sights locked on his target. They'd discussed this strategy already, despite Malin's initial protests about staying together, or letting him go after the prince because he wasn't as *emotionally invested*.

It didn't matter if he had more to lose than the others. Rian couldn't trust anyone else with this. And the rage fueling him refused to let anyone else touch Devlin first. It had to be him or nobody.

One of the Muratians lunged at River as they passed, but Rian knocked his sword aside. He leapt from the horse. The ground here was drier, giving him solid footing to launch at the prince. He tackled him, wrestling the ornate sword from his grasp.

That was easy. Too easy.

Devlin's shock at his shield failing was his second mistake that day.

Even without his sword, the prince struggled fiercely, writhing in the mud and grass. Rian tried to pin him, but he wormed away. They needed him alive. At least for now. Though if Rian had the final say, that wouldn't last long.

"Argh! Get off of me, you Pedite swine—"

Rian lost the last ounce of rationality and punched the Muratian in his stupid face. Then he did it again for good measure. Just to be sure.

Something slammed into his shoulder. *Fuck.* That one wasn't from Devlin.

He was so focused on the man in front of him that he didn't notice anyone around them. Something sharp tore into his shoulder. Either a throwing star or a dagger, he didn't have time to check as Devlin consumed all his attention and breath.

The ground shook behind them. A horse tumbled, a flash of white showing it wasn't River who was, thankfully, smart enough to avoid the chaos.

That split-second distraction let the prince dive at him, roaring. The weapon twisted deeper—yep, definitely a dagger—and a knee slammed into Rian's stomach, sending him sprawling.

He gasped and pulled the dagger out, ignoring the skin it took with it. Cursed Muratians and their serrated blades. They really were the scourge of the ten Rocian Kingdoms.

That was his good arm, or he would have driven it straight into the prince's throat. That lunatic was actually smiling as he spat blood onto the ground between them. "Did you get our message?"

Damn all of Rallion's cursed hells. All thoughts of capturing him alive now evaporated. Fiery rage clouded everything except the man in front. It was Liopen all over.

He had to pay.

Fuck keeping him alive. Fuck taking any of them back alive.

Rian rushed. Despite surprising him with the first attack, Devlin was well trained, blocking most of his punches and landing sharper ones of his own. Rian tried to draw Dark End, but Devlin grabbed his wrist before the long sword could leave its sheath and punched him in his injured shoulder.

A shockwave rippled up his arm. It felt like the dagger wound had doubled, maybe even tripled. It was *just* a punch and Devlin hadn't even hit that hard.

"Better watch that shoulder." The scar on Devlin's chin gleamed as his mouth curled into that twisted smile again. Did he think this was all a game?

Focus, Rian. Focus.

The Muratian wanted him to attack blindly. He *wanted* this.

Fine. If it was a fight he wanted, Rian was ready. His father had drilled him and his brother through scenarios like this since they were children. He had faced his share of foes, including vicious wielders. He wasn't afraid of a *healer*.

The wound on his shoulder throbbed, and his breaths came in ragged gasps, but he didn't let it show. He used the brief reprieve to finally draw Dark End.

Devlin didn't reach for a weapon of his own. His sword lay on the ground, though a dagger gleamed at his hip. Perhaps he thought he didn't need it to take Rian down.

Interesting.

That didn't mean he'd go easy on him. If anything, his arrogance fueled Rian's fury.

Fingers flexed over the hilt of his father's old blade and Rian charged, aiming straight for the prince's heart, if Devlin even had one in there.

The prince flailed his hands as if warding off an insect.

A jolt of pain shot up Rian's arm. He stumbled, gasping as if he'd run half the Black Forest and back. There was no blade nearby.

Where did that come from?

Another step, and a searing sliver of pain rippled up his back before bursting outward. Dark End slipped from his grip, clattering to the ground.

Devlin was in front of him. Rian swung a fist, and the prince grabbed it. A tendril of pain snaked from his lower back to his shoulder.

A second fist connected with his face. It was real. Real pain and not his imagination. He recognized it instantly.

Devlin's twisted smile remained, even as he struggled for air. Two more slices of pain clawed across Rian's back, jagged and unrelenting.

A punch to his gut and Rian dropped to his knees. Each inhale shredded his lungs while every exhale set them aflame. What in all twelve gates was this?

Struggling to rise, his vision wavered and hands shook as he searched for Dark End. Another lash of pain tore across his back, and he forgot where he had dropped it.

The third slice sent him crashing into the dirt, directly in front of the prince's muddy boots.

It felt like a scorching blade scraped down his spine, splitting skin and muscle with each pass.

Then another.

And another.

And another.

His entire back throbbed, crying for mercy. He hadn't felt this kind of agony. Not since—

The next strike landed too perfectly. His back arched and his stomach emptied onto the ground. The back of his uniform was soaked and there was no need to check his hands to see the color they'd turned.

"Your princess isn't the only one with unique gifts," Devlin taunted.

A kick to his side added more pain to the one crawling along his spine. His body convulsed, useless against it. He couldn't move, couldn't fight back, and every breath fought to escape without blacking out.

Then a reprieve. One brief, glorious break where Rian was face down, panting into the dirt and praying it wouldn't start again.

"Some nasty scars there, I see," Devlin rasped, a twisted curiosity in his voice. "What other ones do you have?"

Rian lifted his head. The effort sent blinding ripples of agony down his arms and into his fingertips.

Devlin's hands rose, a strange glow starting to emanate. Rian remembered Isla's warning about his healer powers. He'd twisted into something far worse.

Desperate, Rian patted the ground for Dark End or something useful. *Anything*. But Devlin closed the distance and seized his arm, cutting off his options before they could take form.

The scars on his back ripped open fresh. He was sent back to Aurial receiving his punishment. Worse this time. Relentless, amplified, and all-consuming.

It wasn't only the lash marks. It was *everything*.

Pain radiated from his hip, where a dull arrow had once struck. Down his side, where a sword had met flesh. Old bite wounds from a strange creature in the Hattien swamplands. The burn from a dropped pot of stew on his wrist, and up his arm—

Searing fire pounded through muscle and bone, seeking weakness, bursting it open. A pulse burst out, taking Rian's vision, leaving only the brown dirt an inch from his nose.

The mark on his arm bloomed like he was being burned into ash from the inside out. Every old wound, every old scar, funneled into that spot, erupting in one unbearable chorus of agony. Devlin cursed against and released him.

Footsteps thundered closer and Rian braced himself. Let it end. Let it be quick. Then the pain would finally stop.

There was a thud, and something hit the ground beside him.

Nothing happened. He stayed curled in the dirt. Was he dead?

The fading pain told him he wasn't. Not yet, anyway.

Rian blinked and uncurled himself from the ball of flesh he'd become. Malin loomed over him, a stream of blood trickling down his head, standing atop the unconscious body of Prince Devlin.

They... won?

Malin yanked him to his feet. "What in the name of Slin's cursed armpit happened to you?"

Now that he was standing, blood poured from the open lashes on his back with every movement. It hurt, though less than before. Less now that Devlin was out.

If Malin hadn't arrived when he did...

"We need to get you to the healer," Malin said, turning him around. The urgency in his voice did nothing to soothe the tremors still wracking Rian's body. "Where's Ben?"

"No." Rian shook his head. He knew exactly where Ben was. He jabbed Devlin's side with his bloody boot, ensuring the prince wasn't faking it. "Restrain him first. *Before* he wakes up."

Malin grinned. "I found something in that wielder's supplies that I think will work perfectly." He swiveled his head. "You're not going anywhere until the healer looks at you. Can you even walk?"

Rian scanned the small group, keeping his movements minimal. They'd managed to subdue the Muratian prince's group without losing anyone, but the main force could be a different story. Their fighters were ruthless, even against well-trained Velotians.

Something touched his back. He swore his way through every goddess's name. "Don't touch it, Malin."

His friend threw up his hands. "Sorry. Sorry. I had to check if it was real."

"Did any of them get away?"

"No," a hint of pride licked Malin's voice. "We stopped a pair of wielders that almost slipped past, but none escaped."

Rian's blood froze. He brushed past Malin and circled the bodies scattered throughout the grove despite the protests to stay still. It didn't matter, though. His search was futile.

The wielder. She wasn't there.

Twenty
The Princess

They passed another grass-filled grove, identical to the last, though this one was slightly drier. The further they traveled, the less mud clung to their boots, and the less Edmund complained about it splashing his pants. These lands all looked the same, dull to the eyes. She supposed that was why the middle-lands were perfect for farming and harvests. They were practical, but tedious for travel.

She nearly missed the messy tangle of branches marking the edge of the Black Forest. *Almost.*

The sun burst from behind its shield of clouds, scattering drops of honey and gold across the grassy field. Dampness hung in the air, and if she wasn't mistaken, rain might return in a few hours. Perfect.

The only mercy granted today had been somehow convincing Brenner to split his forces into smaller groups to confuse any trackers. The Koliat had bought the story, eager to take most of his men with him, leaving only a dozen behind to guard Isla. He slipped a snide comment about Edmund's incompetence that made her snort against her will.

The brief amusement didn't last.

And here they were—running from their enemy, all because they were *too important*. Stupid.

Isla gripped the reins of her mare, the leather of her gloves rubbing together with a loud squeak. Edmund had given them to her, presumably to hide any potential *incidents* from the men.

When would he stop being ashamed of her? When she was safe, delivered, and trapped in Koliat? Perhaps distance was the only thing that could fix things.

"We can stop for a meal soon." Edmund shifted in his saddle, cracking his neck to the side. "You must be famished by now. We barely ate this morning."

Judging by the way he wiggled in his seat, he was the one who needed the break, not her. She could sit through the discomfort. Ignoring pain was something she'd learned in those mines.

"A break sounds lovely." She stretched her hands, which were beginning to go numb from clenching the reins too hard. A dull pounding started at her temples. She really should have tried to get more sleep last night but having a religious zealot sneak into your tent really affected the ease into which one falls back asleep. Even with Opi watching, she kept jolting upright, imagining every shadow and speck was another one coming to whisk her away.

By now, she must be an absolute mess with dark circles drawn past her cheekbones. If anyone asked, it could easily be blamed on post-escape exhaustion rather than nerves.

Opi pranced along her mare happily, darting between the horses' legs, much to the annoyance of the steeds, and Edmund. At least they'd grown used to the creature since this morning. Edmund's stallion only tried to stomp on him once when Opi got a bit too close to his hindquarters.

They rode alongside a contingent of Divites, joined by a select few Agicae, including the healer, Ben. She still didn't understand why he was sent with them, when their men would clearly be needing his aid, but Edmund had overruled her again, saying it was already decided.

They stopped in an open area dotted with willowy trees and flowering bushes. Any invading armies would be visible long before they reached them, not that Edmund was worried, or so he assured her many times.

Each time he offered reassurance, the tick in his cheek betrayed him. Isla allowed him to think she was oblivious—for now.

Her stomach growled. A meal was a good idea.

She walked through the small group, feeling strangely alone among Edmund's chosen Divites and Agicae, none of whom spared her a second glance, except to ensure she wasn't causing trouble. One with a thick cloak did keep their eyes on her as she passed, but quickly returned to watching Edmund. Their priority would always lie with him, and she didn't fault them for it. He was the heir, after all.

At least the Pedites didn't stare as much when she was with them, though she knew the real reason why, despite what some had seen in the Black Forest. She used to not care about such things, thinking all soldiers beneath her, but that was before.

Isla passed a group she didn't recognize. These ones did spare her a second glance, and she felt the hair on her arm stand on end. Gods, she hated when they stared so intently. What did this group know about her?

Wait. She stopped.

She *really* didn't recognize these ones. They didn't have an Agicae this tall in their group. Did they?

The Agicae tossed back a hood to reveal a blue uniform underneath.

The gasp didn't leave her mouth before a dagger flew past Isla's shoulder and lodged in the man's neck. The others scrambled to their feet just as quickly, and shouting erupted all around.

Freya was at her side, the thick cloak she'd been hiding under now tossed aside. Where had she been all this time? Isla hadn't thought Freya would leave Rian behind, but this wasn't the first time she'd been wrong.

Isla didn't get a chance to ask. She was too busy ducking under Freya's thick axe as it struck the next Muratian perfectly. A second enemy readied a pair of daggers, only to be intercepted by a soldier charging into his path.

Not a soldier. *Her brother*. Had everybody lost their minds?

To her surprise, Edmund moved with precision, matching the Muratian blow for blow. Together, he and Freya took him down.

Freya brushed a streak of blood from her face. "Thanks."

"You were right," Edmund said, holding his ornate sword at the ready.

"Take the princess and go," Freya commanded, motioning to a pair of soldiers, one maroon-clad, the other in Velotian black and silver. "Meet up with the others. We'll handle the rest."

"It's okay, Isla." Edmund nodded at her. "He'll come for you," he added quietly.

Isla stole another glance at Freya, bloodied axe in hand, and then at her brother, standing with a confidence that bordered on reckless. If he wanted to risk himself to prove a point, fine by her. She nodded at Freya, scooped up Opi, and sprinted toward the opposite end.

Two soldiers flanked her, eyes darting in every direction, muscles tense, ready to react to every echo across the open plain they'd stopped in. Everyone was privy to a plan she wasn't. She would scold them later—once they were alive and safe.

How was the other group faring?

Isla reached the white mare, still tied near the familiar bush where she had left her, and tossed Opi on its back, hissing sternly to keep him from squirming. She grabbed the reins from the short-haired Divite.

"Thank you, Montel."

The man opened his mouth and no sound came out. Blood trickled down the corner of his mouth. His eyes were glassy, as he crumpled to the ground, a thick spear lodged in his back. The mare shrieked in panic and toppled over, pinning Opi beneath her as a spreading pool of red stained the ground.

Isla stared at the two bodies, stuck in her own skin and muscles that refused to move. Her hand hovered halfway to her inner pocket, where the dagger lay, but it wouldn't obey.

The effort sent violent shakes through her, each attempt making the world feel like it was rushing up at her, folding in on itself. Like she was trapped beneath those mines again.

Opi squealed, scrambling toward her, but he couldn't make it out from under the horse's corpse.

For the briefest moment, the paralysis lifted, and she finally snatched the blade.

The reprieve didn't last. Footsteps approached and splitting pain burst all over her body, as if claws shredded her from the inside out. She collapsed to her knees and the dagger slipped from her fingers. She was nothing but pain.

Shining brown boots with maroon buckles came into view, kicking the dagger away.

"We're not going to try that again," a voice like twisted ice hissed.

The agony refused to relent, but Isla pushed through it to face the eyes that had haunted both her waking and sleeping hours. The chill of that voice was familiar, and a small, stubborn part of her wasn't surprised the nightmare had finally taken flesh.

In fact, she had been ready for Beretta to show, even if Rian refused to believe her. She'd forgotten how powerful the wielder was and how quick she moved.

What she *was* surprised to see was the maroon uniform Beretta wore. The same one Isla had imagined in her visions. Flashes of red hair, quickly disappearing when she blinked, leaving her unsure of what was real and what was conjured by her head.

How long had Beretta been parading as one of them? The Muratian stretched her shoulders, a fleeting reprieve arriving as she drew a slow breath. Freckles danced across her face as she twisted it in concentration. "Ready for more?"

Isla felt that rush right before the torment hit and tried to roll away, but it was useless. She landed hard on the ground with searing hot pain bursting through every fiber of her body. Inside. Outside. There was no halting it until it consumed her completely.

As abruptly as it had begun, the pain vanished, replaced by a terrifying snarl. Opi was free, his jaws clamped around Beretta's arm.

"Get off me, you stupid beast—argh!"

Opi tumbled through the air, landing squarely on his feet between the horse's body and the bush.

Blinding rage filled Isla. She lunged, tackling Beretta and driving her into the thorny bush that had given Rian trouble a lifetime ago.

"Fucking hells!" Beretta rolled free of the thorns, and before she could even rise, Isla was back on the ground, writhing in the mud. "Don't try that again."

All she wanted was to reduce Beretta into nothing but dirt beneath her fingers. *Her powers...* she shook her head, trying to summon the darkness, but another tidal wave of pain hit before she could gather her thoughts. Again. And again. Relentless and punishing. Every surge knocked her back, forcing her under before she could catch a breath and find the surface.

Finally, after an eternity, the onslaught ceased, granting her a brief, glorious reprieve. Somewhere nearby, Beretta gasped for air, and then it started again.

"Did you miss our friendship as much as I did?" Beretta rasped, the edge in her voice replaced by raw grit.

Isla couldn't even summon the energy to respond.

A weight landed on her back as Opi leapt onto her, trying to physically stop whatever was tearing through his guardian. It did nothing against the onslaught except offering only the faintest ember of comfort, hardly warmer than a dim spark.

Beretta grunted, and the pain doubled.

Laughter echoed in her brain and across the void that now consumed her. Cold and unyielding with a promise of nothing but despair.

Beretta was next to her, yanking at the ridiculously styled hair she had once warned Alynna would cause the death of her, and kicking Opi off.

Then, a flash of blond, and the pain was gone. Isla curled into a tight ball, unsure if it was another trick or if it was actually real.

"You. Stupid. Wretch." The cold voice rang out, each syllable punctuated by a grunt.

Isla dared to crack an eye open. Flashes of silver streaked across her vision.

Freya.

She swung her double-sided axe at Beretta without pause, refusing to give the wielder a moment to recover, each powerful blow met with deft, agile dodges that took her full attention.

Opi curled into Isla's stomach, quivering from head to tail, and she buried her face into his fur, clinging to the tiniest anchor in the storm.

Another powerful strike skimmed the side of Beretta's arm, and fury radiated off the wielder. It was the spark she needed to stop Freya's next swing before it even cleared her head.

Freya screamed, dropping her axe and clutching her head as pure agony washed over her. A pain Isla wouldn't wish on her worst enemy.

And Isla couldn't do anything. She was breathless, drained, and shaking worse than Opi.

Beretta inched toward Freya with her hands extended and her face twisted in concentration. Freya sank to her knees, mouth open, with no sound escaping. Beretta was going to kill her.

Isla forced herself to her feet, swaying violently and nearly blacking out from the movement. Her skull throbbed as if her brain were clawing against it from the inside, and her skin rippled with every nerve-tingling strike of pain.

A drop of blood trickled from Freya's nose, and Isla was frozen. As helpless as the day the villagers were slaughtered. Just like under the mountain, digging for firestone, when all she could do was watch.

The firestone.

The dagger.

It still lay a few feet away. The waves of pain had shuttered it from her mind until now. It had worked against Beretta before.

Her hand closed around the dark hilt, and before Beretta could fully turn, Isla drove it into the back of her shoulder until it struck bone.

The wielder screamed. She whipped around and tackled Isla to the ground, the dagger still lodged in her back.

All the air Isla had fought so hard to draw in vanished as fists rained down, striking anything they could reach.

Then she was off her. Isla blinked.

Edmund stood there, face streaked with sweat and dirt. His broadsword hung loosely at his side while Freya's boot pressed into Beretta's neck. Her axe was back in hand, raised high, pure fury flashing across her face as her chest heaved.

Do it, a part of Isla whispered, begging for it all to end here. For revenge to be taken in swift blood. Then it could all be over.

Freya inhaled deeply and began to swing.

But it wouldn't be over after this.

"Stop!"

The axe slammed into the dirt beside Beretta's head. She cast a quizzical glance at Isla, still sprawled on the ground. "You sure?"

"Don't kill her."

Isla's eyes fixed on the red-haired wielder, the one who had hunted her and Rian across half of Murat, the same who had imprisoned her below and tormented her for weeks without her even knowing...

and who had followed her into Velotia who knows how long ago to continue that same torment.

After everything Beretta had done, she didn't deserve to die. Not yet, anyway.

❦

The light from Ben's hands faded, and relief washed over her like a thick blanket. Her eyelids weighed as heavy as a small horse, but that sensation vanished the moment she heard familiar voices. All her bruises had disappeared and her side no longer ached, so she brushed him off.

He should have checked on Freya first, who had to lay down after the attack, but Edmund had insisted that Isla be helped before anyone else. Typical.

"I'm fine," she snapped. Ben scrambled back. "Sorry. Go check on the others, please," she added more gently, noticing the wielder's eyes double in size. She didn't need him reporting to Edmund that the princess was off and irritable.

She *was* irritated. Though it had nothing to do with Beretta.

It was the fact that she found them huddled together in some sort of meeting *without* her. Edmund and Brenner were in a circle with Rian and the Divite general. When did they catch up to them? And why didn't anyone tell her?

When Rian's eyes cast her way before skirting away, she knew exactly what—or who—they were talking about. She stomped over in a rage, mud flying with each step.

Brenner straightened and adjusted his long coat. The way his maroon outfit still hung perfectly—untouched by battle—only fueled her anger.

"What are you talking about?" she demanded, ignoring the pounding headache that flared as blood rushed to her temples.

Her. They were definitely talking about her. The way none of them would meet her eyes confirmed it. Fine. Let them be like that. She was done being cast to the sidelines.

"Where are they?" she asked.

"In holding cells we fashioned from supplies found in their bags," the Divite general said smugly.

"We have them separated," Rian added. His arm was pressed tight against his chest, his face so drawn and worn that she could feel the exhaustion in her bones. He hunched as if his jacket were too tight. Even Malin hovered unusually close. What had happened to them?

Rian's skin was pale. Too pale for her liking, but he still stood strong. Unlike her, swaying in the mud. They all courteously ignored it, though Edmund edged closer, ready to catch her should she fall.

Edmund glared at Brenner. "We were just talking about how the prince's top wielder managed to break into our ranks and no one noticed."

Brenner shot back an equally disdainful glower. "How was I supposed to know she'd replaced one of them? I've never seen her before."

"Well, *you* have." Edmund scowled toward Rian. "And we've discovered missing soldiers from days ago at least. *Days.*"

Isla swayed again.

"I didn't see her at the camp, and if you recall, the Pedite contingent has been separated from the others, focused on our scouting duties," Rian said pointedly. Graceful phrasing of Edmund's banishment as mere 'scouting duties' instead of what it truly was: a poorly conceived attempt to punish both Isla and him. "If she's a mindweaver, she could have convinced anyone she belonged. Then it would've been easy enough to sneak the others in, slowly."

Isla adjusted the collar that felt too tight around her neck. She *had* seen her before, but any time she doubled back, the Muratian was gone. Could Beretta have been doing that? Or was Isla's mind playing tricks on her again? *Should* she have told someone?

She definitely wasn't going to tell them now. Not with the way Rian watched her, as if he expected her to shatter at any second. Her outsides were fine, even if the insides still carried traces of Beretta and that searing pain.

Could he tell she was hiding something? The way he looked through her made her squirm. She wanted to scream or shout or anything.

Rian scratched his nose. A Pedite ran up to him with a tally of the injured, ignoring the Divite general.

Isla gasped when Rian turned to speak with him. The back of his jacket was soaked. Blood? Please say that wasn't blood.

Where had that healer gone?

Isla lifted her foot, intending to check for herself, but Edmund shook his head. Not here. Not now. Did he not realize she needed to see him? To touch him and confirm he was safe with her own hands.

Once the soldier left, Rian turned back to the group, eyes still locked on Isla. "Was there anything off that you noticed lately, princess?"

Isla hugged her arms to herself and shook her head. This time, it was her turn to avoid their gazes.

"Isla..." Edmund began.

"It's nothing," she said.

"Isla."

Could he stop saying her name?

"I thought it was nothing at the time," she admitted, feeling incredibly small as the muddy ground held her gaze.

"Isla," Rian said, his tone kind.

That may have been worse. She shook her head. "I didn't know it was real."

"You should have said something," he said. "I know these things seem like nothing at the time, but we could have helped you."

"We could have caught this before," Edmund added.

Obviously. If she had known that it was real...

Anger flared, irrational and sharp. What did they expect, cornering her like this? This was worse than being trapped under the mountain. Not really, but right now, it felt equally suffocating.

This was exactly why she hadn't said anything.

Edmund sighed. His neck turned blotchy.

There was something they weren't telling her. Something they were all in on. And this group rarely agreed on anything.

"What?" she demanded, heart hammering against its cage. "What is it?"

Brenner waved his hand flippantly, balancing on the backs of his heels. Isla caught a shared look between her brother and Rian. So, *now* they decided to work together?

Rian glanced at Edmund. Her brother spoke first. "They're both secure for now... but we don't think it's safe for you to be around either of them. We locked them up with firestone chains we found. Still..."

This time, Edmund gestured to Rian. The soldier said, "She's powerful. I've never seen anything like it, and Freya still hasn't recovered from whatever she did to her..."

That was rich, considering the state of *his* jacket.

Rian waved back to Edmund. "It's too risky. We still haven't found all those other zealots, and who knows what brought those Nothings here. Given what the wielder did to you before, she may be able to find a weakness and exploit it—"

"Just get it out already." The ringing in her ears started up again and she was beginning to feel lightheaded. They were all dancing around the truth, and it was impossible to follow.

One of these cowards needed to say it.

Edmund stepped closer. "I know we talked about not using wielders to get you home safely, given how you were when we found you."

Brenner tilted his head curiously. Exactly what story had he been told?

"But I think—we think—" Edmund gestured toward Rian, Brenner, and general what's-his-name. "You should go on ahead. You will go on ahead," he added, more decisively this time.

Isla stepped back. "I'm staying right here. I know them and want to talk to them—"

"I don't think that's a good idea right now," Rian said, his tone gentle. "I know you think you're fine, but we can't risk it."

A heartbeat passed. Then Rian's eyes flickered to where Freya lingered outside their circle. She still looked caught between here and Rallion's first gate, her face flushed with guilt.

A pang of dread twisted in Isla's stomach. Freya knew she'd seen Beretta already. Isla confided to her back in Slomat. She couldn't have told anyone... could she?

Freya looked away.

No. No. They couldn't possibly mean—

Rian's throat bobbed. Yes. That was exactly what they were saying.

Isla stared at Rian, her heart crumbling into a shriveled speck of dust. She expected this from her brother, not him—or Freya. Her fists tightened into balls.

Edmund spoke, but she couldn't tear her eyes away from Rian. "We can send Alynna and Susanna with you, so you aren't alone."

She clenched her hands, digging her nails into her skin. "What about the rest of you?"

Brenner cleared his throat. He found his pitiful voice only to say, "We can get to Aurial in a week if we make good timing, depending on how cooperative the prisoners are."

She took another step back. "No." Blood still pumped furiously against her skull.

There was no way she was taking directions from this lot of idiots. She turned away, aware of more than one pair of footsteps following her. Only when she reached the edge of the camp did she finally stop.

"I'm not going," she told them, aware she sounded like a petulant child. "I feel far too sickly and I don't think it's a good idea."

"Isla," Edmund said. He sounded tired and he looked like shit. She told him as much.

"We'll be right behind you," Rian added.

"Why don't you have the transporters come back for you, then?" She flexed her fingers. "I'm not going there alone."

Rian and Edmund exchanged another glance. *Screw them.*

"I don't know what father's reaction will be when he sees we've taken a Muratian prince prisoner," Edmund said. "We want to question him. Find out what happened and what their plans are, before father either hangs him immediately—or decides to return him with our heads."

Isla nearly laughed. "You plan on hiding this from *him*? Good luck with that."

Rian tilted his head. "We have an idea that may work, but we need Brenner to keep quiet."

This time, she snorted. Everyone had a role to play. Everyone, except her.

Edmund ignored her. "I think I know how to work with him. By the time we reach Aurial, I can convince him, and his men, to stay quiet."

"I can help with—"

"No," Rian cut her off. She clamped her mouth shut. "I don't want them anywhere near you. Not after everything." Despite the pale tone of his skin, his eyes blazed with something she couldn't name, and it stirred something deep in her gut.

"I know you say you're fine," Edmund said. "We can't risk it. If she's been here longer than we expected, we don't know what's been done, what ideas have been planted. And you're the most susceptible."

The weakest. That's what he didn't say out loud.

Isla slowly shook her head. The truth settled in like a bad storm she couldn't outrun or hide from. They wouldn't be convinced.

"I don't want to go back there," she whispered. One last, desperate attempt.

Edmund pursed his lips. "It's either there or straight to Koliat with him... and if it were me, I know which of those two horrors I'd rather face right now."

"This isn't fair." She blinked the moisture from her eyes.

"Don't I know it," Edmund said. "I promise there is no other option."

Isla's gaze drifted to a tall birchwood, its thick leaves rustling in the wind. Foolish to think he'd begun seeing her as an equal, worthy of an opinion. Utterly foolish. And now Rian was in on his witless scheme.

Did they both think so little of her?

She turned to her brother. "You better not drop Opi off in the middle of a swamp, or I'll make you regret it."

"I'll let Opi snack on his knuckle bones if he tries," Rian said. "He won't touch him."

No smile touched her lips. She stared at him, absolutely furious for letting Edmund force her into this. He was supposed to be on her side.

Her side. Not Edmund's.

She turned toward the small camp. If they were determined to get rid of her, she had no desire to endure another agonizing moment in either of their presences.

Rian tried to say something, likely a foolish plea, but she ignored him. Refused to acknowledge him or his words. They would only soothe his guilty conscience and he didn't deserve to feel better about this betrayal.

This was expected of her brother... expectations had always been low for him. Yet this weight on her chest refused to budge and she didn't want it to. He was supposed to be different.

As she walked away, the birchwood cracked and withered into ash.

Twenty-One

Years.

If she wasn't resolved to move forward with her brother, she'd have turned him to dust after watching him expertly weave through the castle tunnels. He'd been sneaking out for *years* while she wasted away. Trapped.

At least he was showing her now, she reminded herself, as they made another turn down a barely lit hallway. If he left her, she'd never find her way back to her room. There was no way he had learned all the twists and turns on his own. Someone had once shown him.

They'd left her room through a series of doors reserved for the help and took several quick turns, finally going down one shadowed tunnel that she walked past the first time, completely missing it. Based on the thick layer of dust coating the floor, no one had used it in years.

It was a good thing Edmund had left his favorite Siica outside her door when he came to get Isla. Any other would surely have reported the odd occurrence between the prince and princess. She prayed his man was as loyal as Edmund had hinted.

They would find out for sure upon their return.

She tugged at the collar of her Pedite military uniform. Alynna had the good sense to clean and hide it for her, just in case. It served her better than she could have imagined. Once they left the castle, no one gave a Pedite soldier and a hooded Agicae wandering the streets a second glance. Most people avoided them.

Still, the ease with which Edmund moved through the tunnels and back alleys irked her. It was hard to remain focused when all she could think of was the burning betrayal. Who had shown him this in the first place? Certainly not their father. And why had he ever needed to sneak around like this before?

"Everyone is excited to see you." The nervous hitch in Edmund's voice betrayed the bold lie. Good.

They should be afraid after everything they've done to her.

They made their way to the camp stationed outside the castle walls. It was always like this. The inside barracks were supposedly too full, despite the scores of empty beds, so the Pedites were cast out. This time, it served as the perfect shield—the perfect cover for what they were hiding.

Horses neighed from a hay-encrusted barn, and she recognized the familiar whinnies of River. If she could sneak away, she planned to give the loyal steed some treats before returning. She missed his calming presence and was grateful he had made the trip unscathed.

Edmund expertly navigated the score of tents, waving to a few soldiers he recognized. Jealousy flared in her chest when she thought of how many times he had visited them since they finally arrived in Aurial—two full weeks after her.

That part stung. The pain of what she considered a deep betrayal still cut her insides apart, making her want to explode.

No. Push that down. *Deep down.*

She promised herself no fiery explosions today. If she let the rage out, she didn't know if she could ever stop it again.

Two weeks on her own had hardly been ample time to calm her enough to listen to Edmund's initial pleas when he returned. Their first reunion was hardly warm. She had made peace with him only to receive updates from the camp.

If she didn't at least *pretend* to forgive him, he wouldn't have brought her.

"Nobody's bothered to check out here since we arrived," Edmund said over his shoulder. The hitch in his voice told her he knew exactly where her mind wandered.

The first day, he had brought a letter with several pages of hastily scrawled apologies and lengthy explanations that she didn't care for. It still lay in her room, hidden from prying eyes and fully wrinkled from dozens of re-reads.

It had been three weeks since, and she had yet to hand Edmund a reply, despite him asking five times. She had no messages to pass on but allowed Edmund to update her on the progress with their *guests*.

Three weeks in which Edmund had been casually strolling in and out of the castle without a thought to bring Isla along and release her from that draped prison she was trapped in. She was stuck inside, and her would-be correspondent was stuck outside.

"Lucky for you," she said, hoping it didn't sound as bitter as she felt inside.

"The wielder... she was affecting some of the soldiers who brought her food, despite the firestone-laced chains. We think she's weaker now, as we haven't had any outbursts in a while."

Isla remained silent. She refused to give him the satisfaction of thinking he might have been right in sending her ahead. She still maintained they were wrong. They didn't understand Beretta's powers and Isla's experiences could have been an asset rather than the hindrance they'd all assumed.

She had plenty of time during those first two weeks—in which her father had put her on bed rest to recover—to craft the perfect rebuttal she wished her brain had thought of back in that camp. And she'd seen enough of her brother to slip them in every chance she got. She may have even yelled once or twice, and he had taken it all in stride.

That made it worse.

Now, she had every intent to list out all the ways she could have helped and every reason they were completely wrong in sending her away. They came to a larger tent—a commanding officer's—and she knew from the pang in her core and the skip of her heart, exactly who it belonged to. The person who had been most on her mind these past weeks. In all the good ways and terrible ways.

A shadow darted out of the tent, barreling straight into her.

"Opi!" She knelt and stroked the smooth head, running her palm down his long spine. Her entire body melted into a puddle of cooing mess when he rubbed against her. Gods, she missed him. The pure and innocent soul who *hadn't* betrayed her.

He'd grown. The last time she'd seen him, he hadn't quite reached her knees, and now he was fully past them. "What have they been feeding you, sweetie?"

"Everything." Rian burst out of the tent. Opi spun in a circle before leaping up, placing his front paws on Rian's shoulders. He was long. "He's been eating anything he can get his paws on, and if not, he yells for hours into the night."

Isla stood, hoping the heat in her cheeks wasn't visible in the night's light. He looked the same as she remembered, despite it being five weeks since she'd last seen him.

Five weeks.

Two weeks alone. And three weeks bitterly sulking while they all lurked beyond the city walls.

Rian opened his mouth, then closed it. He shoved his hands into his pockets while Opi pranced around the pair.

Her stomach flipped every way and her insides tightened. How many days would that make it? Too many? Not enough? It was still unclear.

While she took the time to drink in every inch of him, noticing the new uniform and freshly shaved stubble, he became interested in Edmund's boots. His back seemed fine, especially compared to right after Devlin had sunk his powers into him. It was difficult to string together all the retorts and admonishments she'd painstakingly crafted now that she was in his presence.

Jerk. Idiot. Moron.

"You're late, Edmund." Rian flailed his arm at a dark tent in the distance. "They're waiting for you."

"Thanks." Edmund took a step, then paused. His eyes traveled between the two, and he grimaced. "You can have ten minutes. That's all."

She refused to peel her eyes away from him, and what was that strange rhythm her pulse had decided to take on? Opi nudged the back of her knees, desperately seeking attention.

"I said *ten minutes*, got that?" Edmund repeated, his voice hitching higher this time.

"Understood," Rian mumbled, now choosing to stare at the ground.

Asshole.

For a dragging moment, Isla's heart sank. It seemed like Edmund wouldn't leave. But after shaking his head, he turned on his heel and strode toward the seemingly trivial tent Rian had pointed out.

But things were never as they seemed.

Now it was only the two of them. Standing awkwardly. No words passed for an excruciatingly long minute.

This was stupid. "Aren't you going to invite me in for a drink?" she asked.

A smile ghosted across his face as he finally lifted his eyes to meet hers. Gods, she missed that annoying shade of gray that liked to stare straight into her soul. "You sure you can handle your liquor?"

Her silly stomach rolled over and danced. "Always."

Bastard.

She brushed past him, bumping his shoulder as she did. The tent was the same as she remembered: plain, with little besides a cot, a dented trunk, and three chairs shoved around a small table littered with maps and half-drank cups of ale.

Who had he been meeting with before her arrival?

Surely, her appearance must have been unexpected, as she'd rejected all previous invitations to come. For some reason, tonight finally felt like the right time to face them.

She cast one withering glance at the rickety chairs and settled on the bed instead. Opi jumped beside her, and Rian sighed dramatically.

"No animals on the bed," he muttered. "We've been working on that for weeks, and you've just undone all our hard work."

As if she cared about that.

After a few short whistles and repeated gestures toward the floor, Opi crawled off and curled up at her feet with a groan.

Rian stood in the middle of the tent, bent awkwardly to avoid hitting his head on the roof. The sight of him, unsure of himself, warmed something in her bitter-soaked heart. She didn't know whether she wanted to hug him or slap him. Maybe both, after what he'd pulled. He certainly deserved it.

Prick.

But she hadn't spent five weeks locked up in that cursed castle with preening noblemen only to start a fight now. She said, "If you're waiting for me to beg you to join me, you'll be standing there all night." Alright, maybe she *had*.

He sighed and slunk into a spot next to her on the bed, pulling out two glasses and handing her a cup of—she sniffed it—ale. He leaned against the post at the far end, keeping a safe distance despite the smile creeping across his stupid face.

"How long do you bet until he comes back?" he asked, picking at his sleeve.

"If he said ten minutes..." She scratched her chin dramatically. "Then five."

He settled his drink on the trunk and clasped his hands together. "I'm sorry."

That did it.

She exploded. Words rolled out one after another. Weeks of being isolated in this hell-hold. On her own. Placed there by the ones she cared about most.

"You fucking prick—"

Opi scattered and ran under a chair.

"You have no idea what that felt like, you moronic—"

The seropa whined and curled into himself, daring to crack an eye at Isla.

"Pig-headed, inbred, imbecile—"

Isla went on for minutes. He didn't stop her, though he looked like he wanted to at several points.

When she finished, her chest heaved as if she'd run all the way from the castle. It still felt lighter than it had in weeks.

Rian nodded, his throat bobbing. "I understand your anger."

"And you're a complete asshat," she said.

He smiled. "Where'd you learn that colorful language?"

"Don't try with me."

"I'm not." The smile disappeared. "Not at all. I made a mistake, and I should have listened to you. With what happened in Slomat, and with Devlin—what he did—it took me back to that day in Liopen. That day I pretty much lost everything and everyone. I got afraid and didn't want it to happen again. I didn't want to lose you."

She raised a single, angry eyebrow. A breeze sent ripples through the canvas around them.

"Unless..." His eyes flashed, and his voice hitched. "Unless I already have?"

For a moment, Isla considered her words carefully, weighing exactly how much torture he deserved.

"You're on very dangerous ground right now," she murmured, her voice low. It didn't sound half as threatening as she intended.

"I could beg for forgiveness on my knees if you prefer." His eyes lit up. "I could do other things on my knees if you'd—"

Isla cut him off with a sharp look. "Where are they?"

Rian's shoulders sagged. "We have her restrained, but if you get too close, she can do... *things*. Some of the men have been affected by her, so we've had to keep the shifts short."

Isla already knew that. She crossed her arms and glowered.

Rian added, "We didn't have a lot of options at the time and I let myself be swayed. If I could do it all again, I wish I'd tried to find another way."

"It doesn't change what you did or how it made me feel. I refuse to ever feel like that again."

"You won't," he said quickly. "If it helps, I've been miserable the past five weeks."

Just a bit.

"Not nearly enough." She rolled her shoulders. "If you ever pull something like that again..." She let the threat hang while Opi chirped his agreement from the floor, eyeing the bed like it was his next great meal.

"We ran into a series of thunderstorms after the second day that nearly flooded the entire camp, then Brenner and your brother got into a shouting match by the fifth day. The other generals have been giving my men nothing but problems since we left that battlefield."

"Hm." Another sip of the cold ale found its way into her mouth. She *might* be able to spare a trace of pity for his men, but definitely not for him.

"Our guests weren't cooperative or talkative at all. Some of the soldiers still report lingering headaches."

She was always trying to claw her way in. Isla hadn't realized how powerful Beretta truly was.

"He was just as bad—in a different way."

Didn't Isla know it?

"But I—I think you could have handled it." He chanced another look at her. "We may have acted rash."

"*May* have."

A pause. Then, "I promise to listen to you better next time."

"Next time?" Fire rose into her throat, begging for release.

"No," he corrected quickly. "You're right. There won't be a next time."

"At least you've *finally* learned something."

He grinned, so she shuffled closer.

"Thanks for taking care of Opi for me," she said quietly, focusing on a stain in the canvas across from her. "How's River?"

"Loving the cavalry life." His hand snaked around her waist. She sucked in a breath. He hesitated, then dragged her into his lap. Instead of strangling him, she threw her arms around his neck. "He's been getting all the treats and great care... He's gained a few pounds."

"That makes two of them." She cracked an eye toward Opi, who slowly slunk his way up the bed as if his measured pace would make him invisible. Rian sighed but didn't stop his ascent or bat him away when Opi curled up next to them.

The seropa had definitely filled out and gained several inches in height.

"I missed you," he breathed. "I missed you barking orders at me and messing up my soldiers' camp."

She chuckled and pressed her head against his chest. The steady drum of his heart sent pulses of calm through her. How did he always manage to do that? She could stay there forever, staring at the sandy ceiling.

"I couldn't make it earlier," she said quietly.

The truth was that Edmund had tried convincing her before, but she didn't know what she wanted. She had been too angry and all she could do was ignore everything. Push it all away until something broke.

Rian brushed her hair behind an ear, treating each strand as if it were fine silk. His fingers played with the ends before starting over at the top.

All the stresses from her day—days—weeks—in the castle melted away as she listened to Opi's heavy breathing and the steady thrum of Rian's chest, surrounded by the familiar canvas enclosure.

"Remember that night in the forest?"

"Which one?" He shifted beneath her. One hand heavy on her thigh, squeezing for reassurance.

"When you got stabbed by a thousand tiny thorns," she said smugly. "But I meant the first one."

She pressed her cheek further into him, and a calloused finger feathered across her bottom lip. "That was the first good sleep I'd had in forever. I think it was the first time I'd felt safe—accepted for once."

His hand pressed against the back of her head. "It was a lovely sleep," he murmured, sending shivers down her spine. "How much time now?"

"Two minutes," she mumbled. "Maybe less."

Perhaps she shouldn't have wasted so much time yelling. She should have gathered her grievances into written lists to review with him instead.

He sighed and kissed the side of her neck. "Thank you for seeing me. I'd rather have you yell at me for hours than be parted like that again."

Isla didn't bother reminding him that their lengthy separation had been entirely his fault. He'd never be living that down.

Was she ready for this?

They entered the first tent, stopping behind the thin line of red firestone erected as a barrier to keep their prisoners in. That, combined with the chains they'd taken, formed the makeshift prison for the Muratian wielder.

A proper cell in the dungeons would have been better, especially those built to contain wielders, but they couldn't risk bringing them into the castle. Too many people would talk, and the king would find out. Then they'd lose any chance of getting the answers they needed.

"Did they talk yet?" she asked, unable to take her eyes off the fiery blue gaze in front of her. The one that had tormented her for months, whether or not she'd realized it.

They had decided it was best to start with her, and Isla couldn't agree more. She hadn't seen Devlin in two months and didn't know if she was ready.

At least with Beretta, she knew what she was getting.

"No," Rian said, hanging his head. "Nothing new."

Freya added, "We haven't given them any info either." She'd been giving Isla space ever since mumbling a quick apology for spilling all her secrets to Rian.

The Muratian's face lit up when Isla stepped out of the shadows. "Come to braid each other's hair again?" she asked in a voice like smooth ice.

Rian's hand moved to the hilt of his sword, the wielder's eyes tracking every movement. Her gaunt features flashed, but she kept the smirk steady on her face.

Rian had said that Devlin was in far worse condition, though that wasn't surprising. Beretta had spent months in the mines with her. Watching her and making sure she didn't run away or get herself killed. She'd eaten the same terrible gruel as her, likely grabbing extra rations whenever Isla wasn't around, and had slept on the cold, hard rock with her... all while he stayed above ground perfectly comfortable, warm, and safe.

Devlin had never been exposed to conditions like that. Never eaten measly rations or kept locked up like a common prisoner. Neither had Isla... before all this.

A small part of Isla relished in their despair, and if Opi were here, she was certain he'd be purring at the sight of the downtrodden and disheveled top Muratian soldier.

"We're not in the mood for jokes today," Rian said. "Are you ready to talk yet?"

Beretta moved to her knees, her firestone-laced chains jangling around thin wrists. "We want better conditions," she said sternly, her eyes flicking toward the side where Devlin's tent stood. "I'm not talking until you move us someplace new. *Both* of us."

"Like where?" Edmund asked. "A royal suite in the palace?"

"We need more blankets," Beretta replied without missing a beat. "And something to sleep on other than dirt."

Rian raised an eyebrow. "Anything else you'd like, *Your Majesty*?"

Beretta rattled her chains, kicking up a cloud of dirt. "A decent meal would be great."

When Rian stepped closer, he took great care not to cross the red line. "And if we move you somewhere more comfortable, will you tell us what we want?"

"I'll tell you everything I know."

Freya shifted in the shadows, her hand still on the hilt of her axe. Her face was a fiery wall, and every time Beretta moved, she shifted in unison. "I wouldn't trust this one, Rian."

Beretta's head whipped around and recognition flashed across her cold blue eyes. Something clicked into place in that cunning mind.

"So... you're the one," she whispered. "I wondered why you've been so intent on breaking us."

Freya winced and gave Rian an apologetic look. "Let's go," she said sternly. "I have no desire to play a part in this one's games anymore."

"Don't you? I'm certainly enjoying myself."

Rian didn't move.

How had Isla never seen Beretta's cruel smile for what it really was? She only ever saw what the wielder wanted her to see, and at the time, it had been her doting friend. That version was long dead now.

Beretta shifted forward, still on her knees, and Rian edged over to partially block Isla. That only made the smile on Beretta's face widen.

"I see now," Beretta murmured in a low voice that curled and twisted in Isla's ears, lightly tapping at the corners of her mind as if trying to sneak in.

Isla wanted to run. To hide. To claw her way out of her skin and tear it away. She shuffled back an inch, feeling the outside breeze brush her back and beg to pull her out.

Freya was at their side with her back to Beretta, eyes sharp with warning. "She doesn't know anything. Let's try the other one. Maybe we'll have more luck."

That sounded like a perfect idea. Then Isla's insides might finally stop twisting over and over.

Freya grabbed Rian's arm and began shepherding them out.

"You know, I expected a bit more... but a Pedite."

Rian froze. Pure fury flashed in his gray eyes.

"Don't let her get to you," Freya said. She tipped her axe at Beretta, though the Muratian didn't flinch.

"When we first got to that mountain, I had to work on taking her memories and making something new. It was long and painful. She screamed so much." Beretta rose to her feet, chains clanging as she shook her wrists.

The words rang oddly in Isla's mind, like a distant memory she had long wished to forget but begged to be released.

"She called your name many times, but you didn't come. None of you did." She pushed dirty strands out of her face. "It was absolutely exhausting. It's never taken that much out of me, but I made it worthwhile. Do you know how much energy it takes to completely destroy someone from the inside—"

Her sentence never finished as Rian pulled himself free from Freya's grip and clamped his hands around Beretta's throat. "Say one more word and I'll end you."

But the wielder cackled between rasping breaths. "You. Won't."

Freya jumped in front of Isla, anticipating an attack she couldn't see. "Rian, don't—"

But it was too late. He released Beretta and dropped to the ground, writhing in terrible, unseen agony.

Twenty-Two
The General

Pain.

It was everywhere. It was everything.

His brain couldn't think. It couldn't function. It couldn't breathe.

Neither could his lungs.

Nothing else existed but the invisible knives burning and freezing at once. Across his flesh, his back, his torso, inside every joint and vessel, as if forged from the same fiery pit of despair. His chest collapsed in on itself, crushing every organ again and again.

Suffering was all he was and all he knew. Even his own name escaped him as the torment devoured all else. No part of him remained untouched by pain, and surely, he would end soon.

He wanted it to be over. For him to be over.

It would be better for all.

Only agonizing darkness waited beyond—

A giant wave of relief crashed over him, and he was on the ground in the middle of that cursed tent, struggling to remember how to work his lungs.

The wielder lay in front of him, eyes closed, with Freya standing over her. The butt of her axe hovered inches from the Muratian, ready to strike again if needed.

"Rian!"

A tug at his arm and warm hands pressed against his back, trying to help him up, but his legs weren't his own. Most of his body refused to function, so he stayed lying in the dirt. The hand on his back kept rubbing, and he listened to delicate breaths in and out until his own shaky ones fell into the same rhythm.

That was like nothing he'd felt before. Worse than his punishment after Liopen and what Devlin did to him with his scars. Was this what Isla had endured for months on end? His insides withered and died.

No. It wasn't like that all the time. It was different. Isla had said so herself. Different and horrible at the same time.

Freya kicked the wielder, flipping her over. "I *told* you she's a slippery one."

Right. *Don't* get too close. Easy enough to forget in the heat of the moment, especially after everything she said.

Rian rolled onto his side. Those warm hands remained on him, as if longing for the same contact.

The flap burst open. Edmund rushed in. The guard on duty, Shaw, lingered beyond the tent's barrier. He had half a brain but was smart enough to stay out of range.

Rian, apparently, was not.

"What was all that screaming about?" Edmund asked. He froze at the scene: Rian sprawled on the ground with Isla crouched over him, and Freya holding her axe inches from the unconscious wielder.

"Handled perfectly fine." Freya flipped Bone Breaker and slid it into the holster strapped across her back.

Edmund extended a hand and helped Rian up. "I told you—it hurts worse than Rallion's fiery swamphole, doesn't it?"

Isla's head snapped toward her brother, but he merely shrugged.

Rian groaned and swayed slightly. Pain still rippled through him like some twisted side effect. He double-checked that the wielder was actually unconscious. How could she be so powerful? That was unlike anything he'd ever experienced… and he had gone through *a lot* in his short lifespan.

Edmund dusted his hands and placed them on his hips. "I take it she was uncooperative."

"Extremely," Freya said.

"I wouldn't—wouldn't say that," Rian said, hand on his chest to ensure it was moving properly. "She did give us something."

"What?" Isla's head snapped toward him. Her skin had lost every trace of color and turned as pale as the stars.

Rian felt as if his skull had been battered beneath a thousand hooves, painful pricks still echoing across his head. He shivered.

Still, Beretta's words replayed over and over again. They reminded him of what Isla had told him before.

"I think I know what we can use to get through to them. Come with me."

They stopped before the unassuming tent, taking a moment to plan their approach. It was the same size and color as the last one, and it held someone just as conniving, if not more.

Freya turned fully to face Rian. "We're not going to get close to this one, right, *general*?"

"I know. I know." Rian waved her off. "I let her get to me and forgot myself."

"Don't let it happen again," Freya said sternly. "They're crooked bastards, the pair of them."

After that, he had no desire to let any wielders near his mind ever again.

Fuck no.

Edmund looked directly at Isla, who remained oddly quiet. "Do you want to stay out here?"

Right. Rian hadn't even asked if she wanted to see Devlin. He had marched them straight here, with no regards for what it might do to her.

Isla shook her head and glared, daring anyone to question her after everything. Freya quickly glanced down.

"You don't have to say anything if you don't want to," Edmund said quickly. "Just let us do the talking."

Isla rolled her eyes and went first.

The tent was exactly as it had always been: dark, with nothing but a thick stake to which the prisoner was tied and a thin blanket that served as his bed. Nothing else.

Neither of them deserved it.

Rian had visited the Muratians every day, experimenting with new ways to coax the pair into speaking or hinting at what they wanted. Beretta remained stoic and gave nothing away, while the prince spent his time complaining or hurling insults at anyone who lingered too close. Not a single truthful word had come from either of them... before today.

Now, Rian had a clearer idea of how to approach this.

The Muratian prince looked far from princely today. His once-fine blue uniform had turned a dull gray from the accumulation of dust and grime. Rusty hair clung together in greasy clumps, and his cheekbones stood out sharply, a result of refusing half the food brought to him because it 'didn't meet his standards.' Even as a prisoner in enemy territory, he still maintained his ridiculous demands.

That haughty attitude had since dried up by the fifth day, along with that infuriating air of entitlement. Now, he was a hunched, deflated shell of a prince... yet, like the wielder before him, Prince Devlin still refused to answer *any* questions.

The prince's eyes swept over his visitors, masking any surprise as Isla strode into the tent. These royals were well-trained in hiding their emotions, the Velotian ones included.

"Did you enjoy the taste of my commander's power?" His gaze shifted as each of them entered the tent and he managed a condescending grin while seated on his throne of dirt. "I could hear the screams from here."

Rian ignored him, stepping past Isla, who froze near the exit. There was no way he would rise to their taunts twice in the same hour.

"Are you ready to talk today?" he asked.

Devlin's grin stayed in place, though he shook his head. "I fear I've lost my appetite for the spoken word. All this time in shackles has affected my throat and I couldn't possibly find the strength."

"You certainly seem strong enough when you're complaining," Rian said.

Freya stepped closer, stopping outside the ring of firestone. "I'd like to try convincing him." She drew a jagged dagger from a hidden pocket and flipped it in the air. "With your permission, General?"

Devlin's face fell when Freya caught the dagger in her opposite hand.

"Not yet," Rian said coolly. The goddesses knew this man deserved it. After experiencing the wielder's powers firsthand and truly understanding the torment she'd caused those closest to him, he *really* wanted to grant Freya permission to do her worst.

But torture would get them nowhere—it had gotten them nowhere. They needed another approach.

He kept his face carefully neutral and stood as casually as possible, despite the anger simmering beneath the surface. Perhaps Freya was right. They should have waited longer before confronting the prince. His pride and fury kept him going, despite his friend's protests.

It annoyed him how easily these Muratians could get under their skin. He thought he was better than that. Stronger than that. Yet it wasn't surprising, considering Beretta had been inside Isla's head for months. There wasn't much the mindweaver didn't know.

"Back's all better now?" Devlin asked.

Rian clenched his jaw, grinding his teeth as he imagined pummeling the prince into the ground.

"No? You should really see a healer for it." Devlin chuckled. "I know the perfect one."

Good to see he still had the energy for jokes. Perhaps Rian should have let Freya draw *some* blood, since the prince was clearly feeling much better today.

Rian crouched outside the circle of crushed firestone. He wouldn't make the same stupid mistake twice. "We could get you a healer, if you want. Maybe one for your friend. She's not holding up so well."

Devlin's nostrils flared. He pursed his lips and stared at Rian's boots.

This was going to be harder than he thought. The man hadn't given them anything in five weeks—Beretta either—so he shouldn't have expected much to change.

"The Celestial Solstice is coming up," Rian said. "Maybe you'd like a bottle of sparkling to celebrate while you contemplate all your life's decisions."

"How long?" Devlin asked.

"What was that?" Rian cocked his head.

"How many days until the Celestial Solstice?"

Rian felt the others shift behind him but didn't dare peek back. Didn't dare give this creature anything useful like he'd done with the mindweaver. "Tomorrow. There's going to be a big party. I don't think you'll be invited."

"No." He shifted and sat cross-legged. "I don't think we will be."

"If you tell us what we want to know, I'll have a healer check you and your commander... and we'll get you a better tent."

Edmund scoffed from somewhere behind him.

"I want to see her," Devlin said.

"Not going to happen."

"Then I don't have anything to tell you." He curled his knees to his chest and wrapped his arms around them.

Why did all these royals have to be so dramatic? They must have been sent to the same instructor.

Edmund stepped forward, half of his face lit by rippling torchlight. Devlin watched the dancing flames behind his shoulder as if they held all the secrets to his escape.

"I guess he can wait out here a bit longer," Edmund said. "Take his blankets. I hear tonight is supposed to get quite cold."

"Won't even give me a hint of a flame then," Devlin replied, a twisted smile grazing his lips. "The only ones you'll be punishing are yourselves."

"Nobody is coming for you," Edmund said. His face started to turn blotchy.

"Is that why you have us hidden away out here? Too afraid to tell daddy what you did? Worried he won't approve?"

Edmund shook his shoulders back. "I don't think I need any parental advice from someone whose mother has half a head stuck up Slin's slimy asshole."

A laugh rocked through Devlin's body. "My mother prefers the teachings of Rallion over any of the others, as yours once did."

Edmund's face went oddly blank.

"Didn't know? I thought that would be obvious, given... everything." Devlin shrugged. "Your sister knows. I'm surprised she didn't share with you. Though, given the secrets in your family, I suppose I shouldn't be all that shocked."

Isla shook her head at Edmund. They could talk about it later and argue when there wasn't a wielding psychopath in front of them.

Rian knew bits and pieces from what Isla could remember. It made sense. The crown. The paintings of Isla's mother with a certain wilted flower in them. The queen had left clues for anyone who knew where to look.

Edmund may have been too dull to pick up on any of them, despite being ten when their mother passed.

"Not one for Sister Death, I see." The Muratian prince had more color in his face than Rian had seen in weeks. "Not everyone has the taste to understand the meaning behind the old texts and see the signs. Perhaps you lean more toward Insmia's fiery teachings?"

"I don't favor any of the goddesses," Edmund said heatedly. "Especially not the goddess of fire and flame."

"Poron shines her light on me." Devlin held out a hand, as if hoping to summon the power he had twisted away from the healing goddess' grace. "Some of us are graced by the goddesses more than others, thanks to our bloodlines." His eyes moved to the entrance, where Freya and Isla stood, then back to Edmund.

The bloodlines. They wanted to combine them? Or was it something more?

"I'd hardly call what you do as graced by the goddess," Isla said, her voice ringing strong and solid from behind him. Her footsteps shuffled closer, still keeping herself partially blocked by him and Edmund.

"And what would you call your gifts, then?" he asked, scratching a scar along his jawline.

"A curse."

"Sometimes what we think are curses are actually gifts carved straight from the goddesses' chests. You only need to learn how to work those gifts properly."

Rian scowled. He was growing irritated with these babbling puzzles.

Isla inched closer, now at the edge of his vision; Freya stood within arm's reach of her. "What did you do to those creatures—to those men?"

Laughter shook those bony shoulders again. This time, Devlin allowed sound to escape with it. Rian had never heard anything so eerie.

"Nothing."

"It certainly didn't look like nothing," Isla said. "How'd you send them after us?"

"How? As if you expect me to actually tell you that. Why? I thought you'd want to see them."

Isla scoffed. "Another present?"

Rian shifted to the balls of his feet. What did that mean?

"No," Devlin smiled again. "Not my present, princess. You were the one who let them out."

Time froze. Everything seemed to stand still as they all processed Devlin's words.

Edmund was the first to recover. "You're lying."

"You wish I was." Devlin's eyes returned to Isla. Her expression was unreadable, and Rian's fingers itched to reach for her. He didn't allow them so much as twitch in her direction. "I wouldn't dare lie on the cusp of the star goddesses' sacred year—full of new beginnings and truths, many of which you already know in your heart."

"The gate," Isla whispered.

"We thought it was an old tale, twisted over the years. Apparently, there was some truth to it. It opened the night you left us."

Escaped was the proper term. Barely making it out with her life and mind intact was a more accurate description Rian would use.

"So, close it," Edmund said.

Rian nearly slapped his own forehead.

Devlin scoffed. "Couldn't if I wanted to. Not when there are so many other fun things we can do with it open. After Rallion's comet, and with the Celestial Solstice upon us, I'd wager there are more itching to escape from there... maybe even Rallion herself will manage to crawl up and upset her sister year's peace. She's been known to get jealous in the past."

"That's enough of that rambling," Rian said. He was oddly calm despite the ice chilling his limbs.

The Muratian was starting to sound like one of those heretics. If what he said about his mother was true, he had been raised by one of the more crazed among them. And a mad heretic in power never ended well for anyone involved.

Half of what he said was likely useless, but there may be some truth in his words. Devlin wanted to spook Isla, to scare her into revealing something. Instead, she held strong.

It must be difficult to see her captors again, despite them being the ones in chains. It didn't take away from what they had done to her. Rian had gained no small pleasure from seeing the two reduced beneath their stations and into nothing more than the filthy prisoners they had treated Isla as for months. The goddess of wrath knew they deserved all that and much more.

"Any more questions for me?" Devlin asked. "I'm growing quite tired."

"That's enough," Rian said sternly. They needed to control the narrative. They couldn't let Devlin know how desperate they were for his information. Not if they wanted him to continue slipping it out between insults.

Perhaps tomorrow Rian could work him some more and get finite details about this supposed gate. If that was even a real thing.

They exited the tent, all feeling a little exhausted from the mental battle with the prince, and walked nearly straight into Malin and the newly minted commander.

Twenty-Three

There was no way this was a good thing. Even *she* knew enough to know that.

The newly appointed commander stood with his badge-adorned chest, trying to seem as self-important as he must think he was, given his short stature and disappearing hairline. He stood out in the worn-down camp, among the broken weapons and dirty tents that hid their precious prisoners. Isla had yet to exchange words with him since their introduction but had no doubt he was a pompous prick like the rest of them, based on how he pranced around the castle. Maybe he'd surprise her.

Doubtful.

"Commander Gaines," Edmund chewed out, hardly missing a beat as he brushed past Rian and Freya, pushing out his chest to keep the commander's gaze on him. "What are you doing out here?"

The commander surveyed the group with his angular face, capturing both Velotian royals and the two Pedite soldiers under his deep scrutiny. "I could ask you the same, Prince Edmund. Is your father aware that the two of you are outside the castle walls on this cold evening delivered straight from Hierel herself?"

He stared at the twinkling sky as if the star goddess was attempting to speak through it.

Definitely a pompous prick. There must be a lie solid enough to be believable. Think, Isla. *Think.*

The whites of Malin's eyes had doubled in size as he tried to casually glance between Rian and the commander. "The commander wanted to see the shape of the Pedite camp for himself."

He kept his voice low, but not too low to tip off the commander. They didn't want Devlin hearing anything important. Keeping stolen prisoners safely hidden was *not* an easy task.

"Yes." Gaines tore his eyes away from the sky. "In all his years in charge, I don't believe my counterpart ever made it down this way except for disciplinary reasons." His eyes darkened. "I have every intention of outperforming him. What better time for a change than the eve gazing upon the Celestial Solstice?"

"Surely that won't be difficult now, commander." The words slipped out as if they had a will of their own. She couldn't help the dig.

News of Commander Skallen's betrayal was not widely spread, thanks to her father's meddling. He didn't want news of his top commander's slip-up known to the masses. It would create panic.

Isla didn't care about her father's reputation. She had no love for him anymore, and even less for the dead commander. Everything bad that had happened to her was thanks to Skallen. He could rot outside of Rallion's eight gate for all she cared.

The gate.

The gate.

The cursed gate.

What had she done? It was hard to tell if Devlin's words held any truth. Then she remembered that feeling in her tent when the zealot uttered his spell. It had felt like something was pulling her down and down. Could that have been linked to Rallion's gates?

There was no way she could ask with this idiot commander staring at her as if he'd forgotten how to speak. Apparently, he *did* know about Skallen's betrayal. One thing her father must have briefed him on before throwing him into the role.

Commander Gaines stuttered, "Well, I have every intent—plan to—fully make amends for—that will never happen again, My Lady."

She loved the way he squirmed.

Edmund's eyes turned cold. "I should hope not." He blamed himself for not seeing through Skallen's lies or catching on to the idea of a mole coming from so high up in their father's precious ranks. Skallen was the last person they'd ever expected to betray the king.

Isla hadn't realized it until it was too late either. No one paid a deeper price for that oversight than she did. No one. She rubbed her arms, trying to provide a hint of comfort to her freezing body.

"Can we show you where the armory is, commander?" Rian asked, gesturing away from the tent that held a captive they very much should not have.

Edmund started inching to the side, attempting to lead him away.

The new commander didn't budge. He surveyed Rian, lingering on his Pedite general badge far too long. "So, you're the new general?"

"The same one," Rian said plainly.

Nobody had to ask how Gaines knew about him—or what he knew about him. Everybody already seemed to know Rian's business around here. She didn't like it one bit.

"Promoted by Prince Edmund here." Malin clapped his back. "A well-deserved promotion, if it's not too bold to say."

"It is," Edmund said, straightening his jacket. "Well, commander, it's been a pleasure seeing you. Perhaps we can cover your plans for my battalions at the ball. I hear General Baid had nothing but compliments to say about your excellent planning skills."

"Thank you, Prince Edmund." Commander Gaines puffed his chest out. "I look forward to seeing you at Hierel's Ball tomorrow."

The changing of the goddess years was always marked with fancy feasts and usually a ball or two, depending on the goddess. Slin's ball last year had involved colorful gowns and a maze of delusions that would have made the trickster goddess proud.

As this year was special, her father had arranged a lavish ball in Hierel's honor. It was the only chance to see the sister years in their lifetime, so he went all out—including planning a grand party all while his two children were on the run from murderous Muratians.

While the ball itself would be the height of royal lavishness, guests were only allowed to wear plain silver in tribute to the star goddess. Other kingdoms would likely hold similar offerings.

The masks they'd wear were meant to present oneself to the star goddess as you truly were, placing everyone on the same level. No jewels or crowns to hide behind. Though many courtesans couldn't help themselves, she'd heard whispers of ladies having crystals sewn into their gowns for extra sparkle.

Isla highly doubted Hierel would appreciate that, and those who went against tradition were due for a terrible year, thanks to her ire.

She hadn't put much thought into what she'd wear this year. Susanna and Alynna already had something in mind, and she was more than happy to leave them to their own machinations.

"We'll see you tomorrow." Edmund tipped his head at the commander, taking another step to the side.

Gods, when would Gaines get the hint to leave? The way he sneered at the others was testing her last nerves.

"I hear Edmund has arranged for you to attend, General Rian," she said, giving a pointed look at her brother. "All of you." She motioned at Freya and Malin, who were edging away from the tent and the conversation.

Freya's face lit up in a giant smile, while Malin still looked confused.

Commander Gaines bristled. "It's not common for Pedites, despite their status—"

"I think we can make an exception," she said in a voice like honey. The same one that had always worked on her previous wardens.

"Edmund and the general have formed a strong bond over these past months, and I'm certain he'd make this exception for a close friend."

"Close friend?" Malin barked. He swung his arm over Edmund's shoulders, nearly toppling her brother with his weight. "I'd say they're verging on the edge of becoming best friends."

Edmund looked like he wanted to stab somebody.

Commander Gaines nodded, as if he took Edmund's strangled silence for confirmation.

"Wonderful." Isla clapped her hands together. "The time really has slipped away. If you'll excuse us, soldiers, my brother and I have to be getting back. We will discuss this more another day."

She dragged out that last word pointedly, so they understood she meant the discussion about their guests would happen later. Her mind was still trying to process Devlin's words for herself. If only Gaines hadn't shown up when he did.

"Yes," Edmund said quickly. "We were not supposed to be out this late, commander, but we were reviewing the configurations ourselves and did not realize the late hour. I hope you can be discreet about this."

The commander seemed to struggle for a moment, then a wide grin filled his face. "Of course, prince. And I'm certain we can discuss more about some of my Agicae plans that your father is hesitant about at that time, too."

She had to hand it to her brother... he kept his composure over the thinly veiled threat.

The words Edmund spoke seemed wrenched from his gut. "It would be my pleasure."

"Well." The commander nodded to Edmund, then Rian. "I would like to see the state of our armory, as promised."

"Absolutely," Rian stepped between them. "This way, commander." He looked back at them for the briefest moment. "My prince... princess."

Isla nodded. The only acknowledgment allowed.

After the last weeks of torment, she'd take what she could get. If only there was more time to hear his groveling. All the prior transgressions were quickly forgotten when Beretta sank her claws into him. She'd never been so afraid.

Isla gripped Edmund's arm and tugged at her gaping brother to follow along. With her back turned to Commander Gaines, she couldn't help but let a smile settle across her face, despite everything Devlin had dumped on them.

"See you lovelies at the goddess ball," Malin called out at some point. It was followed by a round of laughter and a loud smack.

Edmund dragged his feet.

"What now?"

"Just dreading tomorrow all of a sudden," Edmund said.

At least that was something she didn't have to involve herself in. As Edmund and her father were so determined to cast her out of any real discussions, her words would have no merit in persuading the commander to keep his silence. She prayed to Hierel that the new commander was keen enough on gaining the heir's confidence that her brother could work out some sort of deal in exchange for his discretion.

Again... that was now her brother's problem to worry about. Any energy siphoned off for worrying was saved for Devlin's confusing words.

The point about her mother being a Rallion follower was something she'd suspected, but only now confirmed. What else didn't she know about her? The fact that Devlin knew more about her family than she did was infuriating.

"Thanks for that, by the way," Edmund said irritably. She couldn't see his face now that they'd made their way back into the tunnels, but she knew the edge of that particular tone as perfectly as she knew the back of her own scarred hand.

"For what, dear brother?"

"Now I have to find some way to get them into Hierel's Ball, or there will be even more questions I have to deal with."

Isla scoffed, slowing her pace as they neared the end of the tunnel and what would lead to her rooms. "You're quite adept at coming up with grand plans. I'm sure you'll figure something out."

His foot dragged and stopped. She turned to face the spot she thought he was standing in. It was hard to see in this place; she'd surely get lost if she ever tried navigating it alone.

"Something the matter, Edmund?" Feigning a lack of intelligence had worked for her in the past. Why not try it now?

She could practically hear his teeth grinding against each other. He was hiding something.

"Nothing," he said quietly. "I'm glad you came tonight."

It was a relief that her face was hidden in darkness, for she couldn't help the shock that had filled it.

"Well..." she began bitterly. "I'm glad people deemed me worthy enough of their excursions this time."

"You're worthy, Isla... I know I don't always make that apparent, but you are to me."

She turned her head, despite the cover of darkness.

"I *am* trying," he said.

"Trying," she repeated, her voice laced with bitter venom.

"Not well, I know. After the ball, I think we should talk... about *everything*." He pushed against the door, and light flooded the dark pathway. "It's late. Try to get some rest. I'll deal with Gaines to-morrow, and anything else that comes up... including the new guests you've dumped on me."

"You mean your best friends?"

Isla graced him with a self-satisfied smirk that would not be dampened. It was rare to get a good one over him, and she planned on holding onto that feeling. She hurried into her empty room and threw her dirty clothes into the deepest part of her closet, where no one would find them.

That smile refused to disappear as she tucked herself into a bed of the finest silks Velotia could find, and it lingered all through the day, only starting to waver when Alynna and Susanna fussed while getting her ready for the ball.

They put her hair up in dual buns, with fine threads of silver woven between the strands. The dress itself appeared simple at first, made of shining silver silk, but flames were sewn into the hem that shimmered when they caught the torchlight at the right angle. The floor-length gown was made from a single flowing swatch of fabric, hitched snugly at her hips, and tied at each shoulder, with the back open deep—deeper than she was accustomed to. But as it was Hierel's special night, formalities could be ignored for once.

Isla turned every way, watching the fabric ripple and sway like a petal in the wind. Gods, these two were geniuses.

Susanna stood back to admire her work while Alynna held out matching silver gloves with a grimace. Those were added, or demanded, by her father.

There was no point in fighting over this. Isla pulled them on, ignoring how the too-tight gloves made her itchy and want to scream.

"You look like Hierel herself walking among us," Susanna said, clapping her hands together.

More like Rallion, given how exhausted she felt, but Isla didn't bother correcting her as they'd done an excellent job of hiding the dark patches under her eyes.

"And here." Alynna plucked a silver leaf mask and tied it on, taking great care not to disturb the work done on her hair.

Despite being home and wearing the finest fabric Velotia could muster, Isla still felt like a stranger stood in her room and wore her skin. Months ago, she would have given anything to be back here. Now, all she wanted was to run far away. The portrait of her mother hung on the wall across from her, the picture of a perfect queen. It only seemed to mock her further.

Alynna tucked a loose strand into place and cast her eyes downward. "I'm certain the night will pass quickly, then you can excuse yourself after the first dances and nobody can say anything about it."

Except her father would.

She'd stay as long as he deemed appropriate and could only leave after he'd introduced her to enough of the richest courtiers and courtesans first. That was how these things always went, and she used to not mind it. This was the first time she absolutely despised the thought of being paraded around like one of his possessions.

But she smiled at Alynna and murmured her thanks before being whisked away by a pair of silver-clad Siicas. She didn't know if she'd ever get used to their stony expressions and lack of emotion or substance. Every day, she thanked the goddesses that there were no Siicas with her rescue party. If there had been, things would have gone a lot differently from the start.

With the mask on and no crown or usual royal jewels, she could almost blend in. *Almost.* The straight-backed guards on either side made sure she didn't, despite their silver uniforms blending in to near perfection, save for the onyx badges they still bore.

Didn't they wish to be garbed in pure silver as an offering to the star goddess or was that against their sacred vows? She wasn't friendly enough with any of them to ask.

She stood outside the double doors to the ballroom and sighed, sending a quick prayer to Hierel for the strength to get through this.

Her pair of guards peeled off behind a thick column. They would watch from a distance, remaining close in case they were needed but giving space for the royals to work the room and attend to their guests without them feeling threatened by their stoic guardians.

She flexed her hand. If only she could retreat to the safety of the shadows with them. A week under that cursed mountain had been better than this. At least she hadn't known the difference at the time she was there. At least she hadn't known what waited for her above ground.

Now she was similarly trapped. Trapped with a taste of freedom—or whatever you called that time before all this. It made everything in Aurial... worse. Sour, even. Like a spoiled meal that had turned days ago. Something sure to make her stomach upend itself.

A group of loud courtesans passed, their faces obscured by silver masks. One of the voices was familiar. Carissa. They'd taken lessons together before, and the woman always tried to compete with Isla, whether for men or attention. Isla made note of the dark-lined velvet dress Carissa wore and resolved to avoid her tonight.

Another group passed while she stayed at the edge of the doors, summoning the same courage that had helped her through the past weeks and months.

When the third group passed, she decided she was done praying to goddesses who had shunned her all her life. If she wanted courage to get through this, she would have to summon it herself.

She tore off her silver gloves and stuffed them into the nearest ornamental vase. She refused to hide and would wear them the same way the soldiers brandished their tattered war armor as a sign of what they had survived.

With a deep breath, she straightened her back and entered the grand room, full of vultures and jackals ready to strike at the first sign of weakness on this night dedicated to the star goddess.

Twenty-Four
The General

"Shaw, get your pack together. They're looking sloppy out there! And Leon, where in Slin's name is the rest of your team?" Rian's voice cracked from straining it all day. Gods, making this group into a formidable team was really pulling at the last thread of his patience.

Why had he decided to give out new promotions *now*? He must have been possessed by the last remnants of Slin's cruel jests, which wormed their way out before the changing of the goddess years.

And yes, he was the one who had promoted Shaw, along with five others, to Private in one of his, hopefully, many steps to elevate the Pedites among the other military branches. Now he had to get these green Privates to a point where they could lead their own groups out there.

Apparently, that was asking for a lot.

Shaw and Leon's crews were both missing at least half their numbers, with the other half failing to get their equipment organized. Any of his work with Aldan to see if the soldier had latent wielder abilities also proved a disaster. Thank the goddess it was time to call it quits for the day, though he had half a mind to assign Shaw extra patrol duties for his constant back talk and inability to control his men.

Though it may be Rian's inability to maintain and lead his own men that had caused all this in the first place. His mind was half here and half in the stars most days, and he often felt like a shell of a general on even the best nights. For that reason, he sent both off with stern orders and a few assignments for the evening, confident they would finish in time to enjoy the later part of the celebrations.

The same celebration for which Freya had been standing off to the side, tapping her foot impatiently while aggressively gesturing at the package she'd retrieved hours earlier. He severely regretted going with her to hunt those down in the first place. What a bad idea. What a terrible idea. The worst he'd ever had.

And now...

This stupid jacket was far too tight and clawed at his skin. He should never have let Malin talk him into such stiff material.

It wasn't like they had many options, given the rather short notice. He had every intention of not showing up at all—until his friends ganged up and insisted he come, as they were certain to be turned away without him. Freya made sure he knew exactly how much she wanted to try the buffet and how miserable she would make his life if she didn't get to try the mini meat pies the cook had been boasting about.

That was how he found himself trudging up the winding alleyways that led to the draped castle—at a brisk pace, as it was absolutely freezing tonight and his attire was clearly not built for a single one of the elements, despite Freya mentioning how perfectly it brought out the gray in his eyes.

There had never been this much regret for every single decision in his life until he strolled up the steps of that goddess-forsakened castle that sparkled like a gem in the last of the sunlight. He should have stayed behind.

Opi had nearly taken apart half the tents in his attempt to follow them. That could have been the perfect excuse instead of leaving the poor guy with Aldan. He could have faked an injury or lingering ailment from that cursed mindweaver. Anything to exempt him from this looming torture.

But nooooo. He hadn't bothered with any of those and now found himself outside the stupidly ornate carved doors that surely led to his doom. Why did his friends let him come dressed as one of Slin's jesters? They should have told him he looked ridiculous.

"Stop pulling on your shirt, or you'll rip it," Freya hissed, flashing the guard a winning smile as they passed. She looked so unlike herself, with a dark silver mask covering half her face and a long-sleeved gown that cascaded to the floor in puffs of silver. Her usual braids were tucked neatly on top of her head.

"I have never regretted our friendship more than I have in the past twenty-four hours," Rian bit back.

Malin laughed, then opened his mouth and closed it as the group in front of them passed through the doors. His face resembled a stunned blackbird.

Rian understood. His own breath caught at the sight in front of them. One that any Pedite soldier could only dream of seeing in their lifetime.

The grand ballroom nearly blinded him as he entered. From top to bottom it was covered in flowing black fabric meant to mirror the night sky. Lanterns hung from thin strings, mimicking the heaven's constellations and reflected off the silver outfits like hundreds of shining stars.

The perfect tribute to the star goddess.

"No blocking the entryway," the guard behind them called. There wasn't the usual note of condescension this time. With their masks on, there was a relieving sense of anonymity. Nobody here knew they were undesirable Pedites, only annoying guests in their way.

Refreshing.

Rian looked at his friends, and they nodded encouragement. They entered the room as a group. Together. United.

One single functioning unit, *as planned*. Facing the vicious hordes as one. Having each other's back no matter what. Staying as a pack.

Until—

"Oooh." Freya linked her arm in Malin's, the hue of their silver attire perfectly matching as it was bought as a set returned by some ambassador and his wife. They reminded him of toddlers dressed up by their mother. "Look at that table of sauces for your meat. Only sauces. So many kinds! Let's try them all."

Immediate betrayal.

Neither stopped to check if he was all right with being left behind. They left him to fend for himself without a second thought.

While they helped themselves to the myriad of tables laden with colorful delicacies, he plotted his revenge. He'd make them pay when it came to duty assignment. They'd be shoveling horse manure until it bled from their pores. The pair of jerks.

He turned the opposite way, desperate to make a turn about the room before running out as fast as he could. He'd already had two overly dressed noblewomen eye him up, undoubtedly judging his hastily put-together outfit, and had no desire to endure any more derisive looks from courtesans hunting for their next prey.

At the end of his circuit, he spotted an annoyingly perceptive royal dressed in charcoal-silver chenille, tailored impeccably. Rian took a sharp turn to avoid any conversation with Edmund, whom he'd had enough face-to-face chats with to last three lifetimes. He didn't need to be lectured on how he'd yet again embarrassed the Velotian army thanks to some unknown slight or another.

That could wait for tomorrow.

A small table filled with dozens of different desserts lay before him. Tiers of chocolate-frosted cakes, sugar-coated cookies, and berry-covered pies glistened in the forged starlight.

He reached for a mouth-watering lemon cake when another hand beat him to it. He recognized the pattern of smooth scars visible in the shimmering light, topped with the impeccably rigid angle of a wrist.

"*Excuse* me," he rang out. Somehow, his mouth still managed to work faster than his sluggish brain. "That was my cake."

She plucked it from the silver tray and popped it into her mouth. "Sorry about that," Isla said between unroyal-like mouthfuls. She turned to face him fully, and those chestnut eyes trapped him. "I didn't see your name engraved on it."

"Rude."

"Maybe try the chocolate-layered one next time. I hear it's to die for, if you're into such things."

He inched closer, highly aware that there were eyes on them he couldn't see. "I've had enough brushes with death herself to risk myself over a sweet."

Those red lips formed a pout. "Too bad. I hear it's worth it. Anything is better than being stuck in this place." She gestured at the wall decorations. "What do you think?"

He shifted from foot to foot. "A bit overdone. And I've never been a fan of Hierel. I feel Rallion watches over me more than anyone."

"Same." She let out a small laugh. "Though I am intrigued by the gifts we're supposed to be showered with tonight."

"Yes." He chewed the inside of his cheek. "A night of new beginnings and glorious truths... if you've prayed hard enough. Been a good girl. All the usual things."

"Have you been a good girl?" She snorted, eyes sparkling as much as the lights above. "Enough to discover something new about yourself?"

"Always." A group of laughing men in long coats passed. He ignored the few lingering glances she received. How long until one plucked her attention away? "I better—"

Isla swiftly cut across him. "Did you see the vintry tables? A lot of wine varieties to try. There may be enough to make this night tolerable."

A warmth wiggled in his chest. "I doubt there's anything strong enough, but it's worth a glance."

She scoffed and made her way to the crystal-laden table. He followed about four feet behind, momentarily stunned when she turned to reveal the gaping line of missing fabric down her back.

His insides flipped.

She shifted her head to make sure he followed. "I've already had to turn down dances with rather loud royals from Prominent. One of the few benefits of having a betrothed is that I always have the perfect excuse."

"Where is that rascal, anyway?" A shimmering sea of indistinguishable silver figures pressed in on every side. There was no way Brenner would miss this preening show. He must be here, lurking behind the safety of his relative anonymity.

"Somewhere parading around. Look for the long coat with crystal buttons that are definitely not to Hierel's taste," she said scornfully. "Last I saw him, he was entertaining a group of merchants from Koliat."

A woman with ashy blond hair and a silver dress furnished with multiple cut-outs stepped in front of him. Emerald eyes stared at him behind a pearl-lined mask, scanning him up and down.

Oh no. One look around the woman and he realized he'd lost sight of Isla.

"Divite?" the woman said, a thin eyebrow peeking up past the silver mask. "Or Agicae?"

"Not interested." He stepped around before she could speak again.

There she was. Isla stood about twenty feet ahead, hands on her hips, mouth set in a deep frown.

The emerald-eyed woman looked at Isla, then quickly scuttled away. Even with the mask, it was easy to figure out who she was. No one could imitate that haughty royal glare that could melt the skin off bones.

"You finished with your friend?" Isla asked when he joined her by the wine-laden table.

"Oh, you know." He surveyed the variety of crimson-colored glasses. "Just making plans to meet up later and run away together."

A sharp pain sliced through his foot as a delicate heel dug into it.

"Ouch." He rubbed his sole. Stupid fancy shoes. They provided no protection whatsoever. "I've never seen jealous Isla before. She seems... fun."

She stepped closer, eyes sparkling dangerously. "Want to test her again?"

He smirked. "Maybe. I want to see what she does next."

Isla opened her mouth, then shut it firmly.

A black-badged Siica was at his elbow, staring him down. "Move along, *you*. Princess Isla, your father requests your presence."

If Isla could roll her eyes without actually making the movement, she somehow did. At least the stalwart guard didn't notice.

That was it. Their precious time together, already consumed for the evening.

They actually got more than he expected.

"I'll find him at once." Her eyes moved toward the glass doors leading to the balustrades before she gave him a slight curtsy. "Thank you, Reginald."

With the guard so close, there was no opportunity for even a quick, mumbled goodbye. Isla barely glanced at him before turning away, a cross expression hidden beneath her mask. The Siica followed her into the crowd, disappearing altogether as he tailed her through the silver masses.

Now that was over, Rian made his way outside, enjoying the quiet and fresh air compared to that stuffy room. The stars were out in force tonight, sparkling even brighter than the overdone, fake ceiling. Did Hierel know the mortals below celebrated her name?

And what did she have in store for them this year? Rian knew better than to expect prosperity or good fortune, despite what the old scriptures said. Her timing was too perfect to be anything but an ill omen, lighting the path for Sister Death after her.

He waited several minutes, hoping whatever was keeping Isla would pass quickly. With what he knew about her father, she would be trapped entertaining visiting dignitaries, Brenner likely among them. The king would want to parade her betrothed in a grand display, pushing the story that the pair had returned after a bout of illness waylaid their journey. Meanwhile, they were keen to return to Koliat to complete the bonding.

From what he'd heard from Edmund, their father had pushed for a small ceremony immediately upon Brenner's arrival, aiming to solidify the marriage and alliance before anything else could interrupt them. Brenner had expressly declined, stating they would wait until back in Koliat, where better facilities could accommodate the lavish ceremony as planned.

Edmund said he'd never seen their father so furious, despite his attempts to remain calm in front of the Koliat dignitary. Isla, apparently, was beyond pleased with the turn of events, but careful not to gloat near the angry king... at least, that's what Rian had heard from a completely biased source.

It didn't change the fact that she was somewhere inside, being attended to and courted by someone else. Someone who could give her everything he couldn't. The thought made his stomach turn.

The doors behind him opened, letting the noise of the party filter into the crisp night air. Rian looked back hopefully.

"Just us," Malin said dramatically. "Sorry to interrupt your brooding, but I thought you'd been left alone long enough."

Freya was right behind him, a drink in one hand and a plate of food in the other. "You really should try some of the spread," she mumbled through a full mouth.

A gong vibrated inside the room. It was time. He really hoped he'd get a chance to see Isla before it started, but she must be held up.

The goddesses were never on their side.

"I saw her in there," Freya said, licking her fingers. "Stuck with who I think is Brenner and some other Koliats."

He sighed as a lump formed in the back of his throat. It was foolish to get his hopes up for more than a precious second of her time, especially in this place, where the vultures circled as if fresh bodies were up for the taking.

The garden doors below opened, and guests began pouring outside. They moved onto the balconies and into the gardens like a waving silver sea. As much as the fancy fabric made his skin itch, together they made an impressive offering to the star goddess.

Malin whistled and shoved his hands into his pockets. "You have to hand it to these royal prudes, they sure know how to throw a party."

The crowd's murmuring quieted to a low hum as a group entered the center of the garden. Rian recognized one figure instantly and watched as Isla joined her father and brother, along with a few others he couldn't identify, forming a semi-circle around the white fountain. He'd never be allowed within ten feet of that group.

The hum died out completely as dozens of lights glimmered in the skies above.

It was nearly time.

The changing of the star-years of the goddesses.

Beside him, Freya held her breath, and Malin wrung his hands together. This was new for them all and they'd never experience it again.

The sky exploded with hundreds of shooting stars, more than he'd ever seen over his entire life. It *was* the star goddesses' year, after all. Flashing light after flashing light filled the night sky, while paper lanterns glimmered below, a poor imitation of the glorious display above.

Isla's group each received a lantern, while castle workers spread extras throughout the crowd. Freya looked confused when one was handed to her. If anyone had realized they were lowly Pedite soldiers, the offering to the goddess would have been snatched away faster than the stars above replaced themselves in their turbulent display.

The silver outfits all the guests wore truly sparkled. He prayed it would be enough to appease Hierel.

"What do I do?" Freya whispered, clutching her small lantern, afraid of releasing it too early.

"Just wait until it's over," Rian said.

Malin stood slack-jawed, still staring at the display in the sky. "I've never seen that many before. What do you think it means?"

"That Hierel is awake and ready to cast her judgment and share her glorious truths and—oh—" Freya jumped and nearly released her lantern.

Rian grabbed the paper-thin edge. He didn't blame her. The sudden burst of colors across the sky made his heart skip several beats.

Painted rivers of blues and purples stretched across the heavens, dancing in tune with the plummeting stars that broke past. The ribbons swirled and twisted, covering every visible inch of sky.

The crowd murmured, and several people fell to their knees, weeping in praise to the star goddess.

The hair on the back of Rian's neck pricked as the swirls flowed outward like vines—or flowers—before transforming into colorful flames.

Malin still didn't move. "What in the..."

The last time Rian had seen the sky this lively was months ago, in Murat. This display was ten times as spectacular. Hierel must surely be reveling in her glory tonight.

Freya craned her neck. "It's magnificent."

The pattern above twisted and curled into the shape of a bird before bursting out one final time. The colors faded into the black canvas, taking the stars' light with them.

It was strangely dark now, save for the soft glow of lanterns rising slowly into the night as attendees released them one by one. It was impossible to tell who sent up which lantern, but his eyes followed one in the middle that twinkled specially for him. A stupid thought, really, but he let his mind indulge the fantasy. It was the start of a new star-year, after all, and the Goddess Hierel was all about new beginnings and blessings from above.

More lanterns joined those already floating, and light spilled across the marble balustrade as the group around them completed their turn.

Rian shifted on the balls of his feet and caught his calluses against the soft fabric of his pants. Nobody said anything, so surely now was the time to release it. Right?

Malin raised an eyebrow, asking the same question.

The group next to them practically threw their flickering lamp into the air. Hierel wouldn't have appreciated the haste or lack of decorum. Releasing even a small paper light carried weight and hidden pressure for some.

Not him. He used to be afraid of the gods. Used to be.

That didn't mean he was above sending an offering every now and then—to make sure they stayed far away from him.

Freya turned to them, holding out the lantern. "Together?"

Rian grabbed the edge, and Malin mirrored him, forming a small circle around their offering. "As we always do."

"Now?"

They released at the same time, watching the lantern drift upward, joining its siblings in the sky and echoing the celestial display Hierel had painted for them.

Hundreds of glowing lights floated against the onyx sky, maybe more. They seemed to glare down at him with the weight of the star goddess herself. He couldn't tear his eyes away, almost hypnotized by the sparkling gaze. The others were just as captivated.

They stood there among the partygoers, frozen and watchful, until the last of the lanterns faded.

Rian lingered even longer and was only brought back to the ground by a tap on his shoulder.

The emerald-eyed courtesan had returned for another attempt. Before she could speak, he shoved Malin at her, who looked suitably pleased with the arrangement. A tall, dark-haired man approached Freya and led her away to dance.

Not a single ounce of jealousy stirred in him, as it might once have, at being abandoned. Tonight, he preferred solitude above all else, even as he felt undeserving to stand among the royals, courtiers, and merchants who basked in the king's favor.

If the king knew who he was, and what he'd done, there was no way he'd be allowed in. The mask on his face offered some comfort as a small shield of anonymity.

He may have stood there for an hour. It was impossible to tell. The raised pitch of voices and the quickening tempo of music told him the party was still in full swing... it may continue until dawn's first rays.

He spotted Malin and Freya near the dance floor, Malin juggling a drink in each hand while gesturing far too animatedly for a sober guest. Perfect timing to slip away before either of his friends noticed.

Drunk partygoers littered the first hall, but he memorized a short-cut and, with a few swift turns, he stepped into an abandoned corridor. The party's buzz dimmed, though his ears still throbbed in time with the distant music.

Before he could take more than five steps, a pair of hands shot out from behind a dark pillar.

Twenty-Five

Beretta

If she had to spend one more hour in this goddess-forsakened dirt tent, she'd use the next stale loaf they gave her for a meal to slit her own throat, no matter how long it took.

If the timing she kept in her head was correct, her next paltry meal would arrive shortly. She silently prayed to the goddess of fortune that it would be the slimy-haired soldier again.

They thought the disgusting food and frigid floor would break her. They were wrong. She had survived the first of Rallion's gates before. She'd spent months under that mountain and years at that cruel *academy* under much worse conditions. This was nothing compared to either of those.

The one unprepared for this—untrained for this—was her prince. He suffered here, and the soldiers confirmed it. She had to get him out before it was too late.

Footsteps dragged along the floor, uneven with every other step indicating the soldier was hiding a slight limp. Her heart skipped a beat. It was him.

The flimsy entrance was ripped open, revealing the slimy soldier with the double-sword badge on his uniform. She was surprised they entrusted prisoners to such low-ranking troops. She had felled countless of these soldiers on the battlefield over the years, and none had ever impressed her.

Just like this one.

Bumbling idiot.

And yet he'd been assigned to watch over her tonight.

The approach carried far too much confidence, as if he believed her completely defeated. He barely looked at her as he set the food down, eyes constantly darting toward the entrance, where the muffled sounds of the party filtered through.

It was the Celestial Solstice. The beginning of Hierel's year. The start of his distraction.

She kept her head hung low, staring at her filthy boots, as if all thoughts had been swept from her mind. Yet a surge ran through her body, from her core to the very tips of her fingers.

The changing of the star-years was underway, and whatever gifts Hierel planned for the mortals of this land were beginning to spread.

Every new star-year carried this same pulse. A subtle, almost imperceptible flow of power that Beretta had trained her mind to sense. Whether others felt the goddesses' sight and touch like she did, as the barriers wavered and thinned, remained unknown. Either way, she'd been waiting for this night, praying that Hierel's year would yield the results she so desperately sought.

Her focus remained on a questionable stain on her boot, though her mind was nudging at the wing-eared, idiot guard delivering her food. Carefully. Slowly. At first. In case her weeks of prodding at this particular weakling hadn't yet taken hold.

The burn of the firestone chains was like shards of ice scraping along her veins, but she was determined to push through. She'd seen enough in that fleeting glimpse of the general's mind to know they were running out of time. Once the king discovered their presence, there would be no escape for Devlin. It had to be today. And it had to be this soldier.

He was the most brain-dead of all, his thoughts always wandering a thousand leagues away. Tonight, he lamented being stuck on guard duty while others enjoyed lavish parties in the castle or the encampment.

Distractions were exactly what she needed on this most blessed of nights.

The time for waiting was over. She knew her mission and had to see it through, no matter the cost. There was no more room for delay.

The soldier, Shaw, as they called him, kicked the still-full plate from this morning to the side. Her stomach screamed, but she refused to look. She'd gone longer without food before. This was a drop in the well compared to that.

She didn't flinch when the plate clattered against the side of the tent. Neither did she wince when he inched closer and crouched in front of her, that nudge in his mind turning into a web of curiosity. One she had planted ages ago, long before her capture. It was almost too easy how quickly the thought had taken hold, nurturing itself and growing quietly over time.

The urge to leave pain flitted up, but she pushed it down. If he knew what she was doing, it would all be over.

There would be time to play later. After she got Devlin to safety. This required too much careful planning. Sneaking that seed into the general's mind had taken painstaking work to remain discreet. The thought that he wasn't good enough, that he wasn't worthy of his new title. That it would be wise to prove himself by uplifting some of his men. This one, in particular.

She shifted in the dirt under Shaw's gaze, keeping her eyes firmly averted.

"Not hungry today?" he asked, tilting his head to get a better look at her. Curiosity bubbled and churned behind his glossy eyes. He stepped closer, crossing the safety of the firestone ring, and grabbed her chin.

His stupid, dark eyes sparkled with unabashed lechery. If she reached out to touch his thoughts, she was certain it would upend her stomach.

Perfect.

He continued as if her silence were some kind of confirmation in his putrid mind. "They'll send someone in if you don't eat. Someone worse. Someone not as nice as I am."

As if she could ever be afraid of them.

They wanted her alive. Both of them. That much she had ascertained the moment they were captured. It made them desperate. Sloppy. Just like their need to hide their captives from those that stayed behind the castle walls.

If Hierel graced them tonight, they'd be long gone before the party was even over.

Another uneasy shift under the soldier's heavy gaze. His sweaty hand still held her chin, thumb tracing lazy circles along her cheek as he waited for her submission.

Disgusting fool.

Another tug on his mind, and she was nearly fully in. She lifted her eyes to meet his, flashing the smile that reminded Devlin of a feline right before it pounced.

This dense soldier almost caught it for what it was. He startled back, shuffling his feet and breaking the circle of crushed firestone around him. The distraction was enough to slip past the fragile barriers in his mind... and they were some of the weakest she'd ever encountered.

But she wasn't as cruel as the others made her out to be. No, she was different from the other one they'd brought in.

She pressed further against his mind, scraping along the edges of his consciousness so he felt each tendril sting. She couldn't help herself as she drank in the brief surge of pain that radiated off him. The only way to stop it would be to release her from these chains. That thought floated in and attached itself to his mind. The all-consuming desire to release her... maybe she'd be grateful. Maybe she'd even reward him for his valor, and he was certain she knew exactly how to extract the most pleasure from any offering.

Her mouth knew the best places to find, and he imagined the way she'd crawl into his lap and melt into him. Those soft hands would run all over his chest, removing the buttons one by one. Delicately, but in a hurry so they wouldn't be caught. Just as those luscious lips would trace every inch of his body, stopping at all the right places.

They could be discreet, and his commanding officer would never have to know. She'd never tell.

He touched her soft skin, wanting more. *Needing* more.

The bulge in his pants tightened painfully against his leg, desperately craving release. Something only she could give him.

But he'd have to remove the chains to get all that and more. And she would show him how grateful she could be, he was certain of that.

His hands trailed down the front of her dirty shirt, wanting to free the buttons there. Needing to undo every single one, like she would do the same to him. Then he could release her from the confines of this old jacket.

But not while she was still in those pesky chains.

Once he removed them, she would be *all* his for however long he desired. Nobody would check on them for hours. Nobody would know.

All they needed was the removal of these simple chains. That was it.

His hand moved on instinct. Reaching within his jacket for the key—then she could *finally* kill this imbecile.

The hand froze. Shaw blinked.

No. No. No.

Godsdamnit. She was almost there. So close.

His eyes, once glazed, now flashed as realization hit him. He shook his head slowly, aware that his thoughts were not entirely his own before. Then something hard struck the side of his head.

Chains clanged against each other and his sluggish, infiltrated mind couldn't react fast enough before she had them looped around his neck.

He kicked and twisted, fighting hard against her. But she was trained for this. Frail as she might appear, she pinned him, legs wrapped around his torso, cutting off any precious air in his lungs. There would be no escape and no calling for help.

As his lips started to turn purple, she reached out one last time, relishing in the pure terror she felt. The surge of control emboldened her, strengthening her more than any meal could.

The pain flashed and the struggle ended. She released the hold and shoved his lifeless body away.

"Pathetic," she spat, turning him over to hunt for that stupid key.

The chains clattered to the ground, and she dusted herself off, admitting she might be a little rusty after all. At least she had gotten it done.

Pure, blissful relief spread through her body as the fetters suppressing her power were fully removed. Gods, she had missed this.

She was alive.

After helping herself to the soldier's dagger and longsword, she gave his body another kick, a payment for having to expose herself to his disgusting mind for as long as it took. Though, she had planned on using him to gain access to her prince's tent. Now she'd need to come up with another method... and quickly.

Every movement she made sent a small rush of power heating her veins. The solstice was definitely upon them.

As was Hierel's grace.

For how else could she be standing outside her prince's tent with no guards in sight? None, except for those she'd already convinced to check out the light show for themselves, unhindered by the glow of the camp.

If she had more time, she might have paused to admire Hierel's heavenly display. But Beretta knew it was a gift from the goddess:

a distraction that graced wielders with a fresh surge of power... and she wasn't one to squander a blessing from the star goddess.

There was no time to waste, so she burst through the tent, her boots nearly freezing to the ground.

The man in the dirt was nearly unrecognizable. That usual straight-backed posture and swaggering grin were all but memories compared to this hunched over, grime-covered, tattered-uniformed wearing prince. His eyes were dull and his cheeks sullen. What had they been feeding him?

He didn't even look up when she entered.

"My prince," she breathed. In two swift movements, she was on her knees in front of Devlin, kicking away the layer of firestone and tugging at his chains. The firestone burned the bones inside her fingers, but she pulled them, using the dagger to pick the lock before throwing the chains across the tent.

She grabbed his chin and forced his eyes upward—softer and kinder than that soldier had been with her. There were no signs of injury or malaise on his face. After a moment, the prince's eyes lit up in recognition.

"How?" he croaked, the effort sending him into a coughing fit.

She twisted every way, looking for water or anything to help him, but there was nothing in this dirty tent.

"We need to get out of here." She grabbed his shoulder, but he refused—or couldn't—move.

He leaned against the tent pole and sighed, the motion deflating his chest. "I can't anymore."

"Yes, my friend... you can and you will."

She closed her eyes and moved her hand to his shoulder, allowing warmth to flow from Hierel's blessings down to her fingertips.

The days spent in the dirt and cold were nothing against his strong will. He'd undergone tough days on the road, and this was no differ-ent. His body was tired, but it could endure. He was strong. That painful hunger and thirst were nothing against years of discipline and planning... and he couldn't let it all go to waste now. He *would* rise and walk out of here as if it were merely the morning after a hard ride.

Beretta pulled the contact, feeling shaky.

Overwriting pain was always difficult. She wasn't trained for this type of work, and it felt as if she took some of the pain into herself as payment. It was worth it.

Devlin shook his head and released a breath, steadier and stronger than before.

He rose to his feet, tugging her along. Despite being coated in layers of dirt and grime, his nostrils flared, and his eyes flashed with that old malice she'd missed.

There were no mumbled words of thanks from her prince... not that they were needed. It was her duty, and she'd gladly bear the discomfort and headache already tugging at the recesses of her mind.

Pain could permeate her body later. She refused to bend to it while still in the stench of this cursed encampment.

"Let's go," she mumbled, clenching her hands at her sides. "I don't know how long we have until those useless guards return."

"Give me the sword," he said.

She passed the scabbard over, keeping the dagger for herself.

They rushed outside, the prince barely glancing at the dancing skies. Was he already feeling the surge from the goddess like she had or were his effects more subtle?

The idiot guards were still away, but others lingered nearby, distracted by Hierel's display. There was nothing but blessings on this perfect night.

The city walls loomed behind them, along with the repulsive draped castle. They needed a pair of horses to make their escape as quickly as possible.

"Have you lost your mind?" he seethed at her suggestion.

"We need to get as far away as we can before they send scouts after us."

"I'm not leaving without her," he said. "We can't go back now. They're at the ball. It'll be easy to slip in."

"I don't care what your mother wants. We can't risk you getting caught again, especially by those inside the castle. We'll never get a chance like this again."

They wouldn't get so lucky twice. They'd deal with Queen Grimha's wrath and Devlin's disappointment later. Beretta could take the brunt of that eruption.

At least they would survive. That was all that mattered. Her mother's sister had possessed similar powers and disappeared thirty years ago after failing an assignment from their now-queen. Beretta had no intention of letting the same happen to her and would do everything in her power to ensure they both made it out.

"I don't care. We are going in." His eyes scanned the twenty-foot wall ahead, as if he hoped to scale it right then and there. "They kept us out here because the king doesn't know. Think, Beretta. Use your head. They won't be looking for us. It's our *only* chance."

"No." They'd get caught and handed over to the Velotian King. That place was too well guarded, the princess especially. Plus, there were factions of zealots still in this city who could be anywhere. "We. Are. Leaving."

"You can go if you want," he said over his shoulder, his eyes darting around in search of anything to help him get in. "I have a mission—"

"And my mission is to ensure you don't kill yourself in the process."

She grabbed him, submissive thoughts flowing to her fingertips, but he snapped his arm out of reach.

The pure venom on his face startled her.

"Don't you ever try that again." His voice was low and dangerous. She recoiled.

"I know you don't want to return with this failure, but we need to think clearly right now. We can regroup once we are at a safe distance and come up with a new plan. If we rush in now, we are as good as dead. It's not worth your life."

He scratched the scar on his chin, eyes darting around dangerously as he contemplated her idea. She'd given him too much adrenaline, and she needed to find a way to bring it back down before he doomed them all.

All of this, to get to *her*. All because an ancient seer had once foretold a union of the two houses would bring forth the reckoning of the goddess Rallion herself, all thanks to the Muratian linkage to *both* of the sister goddesses. The queen believed it. Her sons believed it and that belief had already cost one of them his life. Beretta was determined it wouldn't claim a second.

The High King's line coursed strong through his son down the Muratian line, and Devlin was certain that a joining with the daughter's line, Rallion's line, would create an unstoppable force, one that could make the goddesses themselves shiver in their havens.

In her opinion, all this would do was bring about the death of her only friend.

Twenty-Six

The Princess

"It's me." Isla removed the hand from Rian's mouth before he decided she was an adversary who needed to be dealt with. She pulled up the shoulder of the too-loose gown that she'd switched with Alynna once everyone had separated.

Gods, it felt like that ceremony had taken forever, and her father was too close to make a break for it earlier. There was no leaving while the skies sparkled from Hierel's warm embrace, especially when it felt like the goddess watched her every move. The hair on her arm still stood straight from the odd feeling she had during the ceremony.

Rian turned around and sighed. Not the reaction she was expecting. "How long until someone catches on to you doing this?"

Isla laughed. Soon, probably, and there would be a reckoning when they did. But she had every intention of making those last few chances count before her father or one of his guards finally caught on.

Even now, they only had precious minutes until she'd have to switch back with Alynna, who was pretending to be sick in the privy. She was determined to make the most of it.

"Sorry I didn't make it out there with you," she said. "I couldn't escape in time. And you took forever to leave that balcony!"

"I was busy watching the show." He tugged off his mask. There was that face she'd been missing all night.

The same one she'd been missing for weeks now. Even though she was still rather angry at him for everything, she didn't want to waste any more time.

Her hands trailed up his chest. The silk was foreign against her fingers compared to the thick leather uniform he usually wore. The fastenings were made out of a similar smooth material and she wondered how easy they were to remove.

She looped her fingers through his, pulling him in for a vitalizing kiss.

"Did you feel connected to Hierel during the ceremony? Like a god?"

He pursed his lips. "Not at all."

Based on the darkness that briefly passed through his eyes, she wondered if he felt that same sensation too. For a terrible moment, her powers had flared up and she found herself wishing she'd brought those blasted gloves with her.

At least she'd managed to keep it in check. She wasn't expecting—whatever that was—to happen with the skies. It caught her off guard, but none of her father's guests noticed. Edmund gave her a worried glance before continuing his charade of ignoring her presence as planned... or maybe not planned, just the same as usual. Things were always confusing with him, even now.

Gray eyes trapped her gaze. "Did you enjoy the party?"

She shrugged. "It was alright. But my mind was someplace else. *With* someone else."

"Ah, I see." His eyes sparkled. "Brenner?"

"Hierel's gifts speak true." She chortled, releasing his hands. "How did you know?" Her heels hit the cold wall. "He's been relatively..." The proper word lingered out of reach. "Subdued? Quiet?"

"Plotting perhaps?"

A smile ghosted across her lips. "Likely. What he's planning is anybody's guess. He was more busy schmoozing rich land owners from Shiaarl to pay attention to me." She grabbed the edge of her skirt and swished it back and forth, watching the material glisten and shine. "Did you really get me all alone in here to talk about Brenner?"

"Hey," he said indignantly. "You were the one who accosted me while I was on my way back to camp like a good, innocent soldier. Remember?"

Isla shook her head.

"Then let me remind you, My Resplendent Lady." He closed the distance before she could even suck in a breath.

She didn't need it. *He* was her air. Her sustenance. Her morning sun that cut through the darkest of nights, even if she hadn't realized it before.

He pressed into her, pushing her flush against the wall at her back. If she could melt into his body, she would, but there were far too many layers between them. Her mask bumped against his nose and he paused briefly enough to help her remove it, before returning his lips to hers, right where they belonged.

The blood coursing through her veins boiled and sparked as it made its way, but she was too distracted by the body pressed against hers to care. It was like a thousand stars were lit in her bones and desperately trying to escape. She needed more of this. More connection. More warmth. More... everything.

Memories of that night in the tent were the clearest they've been and she needed a taste of that again. Judging by what she felt between them; he needed the same.

This old room was abandoned and dusty. Closed for the ceremonies and no one would linger past. Alynna was an expert at stalling so, surely, they had enough time.

Rian shook his head. "Not here," he grumbled against the skin at the base of her neck, clutching on to her as if he was equally desperate to keep their connection.

That was nearly enough to send her over the edge and she gripped him harder. "Yes, here. Here and *now*."

She raked her hands over his chest as her heart pumped wildly, needing to burst from its cage and consume her. The groan he emitted echoed in her throat, all while he still ran his smooth lips along her jaw and neck, driving her to the brink of total insanity.

Rallion's cursed name, did he know what he did to her?

"Rian," she murmured. "We don't have much time. Stop playing."

"Fuck," he moaned. His hand slid and cupped her bottom, then it moved down and he started rustling with her many layers of skirts. "Godsdamnit." Eventually he found the hem of her skirt and pressed his palm into her thigh. Slowly inching inwards.

Her skin was alive and thrumming, begging for his touch. Her hips would have bucked if it wasn't for the tight grip he had on her. The hand under her skirt dipped closer, brushing past the fabric of her undergarments. Heat pooled in the bottom of her stomach, leaking everywhere. Taking her sigh as permission, he pressed the perfect spot that made her knees weak. He held her up while continuing to apply that sweet pressure that sent wafts of pleasure along her spine.

Isla tilted her head back and muttered, "Oh, gods."

Rian's laugh was low and throttled. It made her dizzy, unable to focus on anything except him and getting more of him. She closed her eyes and focused on the steady thumping of his heart against hers. It matched her own sluggish pace, singing a melody only their bodies understood.

"I don't think you're praying to the right gods tonight," he said in a gravelly voice.

"Oh?" Her eyes fluttered open. "Am I not?"

"No." He shook his head and captured her lips in his, tugging until it was blissfully painful. Another series of kisses were planted along her jawline. "The only goddess I pray to is right here." He grinned like a predator and dropped to his knees. "And I have every intent of worshipping her the way she deserves."

"What are you—oh!"

The hem of her skirt was flipped up. A kiss was planted on her left thigh, then one on the right. He made his way up infuriatingly slow—she had half a mind to tell him so but anytime she opened her mouth, nothing but small gasps escaped.

Next, his thumbs looped around her undergarments and pulled them to the floor. A cool breeze met her for one second, then his warm lips pressed against her and all she felt was blazing heat.

More. More was needed. She threaded through his hair and tugged—he understood the message. His fingers joined his mouth and her legs forgot how to work. But he kept her standing while pulling her to the edge of the skies and back.

"Rian," she panted, forgetting all other words and thoughts except for his name. It was the only thing that mattered anyway.

He mumbled something and the vibration sent a flit of pleasure across her body. Her back arched and heat blossomed across her skin. "Again. Do that again," she begged.

He laughed, and it had the same effect. Isla closed her eyes and found herself immersed in a sea of fiery sun. Each movement was another ray of desire pulsing through her as ferocious as a shooting star sent from the goddess herself. Surely, this was what it felt like to be worshipped?

A guttural moan formed in the back of her throat. She tried to hold it in, briefly remembering the nearby party. It forced its way out when he cupped her bottom, pulling her to her toes so he could get a better angle.

Whatever noise came out set him off, and he devoured her as if equally hungry. The thought sent her to the edge of the skies, ready to leap off, and fall as freely as the goddesses did.

One last murmur of her name and she did just that. Wave after wave of pleasure hit her, akin to each burst of star against the heavens.

It didn't stop. His fingers worked her through the first explosion into a second eruption that surely sent the entire castle grounds shaking.

When it was over, he lapped at her juices, taking his time. The thought of him devouring her climax and actually *enjoying* it sent her fingers tingling.

"You taste delicious, princess," he said huskily. "So good." He pulled her undergarments up and pressed another kiss through the thin fabric. She tugged him to his feet and pulled his mouth to hers.

That glorious mouth knew every inch of her body and soul. It knew exactly how to twist her mind so perfectly. She licked the inside of his mouth, wanting to see what she tasted like. And he was more than willing to oblige her exploration.

Hardness pressed into her, and her stomach tumbled again. She needed to feel him. To taste him. To have him inside of her and a part of her.

Her hands moved from his hair and roamed his hard chest. The silk material rumpled underneath her touch and though it was thinner than a petal, she decided that it needed to be removed. Yes, that was an excellent idea.

Voices echoed from the nearby hall and she sucked in a breath.

The party. That sounded close.

Rian's eyes flashed and he rested his forehead against hers. She stared into his glazed gray eyes until the rambunctious partygoers' voices faded into oblivion.

This wasn't enough.

There must be some way she could convince Edmund to help her escape her room again tonight. Perhaps she could say an idea bloomed on how to break through their visitors. Then, they'd have all the time in the privacy of his tent to continue.

Rian grabbed the back of her hair and tilted her head to find her lips, claiming her. She allowed it, even wanted it. She was fully his and he was hers. Just like that night in his tent.

The boiling heat spread like a fire that refused to be doused. It seemed like he had the same idea as his breath quickened, and she matched its pace.

His other hand found its way back under her skirts. The first touch sent a ripple across her spine and her hands twitched against his chest.

Rian jumped back, hand touching his silver shirt, and all contact was replaced by frosty air.

Shock filled his face before he wiped it away, dropping his hand, but it was too late. She'd already seen what he was trying to hide.

Shame. Ruthless shame filled her, shattering all the light in its path.

Not again.

The tips of her fingers were already returning to their proper color. The darkness faded quickly this time.

"I am so—"

"No, it's fine," he said quickly. Too quickly. "It doesn't hurt."

The way his face had twisted in surprised pain when it happened told her that was a lie.

She turned her head to stare at a shiny tile next to her toe. What an idiot she was to think she had control over this. That she could pretend everything was fine. Just when she'd dropped her guard, *this* happened. And she'd already seen the marks on his neck that he'd tried to hide from her.

The goddesses had cursed her since the day she was born.

"Don't do that," Rian said. "Don't get in your head."

"If you could cause the harm that I do and *have* caused the harm I did, you'd be the same."

He tilted his head with a wry smile.

"Sorry," she whispered.

Death and destruction were familiar friends to him but it wasn't the same. The havoc her powers thrust upon innocents was different... and it continued to grow despite her attempts at stifling it.

That time in those mines and the way her mind had been twisted had warped her powers. There was no other explanation besides that she was cursed by Rallion herself.

This was no way to live. And what would happen once she was married to Brenner? The marriage scars on her wrists were the least of her problems now. She could accidently kill him and start an even greater war for her family. And Edmund... he'd be left to—

A calloused hand cupped her cheek. She hadn't realized he'd closed the gap again. "I said don't get lost in your head."

For some reason, she couldn't meet his gaze. Couldn't bear to stare at those gray eyes which sparkled like Hierel's stars.

"You're insane, Rian. Why aren't you more mad about this?"

"I can't be mad at you, Isla. Remember what we talked about in that forest many moons ago?" She nodded. "Don't let it consume you. You have to fight to move forward and that's more important now than ever. My father... he gave up easily. He wanted more in life but never could find the way to achieve it and merely lived a half-life. It consumed him... until it didn't anymore."

A lump became stuck in the back of her throat. Rian barely talked about his father, preferring to keep that part of his past buried away. She placed a hand over the one covering her cheek, wishing to soak up that never-ending strength he seemed to possess and claim it as her own.

"My father wasn't able to conquer the demons in his mind and in a way, he allowed it to kill him. I was once the same way and not even my friends could pull me back. And that's when I met the worst assignment in the ten kingdoms." She cracked a smile. "I don't want that to happen to you. It's not a way to live."

"But... it's getting worse," she breathed, barely above a whisper lest the goddesses listened.

The words she'd refused to admit for fear it would materialize further, were finally spoken out loud. And it felt like the weight of a mountain was removed from her heart and lungs.

"It's not," he said sternly.

"You know—"

"Don't look at it like that. Your powers are growing, and you need to grow with them and control them. You keep looking at this like a curse and maybe it is." She frowned. "But the goddesses don't control your destiny, only you do. Maybe... maybe in this year of the star goddess where blessings and fortunes abound, while truths roam free, you turn that curse into a blessing. A gift."

A gift?

"Become an unstoppable force and make the goddesses regret ever turning their backs on you."

"I don't know."

"It won't be easy. But you have to." He grabbed her hands and placed them back on his chest without a hint of a flinch or wavering fear. "I know you can do it... and I'll be there to help you."

A lie. They both knew it was a dream built on Wallienne's gifts, as the goddess of sins and lies watched all. It was still nice to pretend.

"You always know the best things to say," she said.

"Doubtful." He chuckled. "Just ask Freya or Malin how abysmal I can be when it comes to my words. They've seen the worst of it."

She dipped her head, pressing her cheek against his ribcage. The sound of his heartbeat was comforting, like thunder on a stormy day that forced them to stay in for one more day. He wrapped his arms around her, holding her so she stayed pressed against him... as if she would ever want to break this contact?

Perhaps Hierel would grace them with a little more time, now that it was her year. Didn't she owe Isla that much at least?

"How much longer until you need to go?" he asked.

She closed her eyes. "I have time."

"Liar."

It had already been more than the five minutes she'd promised Alynna. At this point, with her muddled brain and confused thoughts, she was half-tempted to throw down with Slin and never return. How much damage would her father truly inflict if he found out—

"Hey!" a sharp voice called out. Isla blinked in the sudden light that flooded their little escape. An unyielding Siica crashed through the door frame, grabbing Rian by the scruff of his fine silver collar. "Get away from the princess, *you*."

Twenty-Seven
The General

Not good.

The grip on his neck was tight and the thunder of his heart was dizzying. Both burns on his chest and arm throbbed dangerously, but he knew better than to fight back against a fully trained Siica—an extremely irate one at that.

Isla tried pulling her hood up but it was already too late.

Stupid idiot. He knew this was a bad idea and that someone could find them at any moment. His refusal to listen to his thick head cost him.

"This man was just helping me with…" Isla trailed off, mouthing silently as she searched for some reasonable explanation that would satiate the Siica's fury—her *father's* fury. Anything. Anything would do.

"The princess had fallen faint and I was helping her."

"Not likely," the Siica said in a deep voice. "You're going to have to do better than that, Pedite."

Godsdamnit. They knew who he was.

So much for anonymity at this thing. Though, he couldn't fault the Siicas for knowing who every guest was under the mask. They were sworn to protect the king and his family from all kinds of threats.

From the king's point of view, *this* would definitely fall under that category.

He would be hanged for sure. There was no way he could do lashes. Not again.

"Banin, listen." Isla stepped up to the Siica, placing her hand on his arm but he did not yield. "This isn't what you think—"

"It looks like this vermin was taking liberties, princess," Banin spat out. Good to know the soldiers inside the castle walls still kept their hatred of the lowly Pedites burning all these years. "The king will hear about this and will—"

The Siica's eyes widened and the grip around Rian's neck tightened before releasing altogether. A knife had worked its way completely through his neck, blood spurting from the gash.

The soldier dropped to the ground.

A woman in frayed robes so dark they were nearly gray was revealed behind him, holding the hilt of a bloody dagger with hands covered in scars. Her bulging eyes were focused entirely on Isla.

Oh, fuck.

If there was one way this could have gotten worse, this was it.

The zealot stepped over the body and Rian's hand jumped to his side to find nothing. That's right. They took all their weapons at the castle entrance. Then how did she make it inside with one?

The woman wore a thin smile with darkened teeth. In the corner of his eye, he caught Isla's grimace.

Fiery blood pounded against his skull. "I'll kill you if you touch her."

The zealot's smile turned into a twisted laugh. She tucked the dagger into her robes and flourished her hands. Every inch of his skin prickled. He already knew what was coming. She was a wielder and he didn't wait around to find out which kind.

With no real weapons on him, he charged and tackled her to the floor, not even registering whatever Isla shouted.

He punched every inch of the wielder he could reach and tried grabbing her hands to stop whatever was coming but she writhed out of his grasp every time. She kneed him in the stomach and he was winded.

"Fuck," he wheezed, grabbing her shoulder and trying to pin her to the ground. One of her loose fists made contact with his temple and he lost his grip. She wiggled out from under him, placed both hands on either side of his head and screamed.

The wielder's hands glowed and he was blinded by a violent flashing light. A *painful* light.

A *lightwielder*, godsdamnit. That was what Isla was trying to warn him about.

He kicked her off, blinking fervently to try to see but there were only black spots and dark waves. Nothing else. He heard the wielder's ragged breath when she swiped and felt the bite of metal across his arm as her dagger grazed the skin.

Without his vision, he was useless. He tripped over something squishy and landed in a pile of warm liquid. He refused to acknowledge what it was.

Heavy footsteps ran at him and the wielder grabbed his collar, something lodged itself into his shoulder, tearing through the muscle and hitting bone. Pain reverberated through him in shockwaves, followed by pure fury and tingling fear.

A dark shape moved in his vision and there was a gargled scream.

The first shape that he assumed was the wielder slumped over, its crushing weight landing on him. Trapping him.

"Rian. *Rian!*"

The second dark shape grunted and the mass was pushed off him. Two hands grabbed his face but he brushed them off, crawling through the pool of what must be blood that he landed in and feeling around for the wielder.

The touch of her skin was still warm. He fumbled around until he found her wrist to check there was no pulse.

"Are you alright?"

"What happened?" He found a second dagger in the woman's stomach. Even without his sight, he recognized the hilt of that old blade. "Thank you," he breathed. "That was a close one."

Those soft hands returned to feel around his body, lingering on the gaping wound on his shoulder. "Too close." He hissed when she pressed against the wound. "Quiet, you big baby of a soldier. We need to stop the bleeding." Something ripped and then more pressure returned as she wrapped his shoulder. "Do you see that?" she asked sharply.

"I can't see." He rubbed his eyes, pressing in to the point of pain before his hands were removed.

"Don't do that. You're covered in blood. You're a mess."

"Thanks for the compliment." He chuckled, holding a now icy shudder. When did it start to get cold in here?

Isla muttered something incoherent. Her hands lingered on his arm, warming him from the inside out.

"We need to call for help," he said sharply. What if there were more of them?

"In one minute," she said a little too calmly. "Let me clean you up a bit."

"I think that's the least of our worries." He allowed her to help him up, slipping on the liquid beneath his feet.

"Then let's move away from the blood and bodies," she said.

It must have been a sight to see. He was briefly glad that his vision wasn't working at the moment. "Nice job with that dagger," he said. "I didn't see but I imagine it was impressive."

"Hardly," she said wryly. "You'd have multiple notes on my form. I was lucky and she was distracted."

"Good work, still," he mumbled, leaning against the stone wall for support. He attempted to move his shoulder but it sent painful waves down his arm.

Definitely not going to do that again. Isla pressed her fingertips against his chest, keeping him in place when footsteps echoed down the hall.

His heart skipped once, then twice as they waited to see who they belonged to. Not having his vision sent all his instincts off-kilter. Did those sound like Muratian boots or Velotian ones? It could be another wielder come to finish them off.

Isla stepped away from him and let out a deep breath. A sigh? "Kaevin. Cale," she whispered. Her voice cracked and let out an over dramatic sob that he'd heard her use ages ago, before they ever got lost in the Black Forests of Murat. She *was* good at this.

"Princess Isla," one of the voices said. They must be Siicas or castle guards. "We heard a commotion."

A third pair of boots lingering at the door turned on its heels as the owner sped off down the hall, hopefully to find reinforcements. Good. There was no telling how many other zealots wandered these halls. She wasn't safe.

"What happened to Banin?" the second voice said sharply. "May Rallion guide him through the gates." The boots scraped against stone as that one bent to examine the bodies. "Heresy," he whispered, spotting the zealot's burn marks for the first time.

The first pair of boots was closer and had positioned himself between where Rian slumped against the wall and Isla. "The Pedite," he whispered. Rian imagined his face was set in a condescending grimace as he said that.

Good to know all the Siicas and guards were told to look out for him and his friends. Despite being invited by the Prince of Velotia, they were still as unwanted as ever.

"Did he have a hand in this, princess?"

"No," Isla said in a firm voice. "I was taking a walk—I wasn't feeling well, you see, and Banin helped me find a quiet space when this—this woman." Another crack of her voice and Rian wished he could see the face she was pulling now, trying to convince the Siica she was a helpless princess on the verge of complete hysterics. "This woman attacked us." A deep sob. "She killed Banin and the soldier heard and came to help."

Rian didn't need his vision to feel the heat of the Siica's gaze on him, formulating his own explanation for why he was in that hall.

"He saved my life," Isla breathed. "Without him she would have—I would have—I'd be..."

"Here, princess." A soft rustle of wind and the shaking of fabric. "You are covered in blood." He must have given her his cloak to cover up and, even though he knew it was stupid, the thought sent a pang of jealousy through Rian.

"I—I fell," Isla said. "And now it's everywhere! Gods, get it off me."

"Calm down," Kaevin said softly, as if speaking to a child. "We will find your ladies to help you in a moment. First off, we need to deal with *him*."

Again, that glare burned through the darkness of his vision.

"Yes," Isla said. "He needs a healer. We need to fetch one immediately."

The silence before the Siica spoke indicated that was definitely *not* what he meant. He must be mulling over his words very carefully. "Certainly, princess. We'll see to it that he is properly taken care of."

Rian picked up on the begrudging tones. If he had his vision right now, then he'd already be halfway back to the encampment before anyone could question him further—or the dungeons. With darkness obscuring everything, he was as useless as a newborn. Moving would make things worse, and there was no way he'd find his friends like this. It was his first time in this castle and he had no desire to blindly wander.

If only he could see himself right now. He wished he could see Isla to make sure she was alright and not only saying that to keep him calm.

More footsteps vibrated. This reminded him of the time his dad blindfolded him and his brother for their practice. Naturally, they fumbled around like fools and complained about it for hours. Who would have guessed that it would come in handy one day?

There were at least a dozen pairs of boots. It was hard to figure out what voice belonged to who when they were all strangers. Rian stayed against the wall while several voices spoke at once, mostly directed to Isla and the Siicas who had moved closer to watch over her. He told himself they lingered close in case more zealots showed up.

"What in Laian's name is going on here?" a new voice cut through. There was a palpable shift in the air as voices paused mid-sentence and cloaks rustled as bodies straightened. Even Rian's tired bones begged to adjust based on the cool authority in that voice.

He still couldn't see her but felt anxiety pouring off the spot where Isla stood.

All Rian could do was remain as still as possible and hope to go unnoticed.

"Who's that?"

Godsdamnit.

"The Pedite," Cale said. "He helped the princess, *supposedly*."

Rian winced. The frosty glare was on him, scrutinizing every inch, including his too-shiny fancy outfit, and judging him unworthy. The remaining gazes in the room shifted to him.

"Ow." A soft shudder as someone dropped to the floor. "I think I twisted my ankle."

The scrutiny shifted away from him and an embarrassing breath of relief worked its way out.

"Fetch a healer, you imbeciles."

"One is already on the way, Your Grace."

"It's not too bad," Isla said. "I slipped in some—some *blood*." The last word was overly high-pitched.

"Whose cloak is that?" the king said sharply.

"Mine, Your Highness," Kaevin said, his voice hitching slightly. "To afford the princess her privacy and hide the blood."

Isla took a sharp breath that Rian could hear vibrate around the room. She must be an equally disturbing sight to see, though Rian guessed he looked worse.

New footsteps approached and Rian instantly recognized one.

"Father. *Isla*! I came as soon as I could." Edmund's voice swept into the room, crossing the distance to where Isla had dropped to the floor. "We have the healer."

"It's only my ankle," Isla said. "But it's feeling much better. The soldier was injured in my rescue."

"I want him gone, now," the king said.

"Wait!" A body shuffled closer to Isla but Edmund stopped them. What was he playing at? "Heal him quickly, then he can be on his way."

A rough hand grabbed his shoulder, sending spikes of pain flooding out of his wound that were quickly silenced as the healer's magic worked its way. He was given only thirty seconds of healing and knew the wound hadn't fully closed before the king ordered him to stop.

"I want a full investigation of how this transpired," the king said. "I want names of who allowed our defenses to lax."

"What about his face?" Isla said to a deaf room. "His eyes are burned."

"I'll lead the investigation," Edmund said. "Send this one back to the Pedite camp. Find the other two that were with him—you know who they are—and they will take him back. There are healers at the camp who can help."

"But—"

"And keep him away from our guests," the king added sharply. "I don't want the sight of him causing a stir, tonight of all nights."

"Yes, sir." A guard gripped his shoulder and he was led around the two bodies and away from Isla and the others.

He wanted to reach out to her. To touch her and ensure she was in one, safe piece. For now, he'd have to trust Edmund to keep an eye out, even if it warred with every instinct he held, and despite the insufferable prince dismissing him so quickly. It's not like there was anything he could do to Isla with what seemed like half the royal Siicas shoved into that small space.

The Siica released his grip once they were out of the hall, though he wasn't certain if it was because he didn't think Rian was a threat or if he was trying to avoid causing a scene like the king had directed.

A second guard joined, with a light hand pressed against his back to keep moving. It was hard to be quick when you couldn't see where your next step was going, and these two didn't help when he stumbled.

The pain from his eyes had expanded to a roaring headache by now, and he half wanted to go back and demand the wielder fix that too, consequences be damned.

But no. He'd be stabbed before he got close.

As the distance between them grew, so did the gnawing feeling in his stomach. Leaving her alone with those jackals was a terrible idea, especially Edmund. And he didn't even see if Brenner was there. He should have checked.

Isla was out of his reach now. The king and Edmund would ensure that.

Perhaps it was for the best, a voice nagged. They were doomed from the start and it was time he came to terms with it. Everything he touched met a dark end, and it would happen to Isla, too. His existence was nothing but a loose anchor, dragging her to the bottom along with him.

The second guard left as they rounded a corner. Based on the thrum of noise that vibrated off the floors and walls, they were close to the party.

"—are supposed to be here, you putrid bag of fleas. We were invited by Prince Edmund himself."

"Doubtful," another voice sneered.

Relief as he recognized that first voice. Malin.

"Rian! Where have you—ohhhhhh fucking hells." The voice trailed off as he caught sight of Rian, burnt, covered in blood, and escorted by the king's personal guards.

Freya's voice came next. "Ah, is there something we need to know about?"

"This soldier is to leave the castle immediately."

"Why?" Freya asked. "What happened to his face? Is that *blood*?"

"Did I ask for questions? It's on the king's direct orders."

Malin snorted.

"Got it," Freya said. Two hands grabbed each of his arms and he felt friendly bodies on each side.

"We'll take it from here," Freya said.

"Back to camp, *immediately*, Pedites. Before the king changes his mind..."

Freya didn't grace him with a response, though Rian pictured the scowl on her face. He'd been on the receiving end of it many times before.

"We thought you were dead," Malin whispered. "Caught doing scrupulous activities or something."

"*Were* you?"

"Was I what?" Rian stubbed his toe on a drop-off they didn't warn him about.

"Caught doing anything you shouldn't have been?" Freya pressed.

"No." He ground his teeth against the brief wave of pain from his head.

"Step," Malin said, guiding him down a flight of stairs.

"I wasn't *caught* doing anything scrupulous."

Freya let go of him and for a second, he thought she was going to push him down the rest of the stairs. Instead, she let out an exasperated sigh. "I told you that's where he was. I *told* you."

"Fine. Fine." Malin steered him around a corner. "You are always right. I'm sorry."

Fresh air hit his face and everything stung.

They stopped and Freya's shoes scraped until she was in front of him. "Nobody's around now. What in Rallion's name happened to you? Why are your eyes so red and why do you look like you went for a bath in what I *hope* is Muratian blood?"

"Not Muratians. One of those crazy wielders." He rubbed his eyes, trying to make sense of the dark blobs that still wouldn't go away. "How bad is it?"

"You look like you stuck your face in Insmia's flame," Malin said. "Can you see anything?"

"Would I be needing your help if I did?" he snapped. He stretched out his shoulder and hoped he didn't break the poorly threaded together skin. "It was a fucking lightwielder."

Malin whistled. "Damn. He got you good."

"She," Rian corrected. "My eyes are burning."

"They look slightly roasted," Freya said. "But I'm sure we can get you mended right up." He felt a light brush of air as something waved in front of his face. "You can't see anything? At all?"

"I can't see your sorry faces, if that's what you're asking... not that I'm sad about it. But it is rather annoying being stuck here useless."

"More useless than before," Freya corrected.

"Thanks."

"We should go before that jerk of a guard returns to run us out of the city walls." Malin paused dramatically. "And you need a bath and a change of clothes. *Desperately.*"

"You're lucky you can't see yourself. You look like Laian's bloody scythe."

Yes. He knew that already.

"Guess we can't sneak back in for a second helping of desserts," Freya added wistfully.

"Actually," Malin said dramatically. "Look what I snuck out."

Rian assumed he was showing her some treats he stuffed into his pockets or someplace questionable based on the resounding 'oooh' that came from Freya.

A new set of scraping boots hurried along and Rian froze, preparing for the worse. He'd never missed his sight more.

"Aldan!" Freya said. "Why did you leave the camp?" She lowered her voice as he skidded into place next to them, cursing when he caught sight of Rian's appearance. "Is there a problem with our *guests*?"

Aldan took several deep wheezes. By the sounds of it, he'd run the entire way to the castle.

Malin's hand left Rian's arm as he aided the soldier. Another pang sliced down the side of his skull and he wavered in place.

"It's the prisoners," Aldan panted. "They've escaped."

Freya gasped. "How?"

"I don't know the details, but Shaw was in charge and never came back from bringing her meal."

Malin cursed every goddess' name, especially Hierel's. That idiot was as good as dead.

"Hush, Malin," Freya scolded. "Not tonight."

Rian didn't have time to chide her superstitious behavior. The goddesses hadn't been on their side for a while and cursing their names would make no difference.

"Fetch us some horses and we can start the hunt right away," Malin said. "Well, *some* of us can."

This wasn't right. How did they manage to slip out despite all the guards and firestone?

None of this added up, especially tonight of all nights. There was something else going on.

"No," Rian said. "We won't need horses."

"What?" Two voices echoed, and he could feel the weight of their questioning gazes directly upon him.

If his vision wasn't already darkened by the lightwielder, then he'd surely be seeing red everywhere. That light scraping against his mind was recognizable now.

The second guard that brought him out. The mindweaver.

They were already here.

Twenty-Eight

The Princess

The warm glow from the healer's hand faded and she blinked the spots out of her eyes. Her heart resumed its slower pace once he backed away, bumping into a second stone slab behind him.

"There you are, Your Grace," the old man said in a raspy voice. Wrinkled hands brushed against his black Agicae uniform. "Any bumps and bruises are all cleared up."

The room they'd brought her was toasty and the walls were much too close for the amount of people stuffed in here to watch as the healer did his work. So much for privacy. Her father didn't even let the first syllable of protest leave her lips before squashing any hopes of dealing with the healer on her own.

"And the ankle?" her father pressed, uncrossing his arms as his polished boots scraped against the shiny tile. He ran a hand through his blond hair, likely missing the presence of his crown on this holiest of nights. "She'll need full use if she's to return to Koliat with all haste."

There it was.

At least he didn't bother hiding the reason behind the rush and faked worry. Nobody showed any signs of surprise at this besides Edmund, whose lips parted slightly. Perhaps he was different with Edmund, but her father hadn't bothered glazing harsh truths from her in years.

"Yes." The healer wiped a bead of sweat off his wiry brow. "Nothing wrong with it now. Must have been a strained muscle. Easily repaired and better than new."

Isla flashed a winning smile at both her father and his royal healer. She rubbed her temples, staving off a headache she didn't have. "Thank you, William. I feel much better now, though the stress of tonight's events have taken a toll on me."

"This should never have happened," her father said over her head, aimed at his two closest advisors.

"Some lunatic bolstered by the changing solstice, no doubt," Commander Baran said. "It's been said to drive the lesser minds mad in some areas."

Tyrone, the king's top advisor with a son he always tried to push onto Isla, nodded fervently, true to his people-pleasing nature. Isla never liked both of them before and especially hated their lingering nature today.

Edmund's eyes whirled as he stared at Isla, trying to pass a message between them. But she refused to look at him for too long and sat still on the cold slab, as if that would help her become invisible.

Yes, she snuck off and they both knew it. Yes, he was mad at her and she didn't care. He could take it out on her when there were less people around.

There was no way of knowing one of those crazed wielders made their way into the castle and managed to find her at the perfect time. At least she'd made it out nearly scratch free.

Her stomach turned on itself. Rian hadn't.

His eyes were so bloody that she worried for a moment back there that the lightwielder had burned them completely. If she hadn't stopped the wielder, he'd be dead instead of blinded. Once he found a healer to take care of him, she prayed to Poron that his sight would recover quickly.

If her father wasn't there, she'd have demanded he healed Rian completely. There was no way to do that without drawing unwanted attention to an already suspicious scenario. The least of their problems was scarring from a crazed lightwielder.

At least the healer stopped the flowing wound in his shoulder—however haphazardly it was—before sending him away. Away from prying eyes. Away from too many questions. And away from a room of vultures who'd leap at any excuse to bring harm to the one who held her heart. She'd never been so afraid as when her father entered that room.

How much did he know or suspect already? It was hard to tell if Edmund had been true to his word. It was even harder to know how long she had before everything collapsed in on her.

A balding head popped through the door. "A change of clothes for the princess, Your Majesty."

Right. It looked like she'd walked through a bloody waterfall and waded in its pools. At least nobody noticed her dress was different. It was hard to tell under the grime and blood and the Siica's cloak which she kept tightly wrapped around herself. Alynna was smart and must have made a quick getaway once she realized what was happening. There'd been no word from either of her ladies since they split up.

A part of her was drenched in guilt for the relief she felt when she remembered the only other person who *actually* knew what happened, Banin, was dead. Now the blame for the wandering princess had fallen solely on the loyal Siica caught in the wrong place at the exact wrong time, thanks to Mannop's cruel swing of justice.

They'd spoken at length about his lapse in judgement allowing Isla to wander down an abandoned hall, and her heart begged to tell the truth and clear the name of the Siica. Yet, her brain knew the cost it would come at.

"Thanks." Isla passed the velvety black dress through her fingers. The Celestial Solstice was over and, apparently, there was no longer a need to appease Hierel anymore.

She preferred black anyway.

"May I be dismissed?" she asked in a raspy voice, feeling a heaviness on her chest.

"No," her father said, threads of venom laced his voice that sent a shudder running over Isla's body. "I'm not nearly done with you."

Edmund peeled himself from the wall. "Father, why don't we—"

"And *you*..." His eyes travelled over his eldest son's face. She'd never seen her father look at Edmund that way. The worst of his putrid looks were usually reserved for Isla. Never Edmund. It was enough to freeze her brother in place.

Baran and Tyrone had both gone still. They waited to see if the king's famous wrath would turn on them or if they'd be spared by the grace of the goddesses.

Luckily for them, his ire was fully invested in his two offspring. "None of this would have happened if you'd have done as instructed and delivered her to Koliat according to our deal with King Everett. You never listen."

Edmund pursed his lips and dropped his gaze. She didn't fault his silence. Their father had always been an intimidating presence throughout their lives. Nothing had changed except the direction of his fury.

"Out." The king jerked his head at his advisors. "Now."

The pair grabbed the healer and couldn't leave fast enough, relief washing across their smug faces.

Assholes.

Those sharp eyes whipped to where Isla stood, still clutching the black dress to her chest. "Don't think for a second that I don't know what really happened here. Why was your lady found wearing your dress, *Isla*?"

Her heart pounded against her ribcage, loud enough for everyone in this stifling room to hear. Any words she wished to speak lodged themselves squarely in her throat and refused to budge for fear of swift retribution. There was nothing she could say to make this better so she settled on biting the inside of her cheek until it bled.

"That bumbling idiot, Carissa, noticed you slipping away after Hierel's display. I know you weren't sick."

Godsdamnit. She knew that leech was going to cause problems for her. They'd need to find out what else she saw.

"What? Nothing to say for yourself."

"Father," Edmund said quietly. "You know about her lady and the soldier. I told you. This isn't the first time Isla's switched with her."

Hot waves of betrayal cascaded over her. What else had he told him?

"It's the last time." Her father leaned forward, his light eyes holding her gaze and she felt years of disdain seeping through that connection. The hatred he had for his youngest all because of something she couldn't control. She despised these cursed powers as much as he did. More, maybe. Her life had been ruined by them time and time again, and yet *he* thought he was the one most inconvenienced.

She held her hands together tightly, pressing them into her stomach in the hopes that her powers would swallow her whole before having to spend another minute under her father's withering glare.

Edmund broke the heated silence first. "Father—"

"Get dressed," the king said. "Now. Before Brenner shows."

"Brenner?" Isla's eyes snapped over to Edmund. He looked just as confused.

What did he have to do with this?

"This has gone on long enough." Their father gestured between them. "Whatever you two are hiding—whatever grand plan you think you are slyly crafting—it's over. The marriage ceremony is going through tonight."

Twenty-Nine

Their father's words echoed in the small room as they tried to process them. Edmund stupidly asked him to repeat himself. Isla was still standing ice-still, lost for words and seemingly trapped in her own mind.

They should have known something was wrong when their father brought them to the medical wing, ordering everyone around with whispered words before shoving them all into this tiny bay with two healing slabs. Normally, he'd have fetched a healer in the privacy of the royal wing. Not here. There was a reason behind every move his father made, and now they knew why.

"You heard me," he repeated, his blue eyes blazing with a fury Edmund had never seen before. "This alliance is balancing on the edge of a cliff and both of you seem determined to jump off at the first gust of wind. I am not about to let everything we've worked so hard for fall apart now."

The king strode across the room, hand on the door when he turned back to Isla. "I said to get dressed."

"No," came a small voice. It was so quiet Edmund thought he imagined it.

His father, unfortunately, heard it perfectly clear.

"No?" The king's eyebrows rose dangerously, hugging the edge of his light hair. "*No?*" He pointed at her blood-stained dress. "Marry him looking like a corpse returned from the gates. I don't care. But you *are* going to complete the ceremonies tonight. Before either of you can sabotage this beyond repair."

"No."

His hand dropped from the bronze handle. "You don't have a say in this, girl."

Edmund winced but Isla remained steadfast and doubled down. "I don't want to marry him. I don't want to go to Koliat. I want to stay here."

"If I have to have you dragged there by force, I will. You either come willingly or you can make things a thousand times worse."

"I don't want this," she said.

"I really don't care." He thrust open the door and called for his advisors to bring the Koliat prince.

He turned back to survey his children one last time, and Edmund wanted to wither away into his own skin. It was only then that he truly realized the years of torment Isla had gone through at their father's hands. Years in which he stood by, happy to avoid their father's ire, no matter the cost to her. When with one simple gesture, he could have fixed everything.

Isla stared at him, silently pleading while a pair of onyx-badged Siicas grabbed her elbows. He was as helpless as she was to deter their father's decision. The same he'd been all their lives.

They were ushered into one of Hierel's temples before either could utter another protest. Isla still clutched the black dress in her hands, refusing to change. He had to give it to her, getting her marriage scars in the temple dedicated to the star goddess, while looking like she had just been dipped in a bloody river was making one hells of a point.

She was quite the crimson backdrop against the crystalline walls that glimmered like the night sky. The sharp arches sparkled shades of purple and blue across the glass floor, adding colorful dots onto Isla's bloody outfit. She'd dropped the Siica's cloak at some point to really *pop* against the backdrop of the holy temple.

Someone had fetched one of her tiaras but she refused to put it on. As nobody wanted to fight with the princess to force her into a new outfit, they let it slide. The irony didn't pass unnoticed.

His father didn't leave their side, after calling half a dozen Siicas to escort them to the sacred temple. It was like he could read Edmund's thoughts and knew his intentions to slip away and attempt to—well, he hadn't gotten that far but was certain some brilliant idea would have popped up once he was clear of his father's ireful gaze.

This was insane.

Their father was past logic and reason at this point. A small part of Edmund didn't blame him, but that was leftover from the *old* Edmund, one he was desperately trying to bury deep and forge anew. Helping his father force through this marriage wasn't something the new Edmund would allow. Yet, he had no power to stop this.

His fists tightened into hot balls at his side. There was *something* he could do... but, yet, he couldn't. The gaze of the goddesses weighed heavy on his shoulders, as they had all night. This time, it felt like they were peering into his soul and casting judgment.

The moment they stepped foot into the temple, Isla spent about five minutes shouting at their father before coming to the same conclusion that there was no reasoning with him and withdrew into herself. Edmund didn't know what she was thinking at this point.

She'd looked at him several times for help while their father berated her but Edmund was equally lost. He'd never seen this side of him before. The king was a man with a purpose and not even the goddesses could stop him tonight. His children certainly couldn't reason with him, and his cowardly advisors wouldn't dare attempt to dissuade him.

There was nothing left to do except wait for Mannop's swift justice.

"What in all twelve hells is going on here?" that annoying voice of Brenner's broke through the putrid silence. The Koliat prince had arrived with a full escort, shoving his arm out of the Siica's grip once he'd spotted King Augustus.

"Ah, Prince Brenner," their father said smoothly. He gestured to join them on the dais, directly in the shadow of a statue of the star goddess and her sister. "Thank you for joining us. Please accept my apologies for the rather rushed summoning."

Brenner's eyes found Isla and they widened. He made his way over. "Princess Isla. What happened to your dress? Are you injured?"

"No, she is quite well," their father answered. "There was a small issue within the castle grounds this evening. The princess was not harmed and those responsible have been swiftly handled thanks to my guards."

That was one way to stretch it.

Brenner's eyes shifted from Isla, who refused to speak, and back over to Edmund and the king, then to the priestess in her flowing ivory robes. "Is there another ceremony to celebrate the solstice? I believe most of your guests have departed."

"Yes, there is to be a ceremony." The king spread his arms. "Considering the events of the evening and the past weeks, we thought that this night would be rather fortuitous to complete the marriage ceremonies."

"The *what*?" Brenner shuffled back, moving to a lower step. "I'm afraid I don't quite understand, Your Grace. Is there to be a marriage ceremony for us to witness?"

"Yes," he said plainly. "Yours." Brenner's gaze shot back to Isla. "I know your family was quite keen on completing the ceremonies in Koliat. However, I believe this is the perfect night to complete it under Hierel's steady gaze."

Brenner's eyes continued shifting around the room wildly. "Forgive me, as I'm not as used to your customs, but is this some poor attempt at a joke? Why is the princess covered in blood?"

Isla opened her mouth.

"This is not a joke," their father cut across. "We have left things up to Slin's cruel humor for far too long. I think it is time we settled this agreement and complete the bonding. You are welcome to throw a grander function upon your return to Koliat—as I believe that is your mother's intent. I think we can all agree that, given the political climate, it is best to tie things up as quickly as possible."

Brenner jerked his head back. It was hard to read his face while covered in sparkling lights from the colored ceiling.

"I mean this with the most respect, but, *surely,* you cannot be serious?"

"I swear upon Rallion's deathful gaze," their father said.

Isla bristled.

"I'm not marrying her in some cursed ceremony in the middle of the night that should be devoted to the year of the star goddess and nothing else." He gestured at the blood-soaked princess, whose stony expression remained unmoved. "Not to mention, she clearly doesn't want this either."

"The princess is upset from the earlier events. Nothing more."

Brenner lifted his chin. "I may be young, but I'm no fool, and I want no part in forced wedlock. This is not a part of your arrangement with Koliat, and it stinks of desperation. Why the rush?"

Their father's carefully crafted mask of casual aloofness slowly slipped away. "I don't have to answer to you."

Brenner stared at the king as if he'd grown an extra limb. "Well, I'm not doing some half-assed rush attempt at this. Do you know what people will say? My parents will never accept this. Our kingdom won't tolerate it."

Edmund had seen many sides of the Koliat prince over the past weeks, but he'd yet to see him furious. What was he playing at?

The king continued on. "Shall we summon your men as witnesses. Will that make you more comfortable?"

"I'm not doing this right now," Brenner said, hands in the air. "Especially considering the state you're in, princess. I'm sorry."

Isla held his gaze for a moment and Brenner slowly nodded as if gaining some unspoken clarity.

"The princess is more than willing—"

"It doesn't look like she is."

"That is of no consequence," the king said. "Are you saying you wish to break your father's arrangement with us?"

"No. Not at all." Brenner took a deep breath, as if steadying himself. "I believe the Celestial Solstice has taken its toll on all of us," Brenner added softly. "My father will *only* accept a marriage ceremony completed in Koliat. Nothing less. I'm happy to discuss this more in the morning once everyone has recovered and cleaned up. Now is not the time and no words you say will convince me otherwise."

The king's nostrils flared but he painted on a forced smile that fooled nobody in that room. "Very well, prince. But if you are insistent, then I'll begin looking into arrangements to expedite your journey as soon as possible. We have a transporter who is strong enough to make the journey over several jumps and it could be completed in less than two days. We shall have you both ready to leave on the morrow."

Tomorrow? *Tomorrow?*

Brenner looked lost for a rebuttal and merely nodded at the king.

Isla's eyes flared to meet Edmund's, and this time he could read the emotion as clearly as if it were written across her forehead. Panic.

There was no way out of this. Not with their father on the warpath. As much as he refused in the past, it was time for drastic measures. Edmund needed to get to the bottom of the terrible truth, no matter how much he wished to remain deaf to it.

Thirty

The Princess

"When do you think he'll get over this one?" Isla asked, holding back a chuckle as she stared at her brother. She kept her voice low, so as not to draw the attention of the shouting voices in the next room.

After the failed attempt at a forced marriage ceremony, Edmund shoved her into a smaller chamber used for personal prayers while her father was distracted yelling at anyone who was close. Good. They all deserved it. And she was more than content to stay away for now, despite the stiffness of their current hideout.

This place was fashioned more like an old courtesan's tearoom instead of a holy room meant for prayers to the star goddess. An altar at the side contained candles that patrons could light in tribute to the goddesses.

"Hm." Edmund rubbed his chin. "Probably the next time Rallion's comet graces the sky."

At least.

Isla lit a candle for a kind old lady who gave her a cloak many lifetimes ago. This wasn't a temple dedicated to Rallion, but it would have to do for now.

Their father wasn't a forgiving one and there would be swift retribution for this, despite it being Prince Brenner who had objected so fiercely.

Another flame for Edith's daughter.

Who would have known her savior would appear, bouncing with untold swagger only to swiftly reject all her father's plots? He was the last person Isla expected to actually *help* them. Thank the gods, that the pompous prince was just as used to getting his way as her father was to getting his own.

While he couldn't lash out at the Koliat prince directly, the king turned his attention to his advisors, and, thank the goddess, Edmund was swift enough to get them out of there before the tides turned against them.

"Well." Brenner burst through the door with a giant glass of whiskey in his hand. "That was all rather stressful."

Isla backed away from the altar and reclaimed her stained spot on the couch.

"What are you doing here?" Edmund said, already standing up to place himself in front of her. "It's fine, Beau." He dismissed his favorite Siica, who followed Brenner in, with a quick wave. "Leave him be."

Brenner took a swig of amber liquid. "I am here to avoid the yelling." He gestured with his thumb at the room next door. "And because—because what the fuck was that? *What was that?*"

Good question.

"I've had a stressful night. I can't deal with your ramblings too." Edmund rubbed his temples and resumed his frantic pacing around the musty-smelling couch Isla was trying to sink into, despite her blood-soaked dress.

"Do you not want a change of clothes?" Brenner asked. "I can summon some for you."

"Edmund," Isla said sharply. Now that they were away from prying ears and watchful eyes, that worry that was gnawing at her since they left the hall now returned in full force. "Have you heard back from the camp?"

"Nothing yet," Edmund said quietly, keeping it vague as Brenner was listening to every word. "I'm certain all the guests have returned for the night. I can send someone to check in the morning."

"Or now," she pressed, catching Edmund's gaze and refusing to release it.

Tomorrow was too far away. So much could happen overnight. She had to know if he was alright. *Needed* to or her body would collapse in on itself.

As long as Ben was able to get to him right away, he should be able to heal his eyes. Her body refused to rest until she knew he was healed and safe. Only then could she relax and stop feeling like prey trapped underneath an iron trawl.

Edmund sighed heavily. He looked exhausted. She didn't care.

"I want you to go. Now."

Brenner looked mildly confused but shrugged and seemed to determine it wasn't worth his time.

A heavy sigh came from Edmund. "It's so late, Isla."

"*Now.*"

"Fine," Edmund said. "If it sets your mind at ease, I will check myself. I'll send word right away. There's something I need to do, anyway." He jerked his head at Brenner. "You two can catch up. I'll leave a pair of Siicas right outside if there is anything you require." He shot a dark look at Brenner before adding, "And don't do anything stupid—that goes for both of you."

As if there was anything stupid she wanted to do with Brenner. *Ever.*

The silence settled in for several minutes after he left. Brenner didn't break it and focused heavily on his amber drink. What was that prince thinking about that insane display back there?

"Thank you," she said finally, staring at her foot. "For what you did back there. I know that couldn't have been easy, especially given my father's overbearing—"

"It's nothing," he said curtly, rubbing his wrist absentmindedly. "I just—wasn't expecting... well, *that*."

She allowed a small laugh.

This was the longest day of her life, and at this point, she'd been through enough dreadful days to last a lifetime.

He held out his drink. "Want some?"

Isla shook her head. She still hated taking drinks from others if she could help it, she barely even tolerated it when Alynna and Susanna prepared a beverage for her.

Brenner sighed. He looked tired. Not exhausted from a long night of partying and whatever that was that her father tried to pull but tired all the way to his core and then some.

Isla was brought up better than to point it out.

"Your father's mad," he said matter-of-factly.

"No," she licked her lips. "He's furious... probably on a murderous war path right now but at least it's not directed at us."

She did not envy anyone in that room. Though, the thought of those self-righteous pricks cowering in fear brought her a small taste of satisfaction.

"For now. Tomorrow's a new day."

That it was. Brenner spoke of her father's wrath like it was a familiar friend. Something he had known all his life. There was only one way someone could truly know what she'd gone through.

She asked, "Is yours the same?"

He hesitated and for a terrifying moment, she thought she'd overstepped. But then, "Not the same. Similar. He has—high expectations. Very high." That was something she knew all too well. "Despite what I'm certain you've heard, we're not *all* the same." He placed his empty glass on the ornate table between them. "We can... make the best of this—our situation."

Isla stretched her feet, feeling the bottom of these too-tight shoes against her toes. Overbearing parents with unrealistic expectations was something she could handle. Everything else that came along with it... less so.

"My father will not give up on this," she said.

"Neither will mine. He is determined for this agreement to go through... as am I," he said quickly. "I don't want what happened in there to sway you otherwise, princess. I still want this. It was the manner in which it came about—so sudden."

"Naturally," she said quickly. Somehow, she found the strength to force a smile. "The same goes for me. When the goddesses smile upon the timing and it's not done in haste."

"Exactly. At the correct moment. Which is *not* in the dead of the night on the Celestial Solstice. We don't want to anger the goddesses, after all. Especially not Hierel or her sister."

"Most definitely not." She'd had her fill of irate gods and goddesses already. She'd had her fill of a lot of things at this point. A yawn forced its way out. "You'll have to excuse me, Prince Brenner, as I am quite exhausted and not feeling myself anymore."

Not to mention that she still wore a blood soaked gown that was starting to harden in uncomfortable places. The couch would have to be thrown out after this.

"Of course, my lady." He jumped up and helped her to her feet, not a single grimace in sight despite her abhorrent appearance. "Is there anything I can do for you?"

"No." She widened her smile. "I need my rest, and I'm certain you must feel the same."

"I am rather tired," he said. "I was not expecting to be pulled out mid-party to deal with a heat of the night marriage ceremony demand. May I call upon you tomorrow—if you are feeling better?"

The smile cracked. "Certainly. I look forward to it."

The moment she left the room, a pair of Siicas peeled away from the shadows to escort her back to her chambers. Isla was too exhausted to protest their overbearing hovering.

At least they left her at the doors to change. Both Alynna and Susanna were gone, likely already having retired for the night, and she declined getting another aid to help ready her bed. It was stupid when she was more than capable of shedding these dirty clothes and drawing a quick bath to scrub her own skin clean.

The bath was freezing but she was in and out of it in less than two minutes. By that time the water turned a murky color, and her mind was clearer than it had ever been.

She had to see him. Needed to see him. To make sure he was alright or she'd never sleep. She may even explode and take half of this castle with her.

There were pants and a shirt that Susanna had set out earlier, and she shimmied into them. The blade Rian gave her went with her everywhere, even in sleep, so she strapped it to her leg for a brief flash of comfort. During the chaos in that hall, she'd managed to grab it from that zealot's body before anyone noticed. Rian would never forgive her if she lost his father's blade.

Where was he now? Was he already healed and resting at camp, or did something terrible befall them on their journey?

What if her father lied about sending him back to the Pedite camp and instead threw him in the dungeon for questioning? She wouldn't put that past the terrible old man that she was related to by blood only.

While she had a brief glimmer of hope for a different life away from him, Edmund would never be free until his death. Her brother wouldn't leave either. No. He would never do that to Velotia, for they had cousins—distant relatives that the crown would fall too in his stead—and both she and Edmund dreaded what would happen if that came to pass.

They both had their parts in this life to play.

Isla twisted her hands through the tangles of her hair. She pointedly ignored the sticky parts missed from her bath, and pretended it was from sweet honey instead of the crimson liquid that followed her everywhere now. She formed the strands into a simple braid that hung over her shoulder, remembering a lifetime ago when this was the only way she knew how to wear it.

The plush mattress and thick pillows called to her tired body. Later. Much later, hopefully.

A couple of pillows stuffed under the blanket seemed to do the trick. It almost looked like someone slept there. Despite the fact that the sun would surely rise soon, she prayed they wouldn't check on her for hours.

She approached the hidden passageway. After this, Edmund's ruse would be up and he wouldn't be able to use the tunnels again. He'd forgive her for this, eventually. If she could forgive all he'd done, this was nothing in comparison.

Her brother couldn't understand that overwhelming urge to ensure the safety of the ones she loved. She doubted he'd ever had anyone he cared about like she did Rian. It changed things.

Changed *her*.

The wall swung open and the stale air almost reminded her of those tunnels under the mountain, except this time she wasn't a prisoner who didn't know herself. This time, she understood everything and had no doubts in the depth of her being that this was the only way.

That tug that she'd followed weeks ago into the dark forest pulled her again and she knew where it would lead. To her salvation.

The first step into darkness felt like glorious freedom against her boot.

Thirty-One
The General

"Are you absolutely fucking certain?" Malin asked for the fifth time. "Like, for sure, for sure?"

"I lost my vision, not my mind, asshole." If Rian knew exactly how far away Malin was, he'd have decked him in the jaw already. The way his luck was today, he'd hit Freya or a wall, and he didn't know which was worse.

"Did you see her—I mean—hear her or whatever?" Malin asked. There was the sound of a palm slapping skin.

Rian groaned. "No. But it was *her*. That fucking mindweaver."

That foreboding feeling he didn't recognize as not fully belonging to himself at the time had to be her. Not to mention the tendril of pain left behind that was her signature move.

"But what about the zealot?" Malin asked. Rian pictured his brows knitted in confusion. "Who sent her?"

"I don't know." Rian shifted from foot to foot, careful not to lose his balance or his concentration, which was difficult with his head pounding and his arm on fire. "Maybe it's the solstice or maybe it's all a giant coincidence thanks to Slin's cursed eye that has been following me for the past three years. Take your pick."

"We need to find the princess," Freya said. The voice of calm reason like always. "Do you know where her rooms are?"

Rian threw his hands in the air and winced as it hurt his shoulder. "This is my first time here too, Freya. It's not like I was given the ground tour of the private resting quarters of our Velotian royalty. After what happened in that hallway, I doubt they'll let me within thirty feet of her again, especially while looking like this."

He pulled the front of his tunic, which started to dry and crust under his fingers.

"Let's find the prince, then," Freya said, ignoring his rant altogether. "Edmund will understand. He can help us."

He sensed the pair exchanging a look between them and didn't like that he wasn't at the capacity to glare back.

"I need a healer first," Rian said.

Malin shifted to the balls of his feet. "Well, let me go find my personal—*we don't have a healer with us*. And no one in this cursed castle will help a Pedite, general or not."

"We don't have the time to find Ben if we want to alert the prince," Freya added. "Malin, take Rian with you and return to the camp with haste and I'll—"

"No!" His arm prickled with frustration. It was hard to tell if it was his or Isla's at this point. "Fine. Fine." He rubbed his temples, hoping he wasn't just spreading more blood around. "Let's find Edmund and make sure they're aware. I'm not heading all the way back down there when there's a chance that lunatic is running around—"

"*Those* lunatics," Freya corrected. "There's a chance she has her prince with her and that makes them a dangerous pair."

"Not to mention there may be other zealots strolling about this lovely palace," Malin added unhelpfully. "Wouldn't want to run into them either. Now that we have the sightless weighing us down."

Rian grit his teeth. "I am not useless."

"Oh, yeah?" Freya asked. "Who killed the lightwielder?"

He clamped his mouth shut.

"That's what I thought," she said smugly.

"I helped disarm her first. I had her right where I wanted her."

"About to kill you?" Malin added. "Not my first choice but—"

"*Guys,*" Rian said, another angry prick surged up his arm. "We don't have time for this."

"Are you absolutely fucking certain?" Freya asked. "If not, we are going to get into so much trouble if they catch us. The king banished you back to camp."

"I *know.*" He'd stake his entire lackluster reputation and even his life on it, if it came to it. "I know they're here."

"Yes, you imbeciles, he knows we are here," Freya said, likely balling her hands into fists and summoning every ounce of restraint to not strike whatever soldier blocked her path. "Now let us in or you'll really regret this."

Judging by her tone, they were about five wrong words away from Freya punching her way in. That would get them hanged, not to mention none of them had any weapons and he wasn't sure how much of an impact they would have against fully trained and *armed* Siicas.

"Do you know what ungodly hour it is? Their royal highnesses are resting after an onerous night."

It took them some time to find the right wing that housed the royals, and even longer to find someone willing to point them in the right direction.

They still hadn't found a helpful soul yet.

"Come on," Malin said in a smoother voice. "If you won't let us in, then can you please pass on a message or get him to come to us. I promise you he wants to hear this."

"I cannot let strangers in—especially Pedites—unannounced like this."

"Look at him." Malin waved his hand and sent a draft of air into Rian's face. "He's not a threat. He can barely stand on his own."

The guard scoffed.

Maybe he should have stayed behind while they tried to sweet-talk them... though Freya was doing less flattering and was edging on the verge of full-on threats. He should have known they'd never let a Pedite into those eastern wings, let alone one who looked like he'd gotten into a fight with a wild boar.

"Look," the guard said. Gentler this time. "I can't let you into their private quarters, especially looking like *that*."

Rian felt his eyes on him. This was one that usually guarded Edmund so surely, he recognized Rian. *Surely*, he knew they were telling the truth. That or he was about to throw them in the dungeons, no questions asked.

"Fine," Freya said quickly. "Just let the two of us in and we'll be out of your castle in five minutes. I promise."

"They're not here," the guard said. "But if you feel the need to pray to the star goddess directly tonight, you may find better luck with one of the smaller hosting rooms nearby, as the main one is occupied."

"What?" Malin said.

"The temple?" Freya said. "They're at the temple. Where is it?"

"Down by the southern gates, but you can't get there without an escort." The guard added in his gravelly voice, "You still can't take that one."

Malin grabbed his arm. "What do you want us to do with him?"

Rian wished he could see whatever face the man made, followed by a series of hand gestures passed between them. Next thing he knew, he was being ushered around the corner and sat on a bench like a child.

"Don't move." Freya punched his good shoulder. "We'll be back as soon as we find Edmund. He'll know the severity of this and can get us more men."

"Should I stay with him," Malin said hesitantly. "I mean, he's pretty... you know." Another flurry of air as he made more gestures.

"Maybe."

Annoyance flickered through him that wasn't his own. At least it wasn't panic or fear from whatever linked him to Isla, so she must be safe.

Safe for now. That didn't mean *they* weren't close to her. And he had no blade or weapon anymore. Not to mention the fact that he was completely without sight. He was useless and couldn't protect anyone.

"Go with Freya," he said. "Just in case there's trouble. I'll just..." He shifted back on the cold bench. "Stay here, I guess. And try to remain out of the way of people who I'll have no clue are even there."

"Good," Malin said. "Great plan." He clapped his arm, right above the spot where the mark was hidden. "We'll go and try to negotiate with the arrogant pricks."

"Keep an ear out," Freya said. "And if you see—hear anything... scream I guess?"

Malin snorted.

Both danced out of reach of his flailing arms, and promised they'd be back soon.

There was nothing to do except sit there. Alone. By himself. Unable to see or move or do anything.

It was agony.

He should have gone with Malin to find a healer or tried to force his way past the Siica. Letting his guard down with that lightwielder was a mistake. As was allowing himself to get carried away in that hallway, but there was no helping himself. He was powerless under her gaze and her touch.

And now he was stuck, thanks to his own carelessness. All that training in the corps, all that training his dad ran him through to make sure he was a perfect soldier, to make sure he could take on whatever hardships came his way, and now he was rendered useless without his vision.

The minutes dragged on torturously. Maybe he was wrong and the Muratian pair were already fleeing the city. That would be the smart thing to do. The sane thing to do. He prayed that his initial reaction was off, but the knot in his stomach refused to disappear. That knot spread from his gut into a worrisome headache that promised to split him open.

Footsteps approached. Rian wanted to get up, he wanted his sword or anything really, but all he could do was wait until they stopped in front of him.

"We need to go, *now*," Freya's voice cracked under unusual stress.

"Did you not even make it in?" Rian asked smugly. "Not so easy to do now, is it?"

"We need to find the princess," she said. "And quickly."

"What's wrong?" Rian asked. Her voice was off and she stood back favoring her left heel instead of her right. Where was Malin?

Also, where were the castle guards? He hadn't heard any of them pass by in minutes. Even though it was late into the night, they should be doing their rounds given how many guests were at the party who could just wander about.

His stomach swooped. Something was off.

"Something's wrong," he said.

Silence.

"Freya. Did you hear me?"

"*I said get up*," she hissed. Thin layers of ice crashed through each syllable. Unnatural layers of coldness.

Rian sucked in a breath.

Sharp steel pressed into his side and a voice like fiery ice spoke, "Don't fucking move or I'll gut you completely."

Thirty-Two
The General

"Keep moving," the voice sneered. That vice-like grip on his arm was beyond painful, yet he didn't dare attempt to break it. This one was unhinged at best and he didn't want to set her off.

"I'm trying, but it's difficult at the moment." He pointed at his face, not certain if she could see or was even looking. His shoulder scraped against a wall but she didn't care. Instead, she punched his poorly healed shoulder and pushed him onwards.

What a wretch. An absolute, terrible, wretch.

"Fuck." A shooting pain slithered down his spine and back up again.

How did Isla survive months stuck with the twisted wielder? She was stronger than Rian ever was, in *every* way.

His elbow scraped along the wall, the thin fabric he wore served as a poor shield against the rough elements. Where were they that the walls were rougher? And why did the air smell stale? Could air even smell stale?

If he wasn't being shoved around by a murderous psychopath, he'd marvel at how his sense of smell overcompensated for the lack of others. He snorted; his father would be proud.

Another sharp jab at his back and along his skull as she toyed with the memory he'd brought up. "Ouch."

"Is there something funny, soldier?" she spat.

"Nothing at all."

Only Slin's slippery sense of fate and his quick reversal of fortune from mere hours ago. It looked like Hierel's year was starting off with strange gifts of her own. Clearly, none of those were wanted or even meant for him. Perhaps he shouldn't have spent all night cursing her name like Freya scolded him for. She always said that befouling the goddesses' names led to disaster... and now here he was.

Another turn and his toes scraped along a gap in what he assumed were tiles. They weren't as smooth as the ones in the main castle so they were in a rarely used hall. One the workers didn't frequent with less chance of being caught.

If they were spotted, it wouldn't take much for this wielder to muck up their mind. He had to keep pinching himself to make sure this was real and not something happening in his head.

Another hard jab in his back that nearly sent him stumbling over. It was real. Painfully real.

The pressure at his back released. They'd stopped walking and were—somewhere still in the castle hopefully? It was colder now. They were either near a window or had traveled deep into the castle bowels. There were several winding steps up and then down but it was hard to count how many went which way with his head throbbing from her constant jabs.

He was turned around and that was on purpose.

"That's good enough for now," the wielder said thickly. "Don't try anything funny or I'll skin you alive... that or I'll leave you down here to rot away in the darkness."

Down here. So, they were underneath the castle.

"Wouldn't dream of it," he replied smoothly, as if talking to an old friend and not a deranged wielder with a sharp object pointed at him.

His captor paced back and forth, while he leaned cooly against the wall. If he had to guess, she was nervous about something. Waiting for someone. Where was her prince?

The minutes stretched on and on where he knew better than to talk. Instead, he tried thinking of a way out of this with no success.

Then a noise broke his solitude.

A pair of boots—two pairs—approached. They scuffed to a stop and a mass was thrown to the ground in front of him. A loud sob punctuated the stale air.

His heart leapt into his throat and he was ashamed of the relief that flooded into him when he realized the sobs didn't belong to Isla.

"Alynna," he felt around in the dark until he found something smooth. "Did they hurt you?"

Another giant sob. "N—no. I am alright."

His hands found her arm and he patted the top of her head. "Where is she?"

"Excellent question," a new voice said, cutting through the air with his fire-filled tones. "I had the same one myself."

A hand reached out, as if to strike Alynna. Rian flung out his arm and was hit with a blow meant for her.

"Where the fuck did she go?" Devlin said. "She wasn't there like you said she should be. Where did she go? *Where is she?*"

"Probably someplace safe," Beretta hissed. "Where we should go. We tried. It didn't work. There's only so long until they notice—"

The sound of a palm against skin broke her speech.

"I said no!" Anger wrapped around Devlin's every syllable. "I've already told you—"

"We don't have time for this," Beretta's voice was strained this time. "I don't want to stay in this dreadful place any longer."

"*No.*" Another sob from Alynna as he grabbed her. "Where did she go? Where is she?"

"Leave her alone." Rian launched in the direction of the voices, but a boot caught his chest.

Damn that wielder was fast. His ribs screamed and it felt like one broke off and started stabbing the rest of his insides.

"Don't try that again, scum" she said.

It was refreshing not being hated because he was a Pedite but rather hated for being a plain old Velotian soldier. He wasn't even certain if they had a similar conscript division in their army. Surely, they'd look equally down on them if they did.

"She doesn't know anything, you idiots," Rian shot out. He winced through the twinge of pain that seemed to burn everywhere, and not only from his injuries. This cursed mindweaver was a true menace. "She wasn't with Isla—I was."

He was yanked to the side by the scalp. It felt as if she was actively *trying* to rip out every single hair he had. His hand flexed at his side, longing for Dark End to slice her from top to bottom—or his best guess at where her guts were.

"I know that," the wielder seethed. "I was there. Where did she go after?"

Rian, bolstered by some ill-gotten bravado from Slin, said, "Someplace you'll never find her."

Something sharp hit his cheek as the tempered prince demanded, "Where?"

That same falsified boldness swarmed him in a comforting blanket as a plan took hold. "I'd rather die in Rallion's first fiery pit before I tell you."

"That can be easily arranged," the prince seethed. Another thump and whimper from Alynna. "For the both of you."

"Why don't we—" Beretta began.

"We don't need them. As you've said, we don't have time for this anymore. There are other ways."

"Wait," Rian said, his heart thumping faster now. Not like this. Not here. He moved to his knees, facing the direction of the prince's voice. "If you let her go, I can help you. I meant what I said about her knowing nothing. Prince Edmund and my men are occupied at Hierel's temple, they didn't notice my absence but it's only a matter of time until they know you're here."

Silence as the pair mulled over his offer. The sound was only punctuated by his own heavy breathing and the soft sobs permeating from Alynna.

Footsteps dragged over to him and a second voice spoke up, so close to his face that he jumped. That wielder was as quick as she was heartless. "And why should we trust you?"

He really wished he could see their stupid faces right now. It was hard to tell what they were thinking. "Isla and I had plans to leave the city. She'll be outside the castle walls at our meeting point. I can take you there if you promise to let Alynna go, and if you take me with Isla."

A finger dragged along his temple, its twin dragging through the inside of his skull as she tried to sift through his mind for the lie. To see where the trap was.

There was nothing there but truth. The same plan he and Isla talked about during their time alone in the camp, staring up at the tent canopy and planning what they would do when they walked away from this place together. Finally free of all the trappings of stature and propriety, and free from the all-seeing gazes of the goddesses who've cursed them both since the day they entered this life.

That same pull that steered him towards her pulsed, aching to close the gap to where his heart was. It longed and craved and begged to find her. But he already knew where she would be and how they could make a quick escape. Maybe a life in Murat would be better than *this* here. That was, if they even made it there in the first place. He could figure that part out later.

The painful scraping subdued into a dull throb. The claws lingered at the edge of his mind.

"Well?" Devlin asked, a bite of impatience lacing his voice.

"It's... hard to read," Beretta said between heavy breaths. She must be exhausted after her time in captivity and the journey to the castle. Her body wouldn't be able to hold up with the stress much longer. "They had plans to meet up if anything went wrong. I think he's telling the truth."

"Either way, if what you said is true, then she'll come for him," Devlin said, planting the heel of his boot into Rian's back. Again, Rian found himself face-first in the cold and dusty tile. "Or what's left of him, if he tries to pull anything."

"What about her?" Beretta asked, urgency escaping through the ice in her voice.

He recognized that emotion. She wanted to get away from here as quickly as possible. Before anyone found them. Just as Rian wished to delay things longer so his friends would notice his absence and find them.

A swift kick landed in his lower ribs.

"He is *trying* to delay us," she said. "Leave her. We can't take them both if we wish to make haste."

"Fine," Devlin said. "Take care of her."

Rian tried to stand as Beretta's boots made their way to where Alynna still lay crumpled on the ground. "No!" But the feel of cold metal against his throat halted any attempts at aiding her.

There was a gargled noise, followed by painful silence that stretched on for eternity, then a dull thud as Alynna's body hit the ground.

Rian's pulse quickened, battering against every limb and daring him to strike at his unseen captors. He struggled more and felt the knife pressed deeper against him.

"Relax," Beretta drawled. "She's merely sleeping. A deal is a deal."

Devlin relaxed the knife enough for him to find a pulse. Thank the goddess.

"You know what happens if you try to double cross us," Devlin said, allowing the blade to prick his skin as the threat lingered in the air.

"Take us to your meeting spot."

Thirty-Three
The General

It was hard coming up with a genius escape plan while being pushed around in the dark of his mind with constant threats uttered his way anytime he bumped into something.

The suggestion that this would all go a lot quicker if Devlin healed his eyes was only met with a smack to the head. So, they continued their painstaking way through the castle tunnels with Beretta leading the way based on information she'd dug out of a castle soldier's mind as Rian was utterly useless in navigating this maze. That fact alone had earned him another swift kick when Beretta searched his memories to find nothing helpful.

She really was miserable.

By now, Malin and Freya would have noticed his absence, and Edmund would have raised half the castle guards at the prospect of their prized captives running around the castle. They may have already gotten to Isla before she made her way there. He prayed to a goddess he didn't trust for that outcome. Even if it meant his sure death, at least she would be safe.

"You are a fool," Beretta said calmly. It was only after she pinched his arm that Rian realized the comment was for him.

He didn't want to rise to her bait but the walk had been dreadfully boring so why not tempt the goddesses some more? "How so?"

"To think any plans of escape and a free life were ever in your grip," she said. "The goddesses will never release her from her path carved of destiny—either of you, for that matter. You are an absolute idiot to think otherwise."

Well, *sorry* for allowing a glimmer of hope at a quiet life away from everything. One where he didn't have to worry about attempts on his life—or Isla's life—every other day.

It pained him to think this crazy wielder was right. Even if they had ever made it past the city's walls, there was no guarantee safety would find them. If anything, they'd be in more danger on the run from two kingdoms instead of one. *Three*, if the Koliats were upset about losing their precious bride, which, speaking straight from Wallienne, who wouldn't be?

But he wasn't going to give that damned wielder anything to use against him, so he said, "And what's in it for you? Besides being used by the one you call your prince all for the sake of some ill-gotten glory so that his mommy will love him."

Devlin's boots scraped to a stop and he whipped around with all the fury of a rushing beast. Rian imagined a fist raised in the air and aimed directly at him.

"Sorry," Rian said pleasantly. "A little too close to the truth. I'm sure you have a lot of pressure being the unwanted third son of a second son, I'm a second son of a nobody, but at least my parents loved me. I hear you were shipped off because your parents couldn't even stand—"

"Enough!" Beretta's hand was at the back of his head. A burning pain wrenched through his body and then he was sitting cross-legged on a hay-filled floor with the smell of manure and urine assaulting his senses.

The stables. He knew these well enough as it was the same they'd been given access to for the few horses the Pedites owned. From what he remembered, it was nothing fancy, just a few hay-covered stalls and several plain benches lining the walls.

Sweat from a walk he didn't remember dripped down the back of his crusty shirt and his hands were snugly bound. His jaw hurt like he'd been punched, at least he didn't remember that.

Devlin leaned against the far wall with one leg planted against the wood. His heel impatiently tapped the enclosure, and Rian could feel his lingering glower.

A throttled sigh beside him came from Beretta. She shook her hands to distract from the fact that she was panting from the effort of—whatever that was.

Neat trick.

If he'd known she could do that, he would have acted out sooner. It'd save him the long trip here under the castle walls.

"I still say we should have killed him and been done with it," Devlin said.

Beretta ignored him and pulled out something metal. It sounded like a longsword being released from its sheath. When did she manage to grab that? And how long was he out—or whatever you called that? She moved through the stalls, examining each steed carefully and ensuring there were no soldiers hidden under a pile of hay.

He didn't budge or show any emotion when she moved through a stall that belonged to a horse with one ear.

"Nothing interesting over there?" Rian asked. "There are plenty of sturdy horses here. Nobody would notice their absence for hours. Maybe your wielder is right and you should just kill me and leave while you can."

Beretta scoffed. There was heavy silence from Devlin.

Something was off with the pair, like a small wedge that had been driven between two unmoving rocks. Were they fighting while he was out of it? It certainly seemed like it.

Perhaps he'd poke some more at the cracks already forming. There weren't many scenarios in which he made it out of here with his life, he may as well enjoy some fun tormenting the two who'd tortured Isla for months.

"You know," he began. "With the way you two function, I'm surprised we didn't catch you sooner. It sounds like your entire operation in the red mountains was a bust, so you certainly have a knack for terrible planning."

Beretta grumbled and joined Devlin at the wall. He imagined they shared a sour glance together.

"I wouldn't call it a failure," Devlin said quietly.

"Oh, no? You lost your target and quite a few of your men are dead."

Thanks to Rian's men.

"They served their purpose," Devlin said coldly. "We managed to find new friends in the process."

New friends?

Devlin pushed himself off the wall. "That's enough prodding from you. Don't think we don't know what you are doing." He tapped the side of Rian's head.

Ah, yes. The whole mindweaver thing. He nearly forgot. Rian only heard stories of ones able to do more than measly party tricks on the mind or influence dreams. He'd never seen one this powerful. She must have been through *quite* the training to get this point.

Floorboards creaked as Beretta shifted her weight.

Why were they so determined and focused on Isla? There had to be something else at play besides her unique wielder powers.

The Muratians had put forth a marriage bid for Isla years ago. Their father vehemently denied it and insulted their king and queen at the time. It was with their crown prince Abrax, who it was said was the queen's favorite, unlike this lunatic of a son he was stuck with.

Another sharp jab along his skull directly from Beretta. He lingered close to the truth.

They wanted Isla for *something else*.

And he'd led them straight to their meeting spot like a complete moron. There had to be a way to fix this. *Anything*. But he was on his own. Blinded. With nothing to do except listen to the heavy breathing and dragging footsteps of the Muratian royal and his ally.

Now he'd been sitting here for who knows how long, waiting for the pair to decide whether or not it was worth their time to wait. He prayed they gave up and used the horses like he recommended.

Rian even knew the quickest way to Murat that was less travelled by their soldiers. He could show the wielder the way in his mind. Everyone would get some portion of what they wanted, except for Devlin, naturally. He'd have to live with his failure and come clean to his mom, one way or—

—what was taking them so long?

Godsdamnit.

Beretta whipped around and the heat from her gaze broke through his darkness. "He fucking lied," she hissed. "She's not coming."

Oh, fuck. He'd slipped up. So much for that.

Beretta whistled.

Air billowed from all directions, followed by a light crack as somebody dropped in front of them. Two new pairs of footsteps shuffled their way through robes. Old and tattered robes.

Tattered robes? The zealots.

"Chir. Vrax. The princess isn't here. This one lied to us."

They were working together this whole time.

Well, that was something new. At least he knew what happened while he was out of it. Or did they plan this all before?

"It was a fake memory," Beretta said.

"Obviously," Rian drawled. A glorious, fabricated memory at that.

She was never coming. It was all a wonderful dream. Manufactured for the mindweaver based on the countless ones he'd had. It was as good as a memory as far as his mind—and Beretta—was concerned.

All to get them as far away from the castle as he could. He was useless without his sight or weapons, but he could still lead them away from Isla, and if he could drain the mindweaver while at it, that was an added bonus. It was a surprise he held out for as long as he did.

What he wasn't counting on was drawing the zealots out with this desperate plan. He could have taken on Beretta and Devlin and hopefully eliminated one of them as he went. But now there was more.

"Idiot. Kill this one and get us as close to the castle as you can," Devlin said. "He killed Saroft."

"Fuck." Beretta groaned. "We said *not yet*. We cannot go back to the castle."

"*Take care of him!*"

A small dagger rang as it was removed from its sheath. One of the zealots—the transporter, maybe—made their way over to him.

None of this was a part of his ill-thought-out plan. Not at all.

At least he managed to buy them some time. At least he got Devlin out of the city. That had to be worth something.

The mark on his arm ached desperately.

He squished his unseeing eyes closed as he waited for the zealot to exact their revenge. Would it be the throat or the heart? Perhaps they'd take their time and play with him. He wouldn't put it past this homicidal group.

Air gushed and Rian flinched. Cold air hit his arm as the zealot pulled off the remains of his torn sleeve.

The zealot hissed and backed away. It took a moment for Rian to realize what they were looking at.

The mark on his arm.

"It means nothing," Devlin's cold voice says.

"Touched by the goddess," the closest zealot said in clipped tones. "The touch of Rallion." There was a shuffling as he pulled back the sleeve of his robes, likely exposing the same burn marks all the other heretics bore.

"How did you get that?" the other zealot asked Rian. This one must be the transporter.

Rian clamped his mouth and his mind firmly shut.

"It doesn't matter," Beretta said. "The plan's over. We're going."

"No," the transporter's serpentine-like voice called out. He imagined her with a hooked nose to match. "She'll come."

"Prince Devlin," Beretta said. "It's a trap. He lured us away on purpose. We should leave as planned. If Chir won't take us, there are plenty of horses."

A moment of silence as the prince weighed their options.

The serpentine voice said, "If she won't come, we'll take him with us."

"No," Devlin said. "Definitely not. No way. Kill him and get it over with."

"Not yet," the wielder, Chir, hissed.

Rian wished the other would talk more so he could get a better idea of what he was up against. Somebody crazy, no doubt, but that wasn't saying much in this group.

If he had a choice between dying out here or going with them to serve whatever absurd end, the answer was simple.

He'd been living on borrowed time since Liopen. Since...

"You should do it, you know." He spoke to the spot he assumed the prince stood in. "Wouldn't want to bring a liability around with you, especially not when you're on the run from us and mommy."

He felt the prince stiffen. The mindweaver inched close as if expecting an outburst.

"Get rid of him, Beretta," Devlin said. "He's useless to us."

"No. We keep him alive until we find out for certain." The transporter must have grabbed her arm as Beretta hung back. "We must trust in the path the goddess has set forth."

The male zealot murmured in a strange language and their robes rustled as they made some ancient ritualistic symbol.

Devlin scoffed. Rian would be rolling his eyes if it didn't hurt to think about them. Gods, these zealots were committed, he had to give them that.

So was Rian. "Did the goddess also plan for your brother to die in that village?"

The room turned deathly still, as if a chill froze the night air.

"What was that?" Devlin said, taking a small step towards him while struggling against Beretta's grip.

"Did the goddess tell your brother to leave the safety of his borders to pilfer and raze an innocent village to the ground? Because he most certainly paid dearly for his deeds that day. Not sure what kind of goddess would watch over that."

"How would you know that?" he asked sharply.

"Don't listen to him. He's *trying* to get under your skin, and it's working."

Rian nodded. "I am. It is." It was as good of a time as any to let the truth slip, however terrible and nightmare-haunting it was. He had no plans on being used to bait Isla out. If he had the choice, he'd rather a swift end right here knowing those he cared about were safe.

"He's lying," Beretta said.

The claw scraping along his mind pulled from a memory that he'd struggled to forget. Just as he couldn't forget the smell of those bodies as the villagers of Liopen burned, nor the tormented cries of the Muratians they found responsible. They'd begged to be released, for a swift death, and for grace from the goddesses, but none of it was given that night.

"I'm not lying. Your wielder knows the truth, even if she won't say it." Rian took a shaky breath, aware of the transporter still crouching inches away from his face. "I was there."

"No."

"Yes," Rian said. "I may not have been the one to deal the final blow, but between Wallienne and us... It's hard to be *sure*. I can't even remember his face."

There was a scuffle and a roaring cry. "I'll kill you, you bastard."

The transporter stood quietly, robes rustling as she watched the prince with rapt attention.

Rian continued on. "I may not remember him, but I'm certain he wept and begged for his life... as the rest of his men did that day. He didn't really meet a glorious end. It wasn't all that honorable either."

More scuffling. "Let. Me. Go."

Rian smiled. "Let him try his best. Just like his brother did."

"No," Chir said, thrusting an arm out in front of Devlin's chest. "This matters not."

"It doesn't matter," Devlin repeated incredulously. "*It doesn't matter.* Are you fucking insane?"

Evidently, yes.

Chir pulled back the sleeve of her robe, and shook her arm, exposing the dark scars all these Rallion followers wore. "See, prince? See?"

Devlin did not see anything besides a moronic zealot. The same thing Rian saw through his blinded eyes.

"Why we have the scars of the goddess, hoping to earn the one true mark from Rallion herself. Why we pray and learn the old scriptures and the words. It is the same reason the gates are blurred during the solstice as Hierel becomes distracted with her gifts. The *gates*. The vision linked to the deathpuller and your lineage as well."

"I don't care," Devlin said, his voice shaking. "He dies today."

"The High King's line survived through his son, passed down to all the leaders of the Rocian kingdoms, some stronger than others, while Rallion's line survived through the daughter. The reunification of the lines will unleash boundless power and blessings to recreate the line of High Kings. Just as you wanted."

What?

"It doesn't matter today. He's unrelated to it all."

"Not according to the mark. We need to know *why* he has it."

"Stop it. I'll finish him myself if you won't."

"Do not try, young prince."

"He killed my fucking brother."

"Devlin, no!"

All Rian could do was wince and duck as boots scraped wood. There was a clash of metal against something hard, then a thump as the first zealot fell to the ground.

Did he really just turn on them? The second zealot, the wielder, dropped to her knees. Her breath came in gargled rasps.

Well, that took care of two of them at least.

"You think you can turn your back on our deal," Chir said. Devlin must have gotten her good by the way she struggled to get out each word. "Rallion's retribution is everywhere. She sees and knows everything. And it is the sister years. The twelve gates have never been more weakened than they are now and we need the links."

The transporter wheezed and laughed. Wind brushed by, sending all the horses whining and the scar on his arm burning. Something pulled on him—past him—and towards the wielder. She was pulling some sort of power to her.

The air thickened and his chest turned heavy. His skin grew both hot and freezing at the same time.

It was the same feeling outside of Isla's tent when that wielder tried to hurt her. It pulled through him and his arm flared up, taking all his energy with it. He swayed in place, feeling lightheaded and weak, but it quickly disappeared as a terrible sound scratched his ears.

He'd only heard such things a few times in his life, and it always came with those creatures. His stomach hollowed out as his vision snapped back in full force. It made him wish he was blind again.

The marks.

It was always said they were meant as an offering to the Goddess of the Gates herself. A tethering of sorts. He never realized that *this* was what they planned to do with that link.

Thirty-Four

The Princess

Isla was absolutely, most certainly, totally, definitely lost.

A bead of sweat trailed down her neck and into her shirt. At this rate, she'd be caught before she made it past the castle walls, and judging by the muted stone color, she still had a way to go before she reached it.

How did Edmund manage to find his way around here so easily?

Years of practice, she reminded herself. *Years* where he snuck around doing gods knew what. They never got around to the reason why he'd been using them. There was so much she wanted to ask him, if she ever made it out of these cursed tunnels.

The stitch in her lungs called for a break. She paused with one hand against the wall and the other holding her side. She *really* was out of shape. What happened to all those muscles she created in those mines? They'd withered into nothing from lack of use, as had any of her riding muscles.

At least she'd kept up her practices with the dagger. Late at night, when she had so many frustrations that refused to leave, was the perfect time to let out her aggressions on imaginary foes. Some faceless. Others were a perfect rendition of those that had wronged her... and it shifted nightly depending on what kind of mood she was in.

Those nights stabbing Edmund and Rian's faces as they sent her away had long gone, but she fondly remembered practicing what she would first say to them and which appendage she'd hit the hardest.

Now, she was out here, again, fighting her way against the darkness in search of the one person who could shatter her heart into pieces and repair it stronger than before. That hot asshole knew how to get at her in every way, she thought with an involuntary smile.

But which direction led to him?

Edmund should have drawn her a map.

Footsteps in the distance made her freeze. The sound came from behind. Even though she'd been struggling to keep her breath steady, she willed it into a silent pace as torchlight sent shadows dancing on the wall. Who else was down here? These halls were abandoned the last time she came with Edmund.

The boots belonged to a soldier.

A royal guard with a thick red beard and a white-hilted broadsword at his side. She'd recognized him many times around the throne room and in her father's service but didn't know him well enough to know his name. He'd never been kind to her or spoke to her directly before... not that many of them did.

Isla raised a hand to block out the torchlight. Her eyes had just gotten adjusted to the dark before this and now it was covered in spots. "Can I help you?" she asked as casually as she could.

There was no time for this, and she didn't have the patience.

With nothing to do but press herself further into the wall in the hope he wouldn't recognize her in a plain uniform and without the usual circlet adorning her brow. Gods, those things could be so annoying and heavy. The worst of them would leave blood behind her ears after a long day. And her favorite of them... that one she didn't want to think about anymore.

Unfortunately, Hierel didn't grace her with her gaze tonight. The man made his way and stopped inches away from her. At this proximity, she could count the giant pores on his nose and taste the sour tang coming from his heavy breaths.

That little tug pulled on her again. Down the hall to her right. It had to be that way as she'd felt nothing but chilling silence for over an hour before. She prayed it was because he was out of it while being healed. There was no reason for anything else to have happened on this already cursed night. Either way, she was more determined than ever to confirm for herself.

This was wasting her time and she didn't know how much she had left before a Siica came barreling down these tunnels in search of her, if they even knew about them in the first place. So, she tried to step around the man. He grabbed her arm in an unbreakable grip.

Godsdamnit. She really shouldn't have let herself slip these past weeks. Her heart was racing but she kept a straight face, despite panic filling every morsel of her body. "Apologies, sir, but I have to continue on."

"I know what you are," the guard said, spraying her with a fresh waft of rancid breath that nearly sent Isla to her knees.

"I don't have time for this," she managed to twist her arm away and stepped around him, but he blocked her again.

This was getting irritating. Had she been a bit too demanding of this one in the past? Maybe she ignored him one time too many and he was out for retribution. He definitely shouldn't be down here, though neither should she.

She opened her mouth to tell him exactly where to go, but he was quicker.

"A curse upon Hierel's grace is what you are. You'd be better as a gift sent back straight through Rallion's gates."

Fuck.

She wasn't in the mood for a heretic's rambling, she heard more than most people should have in their lifetime. But this man would not let up. Isla's hand inched towards her thigh. Down to where Rian's blade was securely strapped.

As her fingers graced the hilt, she was slammed against the wall with an elbow pressed into her windpipe. The man's free hand blocked hers from moving any closer to the dagger.

Isla gasped for air, as her feet dusted the ground beneath her. Something fluttered through that small pull she felt, something worrying, but she couldn't focus past her desperation to get one good breath in.

Her vision darkened at the edges. This was surely the end and she'd never see him again. Never smell him again. Never hold him again.

She cursed the goddesses for letting her die beneath the ground.

The darkness had nearly closed in. Then the elbow against her windpipe was gone and she dropped to the ground.

The cold stone against her fingertips soothed her and she took several giant gulps of gloriously stale air. Her body wracked with vicious shakes that wouldn't subside. She truly thought it was over for her. Stupid idiot running around on her own, especially after what happened with the lightwielder.

Silver boots appeared and a blond-haired, silver-banded soldier helped her to her feet.

"Thanks," she choked out.

"Oh, don't mention it," Malin said casually, kicking the body over to make sure the man was truly out. Two Siicas stood straight-backed behind him, closely flanking—

"What are you doing down here, Edmund?" Isla asked between raspy breaths.

Edmund pushed past the Siicas and brushed hair out of her face. He was still wearing his ball attire with flames etched into the silver chest. "Why are *you* here?"

Guilt swirled through every inch of her body. Wandering off on her own was *definitely* not the best idea she'd had tonight. "I was going for a walk."

"Isla," Edmund warned, his voice heavy.

"I'm sorry," Isla rasped, holding back tears. "I was going to see him. I wasn't going to be gone for long, I swear upon Wallienne. Nobody even noticed."

She would never be allowed outside her room again. Edmund would have that passage boarded up before the morning rays hit the castle.

Freya's brows furrowed. She still wore a shining silver dress from the night's festivities. "You were trying to get to the camp?"

Isla nodded. She'd never felt so small. "Just for a little bit."

Edmund was staring at her, taking in the uniform that she'd changed into.

Her brother sighed. "*Isla.*"

"You're the one who's been sneaking out for longer than I've been alive, Edmund. Don't you dare try to scold me now."

Edmund exchanged a dark look with Freya.

"Wait." Realization came at Isla like a hammerboar in the forest. Didn't her father send Rian off *with* his friends? "Why are you two here? What's going on?"

Malin looked over his shoulder at Freya as he bounced on the heels of his feet. "Oh, nothing unusual but have you happened to see two crazed Muratians and possibly a blind guy during your little sojourn down here?"

Isla was certain that her shrill tones must have echoed through half the castle. "*What*?"

Thirty-Five

The Princess

"Why did you imbeciles let him go alone?" Isla asked, not even stopping to glare at the pair as Edmund led them through the vortex of tunnels. There were only five other people around, so they were forced to bear the brunt of her wrath, even if she could barely make out their faces. "He can't see, you pack of morons."

"It was *his* moronic plan to go off with them," Freya said. At least she was as unhappy with this as Isla.

"Just like yours," Edmund added. "Except yours is worse." He looked back at Beau and Mada, his closest Siicas, who he swore wouldn't speak a word of this to anyone, despite Isla having doubts about bringing them. "I still think someone needs to take her back."

Isla ignored him and focused on Freya, keeping pace with the fierce warriors' strides. Frenzied rage tumbled through her veins, fueling her. Let them try to touch her—to stop her—she was *not* in the mood for being coddled. "Are you certain they went this way?"

"Yes," Freya said. "He told Alynna where he planned on going and something about a meeting place."

"Alynna?" And what meeting place could he possibly be talking about?

"She was hurt but was able to go back to the castle on her own," Malin said, ducking under a low beam. "I'd have gone with her but as you can see, our little hunting party was down to five and we can't afford to lose a member."

"Unless Edmund wants to take you back himself," Freya said pointedly. "I still don't like this idea. I don't like *any* of our ideas so far."

Edmund turned on his heel and nearly collided with Freya. The warrior didn't scurry back, and held her stance. "Seeing as Isla spent the better part of an hour going in circles, I'm going to guess that the two of you would have fared much worse. Plus, he is *my* prisoner, and *I* will ensure we get him back."

Freya scoffed, as if the prospect that Edmund would be doing any of the dangerous sword-lifting was laughable. It really was. But Isla was not in the mood for laughing at anything right now.

Even Beau gave him a questionable look at this and that Siica had been with him through everything. *Years.* Who knew what secrets about her brother were held behind that stony face.

"I think..." Malin said carefully. "I think that a certain someone would not want us all rushing into danger like this—especially *some people.*"

Isla's hand feathered over the blade. "Don't even try it."

"I was just verbalizing my concerns," he said casually. His throat bobbed. "That's all. No need to get all stabby. I'm not in charge here."

Neither was Edmund. She refused to listen to him and continued on as if nothing had happened.

The group didn't pause when they left the tunnels, nor did they break as they made their way through the deserted streets. The rest of Aurial had partied late judging by the streamers and leftover lanterns strewn everywhere. Isla got tangled in a chunk of string decorations but Malin helped free her.

What possessed them to leave him alone like that? She didn't care if the pair was trying to find them. They should have known better. When this was over and she had him back safely, then she'd give them a full piece of her mind.

It hit her then. They were surprised to find her in the bowels of the castle. They'd planned on confronting Devlin without her. They were going to rescue Rian... *without her*. Only a chance of fate led her to the tunnels. If she hadn't gone, she'd be long asleep without a clue what was happening. With no clue of the dangers resting beyond the city walls.

Nobody saw her as an equal. None of them, at least.

"Are we close?" Freya asked.

"Less than five minutes," Edmund huffed.

A chill filled her, unrelated to the warm breeze that filtered through the sour beer-scented streets. Her pulse quickened and sweat formed at the base of her neck.

Something was wrong. Terribly wrong and she didn't know exactly what or where—and that made it all worse.

Fuck. Why was this all happening now? On today of all days when she was hoping for new beginnings. Was this a taste of the year ahead?

A gust of wind burst past and Isla stumbled. The rush of air pulled into her and dragged her down. All the breath was snatched from her lungs and stars filled her vision. She swayed on her feet, and Malin grabbed her shoulder.

"Are you alright?" he asked. Worry glazed his eyes and she sensed the request to stay behind lingering on his tongue. They didn't understand. *Couldn't* understand.

She shook out of his grip, brushing off whatever had sapped her strength. It came from the same direction that tug had been pulling her. "I'm fine. It's just the darkness. Let's keep moving."

Mada, the giant Siica, looked back at Edmund for instructions. If Isla wasn't so worried about Rian, she'd be jealous that Edmund had Siicas who clearly listened to him and trusted his judgement. She had nothing like that in all her years in Aurial, except maybe Alynna and Susanna, but they weren't allowed to move through the castle as easily as the Siicas.

The stars above winked at her. They mocked her as they waned in and out of sight.

Something was wrong. Even the goddesses knew it.

She was drained. Weakened, somehow. Like a part of her was ripped away, with drops still leaking off her to someplace else.

If they knew what just happened, they'd drag her back home and she couldn't let that happen. Whatever caused it was not here and she knew exactly where it all led to. Those two had to be at the center of all of this and Rian was with them.

Rian.

The other half of her heart. The one whose soul sang to her even while separated by a mountain.

She brushed aside any of the helping hands and took off in the direction of that pull, ignoring Edmund's exasperated sigh. It didn't matter what waited at the end, *he* was still alive and she had to find him.

They followed it to the edge of the city. They were close.

The towering Siica, Mada, held up a hand to stop them. "I don't think we should leave the city walls, Prince Edmund. There is something in the air tonight and we shouldn't risk it."

Isla scowled. Since they were all determined to ignore her wishes, she was going to ignore them. She sidestepped the two Siicas and continued her path forward.

She was through with being the quiet, weak princess that needed to be coddled and saved and passed around. That spoiled, useless girl died in those mines. Violence and retribution were all that remained in her bones.

They ducked under the main portcullis and neared the quiet Pedite camp—

That couldn't be right. This was where Beretta and Devlin were being held before. They'd already escaped and made it into the castle. Why travel all that way, only to return to the place they'd fled?

There were no castle guards stationed here, and the party from the Pedite camp was still in full swing with vigorous music assaulting her ears. The sentries should have noticed something was off, but they were gone from their posts.

Isla knew why.

The stars blinked into darkness, then lit back up again. None of this was good.

The tug didn't lead her towards the heart of the camp, instead, she turned to the far edge where a simple wood structure stood out amongst the canvas shelters.

The stables. The same location her power was leaking from. She lifted a foot—

Malin flung out his arm. "What in all of Rallion's flimsy gates is that gods-awful sound?"

Isla tilted her head, her ears straining to pick up what his years of training so easily did. It took a moment, then she realized it sounded like all twelve gates had been cracked open.

And the noise poured out from the stables like a deathly lament.

A creature galloped their way. Her heart pounded in unison with each hoof step as it ran closer and closer. The sound echoed across her bones and sent the hair on her arms straight up.

It was only a horse.

The stars gleamed in full force, shining their celestial light on the animal. Her heart stuttered and pulsed.

No, not a horse. Something otherworldly and yanked back from the first gate itself. Its eyes were deep hollows and bone-white skin was pulled taut around its torso. It was the same with the dweller and the villagers.

How did it get here? Devlin said the gate was deep within the mountain and he was held captive under firestone chains—*was* held, she reminded herself. He couldn't have gotten one here so quickly. Not without help.

Behind her, the Siica Beau muttered curses upon Rallion's name. Fitting, as Sister Death was certainly the mistress of these creatures. Isla was not afraid of the Goddess of the Gates anymore for she'd passed through several of them and made it back intact.

The creature bared its teeth—or at least, the gap where its teeth should be—and hurtled at them, its charred hair flapping in the wind. If she hadn't seen similar creatures in the woods, she'd have thought Beretta scrambled the last dredges of her sanity.

Alas, it was all too real. She knew exactly how destructive these creatures could be.

Isla only had the small blade at her side, which would do nothing against the giant beast. This time she was not alone. And she definitely didn't have time for this.

The stars faded again. The horse ran straight for her and she dove to the ground, miscalculating how close it was and bumping her chin. As she rolled down, the creature jumped, perfectly launching itself over her and crashing straight into Malin and Mada behind her.

The scraping sound from the Nothing-horse running into them sent a shiver through her body. It was followed by a lot of grunts and high-pitched snarling. The ground crunched under her body as she heaved herself back to her feet. There was no looking back. The others were on their own as her focus was getting to the creature's origin.

The stables. They were there—all of them.

"Get it off me!"

"It's head. Go for the head."

"Isla, stop!"

Her body didn't know how to. She passed a half-dozen living horses running for their lives, River among them, but she didn't pause to catch the frenzied beast. One clipped her shoulder and she swore it dislocated something. Yet, her feet still carried her forward, unable to halt.

As she approached the stable, the stars burst into view again, lighting up the doors which were torn off their hinges. Isla froze.

Two giant wood pillars groaned as they were twisted and strained past their usual load. Horses screamed from their prisons against the walls while pale creatures tore their flesh apart, and blood pooled from two robed bodies laying in the scattered hay.

Isla's chest rumbled, shaking the rest of her body with it.

The middle of the floor was torn open. A giant crevice blared hot white flames that nearly blinded her. The fissure was deep. Too far to see but Isla knew that was what drew on her powers. It beckoned to her, begging to pull her in, but she severed that connection as best she could.

Another pulse ripple through her body—or was it the ground that trembled?

Rian was huddled against the far wall, a crimson-covered figure facing the two humanoid Nothings that closed in on him. He was next to an open stall and carried a scythe—she had no idea where he'd grabbed that from and was too busy keeping them at bay to notice her.

Wait. His sight.

It was returned, thank the goddess—and she wasn't sure which one at this moment. The burns remained but his eyes moved normally, following the motion of the creatures in front of him. He was sporting new bruises and his outfit was ripped in several spots. How did they let this happen to him?

About twenty feet away stood Beretta and Devlin, side to side with weapons raised. The usually coiffed Muratians were disheveled and looked distressed at the chaos they'd caused. Five Nothings, including two boar-looking creatures, who could devour them whole for all she cared, circled the duo. Beretta edged in front of Devlin with a jagged dagger brandished. At least she had loyalty to *someone*.

For a moment, Isla was torn between jumping across the fissure to get to Rian, or diving to the side to stab either of those Muratians in their hearts, if they even had them anymore. Revenge or saving the one she loved? It seemed like an easy option, if her head wasn't so distracted by the hot flames.

"*What the actual fuck?*" A bloodied Malin slid to a stop beside her, grabbing her arm as if he thought she was about to jump into the hole.

Isla hadn't even noticed her feet had carried her forward, and she was nearing the edge of whatever gate from hells that was. Hot flames curled at her fingertips, heating her already burning body into a pyre that was ready for consumption.

There was new noise behind them, as Edmund and the others caught up. Malin must have run ahead to get to her.

A Nothing-boar with a gash down its side ran at Devlin. Beretta tried to get it with her dagger but the added slash did nothing to slow it down. They hadn't faced these creatures like this before and didn't know how to handle them.

Isla allowed herself one beat of pleasure to watch the creature tear them to pieces. It jumped towards the Muratian prince with its jowls ready to devour all.

"Aargh." Devlin raised a hand, streams of sweat dripping off his chin, and the wedge down the creature's side expanded until it split in two.

"What the fuck?" Malin hissed.

Isla jumped, forgetting he was there. She pulled her arm out of his unnecessary grip, yet he continued to hover, ready to grab her at a moment's notice.

"Do something besides standing there and yelling," she scolded, pulling her hands back from the blazing inferno.

"But—but—"

A creature turned and its pale eyes found them before jumping to the open doors beyond. Malin's sword appeared in his hand faster than Isla could register what was happening. He didn't charge at the beast like he usually would. Instead, he kept hovering around her.

"Stop worrying about me."

"I can't—"

"Keep them from escaping," she yelled, the words ripping along her throat.

Malin gaped at her. "The prince?"

Idiot. "No. The creatures. Stop them."

The city. They couldn't let them reach their people unawares. Not again.

Across the fissure, Rian still battled the towering Nothing. Isla took her guardian's distraction to run around the gap, focused on reaching him, but a Nothing jumped in her path. Its claw-like hands swiped the air in front of her. She stabbed its torso with her dagger and it kept moving past her, focused on the entrance.

Malin was right behind her, digging his sword into the Nothing's shoulder. Dark ichor leaked from the wound, slowing it down, but still not stopping it.

"The head," Isla grunted. Then she was shoved to the ground.

Malin's next swing missed and the creature jumped on him, throwing him on top of her. It clawed his arm, spewing blood everywhere, and raised its head. Hollow eyes focused on Malin's throat for the killing blow.

No!

Isla raised her hands, heart chafing against its enclosure. One brief thought and the creature turned into a pile of ashes that fell onto the sputtering soldier.

That was new. Isla struggled to her feet and tried catching the breath determined to escape her. Sparkling dots appeared in her view, making it hard to see more than ten feet in front of her. New and poorly timed, as calling on her powers had never sapped her strength like that before. That took nearly every ounce of energy out of her.

The cursed gate was causing this. It had to be.

Not now. Not when she needed it more than ever.

Malin spit out ash and gagged. "Gross."

There was no time to talk as another was right behind it. He was up and wrapped an arm around her shoulders, pinning her against him. One spin to turn them around and he handled the Nothing with his free hand.

"Stop trying to get yourself killed," he said between swipes. "Rian'll murder me."

"Let me go," Isla grunted as she struggled against his crushing grip. Her breath refused to cooperate and another dizzy spell consumed her.

Stop it. Stop it. Stop it.

"You're going to get *him* killed," Malin grunted.

Isla's limbs sagged. What?

"Let him do what he needs to do. You'll get in the way."

One beat of her heart. Then another pathetic crack as it tried to remember how to function. All she wanted to do was help. Couldn't they see that?

Someone cursed. Not Malin, for once.

A group of Nothings closed in on Devlin and Beretta, while Edmund was being protected by Freya and Beau. Had Mada not made it in with the others? She'd been too preoccupied to notice.

This was a disaster and it was all her fault. Death followed her and she couldn't protect the ones she cared about. The only weapon was Rian's dagger, Shadow Death, and even now she was too weak to make much use of it. But she had powers. Powers that were being drained with every movement she took. Drained and stolen and reforged into something twisted.

For that's what that gate was. An ungodly structure filled with death and decay and... something else. It called to her. Beyond that putrid veil was a hint of a glorious horizon, beckoning to—

Isla was slammed into the ground with Malin on top of her again. Her head spun so badly she could barely make sense of which way was up and which was down, except for the fact that she was face-first in a pile of hay and dark blood.

A snarling jaw was inches away from her face when another body flew into it. She recognized that yelping.

"Opi!"

The seropa tackled whatever Nothing had just gotten the jump on Malin, who was bleeding from the head but still somewhat with her.

"Are you alright?" She wiped blood from his face. He bore a giant gash in his shoulder where it had taken a chunk out of him. That, plus the shredded skin in his arm, made him look like he had one foot through Rallion's first gate.

Across the way, Beretta stuck a sword into the belly of a creature and Devlin tore it into pieces from the inside of its injury. They worked as a team, with him using his powers to grab a hold of their weaknesses, their wounds.

Neither cared for the soldier less than ten feet away. The one *they'd* endangered to begin with.

Rian was on his own, trying to keep himself alive and hold the creatures at bay. There was nothing she could do for him. There was nothing she could do for anybody. Several creatures ran past the door, headed for their sleeping citizens or the nearby camp.

Opi was thrown to the ground and the creature turned back to finish off his victims. Isla held Malin's shoulders. She couldn't even summon a hint of darkness and ash at this point, she was so drained. Emptied.

The winged creature with a shelled back stalked towards them, Isla's body trapped by its gaze. Malin tried to get up, but his injuries were too much. His sword was long gone at this point. The flames from the cursed gate were too high to see anything except for the creature's hollow eyes that seemed to go on and on and on. All sound was sucked into the pit of death, except for the pattern of her own desperate breathing.

In the hollow darkness that threatened to consume her, a glimmer of sunshine rustled. Small at first. Yet, it refused to be smothered. It sprouted and flowered. A small, single root taking hold with a firm grasp.

Don't give up.

She refused to let it take them. Not like this.

Isla dug deep into herself, further than she'd ever gone before. Happy memories evaded her and all that came was the pain and betrayal and—

A shudder shook the ground and darkness flooded her vision. She fought to regain it and keep herself upright as the last of her reserves were sapped.

The Nothing raised a giant hoof-claw, staring right at her. This was it.

"Isla!" Rian called from beyond her sight.

Isla turned but all she could see was Edmund waning on the edge of her blurry vision. His hands stretched to her.

The creature paused, tilting its head curiously. It burst into flames as if a fire had exploded from the inside. Bone-like skin melted and it withered completely.

Wielder flames.

A firewielder.

Transfixed by the dying flames that remained of the Nothing, Isla sat there. Black ichor seeped from the remnants and turned everything it touched to ash but she couldn't care about that. Her body couldn't move and her brain had long since stopped working.

Freya looked at Edmund like he'd grown an extra head. Beau didn't flinch.

A wielder?

A wielder.

There was no way he was a wielder. Somebody would have told her. *He* would have told her. He wouldn't have left her on her own if he was.

A large feline charged through the flames. There were too many of them, and they kept appearing out of that fucking fissure. Opi whined and hunched down beside her. She half wanted to join him. It felt like her insides had fully died.

He never told her. How could he do that after everything? *Everything!*

Another wielder in their family and she had been oppressed and mistreated and shamed. Someone should have known.

Rian's scythe dropped to the ground. The hay absorbed its clatter but Isla felt it *inside*.

The only one true to her.

"No!" She threw her hands and channeled all that fear, all that rage, the betrayal, and the hatred outward. It didn't matter if she could barely breathe or move. It didn't matter if she had nothing left to give.

One last push, before it was all over.

The Nothing about to jump on him turned to ash beneath her power, dusting his face before he could blink. Her vision wavered in and out. The bones in her body trembled, shaking the ground with them.

The darkness spread and spread. A thirst that couldn't be satiated. It crept towards a creature feasting on the remains of a horse, then to one that neared the entrance. It slithered past the humans, though she didn't want to at first. Let it devour them, destroy them like they'd done to her. It wouldn't be the first time she had allowed it to destroy everything in her path.

Visions of frightened faces, moments before they were turned into nothing came to her. The villagers.

But she couldn't.

Not again. She promised not to lose herself in her head. In her fury.

The city. Her people. They were too close.

Her fingers trembled.

If it ran wild, she'd never be able to rein it in. It would destroy the few of those she held dear and loved, despite her wanting it to consume the others. One taste of human flesh and there'd be no end to it.

She couldn't be responsible for the death of any more innocents.

Another shudder from the center. The strain on her weak body was too much. Time to stop this. Rein it in.

Focus, Isla. Summon it and control it.

Control it, that thread of sunshine whispered.

Control it!

Isla answered to no goddess. Destiny bent to her will, not the other way around. And so did her powers. This, she could do. She *would* do.

A shuddering gasp to take in all the breath needed for one final push. Focusing the last of her strength, she beckoned the darkness back into herself, pulling tighter and tighter.

It pulsed once. Then twice, flames flickering in unison.

It refused to come. Refused to obey. Something was wrong.

Opi whined and clawed the ground.

The hole. The fissure or gate or whatever, was growing larger. It wasn't stopping at all. Neither was the spread of her power. Flames took over everything. Larger and brighter with white ash drifting out of it.

The gate wasn't closing. It was flourishing. And it was taking all her power with it.

Thirty-Six

The cavern grew and stretched like an endless sky ready to devour all. It pulled in all nearby light, hungry for any glimmer of brightness, and left a dreadful frost in the air and in his bones.

It would snuff out everything if it was allowed to continue. The Pedite camp was close and so was the rest of the city.

"Isla!" Edmund yelled, staring at her with wide eyes.

She was on the ground, her fingers blackened, and it looked like she was struggling against an invisible pull. Rian could almost see it; he could definitely feel it.

The Nothing he was dealing with was reduced to ashes mid-leap, covering the half of him that wasn't already soaked in blood. With the path clear, Rian longed to run to Isla, as he'd been trying to do since first spotting her.

He wasn't sure when she initially showed up, and the first time he had tried to reach her, a Nothing clipped his injured shoulder. Then Devlin and Beretta blocked the other free path. By now, that twisted pair seemed to have forgotten about him. Initially, they were content to abandon him to deal with the deadly demons on his own before their escape was blocked off. Then it all went to Rallion's hells and time started behaving wonky.

Now Isla was here with Malin and the others, lingering just beyond his reach, despite every fiber of his body yearning to close the gap.

The ground shook and he crashed against the back wall. Every time he tried to move, the floor shoved back as did the creatures.

Devlin's side was wet and Beretta hovered close to him, frozen as she stared at the center of the hole. Opi cowered beside Isla, nudging her with his tail but likewise powerless to help. He whined and backed away from the edge of the opening, which wouldn't stop growing.

Rian's insides chilled as he stared into the vortex darker than a night sky... if the sky was overflowing with ungodly creatures. Truly was a curse sent from Rallion herself.

The gate would suck her dry. Whatever was powering it lingered on the edge of his insides, hungry for any morsel it could find. Nothing was enough to satiate it.

"Stop it, Isla," Rian called across the growing hole. He didn't dare move, not at the rate this thing was expanding. Knowing his luck, he'd fall straight into the center. "That's *enough*."

"I can't," she breathed. Her eyes widened as the darkness reached her elbows.

"It's going to kill everyone," Devlin said. He stared at the ground and kept shielding his eyes from whatever he saw in the gate's depths.

They were the closest to Isla, and that frightened Rian more than the darkness consuming everything. The Siica had an arm across Edmund's chest, stopping him from getting closer to both the gate and Isla, as if she were something to be feared. Malin was on the ground, transfixed by the opening, and no amount of shouting could break him from his spell.

The Siica was yelling at Edmund to leave. Fleeing was pointless. It would take over everything, including Isla and the entire city. Every innocent soul beyond the city walls was at risk. Rian *knew* that. Couldn't the others see?

There had to be another way to get it closed. Some method to shove the darkness back into its cage. Maybe it was time to throw a desperate prayer to the goddesses, if any bothered to listen tonight.

Beretta yanked a dagger from the body of the closest Nothing and turned to Isla with her arm raised. Rian's heart stopped as he realized her intent a second too late. He'd never make it.

The mindweaver planned to close the gate the quickest way she knew how. To sever the link to its power—through Isla. Before Rian could take his first step, and before her hand could release the dagger, a black flash latched onto her arm.

"Aargh," Beretta screamed, throwing Opi through the splintered wall.

Rian stepped towards Isla but the board under his shoes cracked and swayed. *Fuck*. Not that way.

The Muratian wielder froze, transfixed by her wound. If this was another game, what was she trying to pull? Beretta blinked. Then dropped to her knees, shaking and clutching her arm.

She tried to get up but her limbs dangled out of control. It was like her muscles were momentarily numbed.

Rian cocked his head at Opi. The little terror's venom had kicked in. Beretta was lucky he wasn't fully grown yet. He edged around the side, slowly making his way towards Isla without startling her or stepping onto a dark patch. He didn't think she would hurt him but it was hard to know for sure given the rapid spread of darkness that moved up her arms and straight into the gate of the first of Rallion's hells that stood between them.

This was the worst he'd seen her powers. Even she was frightened beyond recognition—he could feel it through their link.

The gate to the hells had been set off by her, and she needed to close it before it consumed her... and took the rest of them with it.

"*Isla!*"

Her eyes had turned fully black and her face drained of color. Rian felt the strength leaking from her into that—that thing. He could feel her fighting it, desperately trying to keep it back but she was not enough.

How do they even stop a force from the goddesses like that? It didn't matter *how*. He had to try... or they'd go down together.

Another pulse and the pit stretched three more feet, the darkness snuffing out most of the light around them. It didn't matter if he couldn't see her, he knew where she was.

The cavernous hole in the ground was something he sent a prayer to the goddess to help him miss. Rian sprinted for her, but another figure shot out from the darkness.

It was Devlin... and he was closer.

For a terrifying moment, he thought the Muratian was intent on killing her. Instead, he scooped up the dagger she'd dropped earlier. Isla didn't move or flinch when he grabbed her hand and dragged the tip along her palm.

Burning pain trickled down Rian's arm.

Isla shuddered, free from the spell. Devlin looked over his shoulder at the fissure, watching as a terrible tremor ran underneath them. Whatever his plan was, it seemed to have worked as the darkness faded from her hands, lingering only at her fingertips.

Rian was unsteady on his feet and toppled to his screaming knees. Every part of his body was in pain at this point. He looked across the gap and caught Isla's gaze. Even if he couldn't make it to her, he was with her. He trusted her.

One nod aimed solely for her. One small tug along that frail thread that led to her.

Finish it. You can do it.

She'd survived months in those mines. There was nothing she couldn't do. No one that had been through as much as she had and came out stronger on the other end. Even he couldn't have done that and survived.

A small glimmer of hope sent back along the thread.

Fight back! You control it.

Isla took a couple of deep breaths. Her body shook so violently that Rian felt his bones quiver. This was it. She held her arms out and an avalanche of darkness poured into her.

More and more darkness, clawing its way out and into the only suitable vessel. It took all the flames with it. For a moment, Rian thought he'd lost his vision again as everything turned completely black.

Then a blinding light shot out and Isla dropped to the ground.

"Well, that didn't work out nearly as terrible as I thought it would," Devlin said, twirling what he now realized was *Rian's* dagger between his fingers as he kicked over the last of the dead Nothings. He bent to examine the deadened wood beneath the body.

He had to be joking. No one could be this dense. Also, that was *his* father's dagger. How dare this depraved prince touch it?

Devlin spoke as if discussing the day's weather, instead of a targeted attack that almost killed them all. An attack fully caused by the two Muratians standing in this shattered stable.

Rian tore his eyes from the spot the gate once was, still picturing it vividly in his mind. All he could think about was exactly how he planned on throttling every ounce of air from Devlin's body.

Freya looked as if she wished to hack the hole apart again, only to throw the Muratian prince in it.

Devlin flipped the dagger in the air and caught it with his other hand. Rian rested his hands on his knees and took a moment to catch his breath. There was definitely some internal bleeding and a cracked rib or two, but he couldn't believe they made it through that with their lives intact.

Devlin crouched over the transporter zealot, Chir. He touched her shoulder, checking if she was still alive.

Freya inched over to where Beau helped Edmund tend to his arm, keeping an eye on the Muratian and blocking his way. Rian shuffled closer to Isla, trying to keep attention away from her before the Muratians remembered why they were there in the first place. She looked out of it and fully drained. He wasn't certain if she registered what was happening right now.

Malin had made his way to his knees beside her, clutching his wounded arm.

Devlin backed away from the transporter, his eyes shifting to meet Rian's as he tossed the blade in the air again. "You good?" he asked to Beretta only.

She nodded. Her face still pale and expressionless as she shifted on the floor, movement slowly returning to her limbs.

Devlin nudged the zealot with his boot and stepped to the side.

Freya had her axe ready, glaring at the Muratian prince. "Somebody fetch those firestone chains."

Devlin scoffed and spread his arms. "After we worked together so nicely? I can't believe you'd double-cross us like—"

"Don't even finish that," Rian said. All it would take was one simple word and Freya would have his head nicely removed from those rigid shoulders. They could deal with the mindweaver later. After what he'd done to those Nothings, and how he manipulated Rian's old scars on that field, he now realized that Devlin was the biggest threat standing in these stables.

The Muratian spun the dagger between his fingers, staring at the blade for a moment. "Nice work there," he said. "I didn't think you'd had it in you, but I guess you managed to survive the Black Forests—twice."

Rian bristled. He didn't need this murderer's approval.

"Apologies," Devlin said slowly. "But I'm afraid our temporary truce is over." He whistled.

"What are—"

The zealot sprang to her feet and tossed a discarded blade at Freya while Devlin dove for where Isla and Malin were.

The soldier was slow from his injuries, and it took one touch from Devlin for them to tear even worse. Malin crumpled to the ground in a pile of blood.

A burst of flames shot at Chir, and she backed away before it landed. Fuck that *really* did come from Edmund. He hadn't imagined it before.

The transporter hissed. There would be time to worry about Edmund when they weren't stuck in a barn with murderous foes.

That bastard healed Chir. He healed her. Fucking *healed* her.

They should have killed him when they had the chance. Beretta sluggishly jumped to her feet. Rian shoved her to the ground before she could reach her prince. He dug his heel into her back.

"Don't fucking move." Devlin pressed Rian's old blade into Isla's side, his eyes whirling dangerously.

Freya edged closer to the transporter, shifting to the balls of her feet as she waited for an opening. Edmund was still crouched on the ground, with his Siica hovering next to him. That one wouldn't leave the crown prince's side, not even to save his sister.

"Drop her," Rian said, digging his boot further into Beretta's spine.

Isla's eyes were lidded but blazing with fury. She was drained from the Nothings, and with the firestone blade pressed against her, there was no fighting back. He had to get her out of here.

And this fucking Muratian prince needed to die.

"Chir." Devlin pointed at the zealot. "If you want to live, you'll get us out of here."

The zealot's bloodshot eyes shifted around the room. No way she'd trust Devlin after he turned on her only twenty minutes ago. No way she was *that* crazy.

"They'll kill you if you stay," Devlin said. "But we." He pointed a thumb at his chest. "Have similar goals. We've worked together

before and I can guarantee your safety and the supplies you're after...
if you help us get out of here."

Chir shuffled her feet, edging closer to Devlin and Isla.

Flashbacks of that transporter in the Ashenwoods came to him.
That was where he nearly lost Isla the first time. He vowed to Laian
he wouldn't let it happen again.

Devlin clearly had other thoughts. "We disagreed on the prior
approach and lost. We can regroup and still work together. Our
goal remains the same. I understand that and we can accomplish
everything we want *right now*."

The wielder's eyes glistened.

"You touch her and I'll kill you," Rian said.

"Nuh-uh." Devlin pointed the end of the blade at him. "You're
not going to do anything." He dragged the blade along the side of
Isla's arm, carving a thin line near the crook of her elbow.

Isla screamed. A tendril of pain jolted up his arm and he nearly
lost his grip on Beretta, who tried to wiggle out from under him,
still not fully recovered from Opi's venom. The seropa was hunched
back, waiting on an order from Rian or Isla.

Not yet. If Devlin was determined to get what he wanted through
any means, so was Rian.

He grabbed another dagger from his pocket and pulled Beretta
back up. "You two can leave." Rian pointed at Devlin and the transporter. "And you can take your soldier with you... but not Isla."

Never her. Not while he still had movement in his limbs and life
in his veins.

Devlin laughed, running the blade along Isla's skin and twisting
it past the surface like he was whittling a design. Bile reached the tip
of Rian's tongue. "I'd never trust a Velotian. No deal."

"That's the only deal you get," Rian countered. "Take your
wielder and get the fuck out of here. You can have your lives and
your freedom."

The transporter was close now, and Devlin was inching back towards her.

"She's weak." Rian pointed at Chir. "And can't take three of you. You'll never make it."

"He's right," Beretta wheezed out. Rian twisted her arm behind her back. "It's okay."

Devlin kept looking at the transporter and to Beretta, then to the prisoner in his grasp. Beretta closed her eyes and nodded. A weighted acceptance settled in Devlin's blue eyes and he turned towards the transporter.

Oh no.

Fuck. They really were that crazy.

Freya's head whipped to meet his panicked gaze; she understood as well. They'd never make it in time.

Rian twisted the mindweaver in his grip and plunged the dagger straight into Beretta's abdomen. Dark blood pooled around his hand as he twisted it in, ignoring his stomach's plea to empty itself.

Isla stared at him, dumbfounded. Devlin froze in shock for the longest second that seemed to never end and Rian feared his gamble hadn't paid off.

He pulled the dagger out of her gut, ignoring the squelching sound. He released the wielder. Beretta dropped to her knees, holding her wound as blood pooled over her hands and onto the floor.

A cry ripped from Devlin's throat. "No!"

Beretta tried to speak but all that came out was an awful gurgling. Blood trickled out of the corner of her mouth, choking her.

Devlin adjusted the grip on the dagger, his eyes pivoting around as the puddle around Beretta grew. Rian stepped away from her, leaving the path clear.

"You have seconds to decide now." He looked back at Beretta, gasping for air and turning dangerously pale. "The offer is still there. We don't have any healers around and I don't think she'll make it. Go. Now. You fucking asshole!"

Devlin cursed Hierel's name, then threw Isla to the ground. He dove for Beretta with the transporter right behind him, pulling her into his arms.

"I'll fucking kill you for this." His eyes blazed straight through Rian's soul.

"Guess I'll see you around, then," Rian answered, feeling foolishly bolstered by Devlin's rage.

With that, the transporter and the two Muratians were gone.

Rian crossed the room and gathered Isla into his arms.

"What the fuck was that?" Malin said, sputtering through a mouthful of blood as he dragged himself up to sit. "That was fucking crazy is what that was. I'm a little impressed and a tiny bit scared."

Freya ran over to Malin. "I thought you were dead, you idiot."

Malin coughed and clutched his chest. "Almost there."

Rian focused on the one in his hands. He caressed Isla's face and swept strands of sticky hair out of her eyes. Any hint of darkness already had pulled back from her hands. She was barely with it though and couldn't focus.

"Hey." He brushed a finger across her cheek. "You're okay. You're fine now. They're gone. I've got you."

Isla's eyes rolled to the back of her head and she slumped over in his arms.

Thirty-Seven

The Princess

Isla's body felt like it had been thrown around in a giant rockslide before being doused in boiling water. If everything didn't hurt so much, she'd have thought herself dead. An eye cracked open to find that she was back in her room, despite the spinning ceiling.

What happened again? Dark flames burst and she was being drained. Then everything collapsed and someone carried her to the castle. Rian?

No. He was stopped at the castle entrance and Edmund took her the rest of the way. Her stomach churned. Edmund. The sting of hot betrayal leaked from the corner of her eyes and dropped onto the pillow.

Why didn't he ever tell her?

Her own brother was the same and yet different. And all this time she never suspected. All this time her father hated her for being exactly what Edmund hid. She had been forced to walk this path alone for years... while her brother concealed the worst secret of them all.

A part of her didn't blame him. If she could have escaped the criticism from her father all these years, she would take that chance. But *never* at the expense of her own flesh and blood. She had more loyalty than some.

"Argh." She punched a furry pillow straight into her ornate table, sending its contents flying.

"What'd that table do to you?"

Isla sat up so quickly that her head spun.

"Whoa. Whoa. Not so fast." Rian grabbed her arm and helped her to the edge of the bed. "You should be—"

"Don't," she bit out, then went into a coughing fit. Rian handed her a glass of water, tilting his head to watch her every movement. Gods, how bad was she out of it after the barn?

It wasn't like she was the worst of them.

Finally remembering herself, she grabbed his face and pulled him closer. He was cleaned up and out of those bloody clothes. The injuries to his eyes and shoulder were all forgotten. He merely looked like he'd had a three-day ale bender and hadn't slept a wink.

"I'm fine," he said softly, covering her hands with his. "Edmund helped sneak me in—I think he felt bad after everything. It involved me wearing one of Alynna's cloaks so don't you ever bring it up again."

That traitor's name sent her blood boiling. She didn't want to hear it uttered in her presence ever again. Just as she never wanted to see him.

Now, Rian hiding under a woman's cloak and trying to pass as one of her ladies, she'd give half her jewels to have seen that. He refused to elaborate further. She was glad he was here and planned to pretend like he'd never mentioned Edmund.

"Thank you for coming," she whispered. "Thank you for saving me."

"You were the one that came and saved me, remember?" He kissed the palm of her hand. "Do you want to talk about it?"

Isla shook her head. Definitely not.

No talking about Edmund. No talking about anything. There would be time later but right now she wanted to forget the sight of those creatures, how they were brought here, and how the mere thought of it made her insides feel like she was slowly turning to dust. She wanted to hide that power deep within herself and burn it into nothing.

Deathpuller.

Now she knew why the nickname was given to those with powers like hers. Why they were said to be inherited directly from Rallion herself. Had her mother known when she became one of her devotees? Did she always pray to Sister Death like those zealots? There was so much she wished she could ask, but that chance was gone.

If Isla had known that's what her powers were capable of, she would never have learned to control them in the first place. Now, this curse had twisted and spread into an even more unimaginable burden. She needed to find a way to fix this.

"What did you see in—in there?" he asked hesitantly, averting his gaze.

"What?"

"It didn't look the same to all of us," he said. "Mine appeared as an endless dark sky. Freya said it was a turbulent ocean, Malin saw only bright light, and Edmund wouldn't say."

The thought that everybody saw something different never occurred to her.

"Flames," Isla said darkly. "I saw all consuming white flames."

What did it all mean?

"I don't know. Maybe it's linked to the goddesses in our lineage, maybe we all hallucinated different things." His brows furrowed, and she traced the line between them. "Edmund sent some men to find Devlin and Beretta. They found no trace left behind."

Isla was certain those two were long gone by now. Long gone and formulating a new plot to ruin her life altogether. Isla knew in the cavern of her heart that it wasn't the last they'd see of those two.

A shiver ran over her body. Rian's eyes flashed with concern. She scooted back on the bed, pulling the topmost blanket and gesturing for him to get under. They could escape in the warmth if they wanted to, only for a little while.

The outside world was too cold and cruel. She had no desire to return anytime soon.

Rian shook his head. "I can't stay. We've been given new assignments and leave tomorrow."

"Tomorrow?" Her head snapped to the window. The sun began its ascent over the distant rooftops. She must have slept an entire day. How long had he waited for her to wake up?

"It went by quickly," he said. "I passed the time listening to the delicate rhythm of your snores."

As if *his* weren't any louder. "Don't change the subject."

His eyes darkened and he threw himself on the bed, tugging her so she was cradled against his side. She threw a leg over him in the hopes of trapping him with her.

"I wasn't." Fingers brushed the sensitive skin at her ankle, pushing the edge of her nightgown before hitching her leg up higher. "We've been given new orders to help with the warfront. Heading out with Commander Gaines and four whole battalions. I'll be leading the Pedite squads."

Straight into a death trap if what she knew of Velotian tactics was true. The Pedite contingents were always sent first and to the most dangerous locations. Why wasn't he more mad at this? If anything, he seemed resolved to his fate. Years with the Pedites had done that. She'd try to talk to her father about this, if he was still speaking to her.

"I don't want you to go," she said, realizing she sounded like a spoiled child. It didn't matter. They wanted him to leave her, right after she almost lost him thanks to those lunatics.

"Me neither." He pulled her so her head was against the crook of his neck. She planted a kiss against his pulse. The smooth patterns he traced against her thigh were the only comfort against the cold darkness that tugged on her. His heartbeat against her cheek steadied any nerves or anxieties she held.

"I was afraid I'd lose you," she said.

A beat, then, "Me too."

"One day," she said longingly. "We'll run away for real. Someplace warm. I've had enough of the cold. Near Bluemoon Bay or along the coast so we can wake up every morning to the smell of salt and sun. Nobody would know our real names or who we are."

His laughter shook her body.

"Then you'll have to make your own pastries and run your own bath. I'd have to teach you things like how to scrub the clothes and hang them so you don't stink like a horse's ass."

She clawed the exposed skin by his neck. "Rude. Ungentlemanly."

He'd be fully cleaning his own smelly uniforms. There was no way she would touch those dirty linens except to burn them.

"We've already established that I'm not a gentleman." The hand stopped making those glorious patterns and squeezed. "Or would you like me to return to being a respectful soldier?" Cold air replaced the warmth on her thigh. "Because there are only indecent thoughts running in my head right now."

In one swift movement, she flipped herself to straddle his torso. All tiredness washed from her limbs and was replaced with fiery heat that infiltrated every vein.

"Only improper thoughts allowed in here," she said. Her hands flinched against his muscled chest, digging into the rough material of his general's jacket. One of far too many layers between them.

"I can tell." He gripped her waist. "Because I was thinking how I've never been in a room as outlandish as this." He jerked his head at the jewels that sparkled from their display and the multiple chests with gold finishings. "And I've never been in a bed as soft as this, with as many unnecessary pillows or drapes around it."

She grinned. "That's because nobody would dare invite a scoundrel like you into their chambers." A finger poked the stubble on his face to emphasize her point.

His lips formed a large circle of mock indignation. "How dare you?"

She wiggled against him and felt his hardness rise. Heat bloomed in the pit of her stomach, spreading its way outward when she trailed down to his jacket and played with the first tarnished silver button.

He frowned. "Are you certain you are—?"

"Do not even finish that sentence."

"Whatever you say, Princess." His hand made its way to her thigh, finding her undergarments and starting to stroke her sensitive areas. "As always, I am yours to command."

Those words sent her insides spinning. Her organs fought for dominance as they were turned inside out. There were so many things she wanted him to do, especially with those glorious lips and those fingers that knew the right spot to hit again and again.

When she tried to speak, her mind forgot how. It could barely remember to breathe under his touch. The only thing her body knew was *him*. And it wanted to be consumed by him. Fully and completely until it wasn't clear where she ended and he began.

Burning heat migrated to her pit. He'd worked her into a heated frenzy. She wanted him. Now. All of him... belonging to all of her.

She managed to get the first few buttons undone and dragged her fingers down every inch of chest she could reach, his skin smooth velvet under her fingers. That resulted in one, low hiss.

The sound rattled Isla's bones and she couldn't take it anymore. This was not nearly enough. Not at all.

More. She needed more. She raised her hands up expectantly and he pulled himself up long enough to drag her nightdress over her head, all while keeping her settled atop his lap. Once she was free from the constraining fabric, she finished with the remainder of his buttons. His tunic joined the jacket on the floor and she shoved him back to the bed. He let her overpower him, as she was certain he could throw her around if he wanted to.

She liked them right where they were—with him laying on her bed, ready for whatever she wanted to give, and her fully in control.

Control of herself and her mind and her emotions... but most importantly, she wanted to be in complete control of *him*.

"What do you want?" His voice was raspy and it sent her organs tumbling all over each other in a quest for dominance. Her insides were burning and there was only one thing that could satiate that blaze. One person.

"I want—I want these off." She tugged at the loop on his pants.

"Happy to oblige, My Lady." He lifted his hips and tugged his pants off, kicking them to the ground. His throbbing member sprang up to caress her inner thigh.

He closed his eyes and leaned his head back. The flush grazing his cheeks made her insides purr. But the hard cock heating against her skin desperately called to her, and her mind couldn't focus on anything else.

She scooted down his body and kissed the hard lines of his stomach, trailing her mouth across his silky skin. Every touch of her lips against his skin was like smooth, melted honey for her soul.

A tremor ran over Rian's body and into hers. Gods, she needed this. She pressed a kiss to the side of him before taking his entire length into her mouth. The moans he made nearly pushed her off a dangerous cliff, so she remained focused on moving her mouth, and taking time to explore every inch of him until he moaned her name.

This wasn't enough. Not yet.

She savored one last salty drop, and crawled up his body to kiss him once more.

"You're everything to me," he said softly. "The reason I breathe and live."

The warmth that bloomed from her insides was different this time. It was sustenance and comfort and home all mixed into one blazing stream. "Same. I don't ever want to feel like I did last night. Never again."

He nodded, incapable of words. She didn't need any from him, she *felt* his affirmations budding inside of her, along with his fervid impatience.

No more waiting. One of them would combust if they did.

She settled back on her heels and wiggled into place above him. Rian grabbed her hips and helped guide her. When she lowered herself onto him, stars flashed before her eyes. He stretched her so fully and perfectly.

"You okay?" he asked.

Her body hummed in smoldering response. Surges of pleasure worked their way through her veins and all she could do was nod while pushing down to fully devour him.

Once she'd adjusted to him inside her, she started moving. She wasn't exactly sure what to do but went with what felt right. She rocked her hips, feeling him hit her insides.

When it wasn't enough, she rose on her knees until he was almost out of her, then came crashing back down onto him. Her skin was on fire and he was the timber, ready to set her, and the world, ablaze.

Rian's eyes had fully darkened and his grip kept tight on her hips, guiding her in and out like smooth waves crashing against the shore.

"That's my girl," he purred, cupping her face. "Not yet."

This feeling should never end, not until she'd felt every part of him she wanted... and she wanted *every inch*. They settled into a slow rhythm that matched every pulse soaring through her body and into his, all while she stared into those gray eyes. Those gorgeous eyes that were flecked with hues of honey and sapphire and emerald that sparkled straight to her soul.

"Fuck it," he grit out. Without stopping the rhythm, he flipped them around so she was on her back. She kept her legs wrapped tightly around him to keep them as close as possible.

Each movement was silky torture, but he never broke their eye contact and she was trapped by his fiery gaze. Fully at his mercy as he claimed her. Just when she thought she couldn't take anymore, he quickened the pace.

Every touch feathered across her skin, *into* her. Each sound echoed in her heart. Any breaths he released filled her lungs with sustenance. She was close. So close. She bit his shoulder to keep from being torn out of her skin. Her fingers dug into his scarred back—her blackened fingers.

No!

She yanked her hands away and he stopped. Understanding quickly dawned on his face. He pulled her hand into his and kissed each of her curse-touched fingers, resuming his movements.

"I got you," he murmured, and her stomach fluttered in response.

A swell of pleasure flowed and her power urged to erupt just as her insides were shattering. The only thing she knew was that she couldn't let it out. She didn't know what to do and considered grabbing the oak headboard as a conduit.

Between shallow breaths and deep thrusts, Rian nodded. He placed her hand over his heart, on top of the dusty marks she'd made in that hallway. The frantic beating beneath her palm sang to her. *Begged* her. So she unleashed it. The skin underneath his hand glowed briefly, then darkened.

He hissed and closed his eyes.

At first, she thought she'd hurt him but his eyes snapped open and they were absolutely feral. He pushed into her, deeper and harder, until he found the core of her soul. Riding out the pain as her unfiltered power pulsed into him and claimed him as hers. She was a part of him, everywhere, all over, and yet it still wasn't enough.

One final, deep push had him groaning as he found his edge, hers right behind him.

Stars skittered across the sky, as bright as the morning sun. Her insides twisted and vibrated as she felt him spill into her. They slowly dove over the edge and into the crashing waves together.

She savored him on her skin and inside her, but she especially loved the taste of him flowing through her veins. Like a toxin she craved more and more of.

The darkness at her fingers slowly faded, taking another full drink of him to satiate her appetite. He was the only nourishment she needed.

Hot air tickled her skin as he rested his forehead on her shoulder. She didn't know where she left her breath behind, except that it slowly came back in giant gulps. It was as if she'd been underground her entire life before this.

The removal of her hand sent a second shudder running through his body and into hers.

"Fuck," he moaned into her neck as they lay there, connected. "You're so perfect, princess." He tilted her chin while he pulled out.

Coldness greeted her, her whine was silenced by another kiss.

Rian's hand had worked its way down and started its movements again. Quicker this time, to pull her over the edge again. Gods, he knew exactly how to unravel her completely. She found herself thrown across the skies again as wave after wave of unimaginable pleasure overtook her.

This was what it was like to be a goddess with the world at your fingertips. He led her over the edge and back home again, all while he murmured sweet promises against her skin.

Lips pressed against her neck, her collarbone... every inch he could find. Her skin was alive and yearned for his touch, and he was more than happy to indulge her every whim as if equally hungry. She was the night sky and the day sky, and he was the ground turning beneath her.

Once he found every morsel of skin he hadn't met before, he returned to reclaim her mouth.

The power within had quietened, only stirring momentarily when she came for the third time that night. But there was no darkness at her hands begging to be unleashed.

They laid together for some time in the comfort of her over-pillowed bed, though most had toppled to the ground by now. It was hard to feel so complete and whole when she knew deep down that a terrible ending loomed near.

Thirty-Eight
The General

Salty seawater sprayed his face while the sun's first ray hit his back. A warm ember heated his chest and spread over his body, keeping him upright against the turbulent winds.

Loud pounding came from the clouds above and the water below. Bellowing. Demanding to be let in. Annoyingly so... familiarly annoying.

Fuck.

Rian's eyes fluttered open. Isla was still tucked under his arm, emanating heat and peaceful stillness that reached into his bones. Her dark hair was splayed across his chest—smelling like a field of lilies—and her arm was wrapped tightly around his midriff, holding him, keeping him, claiming him. An interruption had never come at a worse time.

Until the source of that loud pounding decided to barrel through the door.

Isla shot up, dragging the silk sheet to cover herself. "Edmund." The fiery hatred in her voice sent shivers across his body—the bad kind. "*Get the fuck out.*"

When did she start swearing so much? Darkness flashed at her fingertips.

"You get out," Edmund said, just as heatedly. His words weren't directed to Isla but rather to the intruder in her bed. To *him*. That seemed to anger Isla even more.

This needed to be defused before one of them exploded, and Rian was right in the middle of them. He sighed and scooped his pants up from the floor. The slow movements seemed to irritate Edmund further.

"You were the one who helped me get here," Rian said calmly.

Edmund threw a shirt at his face. "To stay with her while she was recovering."

"Well," Rian said smugly. "She's recovered."

That one came out on its own. He couldn't help himself.

Edmund's entire body shook with what was likely suppressed rage. "Then what in Slin's name are you still doing here? No... wait. I don't want to know. Just *leave*."

Isla, who had snapped awake so quickly and so loudly, hadn't moved since. She stared at her brother with unfiltered rage.

Right. *That.*

The wielder powers. How the fuck did he hide that for so many years? There was no way the king knew about that and kept it quiet. No way.

That made it even worse.

Edmund finally observed her ire and straightened his back, scratching his blotchy neck. "Our father is coming," he said quietly. He pointed at Rian. "The commander has noticed his absence. He needs to leave. *Now.*"

Oh, gods. What time was it?

Judging by the sun's position, they had fallen asleep for a couple of hours. Fuck. He missed a meeting with Gaines. Not a great way to start off with his new commander, who already hated him because of the 'suspicious circumstances of his promotion.'

Edmund was still staring at his sister, some sort of desperation flashing in his eyes. "Look Isla, we need to talk."

Isla turned away from him.

The mark on his arm erupted with an emotion he knew all too well. Raging fury. Rian winced at the force of the emotion thrust upon him. "I don't think now is a good time, Edmund." He tugged his tunic on and approached the prince cautiously.

Edmund's eyes ran down the length of him. "You don't say."

Why did he have to be here every time? *Why?*

Rian jerked his head at Isla. "Give us a couple of minutes."

"You don't have that time," Edmund said slowly. "You can have sixty seconds."

That's all he needed.

"I'll try to stall him." Edmund turned on his heel. "Don't say I haven't done anything for you." Another flicker of anger. Edmund turned his head when he reached the door. "And for Hierel's sake, put your clothes on, Isla. I'll be outside."

Why did the man not have a lick of sensibility in him? After all this time, he still didn't know how to treat her properly, despite his ghastly loud attempts. Rian didn't want to see what a poor effort was, if this was him doing his best.

Rian was already at Isla's side before the door clicked shut. "I'm so sorry." He grabbed her head and pressed a kiss to her temple. "I have to go."

That boiled anger evaporated as she stared at him with wide brown eyes. "Don't. Don't go."

"We'll have a thousand worse problems if I'm still here when your father shows. We can figure things out later."

"Later," her voice rose. "What *later* do we have? You're leaving. Tomorrow! There's no time."

They never had time on their side. Only borrowed moments that the goddesses deemed fit to sprinkle their way when things got too much. That was all they were allowed. Nothing more.

"I... I will write to you when we get to the border. And maybe we'll see each other again when you are—"

"On my way to be sold to the Koliats," she finished angrily.

Not quite the wording he was going for, yet he had no rebuttal. He wrenched his gaze away from hers.

"I don't know what choice we have. And you'll be safer there. Further away from the Muratians. We can look into the gates while we're apart. I'll ask around and maybe you can access the archives and get the answers you need."

She clamped her lips together in a giant frown. He hated that. Anything that brought her pain was unacceptable.

"I don't want this," he said quickly. The mere thought of parting was already sending his heart into a vicious trot. "But I'm not seeing a lot of options."

Being pulled so far away from her would be nearly unbearable. The mere mention of separation curled inside his chest and stayed there, a mountain atop of blade of grass.

"We'll find something," she said wistfully. Her shoulders shook as she came to the same daunting conclusion he already had. "I don't want you to go."

He pulled her against his chest, cradling her there as if he could suck her warmth and take it with him. "Me neither."

It wasn't like they had much choice in the matter. That had been taken away from them at birth.

"How would you even write to me?" she murmured against his jacket.

It wasn't the *how*, more so how he expected to reach her when the king would certainly be filtering any communications sent her way. "I'll take up writing to my new best friend. Edmund will require constant updates on our progress."

She stiffened underneath him. There wasn't enough time to talk her through what happened with Edmund and he didn't want to waste any more precious seconds on that man.

That idiot prince had done a lot of wrong by his sister, especially in this past year. It was hardly forgivable by any sane means, but things were different now and Edmund did seem to at least have Isla's best interests at heart... most times. That was more than anyone else here.

Rian hoped she could find a way to move past it or it would get lonely in this castle. She'd have to talk to Edmund if she wanted the letters he planned on sending. They would need each other.

Gods, *was* Edmund his friend?

No way. He refused to call him that.

They stayed together for the fifteen seconds left before Edmund came barreling in to push him out the door and back to where he belonged.

Rian made it to the Pedite camp in record timing. He was sweating through his jacket and the side of his ribs felt like a dagger was being dragged along his lungs, but he made it.

"Thanks for showing up," Commander Gaines said as he skidded into place. He was already decked out in his formal attire with shining buttons and newly pressed badge on his puffed out chest. A parchment was clenched in his spare hand.

The camp was in disarray with half the tents already packed up and bundles of supplies stacked and ready for the morning. Rian had every intent of inspecting the Pedite portion himself to ensure the men weren't missing anything that would get him into trouble later.

Opi jumped off a stack of bags and bounded over but Freya intercepted the creature. He'd been famished since the gate and ate everything in sight. Rian knew the seropa was pressing Slin's luck with most of the soldiers here.

"Apologies, commander," he wheezed out, clutching the pulsing mark above his heart. A hollow cave had begun forming in his chest, expanding with each step he took away from the castle.

Freya flashed a warning look that was hardly needed. He was playing with fire and had pushed things too far. Exactly *how far*, was yet to be determined.

Guilt swirled within. He wanted to be better than this, for his men. He planned to throw himself into focusing on the Pedites, not only as a distraction but as a promise to the younger version of himself that was first thrown into training to settle his father's debts.

All he'd done so far was fail spectacularly.

"Any reason you've been missing half the afternoon while your second has been delegating orders on your behalf? Are our meetings not riveting enough for you?"

Think, Rian. Think.

He was a commanding officer. One who'd just missed an important meeting with his superior. There had to be a pretty good reason for missing that. Anything... anything that wouldn't implicate Isla and what they were just doing.

His arm prickled. Things must be going just splendidly with their dad. Would that link still be there when he was halfway across the kingdom? Would the bond stretch?

It did when she was in those mines, however faint.

"I was meeting with the prince," he said quickly. The only logical explanation he could muster. It was overused and it wasn't a great one, as Edmund was as likely to rebuke his lies as anyone, but that was all his dull brain came up with.

The commander surveyed him with a frown. He didn't buy it but Rian was hoping there was too much to do that Gaines wouldn't bother confirming his story.

"Well, thank you for deciding to grace us with your presence, *General*." Any of the fake formalities Gaines showed while in Edmund's presence had now fully dropped. Rian may be a general, but for all anybody cared, he was still a lowly Pedite soldier not worth their time.

"It won't happen again, sir," he bit out, fighting against every instinct he had. Opi whined and wiggled beneath Freya's grasp.

"No, it won't," he said smugly. "You may have had leniency under the prior commander." That was leniency? "And you may have somehow gained favor with our prince." That was laughable. "I see through the washed-up uniform and false titles."

Rian looked down at his uniform, freshly ordered and pressed, and tried to find what was wrong with it.

Gaines' face darkened. "There is something going on in this camp that I don't like, and I will figure out what that is, sooner or later."

"What do you mean, sir?" Rian had to really pull it together to make that last part sound respectful.

The commander's eyes sparkled dangerously. "Unfortunately, we'll have to sort through this on a different day. Time to get your men together, Pedite."

"What? Why?" Rian asked, ignoring Freya's exasperated groan. They were leaving in the morning. That's what Gaines had told him.

"An update to our orders from the castle," Gaines said smoothly, brushing the sleeve of his jacket. "It also includes some very concerning details from the king regarding your part in the solstice fire we experienced." Rian's chest tightened. "Lucky for you, there have been many reports of Muratians crossing the borders and causing chaos in our kingdom. Every soldier is needed. You're to take the Pedites and scout the route ahead. You leave within the hour. And get that creature under control before we make it our next dinner."

Thirty-Nine

The Princess

"This is over. Now!" Her father swept his arms out, seeming to suck all the light from the fire and crystal torches that lined the walls. That anger had popped up many times over her life, especially these past weeks, but this was new. She wouldn't be surprised if his head popped off completely and sprayed her room with his insides.

His entire face and neck had turned from a blotchy red to a deep purple that matched the velvet couch. The blond moustache quivered with every syllable and the chandelier's light glazed his eyes with a fiery hatred.

For the first time ever, Isla didn't care.

Not that he was mad at her. Nor that he blamed her for everything. And she especially didn't care that he didn't hold one ounce of room for her in his heart.

It was freeing to finally detach from the pitiful need to please him.

Edmund had turned pale and was slowly inching away from their father until his back hit the stone wall. She didn't spare him more than a second glance or thought. Not after tonight. Not while the bitter sting of his betrayal still burned her tongue.

How could he?

After everything. All these years and he never said something. Their father didn't know or he'd have been given the same deplorable treatment. All these years and Edmund kept quiet to save himself.

He didn't deserve any more space in her mind or her mangled heart. Believing he had changed was a mistake. And listening to any more of his pleas to talk would be another misstep.

Thank the goddess that her father already sent everyone running from her room so he could tear down his children in private. Though she had no doubt that there were listeners nearby, given the volume of her father's roaring dribble.

Dribble she barely paid any attention to.

At first, she tried saying she was kidnapped again, but her father quickly squashed that lie. So, for now, she refused to confirm what he suspected. There was nothing more she owed him.

"I'm not marrying him, father," she said into his angry face. That was the most certain she'd ever been in her life.

"Say that again," the king said, his eyes glowing dangerously.

"I'm not marrying him. I am not going to fucking Koliat. I'm not getting married."

"Father—"

"Shut up, Edmund. I don't need your help."

Her father stepped closer. Isla focused on the dark oak panel behind him. "You're going to need a lot more than his help if you try to disobey this. The deal has already been done. The ink long since dried. It is over. You have to marry him or we will face total ruin."

"I don't care." Isla shook her head, her thoughts never clearer than they were now. The Isla of a year ago would be proud of the way she stood her ground. "And you can't force a screaming and kicking bride into that temple. No priestess will accept that and Brenner won't either."

"He *will*," the certainty in his voice made her pause. "As will you or I will make your life seem like a regular day past Rallion's fifth gate. I don't care if I have to force you and say the words myself, you will be getting those marriage scars and you will be bonded to Prince Brenner for life, as promised."

Edmund rubbed his wrists. Fucking preen. This had nothing to do with him and his disintegrating marriage.

"I'd sooner throw myself off the highest tower before I allow that to happen."

No way had she survived everything just to live like this. A life with a strange prince in strange lands with no one she knew. Not to mention the powers that she could barely control that seemed determined to eat her from the inside.

Perhaps it showed on her face, but something made her father pause. She pounced on his momentary weakness.

"I mean it, father," she softened her voice. "I can't do it. I can't marry him anymore. I'm sorry, I know we need this but if I go there, it *will* kill me. I won't make him happy. I can't be that person. Not after everything. I need you to understand, *please*."

Something shifted in his eyes, but his expression quickly changed into a guarded mask. "You know what. Have it your way. Why not? You win. I don't care anymore."

"What?" Even Edmund unfroze from his spot at the wall to stare at their father in disbelief.

A simple beam of light edged into her vision. Was that hope?

"I'll send a notice to King Everett. I'll reason with him to make some amendments. There's nothing that a little more gold can't fix."

"What do you mean?"

"We'll prepare a new delegation. You can have what you want and I'll make arrangements for the new additions."

"New additions?"

Their father turned on his heel and paced the pile carpet. "Take Alynna and Susanna with you. Hierel knows they're more loyal to you than this kingdom. I don't want them here after what they've allowed you to pull."

"I don't understand."

"You can take your traitor maids with you. And you're taking that fucking Pedite rake—as a part of a security detail or something. I don't know how we'll word it but you can have your fucking whore. I'm sure they'll let it slide. Dia knows that Koliat prince has his own share of them from what I hear. Happy now?"

Isla's mouth dropped. That small morsel of hope snuffed out completely.

Her father stopped in front of her. "Take your disgrace of a Pedite lover with you and do whatever you want with him... in Koliat. You will marry Brenner and you will become their princess."

An explosion came out of her mouth and she couldn't stop the tirade of curses that slipped through. "That is not what I meant!" her voice shook with waves of suppressed rage.

"You are going to Koliat no matter what, Isla."

"Then I'll end it all before we get there."

This time there was no softening of the eyes or understanding expression. Whatever emotion she'd seen before was clearly wrong. "If you do, then I will have him hanged for his treasons against the crown and his crimes that led to this war in the first place. If you choose not to marry Brenner, then I will find the rest of his family and take everything I can from their already pathetic little lives. I will send Alynna and Susanna to work the lower wards until the day they die, and I will find every one of that Pedite's allies, friends, acquaintances, and send them to the stocks. Do you understand me *now*, Isla?"

Isla stared into those eyes. "You're fucking insane."

"I'm deadly serious about this. And I'll keep piling on the consequences every time you try to delay this. We need this. And I need you to accept that."

All she could do was shake her head and focus on keeping that rush of darkness at bay—a near impossible feat when staring into the eyes of a man wanting to ruin her entire life.

"I hate you," she said. Behind him, her mother's portrait mocked her with her half smile. Now that Isla stared at it closely, she finally spotted the hint of burn marks at the collarbone. How had she never seen that before?

"You know," he said slowly. "When you were born and tearing the life away from your mother, the healer said that she smiled before taking her last breath. I will not let you be the death of me too. I will not let you tear this family down."

It would have been better if he'd slapped her. Isla's breath slowed to a deadly pace. Even Edmund turned oddly pale.

"Now, stay here until you are summoned." He turned on his heel and paused. "And for Hierel's sake, properly clean yourself up. You're a disgrace of a Velotian Princess, which you still are, despite how much neither of us want that."

With that, her father left. All her hopes and dignity were whisked out the door with him. She was alone with her traitor brother who stared with panicked eyes. If he was worried that Isla was going to expose his secret to save herself, at least now he knew he was safe. She wouldn't stoop that low.

She wasn't him.

It became too much to stand there, fully defeated, with nothing but her brother as company, so she strode to the door and held it open until he removed himself from her presence.

Isla stayed in the confines of her room for another hour or two. There was nothing to do but pace and pace as she waited for someone to come back and deal more devastating news.

She found her bloody clothes and tossed them into the fire, watching the flames lick the material before fully consuming it. Fucking flames. *Fucking firewielders.*

The sun was halfway through the sky at this point, officially making it the longest and worst day of her life... and that was saying something.

She was a fool for giving into that sliver of hope. Now that it was fully snuffed out, things felt even worse than before. That pool of despair threatened to open up and consume her if she didn't do something.

Where were Alynna and Susanna? She needed a stiff drink. *Now.* She didn't care what hour it was or what her father ordered.

She paced the length of her room and into the attached hosting quarters, knowing there was no chance of escape. The door was there. The hallway was there, but consequences, and likely many Siicas, blocked her from moving towards it. She was trapped. Worse than when under that mountain.

The reminder of dark tunnels and stale air was too much. Just as the reminder of the terrible coldness from that hole in the ground and the way the blood from those Nothings turned everything to ash.

Her breath came in sharp rattles. No matter what she did, it kept getting worse. And the heat from the fire grew unbearable, despite being one room over. She couldn't do this.

Darkness crept from her veins into her fingers. At this point, she wasn't certain if she had the strength to pull it back. It could consume her from the inside out for all that she cared. It could grow and grow until she was nothing more than a pile of ash... like those villagers.

A rap on the door startled her. Her knees gave out and she sank to the ground.

There was nobody she wanted to see. Nobody that was allowed in here at least. The hollow halls of this place contained only gossipers, elitists, and soldiers loyal to her father.

Another sharp rap.

Go away.

She closed her eyes and prayed to Hierel for a moment of peace. The goddesses never graced her a hint of mercy. That's why Edmund strode in, closely followed by Beau. His Siica had been around for longer than she could remember, always by Edmund's side. Hells, he was probably older than their father.

Get out!

She couldn't form the words. Didn't want to waste a breath on him despite the fact that he took up so much of her thoughts already. She settled on sending him a fiery glower.

"I know you don't want to see me right now." The understatement of this cursed year. His eyes trailed to her hands and he froze.

Typical.

Edmund's gaze snapped back to hers and he closed the distance. He knelt and grabbed her darkened hands in his. "I'm sorry I never told you."

There was no way she could meet his eyes so she focused on one of his stupid engraved silver buttons. She traced the lines of the flames in her mind, wishing to be engulfed by their imaginary heat, and ignoring their blatant irony.

The Siica remained by the door, observing, but made no movement to stop Edmund or move him from the looming danger. They must have talked about this before.

Edmund's eyes followed. "Beau knows. He was our mother's personal Siica and the only other person who knows the truth."

If he thought that made everything better. It didn't. One more person that knew about Edmund's powers. One more person who could have saved her from years of torment and shame at her father's hands.

Wait. He wasn't the only one. Their mother had known. She'd known about him. And Devlin said something about Insmia, the goddess of fire. Did he know or was that a lucky guess?

Edmund swallowed loudly. "I don't know when I figured out what I could do, but mother made me swear to never tell another living soul. She taught me how to hide it and how to control it. I think she knew what our father would say if he found out. Beau helped me in the beginning years, alongside our mother. When she—when you were born and she was gone, I was so alone. I didn't know what to do. I was only ten and just lost my favorite person and I didn't know you except what father said about what you'd done."

Isla continued tracing the flame in her mind.

"And when father was so mad about your powers and I saw how he treated you, I got scared. I was too afraid to tell anyone else. I didn't want what happened to you to happen to me, and I was such a coward."

The first truthful words she'd heard. It still did nothing to calm the raging gale within.

"I wanted to tell you, but there was never a good time. After we found you again, I thought it was my chance. To make everything better. To finally fix things with us like I know she'd want. Every time I tried to tell you, the words wouldn't come. I knew you'd be so mad, rightfully so, and I couldn't bear causing you more pain after all you'd been through."

Isla's pulse surged. The darkness was gone from her hands, yet Edmund still gripped them in his own. Was this the first time he'd really touched her in all their years? At nearly twenty-two years of age, it was far too late.

"I know there's nothing I can say to make this better. I hope that with time you can understand that I was—I still am—a scared boy who didn't know what to do." He looked at Beau, who peeled himself away from the wall.

"Beau stayed loyal after our mom died." His hand flinched over-top hers.

After *she* killed their mother. That's what he was thinking, despite not uttering that out loud. He'd said as much before.

Isla finally dragged her eyes to meet his. She felt nothing anymore, *especially* not for him.

"I haven't been the best brother, despite my efforts these past months, which I know were lackluster. It's not nearly enough and will take a while to earn that trust back from you, but I hope this is a start."

Beau pushed back his silver cape and passed a bundle of cloth to Edmund, who finally released her hands. She tucked them behind her back before he could grab them again.

Disappointment flashed in Edmund's eyes. He placed the bundle beside her.

What was that?

"The troops are readying to leave for the border, where they'll reinforce our contingent already there. Alynna and Susanna have been sent with some of your supplies."

Isla's eyes flickered back up. Is that where they've disappeared to?

"I have new orders for Beau to give Commander Gaines direct from the *king* with his personal seal. The princess will be joining the efforts at the border to ensure a smooth transition between groups. Beau can get you there safely and *I* will deal with our father."

But his threats. He *promised*. There was no way she could leave now.

"I don't care what he said before. I won't let him." What power did Edmund have over him? "Once you're gone, he'll have to acquiesce that someone broke in and doctored fake orders. He's too proud for that, especially if he has to admit it was his own heir."

Isla's heart dared to shudder at this.

"I don't know what the future holds or how much time until he comes up with another way to push this through, but it's a start of how I can make amends. It's not the last. I'll do what I can to help from here and keep Brenner occupied," he finished that last part bitterly. He gazed at the bundle of clothes and back to her face. "There's one of our mother's old diaries in there. You can have it. She was the one who first showed me the tunnels. We used them to—to practice." Isla's heart snapped in half again. "You have to go now, and make sure you don't show an ounce of hesitation if that no-brained commander pushes back. You are a Princess of Velotia, and I'm proud to call you my sister."

He jumped to his feet, hesitated, then laid a small kiss on her forehead. "I am truly sorry, sister. Until we meet again."

With that, her brother clapped Beau on the shoulder and left her in the middle of the floor. Alone except for the mute Siica who watched. Waiting for her decision.

Could Edmund's word truly be trusted? It may be another trick orchestrated by her father to entrap Isla.

"My lady," the taciturn Siica said. "I do not mean to overstep but if you wish to travel with the soldiers, we must leave now."

Isla finally picked up the black and silver uniform that she'd grown accustomed to seeing. This one differed from their troops' outfits, with a large patch over the chest containing the royal flame insignia wrapped in thorns.

She nearly snorted. Flames. Of course. How'd she never see it before?

It was an outfit made for a travelling royal. An outfit made for her.

"Princess Isla," the Siica urged again.

The options weighed carefully in her mind. There was no way of knowing until it was too late. She needed to decide if she was taking the risk or not... and *now*.

But the outfit had been made with so much careful detail. It fit her size and stature and was designed for *her*. This wasn't a spur of the moment garment made with hasty alterations. It had been carefully crafted, likely over several days before all of this.

"Princess."

Isla stood, running the uniform through her fingers. The time for hesitation and self-doubt had long since passed.

Her mother was dead because of her. Rian nearly died because of her. She was done waiting for bad things to happen and was ready to take destiny into her own hands. Whatever goddess her mother once prayed to meant nothing. *She* was the only one who decided her own fate from here on out.

"*Princess Isla.*"

It was time to go. Consequences be damned to Rallion. Now was the time to take her destiny into her own scarred hands, once and for all.

Forty
Prince Edmund of Velotia

Edmund flung himself into the wood chair, nearly toppling himself over backward. The circular room was larger than Isla's set of quarters but felt oddly stifling today with its dusky colors and shelf-lined walls filled with hundreds of tomes, all of which he'd read at least once and were proving utterly useless. He ran a finger along the carved thorns of the armrest, imagining the soft wood slicing his skin open.

That would have been better than the verbal lashing he'd received courtesy of his father. Though it wasn't nearly as harsh as he'd been expecting. His father had a hint of resignation when he had been yelling, and Edmund didn't know if that was worse, almost as if he'd expected this and was planning something instead.

When Edmund dropped the last piece in his arsenal, his father stewed in hateful silence before storming off. There was nothing he could do to refute the final piece of the puzzle that Edmund had assembled, and they both knew it would destroy the king's legacy. If Edmund hadn't laid it all bare to his father, he was certain he'd have sent an entire battalion after Isla as promised.

Edmund counted it as a temporary win... until his father came back with something of his own. The year of Hierel was starting off just *lovely*. Edmund didn't know what other set of truths and new beginnings she had in store for them. This was not the year for anyone hiding secrets, the goddess made that much painfully clear.

The royal beside him sighed annoyingly.

Right. It was rude to ignore his guest. Not after Beau so carefully extracted him from whatever trouble he was doused in, to bring him to Edmund's receiving chambers. As much as he wanted to, he couldn't push it off, despite being sleep deprived. This needed to be dealt with right away or his father would know.

A steaming cup of tea waited on the table next to him, but he decided it wasn't strong enough after the day he'd had, so he marched over to the dark cabinet, and pulled out the strongest, oldest whiskey he could find, along with two glasses.

"Long night?" Brenner asked as he set a glass in front of him. "Normally I'd say it's a bit early to start indulging, but given the pallid color of your face, I assume you've been up since yesterday. Party ran a little long?"

Edmund grimaced.

"Not in the mood." Brenner sipped the dark liquid. "I get it. Your father was quite ah, *enthusiastic*, the other day."

That was a mild depiction of his father's fiery cacophony. Their confrontation at the temple felt like years ago, instead of two days.

Brenner's eyes searched his. "What else happened? I heard rumors of a blaze outside your Pedite camp that left some terrible markings behind. I hope they caught whoever was responsible for it."

Edmund's pulse quickened. His face remained steady. How much Brenner knew was still unclear, and he was reluctant to give out more than necessary. Either way, there was no point in hiding the obvious.

"Our guests decided to take their leave," Edmund said measuredly. "They took out the barns with them and killed one of those religious zealots."

Brenner nodded. "I see. And your father—"

"Doesn't know the full extent of what happened." Thanks to the loyalty of their men, and who knew how long that would hold up. "He knows that our lines were breached, but he doesn't know exactly who did it beyond their ties to the Muratians."

Despite that, he still didn't think the zealots were a legitimate threat worth his time. Not when Murat was pushing into their border lands so fiercely.

"And you'd like it to stay that way?" Brenner said, raising an eyebrow.

Edmund took a giant gulp of the liquid, enjoying the way it scorched his throat. The acidic raze was better than the burn of regret which had so expertly worked its way into every pore of his body he was surprised it hadn't started seeping out yet.

"For a start." Edmund rubbed his temples. "The princess has been sent away on assignment with our troops."

"Oh?" Brenner's eyebrow inched further up.

It was hard to read the temperamental Koliat. Edmund couldn't tell if this was news to him or not. There was no time to put things delicately. It was time to lay all their stories bare.

"There will be delays in completing the marriage ceremony—obviously." Significant delays. And his father was furious when he found out about Isla's adventure with the army. If she ever made it back to Aurial, he would make her life an even worse hell than it already was.

"Hard to do the ceremony when the bride is absent... unless your father—"

"No," Edmund quickly cut off that thought. It would be sacrilege and the goddesses wrath would rain down from the heavens in one swift tide. "Once she is back, things are to progress as planned."

Edmund's heart sputtered pathetically. Isla wouldn't even look at him before she left. Would he ever get a chance to fully explain himself?

"This is..." Brenner rubbed his chin. "Not as was agreed upon. I am unsure—"

"Let's stop with the pretenses," Edmund said, crossing one knee over the other. A finger traced the rim of his glass. "Despite what you have said, I know you are loath to rush into this marriage."

At least Brenner was adept as faking surprised indignation. "I would never—"

Edmund cut him off with a wave. "I don't care what your motives are or aren't in the matter. We don't need to pretend here. It doesn't matter anymore."

Brenner clamped his mouth shut. A first.

"I believe a delay can benefit all involved parties. The king is prepared to add an additional ten thousand gold coins to the promised dowry, along with substantial lands near our borders." Lands that should have gone to Edmund and his future heirs. A fact that his father was all too happy to reveal.

At this point, Edmund didn't care. Those lands could wither and burn away under the guidance of the Koliats.

"That won't satisfy King Everett," Brenner said slowly. His eyes snapped up. "Twenty thousand gold coins, delivered immediately as a sign of good faith."

Just as Edmund had guessed. For a kingdom that boasted about their wealth and reserves, Koliat was struggling after years of terrible harvests and a blight that had spread all the way to the edges of Shiaarl. He'd heard as much from his sources in the neighboring kingdom.

No wonder the prince was so interested in travelling their lands the long way. He wanted to see for himself if they were likewise affected. Maybe find answers why it was happening in Koliat. The kingdom wasn't as prosperous as it once was.

The drought and blight were running Koliat's gold reserves dry. What they did have in abundance was—

"My father will want the promised troops ahead of time."

"Insanity," Brenner said. "They will never approve that without the completed ceremony."

"Two battalions, then. Sent to the Muratian borders—once the gold has reached Gea, naturally."

"And what am I to do?" Brenner leaned back in his seat. "Return home—bride less?"

"You get your delay, and you can focus the blame solely on us. Plus, you'll receive a portion of that generous dowry in advance, which should satisfy your king." Edmund waved his hands, holding back his wince. "You are welcome to stay here as our guest instead of returning to what I am certain is a *loving* and *welcoming* home." Brenner grimaced. "We have a large archive entirely dedicated to botany and historical droughts that you can access while here. Perhaps, you'll find the answers you require there. In two months' time I plan on joining my sister at the border and you may come, if you can stomach it."

Brenner huffed. "I am not afraid of a little fighting."

All of his experience with the Koliat Prince indicated that was a bold lie. Brenner was adept at changing himself depending on the audience, likely having to hone that skill while aging in a royal court. He was a lot of things. A fighter, he most certainly was not.

"I want to know more about those creatures you've come across," Brenner said. "I want to see that barn for myself."

"What's left of it," Edmund corrected. "I doubt you'll find anything there that can answer why your crops are failing."

"I need to check every possible link." Brenner crossed his legs and hesitated before asking, "Why do you think they are so intent on your sister, besides the obvious? I don't understand *why*?"

"Potential heir to Velotia," Edmund said, shrugging. "Ransom. Who knows?"

"They can do that with anyone, though... It's her powers."

"I'm not certain *exactly* why. If you follow the old bloodlines back to the High King, there is a link there—"

"Through your father *and* your mother."

"Yes." Edmund grimaced. "Stronger on her side."

Painfully strong.

Where those powers came from was anyone's guess. Very little was known of his mother before she came to the castle and caught the eye of the crown prince.

Brenner pursed his lips. "I guess it's good to settle all of this before returning to Koliat. They'd follow us and I won't put my people in that kind of danger, not after everything."

"I know you, Prince Brenner," Edmund said carefully. "You may have hidden your true self well enough from Isla, but I see through you."

Brenner's face turned to stone and he twisted in his seat. "Not as well as you may think, prince. In the matter of the terms you have presented, I find them acceptable."

"And the other part?" Edmund asked, his voice hitching and his confidence cracking. Gods, he needed a long rest after this.

"I won't tell your father what you've been up to all this time," Brenner said. "Not yet, anyways."

So, he would wait until the opportune moment. For when he could cause the most damage.

"And you'll keep whatever you know about Isla to yourself," Edmund pressed. He didn't just mean her powers.

"Naturally." Brenner dipped his head. "You may think quite low-ly of me, but I wouldn't do anything to jeopardize the reputation and integrity of my future bride, despite what she may be off doing at this moment. We will be bonded by the gods soon."

Edmund rubbed the scars on his wrist. There was no escape from a bonded mark etched into your flesh. The old texts said it changed you, and some days he believed it. Those crazed zealots certainly lived by those words, judging by the state of their skin.

That bond could never be erased in the eyes of the goddesses.

"You know some of the ancient, stronger bonded of legend were even told to share the same powers," Brenner mused. "That's why the old High King was so strong—if you believe he actually bedded the goddess herself and not just a deathpuller on a power trip.”

Edmund eyed him carefully, refusing to give anything away. “Is that what you’re after then?”

Brenner scoffed. “Fuck, no. I didn’t know until recently... and trust me, I have no desire for a taste of that darkness—no offense,” he added with a shrug. “I don’t envy wielders in the slightest. There’s always insurmountable pressure to impress your king and your goddess.”

Didn’t he know it?

Edmund knew exactly what it was like to be thrown into a union you weren’t too fond of or excited for. Exactly. The way Brenner spoke of it, indicated he had similar feelings.

“What’s her name?” Edmund asked. It may have been too brazen, but there was no other explanation for his actions. His hesitation.

Brenner laughed into his drink. “*Her* name?”

“I see.” That explained a lot. Edmund raised his glass and tipped it against Brenner’s. “To the future, then.”

“To a fruitful new alliance and getting through the dark times.” Brenner drank his cup without hesitation. Then he shook his head and sat up, his expression set. “Since we’re now being more upfront about our situation and convoluted agreements, I want to know... why exactly did your father make that deal with mine when he already ordered his commander to hand the princess over to the Muratians for death?”

Forty-One
Prince Devlin

The iron-wrought doors swung open as if he hadn't been absent for over a year. The room beyond was flushed in cascading beams of yellow, red, and orange thanks to the stained glass mimicking the sun's rays. Sage curtains billowed around oval windows that overlooked the rolling hills beyond.

The colors of home always calmed him, especially compared to *that* place. Familiarity was needed after the uncertainty that had plagued him since Aurial. He thought he knew his mission. His one true calling. But if things were so difficult, almost impossible with the princess, then what was left for him? The path he treaded was not as clear as it once was.

If anyone knew the answers he sought, she would.

The guards barely gave him a glance as he strode past, Beretta on his heel as always. She'd bounced back to full health over their excruciatingly long journey home.

Chir transported them out of Aurial and they were able to negotiate a new agreement that would benefit them all. The duplicitous Follower refused to take them the rest of the way home and dumped them at the border. It took three weeks to make it to Mirabello.

Idiot. Next time their paths crossed, he planned on removing a finger for that. And there *would* be a next time. When exactly that was, was still to be determined.

Before he did any sort of plotting or bathing or eating, he had to see her. Their path turned toward the throne room—her favorite and most likely spot she'd be during this time of day. His pulse quickened with each echoing step he took.

If he hadn't been in that barn and seen it with his own eyes, he'd never have believed what happened. The gate opened, *right there*, thanks to Chir's betrayal. He thought they needed the unification of the bloodlines before anything like that could happen—another thing she'd lied to him about.

Maybe it was because of the Celestial Solstice throwing things off. That had to be it. The only *sane* explanation.

Before he could get past the arched doorway, a thickset man half a head shorter stood in his path. Annoyance replaced any prior nerves Devlin had.

Graeme was on his mother's new council and was as close to a sniveling ground-weasel as one could get. He knew everyone's business and had inserted himself into Devlin's past assignments, no matter how little his help was needed or *wanted*.

Yet, his mother always had an ear to give to this listener, no matter the hour.

Gods, what a terrible man.

"Prince Devlin, while I am certain your mother will be relieved to see you arrived in good health, she is entertaining—"

Fuck that.

Devlin brushed past with no acknowledgment, leaving his mother's aid sputtering in the hall. He had to see her. And *now*. If she found out he did anything first then there'd be all hells to pay.

Before crossing the final set of painted glass doors, they paused. Beretta was suddenly interested in an old portrait of his father, grandfather, and uncle—the true firstborn son of Murat, before he disappeared.

He nodded at Beretta. "Go. You don't need to be here for this."

Relief flooded her face that she didn't bother to hide—it wasn't needed with him. She nodded and turned on her heel.

Devlin crossed into the ornate throne room, decorated the same as the halls except this one had gold trimmings everywhere you could imagine. A little over done but other kingdoms were worse. The throne settled on top of the dais was made of an old oak giant and laced with gold carvings. He'd never been a fan of it, even when his father sat upon the opulent seat.

Queen Grimha wore a rich sapphire dress with matching cape and was draped over the arm of the tallest chair—fussing about his brother as usual. She didn't stand when he approached, despite it being over a year since they'd last seen each other.

There was no shock on her thin face either. She knew he was coming.

"Brother. What a pleasant surprise," Kai drawled. "You look well. Considering the stories we've heard, I was half expecting your body to show up any day." His gaze flickered to the empty space at Devlin's side. "Where's your little shadow?"

Their mother smiled at his words, though the gesture didn't reach her cold eyes. She adjusted the thin crown atop her chestnut hair. "Be kind to your brother, Kai. I'm certain his journey has not been easy." Her eyes travelled the length of him. "I take it you did not succeed?"

Devlin's eye twitched. Obviously not.

"The task proved more difficult than we first thought." He focused on his mother instead of the gloating expression on Kai's stupid, freckled face. "She's better guarded than we thought. And her powers have grown exponentially."

"Our one gods-given chance was squandered when you took her to that mountain instead of straight here." His mother clicked her tongue. "And now you've waited until after the solstice, where we knew this could happen. If you would have done as directed in the first place…"

Devlin tuned out the rest of her tirade. He had his reasons for taking her to the mines first. She needed to be molded and trained before anyone tried to break her. If he'd brought her straight here, then he knew what would have happened, and they'd all have paid the price in ash and death.

His mother and brothers were less calculated. More brash. They didn't think things through with a vision for the future like he did, and his mother's current rants were confirmation enough.

What he wouldn't give to wipe the smirk off of Kai's face. His brother didn't even try to hide it as they both knew their mother would never berate him. If Devlin even tried to pull a face… there would be a much different outcome.

It must be nice being the favorite… well, the *new* one.

Abrax had been preferred above them all. Always had been. Now that he was gone, Kai relished in gaining her full attention and love. Perhaps it was because they shared the same brutish temperament. Whatever the reasons, his mother never gave a care for the son she abandoned to the wielder camps and constantly forgot existed.

"Devlin! Are you even listening?" that voice scolded, sending a shiver up his spine.

"I am, mother," he said quickly. "And I'm sorry."

"We had reports that she's left their capital," Kai said smoothly. "It'll be easier when she's near the border."

"If that is still the plan?" Devlin asked hesitantly.

The gods had it out for him, he was certain of it. There must be a way to garnish their favor again. The blood of the High King ran through his veins, passed down from his father. He was destined to reunite the bloodlines and reforge the old kingdom, he knew it. He just didn't know *how*.

"Of course it is," his mother rang out in cold tones. "Nothing has changed because you failed. History has shown the power a deathpuller wields, and the power she can bestow. It's the only way for our kingdom to move forward. Your brother will help you this time."

"No way am I—"

"But I—"

"Enough!" Her tones were resolute. Final.

Both he and Kai grimaced. Hierel grant him strength to get through this with his sanity.

His mother rose. A blue sleeve shook back to reveal fresh scars glistening above her elbow. Burn scars. Now, *that* was new.

He shouldn't be surprised. Especially given her ravings of late. No wonder she formed an alliance so easily with those followers. They all believed the marks were the purest and fastest way to the goddesses blessings.

If Devlin didn't know any better, he'd say she was one of them from birth. His mother was always evasive about her upbringing before she came to the castle with an eye on the heir at the time, their uncle. She never secured that proposal but managed to snag the second Muratian son through some will of Slin's. Devlin had an inkling that was all part of some grand design she'd yet to reveal.

"Is that all you have to report, Devlin?" she asked sweetly. Cloyingly sweet. He knew she was done with him. "I am rather busy at the moment."

It hardly looked it. But Devlin knew better than to say that out loud. Instead, he planned to bide his time and figure out a different approach, one that didn't involve working with Kai if he could swing it.

The time to grab hold of the pommel of destiny was now... no matter what wayward plans his mother had. *She* was not an heir of Murat, merely a steward. Soon her time would be up and she'd have to acquiesce to one of her bloodborne sons. While she was focused on grasping Rallion's powers for herself, Devlin remained intent on raising Murat to its former glory under the old High Kingdom.

It was their destiny in all of this. Which reminded him—

"One more thing." Devlin dug into his jacket and tossed the firestone blade at his mother. It skidded across the floor and stopped at her feet. She didn't move.

"What is the meaning of this?" she asked sharply.

He jerked his head at the blade. "It's faded, barely there, but check the hilt."

Sharp eyes stayed on him while she picked up the blade, turning it over in her hand. "Where did you get this?" she asked in a strange voice.

"Off of *her*," he said. "I thought you wanted her power but Chir said there was more to it. I know it's about uniting the blood lines, so tell me why she had *this*." He pointed at the dagger. "I recognize the bell etching, faded as it was. It's a Muratian blade. And I've seen only one other like that before."

His mother pursed her lips and handed the blade to Kai. "I don't get it," he said stupidly.

Devlin rolled his eyes, hiding balled up fists behind his back. "Our father carried a similar firestone blade, with the same bell carving. He and his brother were gifted a matching set by our grandfather. I don't know how many others there are like this."

"Yes, he had a similar one," she said in clipped tones.

"So where did *they* get this from?" Devlin asked. "Why did *she* have it?"

His mother stared at the faded dagger, blotches forming on her neck. The heavy silence weighed on him.

"Well?" Devlin demanded. The pungent smell of tension and deceit permeated the room.

"It can't be hers. She must have taken it from someone..." Her eyes finally lifted from the blade. They were sharp, cold, and as unyielding as always, but there was something else in there. Was that a hint of contrition? "Sit down, boys. There are things you need to know... about why we sit on this throne and what happened to your uncle."

Cadence is a Canadian author who enjoys reading any Science Fiction and Fantasy novels she can get her hands on. Disappearing into a great book with a glass of wine is one of her favorite past times. She loves writing new characters and getting to explore new worlds, creatures, and magic (maybe with a little heartbreak sprinkled in there, too). In her spare time she tries to get outdoors as much as she can and spends time cuddling her cat, who moonlights as her personal assistant!

The goddess years

The Star-Years of the Goddesses:
Leto: Overseer of harvests
Neme: Goddess of birth and fertility
Halia: The one-eyed watcher of mountains and forests
Insmia: The fire goddess
Poron: Goddess of health and healing
Slin: The trickster goddess of chaos
Kiemp: Goddess of the oceans and rivers
Wallienne: Goddess of sin and lies
Laian: Warden of wrath and retribution
Imoten: Guardian of fortune
Mannop: Deliverer of justice
Kheppi: The morning sun goddess
Dia: Watcher of the unknown

The sister goddess years, as foretold by Rallion's comet:
Hierel: The star goddess
Rallion (Sister Death): Goddess of the gates

www.ingramcontent.com/pod-product-compliance
Lightning Source LLC
Chambersburg PA
CBHW050111120726
47904CB00004B/1301